THE SIN-EATER AND OTHER WEIRD STORIES

The Hippocampus Press Classics of Gothic Horror Series

CLASSICS OF GOTHIC HORROR

Edited by S. T. Joshi

Johnson Looked Back: The Collected Weird Stories of Thomas Burke
The Harbor-Master: Best Weird Stories of Robert W. Chambers
Lost Ghosts: The Complete Weird Stories of Mary E. Wilkins Freeman
Back There in the Grass: The Horror Tales of
Irvin S. Cobb and Gouverneur Morris
The Mummy's Foot and Other Fantastic Tales by Théophile Gautier
The Were-Wolf and Others: The Weird Writings of
Clemence Housman
Twin Spirits: The Complete Weird Stories of W. W. Jacobs
The Sin-Eater and Other Weird Stories by William Sharp
and Fiona Macleod
From the Dead: The Complete Weird Stories of E. Nesbit
The Whispering Mummy and Others by Sax Rohmer
Phantasmagoria: The Weird Fiction, Poetry, and Criticism of
Sir Walter Scott
Frankenstein and Others: The Complete Weird Fiction of Mary Shelley
If the Dead Knew: The Weird Fiction of May Sinclair

The Sin-Eater and Other Weird Stories

WILLIAM SHARP AND FIONA MACLEOD

Edited by S. T. Joshi

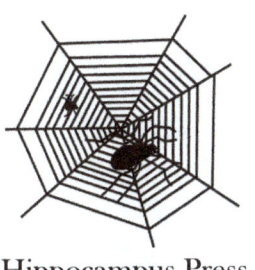

Hippocampus Press

New York

Published by Hippocampus Press
P.O. Box 641, New York, NY 10156.
www.hippocampuspress.com

Cover art and design © 2025 Daniel V. Sauer, dansauerdesign.com
"Classics of Gothic Horror" logo by Daniel V. Sauer
Hippocampus Press logo designed by Anastasia Damianakos.

First Edition
1 3 5 7 9 8 6 4 2

ISBN: 978-1-61498-467-2

Contents

Introduction 7

Stories by William Sharp 17

    The Gypsy Christ 19

    The Graven Image 52

Poems by William Sharp 63

    The Weird of Michael Scott 65

    The Deith-Tide 79

    The Willis-Dancers 82

    A Dream 86

    The Twin-Soul 87

    The Isle of Lost Dreams 88

    The Death-Child 89

Stories by Fiona Macleod 91

    The Sin-Eater 93

    The Anointed Man.. 119

    The Dàn-naṇ-Ròn 124

    Green Branches.. 149

    Silk o' the Kine 162

    The Washer of the Ford 168

    The Last Supper 180

    Cathal of the Woods 187

    Mircath 213

    The Laughter of Scathach the Queen 216

    Ula and Urla 221

By the Yellow Moonrock 227

The Herdsman 240

Appendix **275**

By the Yellow Moonrock [beginning] 277

Bibliography **293**

Introduction

William Sharp may appear to be an unlikely contributor to the weird tale, as the bulk of his work—especially that written under the female pseudonym Fiona Macleod—consists of retellings of Celtic myth and legend; but since such legendry is full of weird elements, ranging from metempsychosis to doppelgängers to revenants, it is unsurprising that Sharp has belatedly been recognized as a distinctive author of weird fiction and poetry.

Sharp was born in Paisley, Scotland, on 12 September 1855, the first child of David Galbraith Sharp and Katherine Brook Sharp, He would eventually have two brothers and five sisters. As a boy he engaged in vigorous outdoor activities; as he wrote later, "I think I sailed up every loch, fjord, and inlet in the Western Highlands and islands."[1] Although he was a voracious reader in youth, his parents sought to dissuade him from a literary career, and he entered a law office in Glasgow. His father died in 1876; subsequent ill-health on Sharp's part compelled him to travel to Australia to recover. It would be the first of many voyages that the peripatetic writer would undertake over his relatively brief life. The trip to Australia necessitated his withdrawal from the University of Glasgow, and he never completed his degree.

Sharp came to London in 1877, initially working at a bank; but his irresponsibility caused him to be fired. A chance meeting with the writer and artist Dante Gabriel Rossetti in 1879 radically altered his life and career, resulting in his meeting many of the leading literary figures of the day—A. C. Swinburne, William Morris, Robert Browning, and many others. He adopted the principles of the Pre-Raphaelite painters, vaunting the bohemian lifestyle, a devotion to "pure" art without thought of

---

1. Quoted in Elizabeth Sharp, *William Sharp (Fiona Macleod): A Memoir* (New York: Duffield, 1910), 12.

remuneration, and an awareness that aesthetic richness can only result from a deep connection to one's native land and heritage. A volume of poems published in 1882 betrays the influence of Shelley, Wordsworth, Emerson, and Whitman.

Over the next several years, however, Sharp engaged in precisely the literary hackwork he professed to despise. Shortly after Rossetti's death he generated a laudatory biography (1882); it was later followed by biographies of Shelley (1887), Heinrich Heine (1888), and Browning (1889). He also established himself as an art critic, writing for the *Glasgow Herald* and the *Art Journal.* He had already visited Italy in February–June 1883, canvassing the museums in Rome, Florence, Venice, and elsewhere. In addition, he wrote two more volumes of poetry (one of which, *Romantic Ballads and Poems and Phantasy* [1888], contains some of the earliest of his work that could be classified as weird) and two novels. During this time he evinced a growing distaste for the urban environment of London and its corrupting influence on the imagination. A travel essay of 1885 expresses his sentiments: "The writer is one of those persons on whom the sense of the sublime in nature is most borne where there are vast spaces . . . He feels the grandeur of mountains to be less impressive than that of boundless sea or limitless desert."[2]

Sharp's travels continued: Paris in April–June 1884; Canada, New England, and New York in August–November 1889; Argyll, Scotland, in the summer of 1890; Antwerp, Bonn, the Rhine Valley, and Stuttgart in the fall of 1890. By the end of 1890 he apparently decided to settle permanently in Rome, but he ended up returning to London less than a year later. Nevertheless, according to his wife, Elizabeth Sharp (a first cousin whom he had known since childhood, and whom he had married in June 1884), this whole period constituted a strong break from his life as a London littérateur. The visit to Argyll may have contributed to his growing awareness of the need to re-establish ties with his native land—both its topography and its distinctive culture.

It was, indeed, sometime in 1891 that the development of the persona of Fiona Macleod came to him, even though the first work pub-

---

2. Quoted in Flavia Alaya, *William Sharp—"Fiona Macleod" 1855–1905* (Cambridge, MA: Harvard University Press, 1970), 63.

lished under this pseudonym did not appear until 1894. The persona testifies to Sharp's interest in both the racial/ethnic element in literature and his own sense of hermaphroditism. Elizabeth Sharp reports that a Highland nurse named Barbara had early inculcated Sharp in Celtic folklore: "it was she who told him stories of Faerie, crooned to him old Gaelic songs, and made his childish mind familiar with the heroes of the old Celtic Sagas, with the daring exploits of the Viking rovers and Highland chieftains."[3] Sharp himself elaborates upon this account:

> My Hebridean nurse had often told me of Shony, a mysterious sea-god, and I know I spent much time in wasted adoration: a fearful worship, not unmixed with disappointment and some anger. Not once did I see him. I was frightened time after time, but the sudden cry of a heron, or the snort of a pollack chasing the mackerel, or the abrupt uplifting of a seal's head became over-familiar, and I desired terror, and could not find it by the shore. Inland, after dusk, there was always the mysterious multitude of shadow. There, too, I could hear the wind leaping and growling. But by the shore I never knew any dread, even in the darkest night. The sound and company of the sea washed away all fears.[4]

Sharp goes on to note that, when he was a teenager, a fisherman, Seumas Macleod (from whom, presumably, he adopted the surname of his pseudonym), instructed him in the Gaelic language and took him out to sea on numerous occasions.

Sharp's uncanny sense that a woman was trapped in his body is verified by his wife's recollections. "I remember he told me that rarely a day passed in which he did not try to imagine himself living the life of a woman, to see through her eyes, and feel and view life from her standpoint, and so vividly that 'sometimes I forget I am not the woman I am trying to imagine.'"[5] Sharp may also have been inspired by a female friend with whom he fell in love in 1890—Edith Wingate Rinder, whom he had met in Italy in 1890–91. He dedicated to her (under the initials "E. W. R.") the first work published under the Fiona Macleod pseudo-

---

3. Elizabeth Sharp, *Memoir* 5.

4. Quoted in Elizabeth Sharp, *Memoir* 7.

5. Elizabeth Sharp, *Memoir* 52–53.

nym, the novel *Pharais* (1894). Edith also urged Sharp to return to his Scottish/Celtic roots. He began associating with a group in Edinburgh called the Evergreen (it published the magazine *Evergreen* in 1895–96]), one of whose members was Patrick Geddes (1854–1932), a Scottish professor of botany at the University of Dundee who published some of the Fiona Macleod volumes. Under his own name, Sharp compiled the anthology *Lyra Celtica: An Anthology of Representative Celtic Poetry* (1896).

But in the period 1895–1904 a majority of the books Sharp published appeared as by Fiona Macleod. These include the novels *Pharais* (1894), *The Mountain Lovers* (1895), and *Green Fire* (1896); the story collections *The Sin-Eater and Other Tales* (1895), *The Washer of the Ford* (1896), and *The Dominion of Dreams* (1899); the plays *The Immortal Hour* (1899) and *The House of Usna* (1903); a retelling of Celtic legends for children, *The Laughter of Peterkin* (1897); the poetry collection *From the Hills of Dream* (1901); and even several volumes of nonfiction, *By Sundown Shores* (1900), *The Divine Adventure* (1900), *Iona* (1900), *The Winged Destiny: Studies in the Spiritual History of the Gael* (1904), and *Where the Forest Murmurs* (1904). Sharp made elaborate efforts to convince the literary world that Fiona Macleod was an actual person; he wrote letters to leading literary critics and signed them under his pseudonym, and the identity of Fiona Macleod was a closely kept secret until after his death.

The tremendous productivity—which also included the story collection *The Gypsy Christ and Other Tales* (1895), published under his own name—that Sharp exhibited at this time bespeaks an outpouring of creativity based upon the Celtic legendry he had absorbed over a lifetime. And it came as he and his wife continued their wide travels. From 1892 until only a few months before his death they ventured to New York, Paris, Algeria and Tunisia, the Hebrides, Venice, the Lake Country, Ireland (where he met leading figures of the early stages of the Irish literary renaissance, including Douglas Hyde and Lady Gregory), Holland, Sicily, Athens, Wales, and elsewhere. Sharp, plagued by ill health during his final years, died at Castello di Maniace, Sicily, on 5 December 1905.

*   *   *

There is some reason to doubt that Sharp—in spite of his early comment, "I desired terror"—set out to be a writer of "weird fiction" even occasionally. At the time when most of the Fiona Macleod works were written, in the 1890s, the genre was still in the process of separation from mainstream fiction. This period may have been the heyday of Arthur Machen, whose *The Great God Pan and The Inmost Light* (1894) and *The Three Impostors* (1895) created a furor, and when such landmarks of weird fiction as Robert Louis Stevenson's *The Strange Case of Dr. Jekyll and Mr. Hyde* (1886), Oscar Wilde's *The Picture of Dorian Gray* (1890), and Bram Stoker's *Dracula* (1897) appeared; but even these works were not regarded as radically distinct from other literary work of the Yellow Nineties, when the palette of English fiction was expanding well beyond social realism to incorporate myth, folklore, and legendry of all sorts.

Indeed, there is also a difficulty in identifying as "weird" the Macleod works that utilize these same elements, sometimes extending into the use of explicit motifs from Christianity or other religions. In one of the two tales in this volume published under his own name, "The Gypsy Christ," set in the Peak district in northern England, we are introduced to a man, James Fanshawe, one of whose ancestors was crucified as the Gypsy Christ. He reports that gypsies do not "worship [God] nor propitiate him nor fear him"; they also do not believe in an afterlife. Fanshawe claims to be the lineal descendant of a gypsy woman who had laughed at Jesus on the cross. All these religious elements fuse into a tale of the bizarre that features Christian imagery at every turn.

This story is worth comparing to the Fiona Macleod tales "The Last Supper," an allegory of Jesus and the twelve apostles at the last supper, and "Cathal of the Woods," where the conflict of pagan and Christian is the focus. Here, a monk named Cathal meets a pagan woman, Ardanna, and renounces his chastity. But Ardanna's father, Ecta, has just become a Christian. The two lovers are seized, and Cathal is thrust into the hollow of an oak tree. Days later Ardanna comes to him—but is she a human being or something else? She herself declares, "I am of the green people." Other "green phantoms" later emerge, and it is stated that "the green fire of life flamed in [Cathal's] veins." Twenty years later, Cathal meets a former colleague in his monastery, Molios, and declares that there is indeed a heaven and hell—"but not what Colum taught, and you taught." He shows them the "soulless" offspring of himself and Ardanna. The entire tale asks us to find terror and weirdness in the non- or anti-Christian entities that people the story. It is worth noting that Sharp put forth Fiona Macleod as a Catholic, possibly as a gesture of disapprobation of the Calvinist/Presbyterian heritage of Scotland.

But "The Dàn-nan-Ròn" takes a somewhat more positive view of paganism. Mànus MacCodrum "adheres to the old faith"—i.e., the faith of the pre-Christian settlers of Scotland. Anne Gillespie is engaged to him, but her cousins, the Achanna brothers, do not wish her to go. (They appear to be keen on keeping her to their side to cook and clean for them.) In protest, one of the brothers, curiously named Gloom, plays the "Dàn-nan-Ròn" (the song of the seal). Is Mànus a seal in disguise? Why does he later develop a taste for eating raw fish? This mesmerizing tale hints at metempsychosis without ever explicitly avowing the reality of Mànus's transformation.

This is one of several tales about the Achanna clan. The first such story is "The Anointed Man," a narrative of Alison Achanna, who is deemed at the outset to be "fëy"—endowed with unspecified supernatural abilities, such as clairvoyance. In this case, Alison can see beauty in what others only see as ugliness: the "squalor and hideousness" of industrialized cities is to him full of a latent loveliness. In "Green Branches," a direct follow-up to "The Dàn-nan-Ròn," there is doubt in James Achanna's mind as to whether his brother Gloom, who appears to have drowned in the earlier story, is alive or dead. (James is sometimes referred to as Sheumais.) Here again a romantic quarrel—James loves Katreen Macarthur, but so did Gloom; and now she has been promised to her cousin, Ian Macarthur—leads to a weird denouement. "Silk o' the Kine" and its sequel, "Ula and Urla," deal with love triangles that end with a supernatural climax.

Rory MacAlpine, the protagonist of "By the Yellow Moonrock," is also said to be "fëy." This piper has developed a reputation for drunkenness and lechery; but he becomes involved with an enigmatic woman who, he is told, is a Serpent Woman—"a woman who could suck the soul out of a man through his lips." Whether this is merely myth or a baleful reality is something Rory learns to his regret.

Sharp/Macleod's most famous weird tale, "The Sin-Eater," is undeniably pagan. The concept of the sin-eater—a stranger who comes to the place where a dead person is laid out prior to burial and eats a cake placed on his or her chest, thereby taking away the sins of the deceased—is an element of the ancient folklore of Scotland, Ireland, and Wales, but also has analogues with similar practices in Meso-America and elsewhere. In the story, there is nothing explicitly Christian in the concept or its attendant ceremonies. And when Neil Ross, who seeks to be the sin-eater for the recently dead Adam Blair, violates custom, which states that the sin-eater must "above all bear him no grudge," his fate is sealed.

A succession of narratives, chiefly based on Norse myth, provide interesting anticipations of the future subgenre of sword and sorcery. "The Washer of the Ford" and "Mircath" are the chief examples, and their stirring battle scenes—interspersed (as are several of the other tales in this volume) with hypnotically rhythmic verse—are enough to evoke the later work of Lord Dunsany ("The Sword of Welleran") and Robert E. Howard.

The weird poems that Sharp included in *Romantic Ballads and Poems of Phantasy* range from "The Weird of Michael Scott" (a powerful weird ballad in which the "wizard" of the title encounters his own soul—a theme that Sharp utilizes in the final story in this volume, "The Herdsman") to "The Willis-Dance" (about a dance of the untimely dead) to briefer and more ethereal works that underscore the obscure but terrifying borderland between life and death. Sharp's notes to the poems underscore their derivation from Celtic myth.

What distinguishes Sharp's tales—especially those written under the Fiona Macleod pseudonym—is a gift for poetic diction, derived largely from his use of Scots dialect and the innately metaphorical language of the primitive peoples he puts on stage; and these elements vivify the ancient myths he has refashioned for his own day.

How Sharp/Macleod became a minor but notable figure in the weird fiction of his time is far from clear. The first occasion in which one of his tales was reprinted in a horror anthology occurred only a few years after his death, when William Patten included "Green Branches" in *Great Short Stories II: Ghost Stories* (1909). The tale was subsequently reprinted in Joseph Lewis French's *Great Ghost Stories* (1918). French went on to include "The Sin-Eater" in *The Best Psychic Stories* (1920), where H. P. Lovecraft read it and borrowed some of the Gaelic curses for the cataclysmic conclusion of "The Rats in the Walls" (1923).

The sin-eater theme was subsequently used in brilliant fashion by Christianna Brand in "Sins of the Fathers" (1964; subsequently adapted on *Rod Serling's Night Gallery* in an episode that aired on 23 February 1972) and by Ramsey Campbell in *The Long Lost* (1993).

The lengths to which William Sharp went to fashion the hoax of Fiona Macleod as a mysterious female writer of Celtic lore is a striking testimonial to the complexities of his own psychological makeup as well as the depth of his absorption of the rich body of myth of his native Scotland. His bountiful production under the Macleod pseudonym during a relatively brief period points to the fervency of his desire to draw upon this body of legend and render it fresh and vital to his audience. It remains so more than a century after it was written, and we can do no better than to admire his infusion of weirdness into scenarios that probe some of the most fundamental and vital of human emotions, all set in a wild and remote landscape that in itself is evocative of the unearthly.

—S. T. JOSHI

A Note on This Edition

The stories in this volume are taken from the original editions of story collections by Fiona Macleod: *The Sin-Eater and Other Tales* (1895), *The Washer of the Ford* (1896), and *The Dominion of Dreams* (1899). The texts of these stories differ from the versions included by William Sharp's widow, Elizabeth Sharp, in her seven-volume edition of *The Works of Fiona Macleod* (1910). Although Elizabeth Sharp claims in some cases to have used manuscript sources, in my judgment the texts in the original edition are almost uniformly superior to those in the *Works*. The majority of changes are in matters of punctuation and a few proper names. The one exception is "By the Yellow Moonrock." This story exists in a much longer text in *The Dominion of Dreams* (1899) than in the reprint of that book in volume 3 of the *Works*. In a bibliographical note at the end of that volume, Elizabeth Sharp writes: "The curtailing of the opening portion of 'The Yellow Moonrock' [*sic*] is the work of the author." I have decided to use the shorter version because it is more focused on the weird events than the longer version. I print the excised portion of the story in an appendix. I have used the title "Cathal of the

Woods" from the *Works,* volume 2, but the text from *The Washer of the Ford* (where the story is titled "The Annir-Choille"). All the poems are taken from Sharp's *Romantic Ballads and Poems of Phantasy* (1888).

—S. T. J.

Stories by William Sharp

The Gypsy Christ

I

There are, among the remote uplands of the Peak district, regions whose solitude is that of a wilderness. Over much of the country there is a frown. When fair weather prevails: though these lofty plateaux are seldom wholly free from cloud-shadow: this frown is merely that of a stern man, preoccupied with sombre thoughts. When there come rain and wind, and still more the dull absorbing gloom that floods out of the east and the north-east, the frown is forbidding, minatory even, at times almost tragic. Viewed anywhere from High Peak to Sir William, these uplands are like the sea. They reach onward, lapse, merge into each other, in a similar succession of vast billows: grand as they, as apparently limitless, and, at times, as overwhelmingly depressing.

The villages are scattered, insignificant: built of dull, grey stone: gardenless, flowerless. The people are uncouth in speech and manner: cold, too, as the stone of their houses, and strangely quiet in the ordinary expression of emotion.

In all regions where the wind is the paramount feature in the duel between man and the powers of nature, as upon the seas and great moorland tracts, it is noticeable that human voices are pitched in an unusually low key. In remote islands, upon mountains, on the billows of hill-land that sweep up from the plains and fall away in dales and valleys, on long flats of grass, fen, or morass, and upon the seas, the human voice takes to itself in time a peculiar, and to those who know the cause, a strangely impressive hush. Here, it is as of men subdued, but resentful, forever gloomful.

No land is so dreary as to be without redeeming beauty. The hill-region of the Peak, that most visited at any rate, has singular charm. The dales are famous for their loveliness, their picturesqueness; the heather slopes for their blithe air; the high moors for their wide perspectives,

19

their clear windy breath, their glory of light and shadow. Nevertheless, there are vast districts where nature, and man, and the near way and the wide prospect, and the very immensity of the environing sky, are permeated with the inner spirit of gloom, as the cloud-caravans of July with their burden of thunder.

There are reasons why I do not wish to be explicit topographically, in what I am about to narrate: indeed, no one from what I write, could find the Wood o' Wendray, or the House o' Fanshawe. It must suffice, that what I have to tell occurred in the remotest, perhaps the grandest, certainly to me the most impressive region of the Peak-Land.

Far among these uplands; at the locality I mean, from twelve or fifteen hundred to two thousand feet above the sea; there is an almost trackless morass, called Grailph Moss.

The name is by some supposed to be a corruption of grey wolf: for here, according to rumour, the last wolf in England had its lair, and might have been living still (for the huntsmen aver that the grey wolf lives three hundred years!) but for its audacity at the time of the Great Plague. Packmen and other wayfarers have alleged that on wild nights of storm, or in even more perilous seasons of mist or marsh-fog, they have seen a gaunt shape leap towards them from a dense clump of heather or from behind a juniper, or have heard, behind or in stealthy circuit, terrifying footfalls as of a huge dog.

Grailph Moss comes right upon an old disused highway. Along this road, at far intervals, are desolate hamlets: in all save the three summer months, apt to be isled in the mist breathed from the myriad nostrils of the great Fen. At these times, the most dreadful thing to endure is the silence.

Not far from one of these hamlets, and somewhat more removed from the contagion of the Moss: high-set, indeed, and healthy, if sombre of aspect save under the fugitive bloom of the afterglow, or where redeemed by the moonlight to an austere beauty: is a strange house, the strangest I have seen anywhere.

The House o' Fanshawe, it is called in the neighbourhood: though what is perplexing is that the name is centuries old, though for centuries no family of that name occupied the Manor of Eastrigg: nor is there any local legend concerning a Fanshawe, or record of any kind to account for the persistency of the designation.

Long before my friend, James Fanshawe, took the Manor, ruin had come upon the middle as well as the northern portion. In fact, the southern end, which had been the original Elizabethan house, was scarce better, and had been preserved at all only because of its fantastic, often beautiful, and always extraordinary roof and wainscot carvings. These were none the less striking from the fact that they were white-washed. Many were in a fashion suggestive of the Arabesques of Barbary, such as are to be seen to this day in the private houses of the rich Moors of Tlemçen or Tunis. Others recalled the freaks of the later Renaissance imagination: and some were of Gothic rudeness and vigor. But the most extraordinary room of all was a small chamber opening from a large vaulted apartment. All the panels on three sides of the room, and the whole roof, were covered with arabesques of the Crucifixion: no one whitewashed carving quite like any other, though all relentlessly realistic, sometimes savagely, brutally so. The fourth side was of varnished black oak. Against this, in startling relief, was a tall white cross, set in a black stand; with a drooping and terrible figure of the crucified God, the more painfully arresting from the fact that the substance of which it had been wrought had been dyed a vivid scarlet, that, with time, had become blood-red.

A word as to how I came to know this house in this remote and desolate region.

Two or three years ago, when wandering afoot through Croatia, I encountered James Fanshawe. There is no need to narrate what led up to our strange meeting, for a strange meeting in strange circumstances, and in a strange place, it was. It will suffice for me to say that our encounter, our voluntary acquaintanceship, and our subsequent friendship, all arose from the circumstance that each of us could, with more justice than some who have done so, claim to be a Romany Rye—which is not exactly "a gentleman-gypsy," as commonly translated, but rather an amateur-gypsy, or as a "brother" once phrased it to me "a sympathising make-believe gypsy." There are some who can talk the dialects of "Little Egypt," or at least understand them, and many who know something of the folk-lore, habits, and customs of the wandering people: but there are few, I take it, who have lived the gypsy-life—who have undergone, or even heard of, the ordeal of the Blue Smoke, the Two Fires, and the Running Water.

Thereafter, we met on several occasions: frequently in Italy, or the Tyrol, or southern Germany: generally by pre-arrangement. The last time I saw Fanshawe, until I met him in Glory Woods, near Dorking, was in the Hohenheim country, on the high plateau to the southwest of Stuttgart. It was then he told me he had been to England, and had travelled afoot from Southampton to Hull: and that he had at last decided to settle in that country, probably in the New Forest region. I promised to visit him in England when next there. I wanted to fare awhile with him there and then, but as it was clear he did not at that juncture wish my company, I forbore.

James Fanshawe was a noticeable man. Tall, sinewy, ruddy though with dark, luminous eyes, and long, trailing, coal-black moustache, he would not have seemed more than thirty years old but for his iron-grey hair, and the deep crow's feet about his mouth, eyes, and temples. As a matter of fact, he was, at the time I first met him, at the Midsummer's-day of human life; for he had just entered his fortieth year.

One early spring day, when, by the merest hazard, we came across each other in Glory Woods, he reminded me that nearly two years had passed since my promise to visit him. He had not, after all, settled in the south country, but, he told me, in a strange old house, in a remote and wild moorland tract of Derbyshire. While he spoke, I was observant of the great change in him. He had grown ten, fifteen years older in appearance. The iron-grey hair had become white; the strong face, rigid; the swift, alert look now that of a visionary, or of one who brooded much. Perhaps the most marked change was in the eyes. What had always struck me as their dusky, velvety Czech beauty was no longer noticeable. They were much lighter, and had a strange, staring intensity.

But I was glad to see him again: glad to pick up lost clues, and glad to be able to promise to be with him at Eastrigg Manor at the end of the sixth week from that date.

That is now I came to know the "House o' Fanshawe."

II

Eastrigg itself is more than twenty miles from the nearest station. The drive thence seemed the longer and drearier because of the wet mist which hung over the country. Even sounds were soaked up by it. I never passed through a drearier land. Mid-April, and not a green thing visible, not a bird's note audible!

The driver of the gig was taciturn, yet could not quite restrain his curiosity. He was not an Eastrigg man, but knew the place, and all connected with it. He would fain have ascertained somewhat about its owner; perhaps, too, about myself, or at any rate about my object in coming to the reputed haunted, if not accursed House o' Fanshawe, where my host-to-be lived alone, attended only by an old man named Hoare, a "foreigner" too, because come from the remote south country. When, however, he found me even more reserved than himself, he desisted from further inquiry, or indeed remarks of any kind.

It was in silence that we drove the last ten miles; in silence that we jotted along a rude, grassy highway of olden days, heavily rutted; in silence that we passed, first one, then another gaunt ruin,—two of the many long-deserted lead-mine chimneys which stand here and there throughout that country, and add unspeakably to its desolation. Finally, in silence we reached the House o' Fanshawe.

A small side-door, under heavy beams, opened. An elderly man stood, his right hand over his eyes, and his left holding a lantern which emitted a pale yellow glow, beneath which his face was almost as wan and white as his bleached hair.

He looked at me anxiously, questioningly, I thought. Instinctively, I inquired if Mr. Fanshawe were unwell.

"Are you a doctor?" he asked, almost in a whisper; adding, on my reply in the negative, "I hoped you might be. I fear the master is dying."

Startled, I unburdened myself of my wet overcoat and then followed the man along a rambling passage. On the way, he confided to me that though Mr. Fanshawe was up and about, he had been very strange of late, and that he ate little, slept little, and was sometimes away on the Moss or the higher moors for ten or twelve hours at a time; further, that within the last few days he had become steadily worse.

Even this forewarning did not adequately prepare me for the change in my friend. When I saw him, he was sitting in the twilight before a peat fire on which a log, aflame at one end though all charred at the other, burned brightly. His hair was quite white: so white that that of his man, Robert Hoare, was of a yellow hue by comparison. It hung long and lank about his cadaverous face, which, in its wanness and rigid lines, was that of a corpse, except for the dark luminous eyes I remembered so well, once more like what they were in the days I first knew him, but now so intensely, passionately alive, that it was as though the flame of his life were concentred there. He rose, stiffly and as though with difficulty, and I saw how wofully thin he had become. It was with a shock of surprise I realized what vitality the man still had, when he took my hand in his, gripped it almost as powerfully as of yore, and half led, half pushed me into an arm-chair opposite his own.

Yes, he admitted, he had been ill, but was now better. Soon, he hoped, he would be quite well again. The eyes contradicted the lie of the lips.

After a time, our constraint wore off; but though I avoided the subject of his health and recent way of life, he interrupted me again and again to assure me that he would not have let me come so far, to visit so dreary a house, and see so unentertaining an invalid, had he known how to intercept me.

Suddenly he rose, and insisted on showing me over the house. Room by room fascinated me; but that small chamber of which I have already spoken, that with the crucifix, gave me nothing short of an uncontrollable repugnance, something akin to horror. He noticed this, though neither the lips offered nor the eyes invited any remark.

No wonder that from the several ominous circumstances of this meeting I was half prepared for some unpleasant or even tragic dénouement. But, as a matter of fact, nothing happened to alarm or further perturb me; and long before I went to my room I had noticed a marked improvement in Fanshawe,—that is, in his mental condition; physically, he was still very distraught as well as frail, and appeared to suffer extremely from what I took to be nervous cold, though he said it was the swamp-ague. "The Moss Fiend had got him," he declared. He wore a long frieze overcoat, even as he sat by the fire; and all the time, even at our frugal supper, kept his hands half covered in thick mittens.

Naturally enough, I did not sleep for long. In the first place, sleep is always tardy with me in absolutely windless or close, rainy weather; then the absolute silence, the sense of isolation, affected me; and, more effectually still, I could hear Fanshawe monotonously walking to and fro in the room to my right. This room, moreover, was no other than the fantastically decorated ante-chamber. I could scarce bear to think of my distraught friend, sleepless, and wearily active, in the company of that terrifying crucifix, that chamber of the myriad reduplications of the Passion. But at last I slept, and slept well; nor did I wake till the late sunlight streamed in upon me through the unshuttered and blindless window.

We spent most of that day in the open air. The morning was so blithe and sweet, Fanshawe lost something of his air of tragic ill; and I began to entertain hopes of his ultimate recovery. But in the early afternoon, when we had returned for the meal which had been prepared for us an hour before, the weather changed. It grew sultry and overclouded. The glass, too, had fallen abruptly. The change affected my friend in a marked degree. He became less and less communicative, and at last morose and almost sullen.

I proposed another walk. He agreed, with an eagerness that surprised me. "I will show you one or two places where I often go," he added: "places that the country people about here avoid; for the moorfolk are superstitious, as all who live in remote places are."

The day, as I have said, had become dull and heavy; and what with the atmospheric change, and the saturnine mood of my companion, I felt depressed. The two gaunt chimneys which rose above their respective mines were my skeletons at the feast. Otherwise I could have enjoyed many things in, and aspects of, that unfamiliar country; but these tall, sombre, bat-haunted, wind-gnawed "stacks," rising from dishevelled ruins, which, again, overlay the deserted lead-mines, oppressed me beyond all reason.

At one of these we stopped. Fanshawe asked me to throw something into a hollow place beyond one of the walls of a building. I lifted a large stone, and threw it as directed. I thought, at first, it had fallen on soft grass, or among weeds and nettles, for no sound was audible. Then, as it were underfoot, I heard a confused clamour, followed by the faint echo of a splash.

"That will give you some idea of the depth of the mine," my companion remarked quietly. "But it is deeper than you imagine, even now. There are sloping ledges *under* that water in which the stone fell at last; and beneath these ledges are corridors leading far into the caverns whence nothing ever comes again."

"It is not a place for a nervous person to come to," I answered, with as much indifference as I could assume; "nor for any one after sundown, and alone."

Fanshawe looked at me passively, then said quietly that he often came there.

"I wonder," he added, "how many dead will arise from a place like this when the trump of the Resurrection stirs the land?"

"Has any one ever fallen into this mine, or been murdered in it?"

"They say so. It is very likely. But come: I will show you a stranger thing."

So on we trudged again, for, I should think, nearly a mile, and mostly through a thin wood. I wondered what new unpleasant feature of this unattractive country I was to see. It was with half angry surprise I was confronted at last by a thick scrub of gorse, overhung by three large birches, and told that there was what we had come to see. Naturally, there was nothing to arrest my attention. When I said so, however, Fanshawe made no reply. I saw that he was powerfully affected, though whether grief or some other emotion wrought him, I could not determine.

Suddenly he turned, said harshly that he was dead tired, and wished to go home straightway. Beyond a statement about a short cut by Dallaway Moor, he did not vouchsafe another remark until we reached the Manor.

At the entrance, Hoare met us, and was about to speak, when he saw that his master was not listening, but rigid, with moving jaw, and wild eyes, was staring at the panels of the door.

"Who . . . who has been here?" he cried hoarsely; but for answer the man merely shook his head stupidly, muttering at last that not a soul had been near the place.

"Who has been here? Who has been here? Who did this?" my friend gaspingly reiterated, as he pointed to a small green cross, the paint still wet, impressed a foot or more above the latch.

III

Fanshawe was taciturn throughout the first part of the evening. We ate our meal in silence. Afterwards, in his study, he maintained the same self-absorption, and for a long time seemed unaware that he was not alone. The atmospherical oppression made this silence still more obvious. Even the fire burned dully, and the smoke that went up from the mist-wet logs was thick and heavy.

It was with a sense of relief I heard an abrupt, hollow, booming sound, as of distant guns at sea. The long-expected thunder was drawing near. For many minutes after this, the silence could be heard. Then there came a blast of wind that struck the house heavily, for all the world like an enormous billow flooding down upon and all but engulfing a dismasted ship.

Fanshawe raised his head, and listened intently. A distant, remotely thin wail was audible for a few seconds: the voice of the wind-eddy far away upon the moors. Then, once more, the same ominous silence.

"I hope the storm will break soon," I said at last.

"Yes. We'll have one or two more blasts like that, then a swift rain; then the night will become black as ink, and the thunderstorm will rage for an hour or so, and suddenly come back upon us again worse than before."

I looked at my friend surprisedly.

"How can you tell?"

"I have seen many thunderstorms and gales on these moorlands."

I was about to say something further, when I saw a look upon my companion's face which I took to be that of arrested thought or arrested speech.

I was right in my surmise, for, in a low voice, he resumed:—

"You will doubtless hear many another storm such as this. As for me, it is the last to which I shall ever listen: unless, as may well be, the dead hear. After all, what grander death-hymn could one have?"

"You are ill, Fanshawe, but not so ill as you believe. In any case, you do not fear you are going to die to-night?"

He looked at me long and earnestly before he answered.

"I—suppose—not," he said slowly, at last, but in the meditative way of one revolving a dubious matter. in his mind: "no, I suppose not necessarily *to-night*."

A long discordant cry of the wind came wailing across the Reach o' Dallaway. It was scarce gone, when a ponderous distant crashing betokened the onset of the elemental strife to be fought out overhead.

The effect upon Fanshawe was electric. He rose, moved to and fro, twice went to the window, and drew up the blind. The second time, he opened the latch. The window was of the kind called half-French; that is, it was of a single sheet of glass, but came no further than two thirds of the way down, the lower third being of solid wood, and could be opened (drawn inward) only in its glazed section.

He withdrew the fastening, stooped, and peered into the yard. A stealthy, shuffling sound was audible, followed by a low whine.

Fanshawe seemed satisfied, and, having closed the latch, drew together the thick, heavy curtains.

"That was my bloodhound, Grailph," he explained. "I always let him out at night. He keeps watch here. He is a huge beast, cream-white in color, and so is as rare and remarkable as he is trustworthy. I brought him, as a puppy, from Transylvania. The people hereabouts hate and fear him, the more so, because of his name. I have told you about the legend of Grailph Moss? Yes? Well, the rumour has filtered from mind to mind that my Grailph is no other than the original Grailph, or Grey Wolf; and that in some way he, I, and the 'House o' Fanshawe' are connected in an uncanny destiny."

"Are you quite sure you're not?" I interrupted, half in badinage, half in earnest.

He took my remark seriously, however.

"No; I am *not* sure. But who can tell what is the secret thing that lies hidden in the ninth shadow, the ninth wave, and the brain of a ninth child?"

"Ah, you remember what old Mark Zengro said that day by the cavern of the Jällusietch, in Bohemia! How well I remember that noon: how he called you Brother, and . . ."

"Well?"

"Oh, and what a strange talk we had afterwards by the fire, when . . ."

"No; that was not what you were going to say. You were about to add: *'How angry you were when Zengro made with his forefinger the sign of a circle about him; and how you nearly left the camp then and there.'* Is not that true?"

"Yes, it is true."

"I thought so. Well, I had good reason to be angry."

"Oh, his action meant only that he took you to be fëy, as we say in the north."

"No, it meant more than that. But this brings me to what I have wanted to say to you: what must be told to-night."

He stopped, for the roar about the house shook it to its foundations: one of those swift, howling whirlwinds which sometimes precede the steady march of the mighty host of the thunder.

When it was over, he pulled away the smoking logs from the fire and substituted three or four of dry pine and larch, already dusted with salt. The flame was so vivid and cheerful that, when my host eclipsed the lamplight, and left us in the pleasant firelit gloom, the change was welcome, though the wildness of the night without seemed to be enhanced.

For at least five minutes Fanshawe sat silent, staring into the red glow over which the blue and yellow tongues of flame wove an endless weft. Then, abruptly, he began:—*

"You know that I have Gypsy blood in me. It is true. But I do not think you know how strong in the present, how remote in the past, the strain is. In the twelfth century my parental ancestors were of what might be called the blood-royal among the Children of the Wind. One of

---

*His narrative, in its earlier stages, was much longer than my partial reproduction of it; for some of it dealt with irrelative matters, some of it was merely reminiscent of our own meetings and experiences in common, and some of it was abruptly discursive. Interwrought with it were the sudden tumults, the tempestuous violence of that night of storm: when, through it all, the thunder was to me as the flying shuttle in the Loom of Destiny.

them, head of a great clan at that time dispersed, during the summer months, through the region of the New Forest, was named John the Heron. Hunting one day in these woodlands, the king's brother was set upon by outlaws. They would have killed, or at least withheld him against a ransom, but for the bravery of his unknown gypsy ally. The royal duke was grateful, and so in turn was the king. Wild John the Heron became John Heron of Roehurst and the lands round Elvwick. He had seven sons, five of whom died tragic deaths or mysteriously disappeared. The eldest in due time succeeded his father; the youngest travelled into Derbyshire in the train of a great lord. In those days the most ancient, the proudest, but even then the most impoverished of the old families of that region, was the house of Ravenshawe. Its head was Sir Alurëd Ravenshawe, a man so haughty that it was said he thought the king his inferior. Gilbert Heron was able to do him a great service; and ultimately, through this influence, the young man succeeded to the name and titles of a beggared and outlawed knight, Sir Vane Fanshawe. Nevertheless, there could have been no question of the marriage of the young Sir Gilbert Fanshawe (for the name of Heron was to be relinquished) with the lady Frida, though the young people had fallen in love with each other at their first meeting; and, ultimately, it was permitted at all, and then reluctantly, only because of two further happenings. The first of these was the undertaking of the great lord with whom the young man was (a near kinsman and friend of Sir Alurëd Ravenshawe), that the king would speedily make Sir Gilbert Fanshawe of Roehurst in Hants and Eastrigg in the shire of Derby, a baron. At that time, there was no actual village of Eastrigg, but only a small hamlet called Fanshawe, or, as it was then given, The Fan Shawe. These lands belonged to Ravenshawe, and he gave them to his daughter as a wedding gift, on the condition that the king made her betrothed a noble, and that he became known as Baron Fanshawe of Fanshawe.

"All this was duly done, and yet there seems to have been deception in the matter of the Gypsy origin; for about the time of the birth of an heir to my lord of Fanshawe, Sir Alurëd refused to hold any communication with his son-in-law, or even to see his daughter. A Ravenshawe, he declared, could have nothing in common with a base-born alien.

"It was some years after this that strange rumours got about concerning not only Lord Fanshawe but also The Chase, as his castellated manor was called. A wild and barbaric folk sojourned in its neighbourhood, or in the adjacent forests. A contagion of suspicion, of a vague dread, of a genuine animosity, spread abroad. Then it was commonly averred that my lord was mad, for had he not been heard to proclaim himself the Christ, or at any rate to speak and act as though he were no other than at least the second Christ, of whose coming men dreamed?

"One day Sir Alurëd Ravenshawe appeared in the camp of the Egyptians, as the alien wandering-folk were wont to be called. What he learned from the patriarch infuriated him to frenzy. 'Let the dog of the race of Kundry die the death he mocks,' he cried; 'and lo, herewith I give you my bond that no harm shall come to you or your people's goods, though you must sojourn here no more.'

"Then it was that the Egyptians waylaid their kinsman, the Lord Fanshawe of Fanshawe, and crowned and mocked him as the Gypsy Christ, and crucified him upon a great leafless tree in the forest now known as the Wood o' Wendray. Thereafter, for a long period, the place knew them no more. But, in going, they took secretly with them the infant Gabriel, only child of the House o' Fanshawe."

For a time after this, Fanshawe ceased speaking. We both sat, our gaze intent upon the fire, listening to the growing savagery of the storm without. Then, without preamble, he resumed. He had a habit, when in the least degree wrought by impatience or excitement, of clasping and unclasping his hands; and his doing so now was the more noticeable because of the strange tapery look of the fingers coming from the rough close mittens he wore.

"That Gabriel Fanshawe never saw England again, nor yet his son Gabriel. The name was retained privily, though among his blood-kin in Austria or Hungary he was known simply as Gabriel Zengro, the kin-name of the patriarch who had adopted him after the crucifixion of his father.

"Long before his grandson was a man well over forty years,—and it was not till then that the third Gabriel visited England to see if he could claim his heritage,—the lands of Eastrigg, the house and hamlet of Fanshawe, and Wester Dallaway, not only were exempted from all claim upon them by any one of the blood of Gilbert Fanshawe, the baronry in whose name was cancelled, but had, in turn, passed from the hands of the old knight of Ravenshawe into those of the family of Francis, with whom they remained until the fall of the Jacobite dynasty, after which they were held by the Hewsons, until (sadly diminished) they came again into the ownership of a Fanshawe, with my purchase of them.

"But though Gabriel Zengro the third found that he had lost his title and northern inheritance, he was able to recover possession of Roehurst. There he settled, married, and had two children: known only, of course, by his English surname. In the fiftieth year of his age he became markedly unpopular with his fellows. He was seen at times to frequent a rude and barbaric sect of vagrants,—even to live with them; and the rumour spread that his foreign wife was really one of these very aliens. Then he was heard to say wild and outrageous things, such as might well hang a man in those times. The upshot was that one day he returned to his home no more. His body was found transfixed to a leafless tree in the forest beyond Grailph Moss."

"Beyond Roehurst, you mean?" I interrupted.

"No, I mean what I say. His crucified body was found in the forest beyond Grailph Moss, in that part of it called The Wood o' Wendray."

"That is," I interrupted again, "where the same frightful tragedy had been enacted in the instance of the victim's grandfather?"

"Even so. But though Gabriel Fanshawe had been lured or persuaded or kidnapped out of Hants, he was certainly alive after he crossed the Derwent, for a huntsman recognised him among his people one day, and spat on the ground to the north, south, east, and west. The lord of Roehurst disappeared in this mysterious fashion; and none of his neighbours of the south learned aught of his doom, but only his wife knew, the tidings having been conveyed to her I know not how. But from the record she put in writing, it is clear that with the message had come a summons, perhaps a menace; for, together with her two children, she betook herself to the greater safety of London. There the girl died, calling vainly, and uttering strange words in a tongue no one spake or understood. But the boy lived, and in course of years grew to manhood, and on the death of his mother went to reside upon his own lands. Nor was it till after his marriage, and the birth of a son, that he read the record his mother had caused to be writ; and so came into the knowledge that has been the awe and terror of those lineally descended from him.

"But neither he nor his son came to any harm, save the common doom of all. Of his grandson wild things were said, but all that is known certainly is that he hanged himself upon the great oak in front of Roehurst. He too, however, had left a Gabriel behind him as his successor: in due time a good knight and learned man, who brought up his only child worthily and steadfastly. Strange that the heir of two such loyal and excellent men should prove so feather-brained as to love the woods better than the streets, and the wild people of the woods better than courtiers and scholars! Stranger still that the old omens should recur, till, at last, Gervase Fanshawe, after an awful curse upon all of his blood, and terrifying blasphemies, openly set fire to his manor; and himself, with his little daughter (though the young Gabriel escaped), was consumed in the flames.

"Thus, with tragic alternations, went the lives of my forbears; till, after many generations of English Fanshawes, the house of Roehurst came to an end with Jasper Fanshawe."

At that moment so savage an onslaught of wind and rain was made upon the house, so violent a quake of thunder shook the walls, that further speech was impossible for the time. But, save by his silence, my companion took no notice of the tumult. His eyes were very large and wild, and stared spell-bound upon the fire, as though they beheld there the tragic issues to the many memories or thoughts which tyrannised his brain.

"I said that the family of Roehurst," he resumed, as soon as comparative quietude had followed that wild outburst, though the wind moaned and screamed round the gables and among the old chimneys, and the rain slashed against the window-pane in continuous assault,—"I said that the family of Roehurst came to an end with Jasper Fanshawe. This was at the close of the eighteenth century. Jasper was the last of his race, and, the rumour ran, one of the wildest. Almost on the eve of his wedding it transpired, that when, in his youth, he had gone away with and lived among the gypsy-people, he had, as most if not all of his progenitors, married a Romany girl. The union was not one that would be recognised by the English law; but the authentic news of it, and the confirmed rumour that Squire Fanshawe had a son and daughter living, brought about a duel between him and the brother of his betrothed. With rash folly this duel was fought in the woods, and witnessed by no one save the gypsy 'messenger' who kept the squire always in view."

"The gypsy-messenger, Fanshawe?"

"Yes. That is the name sometimes used. The old word means the doom-watcher. The latter is the better designation, but I did not care to use it.

"Well, my ancestor killed the man Charles Norton. The deed was the worse for the survivor, in that Norton was the favourite son of the most influential man in the country-side. In a word, the slaying was called murder, and Jasper Fanshawe was proclaimed. His sole chance lay with his blood-folk. The doom-watcher came into Winchester, and testified to what he had seen, while hiding among the bracken in the forest; but his evidence was overborne, and, rightly or wrongly, he was himself clapped into prison on a charge of rick-burning.

"No trace could be found of the fugitive, nor of the 'Egyptians' with whom he made good his escape. The large encampment in Elvwick Wood had broken up into sections, which had severally dispersed, and all had vanished almost as swiftly and effectually as the smoke of the camp-fires.

"Whatever I may surmise, I do not know for certain the manner of Jasper Fanshawe's death. His son, James, lived for the most part in Hungary; at other times in the wide-roaming lands between the Caspian and the Adriatic. He took in preference the old kin-name of Herne, which, indeed, his father had adopted after his flight from England.

"This James Herne lived to an old age, and became one of the 'elder brothers' of his particular tribal branch. His son Gabriel, however, left his kindred, and went to Vienna, where he studied medicine. Then, while still relatively a young man, he gained an important post at Prague, and in a year or so became what would here be called a magistrate. He was noted for his severity in dealing with all vagrants, but especially in the instance of any gypsy delinquent. At this time, as from his early Vienna days, he was known as Vansar, a Romany equivalent for Fanshawe. On three separate occasions, his life was attempted, though each time the would-be assassin escaped. Gabriel Vansar was not the man to be intimidated; indeed, he became only the more stringent and tyrannical, so that soon there was not a gypsy encampment within a twenty-mile radius of Prague. In his thirty-sixth year he was offered a medical professorship in Vienna. In that city he met a Miss Winstane, a beautiful English girl, the sole child of Edward Winstane, a Justice of the Peace for South Hants, and Squire of Roehurst Park and the greater part of the Parish of Elvwick. Miss Winstane loved her handsome wooer, and the marriage was duly solemnised. Though he spoke with a slight foreign accent, Mr. Vansar knew his paternal language thoroughly; for though 'James Herne' had ceased to be English in all else, he had been careful to teach his son his native tongue, and indeed always to speak it when alone with him.

"Neither Mr. Winstane nor Winifred Winstane ever knew that Gabriel Vansar was Gabriel Herne the Gypsy, or, in turn, that he was the grandson of that Jasper Fanshawe whose flight from Roehurst had been followed by the confiscation of his property, and its disposal to Edward Winstane the elder.

"As a matter of fact, Mr. Winstane died a few months after the marriage of his daughter. Gabriel Vansar now relinquished his post, and went to England to live the life of a country squire. There he had three children born to him: two sons and a daughter. Naomi was the youngest by several years, and at her coming her mother went. Of the two sons, Jasper was the elder, I the younger."

IV

Although not taken wholly by surprise, I exclaimed, "You, Fanshawe?"—adding that indeed the chain of circumstances was remarkable.

"Yes. . . . Well, when my brother was twenty-one, and I nineteen, our father died. He had changed much since our mother's decease, and had become strangely depressed and even morose. There was adequate explanation of this in the sealed papers which he left to Jasper.

"But now I must diverge for a moment. I have something very strange to confide to you. But first tell me: have you heard of Kundry?"

"Of Kundry?" I repeated, bewildered.

"You love music, I know; and I thought you might have heard of Kundry."

"Ah, yes, I know now. You mean the woman in Parsifal?"

"Yes. At the same time, Wagner does not give the true legend. He did not even know that the name is a gypsy one, and very ancient. I have heard that some people think it imaginary; others, that it is old-time Scandinavian. But our people, the Children of the Wind, are far more ancient than any one knows. We had earned that very name long before the Coming of the Christ. We had, however, another name, which were I to translate literally, would be something like 'The Spawn of Sheitan:' given us because we were godless, and without belief in any after-life, and were kingless and homeless and, compared with other peoples, lawless. As we were then, so in a sense we are now: for though we do not deny God, we neither worship him nor propitiate him nor fear him; nor have we any faith in a future, believing that with the death of the body that which is the man is dead also; and kingless we are, save for the common overlords, Time and Death; and homeless, except for the curtains of the forest and the dome of the sky, and the lamps of sun and moon; and, even as the wind is lawless and the sea, so also are we, who are more unstable than the one and more vagrant than the other.

"Nearly nineteen hundred years ago a tribe of our race, 'the first tribe' it was called, because it claimed to be the original stock, was in the hill-country beyond Jerusalem.

"It was in the year of the greatest moment to the modern world: the year of the death of Jesus of Nazareth.

"I need not repeat even in the briefest way details which are universally familiar. It is enough to say that some of our people were on the Hill of Calvary on the Day of Anguish; that among them was a beautiful wanton called Kundry; and that as the Sufferer passed to His martyrdom, she laughed in bitter mockery. Turning upon her, and knowing the darkness of her unbelief and the evil of which she was the embodiment, the Christ stopped and looked at her.

"'Hail, O King!' she laughed mockingly. 'Vouchsafe to me, thy Sister, a sign that thou art indeed Lord over Fate; but thou knowest thou canst not do this thing, and goest to thy death!'

"Then the Christ spake. 'Verily, thou shalt have a sign. To thee and thine I bequeath the signs of my Passion, to be a shame and horror among thy people, forevermore.'

"Therewith He resumed His weary way. And Kundry laughed, and followed. Again, during the Agony on the Cross, she laughed, and again at the last bitter cry of the Son of God; but in the darkness that suddenly came upon the land she laughed no more.

"From that day the woman Kundry, whom some have held to be the sister of the Christ, was accurst. Even among her own people she went veiled. Two children she bore to the man who had taken her to his tent: children of one birth, a male child and a woman child.

"They were in their seventh year, when, in a wild Asian land, Kundry came out among her people and told them that she, the Sister of Christ, had come to deliver them this message, that out of the off-spring of her womb soon or late would arise one who would be their Redeemer, who would be the Gypsy Christ.

"When the young men and maidens of her people mocked, the elders reprimanded them, and asked Kundry to give some proof that she had not the sun-fever or the moon-madness, or other distemper of the mind. Whereupon the woman appalled them by showing upon her hands and feet the stigmata of the Crucifixion.

"But, after the first wonder, and even awe, a great horror and anger arose among the kindred. Three days they gave her within which to take back that which she had said, and to confess the trickery of which she had been guilty, or at least to reveal the way in which she had mutilated herself and so healed the wounds. At sundown, on the third day, the strange and awful signs were still there; nor would the woman retract that which she had said. So they scourged her with thorny switches, and put a rough crown of them round her head, and led her to a place in the forest where there was a blasted tree. And as she went she stopped once, and looked to see whose mocking laugh made her last hour so bitter; and lo, it was the girl whom she had borne in her womb. Then they crucified her, and she gave up the ghost in the third hour before the dawn. But because that the children were so young, and bore no mark of the Curse, and were of the First Lineage, they were spared."

At this point my companion ceased. Leaning forward, he stared into the fire as one in a vision. A long silence prevailed. Outside, the wind wailed wearily, rising at times into a screaming violence. The heavy belching roar of the thunder crashed upon us ever and again, and even in the firelit room with its closed curtains the lightning-glare smote the eyes.

Fanshawe apparently did not hear; perhaps he did not see. I watched him intently, the more curiously because of what he told me and what I inferred. At last a strange, a terrifying cry startled even his abstraction. He sprang to his feet, and looked wildly at the window.

"It was the wind," I said; "I heard it like that a little ago, though not so loudly, or with so weird a scream."

Fanshawe made no reply. After a prolonged stare at the curtained window, and a nervous twisting and untwisting of his fingers, he seated himself again. Then, almost as though he had not broken his narration, he resumed:—

"The son and daughter of Kundry were spared by the enemies of the tribe as well as by their kindred,—or rather they escaped the cruelty of the one as well as the fanaticism of the other; for the tribe was almost exterminated by the shores of the Euphrates, and only Michael and Olah, the son and daughter of Kundry, with a few fellow-fugitives, reached a section of their race temporarily settled some fifty miles to the north.

"There 'the laughing girl,' as Olah was called, partly in memory of her mother, partly because of her own laughter at her mother's death-faring, and partly because of the musical mockery wherewith she angered and delighted the tribesmen, brought unhappiness and ruin among 'the rulers.' There were three brothers of the ancient race, and each came to disaster and death through Olah. But through their death, Michael came to be what you would call the Prince of the Children of the Wind. There was but one evil deed recorded against him: the murder of his sister. But—so the ancient chronicle goes—this act was not out of cowardice or malice; it was to remove the curse of the mother, not only from those of her blood, but from the race. The deed was done in the year when Michael's wife bore him their second child, a girl. Before Olah's death,—and she died in the same way as her mother,—she took the little Sampa in her arms, and breathed her life into it. On the day of the crucifixion, the child turned in her sleep, in her mother's arms, and laughed as child never laughed before.

"The story thereafter is a long one. It is all in the secret record of our people, though known to a few only. I could tell it all to you, with every name and every happening, but this would serve no purpose to-night. Suffice it, that link by link the chain is unbroken from Michael and Sampa, the children of Michael, brother of Olah, the son and daughter of Kundry who laughed at the Christ on Calvary, even unto the three offspring of Gabriel Fanshawe, who was called Vansar, and was of the tribe of the Heron."

Could it be, I wondered, as I looked intently at the speaker, that this man before me was the lineal descendant of that Kundry who had laughed at Christ; that he was the inheritor of the Curse; and that for him, perhaps, as for so many of his race, the ancestral doom was imminent? With an effort I conquered the superstitious awe which I realised had come upon me.

"Do you mean this thing," I said slowly, "do you mean that you, James Fanshawe, are the direct descendant of Kundry, and that the Curse lives, and that you or some one of your blood, whether of this or a later generation, must 'dree the weird' even as your forbears have done?"

"Even so: I am as I say; and the Curse lives; and no man can evade the doom that is nigh two thousand years old."

I waited a few minutes, pondering what best to say. Then I spoke.

"The story is a strange and terrible one, Fanshawe. But even if exactly as you have told it, surely there is no logical necessity why you or your brother or sister should inherit the Curse. There has, by your own admission, been frequent admixture of a foreign and Christian strain in your lineage. Your father was, to all practical intents, no more a gypsy than I am. He married an English girl, and lived the life of a country squire, and was no different from his kind except in his perhaps exaggerated bitterness against gypsies,—though, by the way, not as different in this respect either, for the country gentleman loveth not the vagrant. In a word, he himself, with all his knowledge of the past, would have laughed at your superstitious application of the legend."

Fanshawe turned upon me his great luminous eyes, aflame with the fire of despair. I could see that he was in passionate earnest.

"*My sister* might have laughed," he said in a voice so low as almost to be a whisper, but with significant emphasis: "*my sister* might have laughed, not my father."

"Why, Fanshawe," I exclaimed, startled, "you do not mean to say that your sister is—is—"

"A daughter of Kundry."

I received the remark in silence. I did not know what to think, much less what to say. My nerves, too, were affected by the electric air, the ever-recurrent surge and tumult of the thunderstorm; and I felt bewildered by what I heard, by what, despite its improbability, I knew that I believed. At last I asked him to resume, saying I knew he had not ended what he had set himself to tell me.

"No, I have not ended.

"From what I have told you, you will have gathered that the Curse does not show itself in every generation, but in the third. I cannot say that the death record is unvarying, for I do not know; nor has it been possible to trace every particular of a remote ancestry. But here is a strange thing: that in all but three instances, so far as known, no son or daughter of Kundry has ever had more than two children. From generation to generation that bitter laugh has never lapsed. From generation to generation it has brought about disaster and shame. Many, even as I have done, have dreamed that the Curse might be expiated or outlived; but it may well be that even as in every generation 'the laughing girl' who is of the race of Kundry mocks God, so in every third generation, till the Christ come again or the world be no more, there may be the tragedy of my ancestral woe.

"All this, my father knew ere he died. He had meant to carry the secret to the grave, and by many precautions believed he had safeguarded his children from contact with the people he hated and dreaded, though he was of them himself.

"About the time when my father's morose and brooding manner was first noted, my brother Jasper had fallen ill. It was a mysterious trouble, and no doctor could name the malady. Once, only, I saw my father furious,—on the day when he learned that there was an encampment of gypsies in Elvwick Woods, and that Jasper, who was as impassioned in religion as Saint Francis himself, had been among the wandering people, striving to win them to the Brotherhood of Christ. Our father did not know that I and my sister Naomi had already discovered the camp, and had been fascinated by the dark people and their way of life and the forest freedom,—so that we could think of little else, and yearned to be in the greenwood, even as a bird to spread its wings beyond the bars of its cage.

"It must have been immediately after this that my father made the discovery which changed him from one man to another. Neither Naomi nor I knew aught of it at the time, though we were aware that something dire had happened, something of awe, of dread.

"For when Jasper rose from his bed of sickness there was upon his feet and upon his hands the purple bruise and ruddy cicatrix of the great nails of the Crucifixion."

For a few moments Fanshawe paused, and drew a painful, laboured breath, as of a man in pain or a great weakness.

"After our father's death, Jasper shut himself up in his room, and would see no one. I used to creep along the passage at dusk, and listen to the wild incoherences of his prayers. We, Naomi and I, were very dismal, and it was with relief when, one evening, we fled into the forest, and joined our friends, more mysterious and alluring than ever because of the terrifying things which had been said of them by him who was now dead.

"Our shortest way was by Elvwick churchyard. Perhaps but for this we would not have thought of looking at our father's grave again: for we did not mean to return to Roehurst. Hand in hand, however, we stole to the spot we had already ceased to regard with the first overwhelming awe.

"The shock was greater than even that of his death had been, for we saw that the grave had been rifled. The coffin was visible, but the lid had been forced open. There was no corpse within. Almost too dazed to be frightened, it was some time before I realised that the outrage must have been committed that very night; for the upturned earth had retained its fresh smell, an axe was lying near the grave, and there were imprints of feet in the damp soil.

"The idea flashed across my mind that our father had somehow come to life again,—perhaps, I thought, he knew of our intended flight and had gone back to Roehurst to frustrate it,—and I could scarce move with terror. Naomi laughed, a strange mirthless laugh that made me turn as though to strike her. Then, shivering and sobbing, we crawled away. I think we were about to return home, when a tall figure arose, called us by our names, and invited us to come and see the merry 'Dance of the Wolves' around the camp-fire. I told the man—Mat Lee, I remember his name was—what had happened. To my surprise he did not appear shocked or frightened. He was silent for a little; then in a whisper he urged us to run with him at once, lest we should meet the dead man on his way back from the house to the grave.

"That is how my sister and I went to live among our unknown kindred. The very next day, at dawn, the camp was lifted; a week thence we were in Brittany. It was not till long afterwards I learned that it was the tribesmen who had desecrated my father's grave. 'He had been a renegade, and the enemy of his race,' they said, 'and it was only right that though he had lived in honour he should afterwards be flung back to earth as a dead dog is hurled among the bramble or gorse.'

"Once, only, I saw my brother again. I know that he did his best for us. He traced our flight, and kept in touch with us. A 'commando' was sent to him, forbidding him to come near us, or even to go among his kindred anywhere. I was told I was free to go and come as I liked, and that I had money always at my command. Naomi, however, had to abide with the tribe. For three years I roamed throughout the lands east of Saxony and Bavaria, and as far south as Dalmatia and Roumania. I had been well educated, and was a student; and I learned much, though in my own desultory fashion.

"Then tidings reached me that Jasper had disappeared. It was said that he had been seen in the shore-woods of Lymington, on the Solent; and that he had been drowned, while bathing or boating. An upturned boat had been discovered, in which he had certainly been that forenoon, for he had come in it from Yarmouth in the Isle of Wight.

"I went to England, and in due time entered into possession of the family property. At first (and this was when we met in Surrey), I thought of settling there, for a time. At last, however, I decided to dispose of

Roehurst, and realise everything that had come to me; and I had done this, and was about to leave for eastern Europe when a letter reached me from Derbyshire. *It was in my brother's handwriting.*

"Bewildered, distraught, and angry, I read this strange and unlooked-for communication. The writer was alive, and begged me to come and save him from the enmity of the kindred with whom he had at the end cast in his lot. To narrate briefly what might well be told with lengthy and surprising detail, I reached Sheffield, and thence set out across the wild and remote country (to me at that time quite unknown, even by repute) which lies to the north of Dallaway Moor and Grailph Moss. At the verge of the great forest I was met by a gypsy guide. Late that night we reached the camp. From an hour after my arrival till the last hour of the night I was alone with my brother. He told me all that I have told you, and much else beside; also where his own and our father's papers were to be found. Finally, he declared that the Curse died with himself. He had had this revealed to him in a vision; besides, other circumstances, with which I need not weary you, pointed to this end. He had sworn this to the tribesmen, and they had consented to forego the manner of his death, if he would further renounce all claim to be the Gypsy Christ. The very name gave them a sense of horror and anger; his fervent words of exhortation had made them sullen, and at last resentful; and, over and above this, there was the vague race-legend that, whenever the Gypsy Christ should come, the days of the Children of the Wind would be numbered, and they would dwindle away like the leaves in October.

"An hour before dawn, three of the kindred entered the tent. They put a bandage about my eyes, and secured my arms. I heard them lift Jasper, and put him upon a hurdle of larch-boughs. In the chill air we went silently forth. In about a quarter of an hour we came to a standstill upon a rising ground. I heard Jasper repeat in a husky voice that he was not worthy to be the Christ; that he was not the Christ; and that he prayed that with him might pass away forever the curse of Kundry.

"There was a brief silence after that; then a rustling sound in the air; then, after an interval, a thud, thud, thudding, followed by a splash.

"'No man ever comes back from the bowels of the lead-mine, O James, of the tribe of the Heron, of the race of Kundry,' whispered a voice in my ear.

"When, an hour later, the bandage was taken from my eyes, I was on the moor just above the House o' Fanshawe. A boy was beside me, his face covered with a slouch hat. In a few words, in our ancient language, he told me that I was by the village of Eastrigg, and that twenty miles south of me lay Fothering Dale, whence I could easily go in any direction; anywhere, he added significantly, where the tongue can be silent and the memory dead.

"I made no inquiries about the matter I have told you. Fortunately I had informed no one of the letter I had received. This letter I burned. But I ran a great risk by returning a few days later to Eastrigg. The reason was this: I had learned, from the papers to which my brother had alluded, the whole story of our doomed race, the race of Kundry; and I decided to try one more desperate hazard against Fate, for I could not be sure that Jasper's death would remove the Curse. In a word, I decided to make my home in this place where my ancestor and brother suffered such cruel deaths, and to die here; for I found in my papers an ancient prophecy, both in English and Romany, to the effect that when a woman of the race of Kundry would voluntarily sacrifice herself at the Hill of Calvary, or when a man of the race of Kundry would live and die at the place where one of his kindred had suffered for the Curse, the doom might be removed.

"Thus it was that I became possessor of this strange 'House o' Fanshawe.' But I had something to do before I settled here.

"When everything that had to be done was done, I went abroad to seek my kindred, and more particularly my sister Naomi. Perhaps you guess my object. I had more hope of success, from the circumstance that Naomi was of a passionately enthusiastic nature; and that, of late, she had even dreamed of leaving her people (for one strain in her fought against the other), to enter a Sisterhood of Mercy.

"But my people had gone, and the clues were already old and complicated. I went through Hungary, across Transylvania, hither and thither in Roumania, and from end to end in Dalmatia. Everywhere I was on their track, but the trail was confused. It was not till I had gained the Bavarian highlands that the conclusion was forced upon me I was being misled. This became a certainty after I had followed a sure trail through Suabia and so to the Lands of the Moselle. At Trèves, I was directed southward, and went blindly on a false track that led through southern France towards the Basque provinces; but at last, at a place in Provence called Aigues-Mortes, I met a life-brother (that is, one whose life had been saved when otherwise it would have been lost, and who has vowed his life-service to his saviour, whenever required), whom I put upon his oath. He told me that the Zengri, the Hernes, and two other tribes were not in southern Europe at all, but in England. I had hit upon the right trail between Heidelberg and the Mösel, but, when almost upon my people at Trèves, had been skilfully diverted. And the reason for this was the extraordinary ascendancy of my sister. My heart sank as I heard this tiding. I feared that the Curse had already shown itself; but, my informant assured me, I was wrong in this surmise. It was merely that Naomi had fascinated the tribes-folk, and, particularly since the death of the old Peter Zengro, had become practically a queen. Her word was law.

"Of course I could not tell the exact reason why she wished to evade me. Possibly she feared I might resent her ascendancy, and try to usurp her; possibly she had some reason to fear that the always latent enmity against any of the race of Kundry would be directed against me. As likely as not, she had several schemes to fulfil, all or even one of which might be frustrated by my appearance on the scene.

"Nevertheless, I decided to travel straight to England, and, as soon as practicable, gain an interview with Naomi.

"For some weeks after I reached this country I was again purposely misled. Yet from one thing and another I became more and more anxious to meet Naomi soon. Strange rumours were abroad. At Ringwood in the New Forest, I overheard some words by the camp-fire (when I was supposed to be asleep) which made my heart shrink.

"Once again I lost all clue. Then it was that I remembered Nathan Lee,—an intimate friend of yours as well as of mine,—who, because of his great love for his wife, had sworn never to leave the neighbourhood of Glory Woods, where she was buried. I travelled with all speed to Dorking. From Lee I learned what I wanted to know. By a strange fatality, Naomi had made her headquarters in the Wood o' Wendray, beyond Eastrigg. But was it a blind fatality? That was what troubled and perturbed me. Why had she, why had our particular tribe, settled at the accursed spot where Jasper Fanshawe had met his fate!

"It was at this time that I met you in Glory Woods. The next day I was back in the village of Elvwick, and had arranged with Robert Hoare, the late gardener at Roehurst, and his wife, to come and keep house and generally look after me, at Eastrigg Manor.

"Almost every day after I was settled I rode over to the Wood o' Wendray; but the ban was upon me, and I was warned not to approach the camp. Thrice I set the ban at defiance, and strode into the camp, but on no occasion saw any sign of Naomi. This was the more strange, as, on the third time, I arrived at sunset, 'the hour of the smoke,' when the gypsies meet round the fire to talk and smoke and break their long day-fast. It was after this third visit I was formally warned that my next defiance of the ban would be my last. I knew this to be no idle threat. Thereafter I had to be more cautious. I no longer rode across the moor; but, either in the morning twilight or in the late afternoon, wandered here and there across the uplands: sometimes by the deserted lead-mines, sometimes by the green pool, sometimes even within the outskirts of the Wood o' Wendray.

"I met you in Glory Woods in the spring, and now it is autumn. It was exactly midway in this time that I learned a dreadful thing.

"One day a message came to me, in Naomi's writing, to be at the green pool beyond Dallaway mine at dawn on the morrow.

"I was there, of course. The morning was raw and misty. Even at the margin of the Pool I could not see the further side. Suddenly, however, I heard whispered voices, and the trampling of feet. I called, and was at once answered. I was bidden not to stir from where I was. The voice was that of Naomi, but with a note in it I had never heard before.

"'Is that you, James Fanshawe, of the tribe of the Heron, of the race of Kundry?'

"'It is I, Naomi, daughter of Gabriel. It is I, your blood-brother.'

"'Then know this thing. She whom you wedded secretly, Sanpriella Zengro, is dead.'

"I gave a cry of pain. . . . I have not told you that, during my last year with my people, I loved Sanpriella, the daughter of Alexander Zengro, the brother of Peter Zengro, of the First Tribe. But Alexander Zengro feared and hated any of the race of Kundry; so we loved secretly. This was one reason why I was so eager to find my people again; for Naomi was not, as you may have supposed, my one quest. I knew that Sanpriel-la was with child, and I longed to make her my wife before all men.

"'Is it so?' I cried in a shaking voice, because of my sore pain; 'is it so, upon the oath of the crossed sticks and the hidden way?'

"'I say it. May tree fall on me, and water gain upon me, and the falling star light on me, if I speak not truth. Sanpriella is dead. She lies in the wood of Heiligenberg, beyond the Neckar. And now listen to the doom, thou son of Kundry.'

"My heart leapt at these ominous words, doubly ominous and strange coming from one of my own blood.

"'Unto Sanpriella were born twin children, a boy and a girl. The girl lives, though you shall never see her. She is in a far land from here, and the lines of her life are already known. The boy . . . the boy is . . . dead.'

"'But know this thing, James my blood-brother. The doom of Kundry was upon him. His mother hid the thing, but after her death the Curse was visible. Upon his hands were the bruised wounds of the nails of the Crucifixion.'

"With a shuddering cry I sank to my knees. Wildly I prayed, implored Naomi to say it was not true; that it was hearsay; that some natural cause had been mistaken for this horrible mystery.

"'Therefore,' she resumed unmoved, 'the ban is upon you also. Take heed lest a worse thing befall you. It will be well if you leave this place where you live, and forever. Be a wanderer upon the face of the earth; it will be for you safer so: but avoid the trail of the Children of the Wind as you would the pestilence. And now—farewell!'"

"'My child lives—my daughter lives!' I cried despairingly.

"There was a long silence. I called again and again, but met with no response. Thick as the mist was, I raced round the pool like a greyhound. There was no one near. I ran out upon the moor, but there I was like a derelict boat in wide ocean in a dense fog. I could see nothing, hear nothing. All that day the mist hung impermeable; all that day I abode where I was."

Once more a long silence fell upon Fanshawe. Outside, the shrieking of the wind was appalling. The rain slashed against the house as though all the sluices of the thunderstorm were concentred there. The thunder was no longer overhead, but a raucous blast—distinct from the blind, furious gale—moved to and fro like a beast of prey. I was overcome by the strange and terrible tale I had listened to. Then and there, to that wild accompaniment, it all seemed deadly true, and as inevitable as Destiny."

With an abrupt gesture, Fanshawe suddenly resumed:—

"On the eve of that day I walked swiftly across the moor. The sun was almost on the horizon as I reached the eastern edge of Grailph Moss. Suddenly, I stopped as one changed into stone. Black against the sunset-light I saw a tall figure stand: with head thrown back, and arms wide outstretched from the sides. Was it a vision of the Christ? That was the thought which came to me. Then the figure disappeared, absorbed in the mist over Grailph Moss. I turned and went home. It was Naomi I had seen.

"The next evening I was in the same place, at the same hour.

"Again I saw Naomi, in that sunflame Crucifixion. Once more she disappeared, and across the Moss. I knew of no encampment there, but unquestionably she had moved swiftly westward.

"On the third afternoon I was there again, earlier. This time I had with me my white bloodhound. We crouched in good hiding till Naomi passed. I made Grailph sniff her track. When the sun set, she disappeared as before. I held Grailph in leash, and followed swiftly. In less than an hour I came upon her. She was standing in a waste place, near the centre of a broken circle of tall slabs. These were the Druidic Stones, known almost to none save the most daring explorers of the Moss, for they are in a region beset with quagmires.

"She was speaking, with outstretched arms, as if in prayer. There was no one visible. She was, I saw, in a trance, or ecstasy.

"When, suddenly, she descried me, she leapt like a deer on to a narrow dry path beyond the stones. She would certainly have evaded me but for Grailph. The hound slid beyond like running water in a rapid. In less than a minute he had headed her off.

"When I came up with her, I expected either furious denunciation, or at least a summary command that I should return straightway. She did no more than look at me intently, however. She had already forgotten what had lain between us. She was possessed.

"'*Naomi*,' I said, simply.

"'I am Naomi, blessed among women.'

"I stared, perplexed.

"'Why do you follow me here to spy me out? Beware lest God strike thee for thy blasphemy.'

"'My blasphemy, Naomi?'

"'Even so. I come here to meet the Spirit of God.'

"'Tell me, my sister, is this true what I have heard: that you are with child?'

"Her eyes flamed upon me. But her voice was cold and quiet as she replied,—

"'It is true. The Lord hath wrought upon me a miracle. I have immaculately conceived, and the child I shall bear will be the Gypsy Christ,—the long dreamed-of, the long waited-for second Christ.'

"'This is madness. Come with me; come home with me, Naomi.'

"'The green earth is my home; and the wind is my brother, and the dust my sister.'

"'Come!'

"Then in a moment her whole look and mien changed. The flame that was in her eyes seemed to come from her very body. Her voice now was loud, raucous, imperious. The hound whined, and sidled to my feet.

"'I am the Sister of Jesus, I am no other than Kundry, deathless in my woe until these last days. I am the Mother of the Christ that is to be. And you, *you*, son of my mother's womb, you are ordained to be my prophet! Go forth even now: go unto our people in the woods: declare, declare, declare, to them, to all, that the Gypsy Christ cometh at last!'

"I was shocked, terrified even. But after a throbbing silence, I spoke, and firmly,—

"'This is madness, Naomi. Already the Curse is heavy enough upon us. Do you not know that our brother Jasper was done to death because of this doom of ours; that because of this awful malison on the race of Kundry . . . that . . . my little son . . .'

"'I know all,—what has been, what is, what shall be. Once more I ask you: will you be the prophet of the Gypsy Christ?'

"'No, never, so help me God!'

"'This is the fourth day of this Week of the Miracle. To-morrow thou hast; and the day after; and yet again, another day. Repent while there is yet time. But if thou dost not repent, thine end shall be as that of thy dog. An awful sign shall be with thee this very night; yet another shall be with thee on the morrow; and on the third thou shalt receive the message of the Cross. Then thou shalt waver no more, for whom all wavering is forever past. And now, begone!'

"Broken in spirit, I turned. When, a hundred yards thence, I looked back, there was no trace of Naomi anywhere.

"That night I had the first sign."

Here Fanshawe ceased for a moment, and wiped the cold sweat from his forehead with a hand tremulous as a reed. His voice had sunk into a dull monotony, to me dreadful.

"On the day following, I had the second sign. Drops of blood oozed from the red figure of the Christ that you have seen in my room. Then, you came. To-day I have had the message of the Cross. You saw it yourself: a green cross on the portal of the house.

"Then at last my terror overmastered me. Also, I yet hoped to prevail with Naomi. Thus it was that when I left you abruptly this afternoon, I rode across the moor, to the Wood o' Wendray. I reached the camp, but only the ashes of dead fires were there. Yet I know my people wait, and Naomi has my life on the hollow of her hand."

But here I broke in eagerly.

"Come, Fanshawe, come with me at once, the first thing to-morrow. You must not be here another day. It is madness for you to remain. Why, in another week you would persuade yourself that you too had inherited this so-called curse!"

"Look!" he shouted, springing to his feet, tearing the coverings from his hands, and holding forth the palms to me, rigid, testifying, appalling: *"Look! Look! Look!"*

And as I live I saw upon the hands the livid stigmata of the Passion!

With a cry, I repelled him. A great horror seized me. But the next moment a greater pity vanquished my weakness. He had already fallen. I took him in my arms, and laid him back on his chair.

James Fanshawe was dead.

For some minutes I stared, paralysed, upon the still face that had just been so wrought with a consuming frenzy. A deep awe came upon me. I crossed the room, threw back the window, and looked out. Grailph the hound was not there. Nor could he have been lurking near, for at that moment I saw a man glide swiftly across the yard, and disappear into the gloom.

The rain was over, the thunder rumbled far across the moors; the wind, too, had veered, and I heard it crying like a lost thing, in the deep ravine of the Gap.

I stayed quietly beside my friend, keeping vigil till the dawn. While it was still dark, I went again to the window, and looked out. On the moor I could hear two larks singing at a great altitude. Doubtless they had soared to meet the dawnlight.

I thought of Naomi, whose madness would surely bring upon her, and that soon, the awful ancestral doom. Yet of this I knew I should hear nothing. The Children of the Wind have a saying: The dog barks by day, and the fox by night; but the Gypsy never lets any one know whence he comes, where he is, or whither he goes.

Sometimes the horror of it all makes me long to look upon it as an evil dream. Has the dreadful Curse at last worked itself out? With a sudden terror, I remember at times that James Fanshawe had two children born to him. What of the girl? Did she, too, laugh, when her kindred led Naomi to her doom? Even now doth she move swift and sure towards that day when she shall go quick with child; when she or the child or the child's child shall arise and say, "Behold the Gypsy Christ is come at last!"

The Graven Image

Being the Narrative of James Trenairy

There is an old house in Kensington which is to me, dweller in the remotest part of Cornwall though I am, the most solitary place I know. It is not far from the eastern boundary of Holland Park, yet, I am sure, few even of the residents on Campden Hill, or other Kensingtonians, are aware of its existence.

The house is a small square building, set far back in a walled garden. The approach is by an unattractive byway, which has all the appearance of a *cul-de-sac,* though there is really a narrow outlet which leads ultimately to High Street.

"The Mulberries," as it is called, was, some years ago, occupied by my father's old friend, John Tregarthen: as it was, in years back, by at least three successive John Tregarthens before him. The Tregarthens have always been a solitary and even somewhat eccentric race, but where the last representative of the family differed from his kin was in his dislike to his native Cornwall. He was the most confirmed Londoner I have ever known, though by this I mean only that he never left the metropolis, and seldom roamed beyond Kensington. So far as social intercourse was concerned, however, he might as well have lived in the lighthouse of Tre Pol, or at his own desolate ancestral home, Garvel Manor.

In the autumn of last year, on my way to spend the winter in Italy, I stayed for a few days in London. One afternoon I was in the Campden Hill neighbourhood, vainly in search of the studio of an artist friend, who seemed to me to have done his utmost to make his abode indiscoverable. It was while on this quest that I meandered through small streets and byways, and found myself at last at an unkempt gateway, whereon I could just decipher the words, "The Mulberries."

I confess that I had forgotten the very existence of Mr. John Tregarthen. Several years had passed since my father's death, and I had never had occasion to communicate with the owner of "The Mulberries." Now, however, that I was there, I was prompted by various feelings, but particularly by that clannish sentiment which distinguishes the true Cornishman, to seek Mr. Tregarthen himself.

To avoid needless details, I may say at once, and succinctly, that I found Mr. Tregarthen within; that he gave me a cordial welcome,— cordial, that is, for a man of so austere a life and so sombre a cast of mind; and that I was persuaded to remove my impedimenta from my Bloomsbury hotel, and to spend my two remaining spare nights at "The Mulberries."

When, a few hours later, I drove up to the house and rang the gate-bell, I feared that my host had forgotten our appointment and gone off on some errand or walk. Time after time I rang, but without any result; and as a dull November rain was drip-dripping from the few discoloured leaves still clinging to the chestnuts and elms, my position was not an agreeable one.

At last, however, Mr. Tregarthen came slowly along the garden path and opened the door to me. In the misty gloom, unrelieved by even a flickering gas-jet, I could not discern his features; but I fancied that he spoke constrainedly, and, indeed, as if he had already repented of his pressing invitation.

True, when once we were housed from the rain and chill, and the outer world was, as it were, locked away for the night, he became more genial, and even expressed heartily his pleasure at seeing me there as his guest. None the less, so gloomy was the lonely, silent house, so cheerless the aspect of the room where we sat, notwithstanding the bright flame of a wood fire and the yellow glow of a large reading-lamp, that I could not but regret the cheerful, if commonplace comforts of my hotel, the opulence of light and sound, the pleasant intimacy of familiar things enjoyed in common.

Still, I enjoyed my evening. We had a very simple dinner, for Mr. Tregarthen's one servant, an elderly Cornishwoman, was no vagrant from the culinary straight path to which she had been accustomed in her youth; but the wine was exceptionally good. My host talked well and intelligently, and, recluse though he was, I could see that he took at least a casual interest in the various matters of international policy which were at that time occupying so much attention in the press.

After dinner we adjourned to a small room, which he told me was his sanctum. There we had coffee, and sat for a long time in silence, watching the play of the firelight along the dark bookcases which lined the room, and listening to the dreary intermittent cry of the autumnal wind. Mr. Tregarthen had either forgotten, or had intentionally omitted, the lighting of his lamp. Though in ordinary circumstances, nothing delights me more than to sit and dream by the fireside in a dark room, I admit that on this occasion I should have preferred the serene company of a lamp, or even the unwavering effrontery of a gas-jet. Again, I am a smoker, though indifferent to the pipe, and I could not but yearn for that postprandial luxury to which I had grown so accustomed. No cigar was offered, however, and I was quick to discover proofs that tobacco in any form was not to be found at "The Mulberries."

After a long silence, following some casual chit-chat about the places in Italy where I hoped to sojourn, my host suddenly made a remark that surprised me, wholly inconsequent as it seemed.

"You never knew him, did you?"

Again I noticed that strange constraint of voice, as if the mouth spoke while the mind was otherwise preoccupied.

"Him . . . whom?"

"My brother Richard."

"No, never. I heard—"

"What have you heard?" broke in Mr. Tregarthen, at once so imperiously and so sharply, and with so keen an accompanying glance the while he stooped in order to scrutinize me more fully in the upswing of the flame, that I realised his constraint was due to no mere dreamy indolence of mind.

"Oh, merely that he was always a wanderer, and that he came here at last broken in health, and died of some long-standing but mysterious trouble."

"Ah!" ejaculated my companion, and said no more. I did not care to broach the subject again, for I knew that it was one which could not be welcome. Indeed, I had heard more than I was willing to admit to

Mr. Tregarthen, though I knew not how much was mere rumour. I remembered, however, that my father, a man as exact in the spirit of his statements as precise in the expression of them, had told me of some tragic misunderstanding having long separated John and Richard Tregarthen, and that there was something very strange in the return of the younger to his brother's house, whence he had departed years before with a curse upon him heavy as woe and unforgettable as death. Moreover, I recollected some vague particulars concerning a beautiful girl, one Catherine Tregaskis, belonging to an old family neighbouring our own, whom, as I understood, both men had loved, and who, in the manner of women, was a cause of infinite disturbance to both.

I was about to rise at last, for a fret of impatience was on me. The dull sound of the wind had grown to a moaning sough, that, in my then mood, could be hearkened with equanimity only in affluence of light and comfort. I thought that if I went to the bookcase near the fire my host would suggest the lighting of the lamp; but before I stirred, he broke the silence once more.

"We have scarce spoken of our own parts yet. I wish to know something about our neighbours of old. Tell me, who lives now at Malfont? Is James Tregaskis still alive and well?"

"Yes," I replied, "Mr. Tregaskis is still alive, though he lives in as recluse a fashion as you do. His wife died three years ago. Childless and wifeless, the old man is very lonely. He has never been himself since—since——"

Here I stopped, embarrassed; but Mr. Tregarthen quietly finished my sentence,—

"Since the death of his daughter Catherine, you were going to say?"

I bowed slightly in affirmation.

"Will you tell me the actual wording of the inscription on the memorial tablet which he has raised in the family burial-ground behind the little private chapel on Malfont Heath?"

"Well—to say the truth, I don't know—that is to say, I have forgotten," I muttered, confusedly, reluctant as I was to communicate anything on a subject fraught with so much that would be painful.

"Does it run thus?" went on Mr. Tregarthen, quietly, though with a suggestion of irony in his voice. "Does it run thus, for I am sure you can at least correct me if I am wrong? First, the date of the year; and then—

"'TO THE MEMORY
of
EDWARD TREGASKIS, aged 29: Slain in war.
OLIVIA TREGASKIS, aged 26: Drowned at sea.
CATHERINE TREGASKIS, aged 25: Not yet avenged.'

Tell me, am I right?"

I admitted that he was, and even ventured to add that in our neighbourhood people thought trouble had perverted James Tregaskis' judgment.

"And, of course," I went on, "when he lost his youngest and best-loved child, the third terrible bereavement in a single year, it is no wonder that he imagined vain things, and turned away from those who would have won him to a more generous, if not a more resigned, view."

Mr. Tregarthen looked at me curiously, and I fancied that for a moment a sarcastic smile hovered across his face.

He said no more, however. After a brief interval he rose abruptly, lighted the lamp, and drew my attention to some rare books on Etrurian remains which he thought would interest me, as I was on my way to Volterra and other dead cities and towns of the Etruscan region.

I am not accustomed to late hours, and I suppose that I showed the weariness I felt. At any rate, when my host asked me if I was inclined to go to my room, I assented gladly.

Yet, when I was alone, my sense of sleep was no longer a pleasant languour. The room was a long oak-panelled chamber, both in height and appearance quite unlike what one would expect from an outside view of "The Mulberries." The bed, an old-fashioned four poster with heavy hangings, stood with its back to the same wall in which was the door; beyond it, on the right, was a fireplace, in which one or two logs sullenly smouldered. For the rest, there was nothing but a few stiff chairs set along the dark panelled walls, and a great gaunt badly-carved escritoire and bookcase of bog-oak.

I do not like gloomy rooms, and so it was natural that I should again think with regret of my comfortable lodging at the hotel, where, for old associations' sake, I always put up when I go to London. But I had the good sense to undress and go to bed, hopeful of sleep.

Whether it was the singular silence within, or the moaning voice of the wind without, with a swift slash of rain ever and again upon the panes, or the coffee I had drunk, or I know not what, but sleep I could not. The longer I lay the more restless I became, and at last I thought I would rise and see if there were any readable volumes in the oak bookcase.

There were not, and I turned discontentedly to the fire, which I had replenished before I went to bed. I leaned on the mantelpiece for some time, looking into the flickering tongues and jets of red and yellow flame beneath, when I chanced at last to stand back and look up.

For the first time I noticed that what seemed a large bronze bas-relief was deeply set in the wall. I know not why I had not noticed it before; doubtless because the fire was low and the shadow deep, while I had not moved the candle away from the small book-table near the door where I had placed it on entrance.

I was glad of anything to distract me. So I lit my candle, and held it so that I could scrutinize the ornament, as it appeared to be. I saw at once that it was something out of the common. It seemed to be a sheet of bronze or copper, along the sides and at the base and summit of which were strange and perplexing arabesques and other designs, most notably what I presumed to be flaming swords, somewhat as represented by Leonardo da Vinci.

But in the centre was a head, life-size, which so far as I could tell was moulded in wax, hardened and tinted.

I did not apprehend these and other details till later, for my first feeling was one of startled curiosity, my second of something akin to fear.

The face was that of a woman; no doubt, of a beautiful woman, though the expression was so evil, or, rather, I should say, so forbidding, that I was blind to the native loveliness of the features.

What amazed me was the extraordinary lifelikeness. The face before me seemed almost as though it were alive. The clustering black hair, drawn back from the high pale brows, appeared to droop with its own weight; the compressed mouth, the distended nostrils, the intent staring gaze, simulated a painful and distressing actuality.

For some time I was fascinated by this strange portrait or imaginative study. I regarded it with something of the same blended curiosity and repugnance with which most of us look at some rare and terrible reptile. No, I felt sure, that woman *lived* once; through those sombre eyes came fire of passionate love or passionate hate; from those delicately-curved lips issued words fanged with scorn or sweet with perilous seduction.

At last I scrutinized the base. There, wrought in deep, strong lines, I read:

"THE GRAVEN IMAGE:"

with below it the words,

"Lo, I made unto myself a graven image, that unto the end of my days the eyes of the body should likewise know no peace."

The inscription was mysterious,—nay, I admit that to me it had a terrifying suggestiveness.

I could look no more. Had I not been ashamed of my weakness, I should have dressed and gone down to the sitting-room. Determined, however, not to yield to my nervous disquiet, I went back to my bed. It was with a sense of relief that I felt my weariness growing upon me, and the stealthy tide of sleep draw nearer and nearer.

When I awoke, I know not how much later, it was with that abrupt sickening sensation which is indescribable, but is familiar to any one who has been aroused by the unheard but subtly apprehended entrance of another person into the room.

I lay for a few moments in a cold perspiration, trembling the while as though in terror. Then I opened my eyes.

I did not need to raise myself. The fire was burning dimly, but I could clearly see a woman standing beside it, looking fixedly into its embers. So much of her face as was turned towards me was in deep shadow. She was tall, and of a fine grace of figure, and though simply dressed in a long gown of a soft grey material, I imagined her to be of good birth and breeding.

I know not how it was that for that brief while fear left me, and that I could lie and speculate thus quietly. I perceived, of course, that my visitor was not Mr. Tregarthen's old servant, but it occurred to me that she might be an inmate of the house. For all I knew to the contrary, Mr. Tregarthen might be married; and, if so, this might be his wife or daughter come to my room unknowing me to be there, or, mayhap, as a victim to somnambulism.

But when suddenly a flame spurted upward from the heart of the fire, almost simultaneously with the sound of an approaching step along the passage, and the woman turned her face towards the door, so that I saw it plainly, my heart seemed as though it would burst.

For with a sense of unutterable fear I recognised in a flash the beautiful but terrifying face of the "Graven Image."

Startling as was the discovery, I had no time for thought, even if I had not lain as though paralysed.

The vindictive fury and scorn that shone in her eyes affrighted me. If it was Mr. Tregarthen who had come along the passage and was now knocking slowly at the door, his reception promised to be a dramatic one.

Whether the door opened or not, I cannot say. All I know is that I saw the woman draw back, as a tall dark man, whose features were quite unknown to me, slowly advanced.

Neither seemed to be aware of my presence; certainly they took no note of it.

I wondered he did not quail under that fierce, that inexpressibly malignant scorn.

As it was, he stopped abruptly. What tragedy of love turned to hate was this! In the dark scowl of the man I interpreted an insatiable fury. Yet I shuddered less at this speechless anger than at the lacerating contempt of her unwavering stare.

I looked to see the man spring at her, to do her some violence. But, leaning against the fireplace, he stood watching her intently. On her face was such a shadow of tempest as made me sick with a new and poignant terror.

I saw his lips move; the scowl on his face deepened. He drew himself erect, and as he did so I thought I heard him utter a name mockingly.

She did not answer, did not move. Outside I heard the wind rise and fall, monotonously crying in a thin shrewd wail. The patter of the rain had ceased, but so intense was the stillness that the drip, drip, from the soaked leaves upon the sodden ground was painfully audible.

Then so swiftly that I scarce saw her move, she sprang forward. There was a flash, a hoarse cry, and the man staggered back, with the blood from a knife-thrust spurting from his left shoulder.

She stood motionless. He, staring at her, panted hard as he slowly stanched the blood.

Suddenly she began to scream. I thought my blood would freeze with horror at the awful sound; scream after scream of deadly terror, and yet neither she nor the man moved.

But, looking at him, I saw that murder flamed in his eyes. Before I could spring from the bed to interfere, he leaped upon her like a beast of prey. In a moment both were on the floor, and I could see that he was strangling her to the death.

With a savage exclamation I dashed to the spot, but tripped, and the next moment lay unconscious, for my forehead fell against a corner of the oaken bookcase.

When I woke, or came out of my stupor, I was still on the floor where I had fallen, though the sunlight streamed in at the window. There was no sign of the horrible tragedy that had been enacted before me. With a shudder I looked at the "Graven Image," and recognised, with a new and horrible distinctness, the appalling verisimilitude of the waxen face.

It was impossible to remain in the room. I dressed hurriedly, and made my way downstairs. The front door was open, and I passed into the garden. The fresh air, damp as it was, was cool and soothing to my throbbing nerves, and, before long, I had almost persuaded myself that I had been victim to nightmare.

Suddenly I caught sight of Mr. Tregarthen. He was sitting in his sanctum, and beckoned to me. From the appearance of the room, and, indeed, of himself, I guessed that he had been there all night.

"Well?" he said, quietly: his sole greeting.

I thought it best to be frank.

"I have had a bad night," I began.

"I know it. I heard you cry out."

I looked at him amazedly and in some fear. Abruptly, I demanded, in an imperative tone:

"Who was the original of the 'Graven Image'?"

"Catherine Tregaskis, my betrothed wife."

I was silent, intensely surprised as I was.

Mr. Tregarthen leaned forward and handed to me a vignette portrait.

It was that of a handsome, dark-haired, dark-eyed, black-bearded man. I recognised the face at once, with a thrill of horrified remembrance.

"Who—who—is this man, Mr. Tregarthen?"

"My dead brother, Richard."

I write this a year after my visit to "The Mulberries," which I left that morning. Mr. Tregarthen is dead. "The Mulberries," under another name, is still untenanted; but I should be poor and forlorn indeed before I accepted again the shelter of that roof.

POEMS BY WILLIAM SHARP

The Weird of Michael Scott

(Michael the Scot: fl. circa 1250.) Variants of the Michael Scott legends still exist in parts of the Scottish Southlands: betwixt Tweed and Forth, mainly in the remote districts of the shires of Selkirk, Peebles, and Roxburgh, and north of the Forth here and there along the Fife coast. The most common is that which relates to the magician's power of changing into an animal anyone who crossed him; and it is upon this that Part I. of the following ballad turns. That also is current which relates how Michael the Scot could win the soul from the body of any woman whom he loved. There are several versions of this uncanny kind of wooing: sometimes Michael Scott is said to have seduced the spirit from its tranced tenement, only to find himself eluded after all; sometimes the maiden, unable to resist his spell, comes to him, but over the battlements, and so is killed; again, just as she is about to yield she calls on Christ, and only a phantasmal image of her goes forth, though in the struggle her mortal body perishes (it was upon this version that Rossetti intended to write a poem; his prose outline of it is given in his Collected Works); or, yet again, she comes at her wizard-lover's signal, but when he would embrace her a cross of fire intervenes, and, to save himself from sudden hell-flames which arise, he has perforce to bid her return in safety. I have in Part II. treated Michael Scott's allurement of Margaret's soul not wholly accordantly with any legendary account, yet in superficial conformity with that which most appealed to my imagination. Part III. is in treatment entirely imaginary, although, of course, the germinal idea—that of encountering at the point of death one's own soul—is both old and widespread. The Doppelgänger idea is a most impressive one in its crudest guise, and I have endeavoured to heighten its imaginative effect by making Michael Scott pronounce unwittingly a dreadful doom upon his own soul.

The wild wind moaned: fast waned the light:
Dense cloud-wrack gloomed the front of night:
The moorland cries were cries of pain:
Green, red, or broad and glaring white
The lightnings flashed athwart the main.

The sound and fury of the waves,
Upon the rocks, among the caves,
Boomed inland from the thunderous strand:
Mayhap the dead heard in their graves
The tumult fill the hollow land.

With savage pebbly rush and roar
The billows swept the echoing shore
In clouds of spume and swirling spray:
The wild wings of the tempest bore
The salt rheum to the Haunted Brae.

Upon the Haunted Brae (where none
Would linger in the noontide sun)
Michael the Wizard rode apace:
Wildly he rode where all men shun,
With madness gleaming on his face.

Loud, loud he laugh'd whene'er he saw
The lightnings split on Lammer-Law,
"Blood, bride, and bier the auld rune saith
Hell's wind tae me ae nicht sall blaw,
The nicht I ride unto my death!"

Across the Haunted Brae he fled,
And mock'd and jeer'd the shuddering dead;
Wan white the horse that he bestrode,
The fire-flaughts stricken as it sped
Flashed thro' the black mirk of the road.

And ever as his race he ran,
A shade pursued the fleeing man,
A white and ghastly shade it was;

"Like saut sea-spray across wet san'
Or wind abune the moonlit grass!—

Like saut sea-spray it follows me,
Or wind o'er grass—so fast's I flee:
In vain I shout, and laugh, and call—
The thing betwixt me and the sea
God kens it is my ain lost saul!"—

Down, down the Haunted Brae, and past
The verge of precipices vast
And eyries where the eagles screech;
By great pines swaying in the blast,
Through woods of moaning larch and beech;

On, on by moorland glen and stream,
Past lonely lochs where ospreys scream,
Past marsh-lands where no sound is heard,
The rider and his white horse gleam,
And, aye behind, that dreadful third.

Wild and more wild the wild wind blew,
But Michael Scott the rein ne'er drew:
Loud and more loud his laughter shrill,
His wild and mocking laughter grew,
In dreadful cries 'twixt hill and hill.

At last the great high road he gained,
And now with whip and voice he strained
To swifter flight the gleaming mare;
Afar ahead the fierce sleet rained
Upon the ruin'd House of Stair.

Then Michael Scott laughed long and loud.
"Whan shone the mune ahint yon cloud
I kent the Towers that saw my birth—
Lang, lang, sall wait my cauld grey shroud,
Lang cauld and weet my bed o' earth!"

But as by Stair he rode full speed
His horse began to pant and bleed:
"Win hame, win hame, my bonnie mare,
Win hame if thou would'st rest and feed,
Win hame, we're nigh the House of Stair!"

But with a shrill heart-bursten yell
The white horse stumbled, plunged, and fell,
And loud a summoning voice arose,
"Is't White-Horse Death that rides frae Hell,
Or Michael Scott that hereby goes?"

"Ah, Lord of Stair, I ken ye weel!
Avaunt, or I your saul sall steal,
An' send ye howling through the wood
A wild man-wolf—aye, ye maun reel
An' cry upon your Holy Rood!"

Swift swept the sword within the shade,
Swift was the flash the blue steel made,
Swift was the downward stroke and rash—
But, as though levin-struck, the blade
Fell splintered earthward with a crash.

With frantic eyes Lord Stair out-peered
Where Michael Scott laughed loud and jeered:—
"Forth fare ye now, ye've gat lang room!
Ah, by my saul thou'lt dree thy weird!
Begone, were-wolf, till the day o' doom!"

A shrill scream pierced the lonely place;
A dreadful change came o'er the face;
The head, with bristled hair, swung low;
Michael the Wizard turned and fled
And laughed a mocking laugh of woe.

And through the wood there stole and crept,
And through the wood there raced and leapt,
A thing in semblance of a man;

An awful look its wild eyes kept
As howling through the night it ran.

PART II.

Athwart the wan bleak moonlit waste,
With staring eyes, in frantic haste,
With thin locks back-blown by the wind,
A grey gaunt haggard figure raced
And moaned the thing that sped behind.

It followed him, afar or near:
In wrath he curs'd; he shrieked in fear;
But ever more it followed him:
Eftsoons he'd stop, and turn, and peer
To front the following phantom grim.

Naught would he see; in vain would list
For wing-like sound or feet that hissed
Like wind-blown snow upon the ice;
The grey thing vanished like a mist,
Or like the smoke of sacrifice:

"Come forth frae out the mirk," his cry,
"For I maun live or I maun die,
But na, na mair I'll suffer baith!"
Then, with a shriek, would onward fly
And, swift behind, his following wraith.

Michael the Wizard sped across
The peat and bracken o ' the moss:
He heard the muir-wind rise and fall,
And laughed to see the birk-boughs toss
An' the stealthy shadows leap or crawl.

When white St. Monan's Water streamed
For leagues athwart the muir, and gleamed
With phosphorescent marish-fires,
With wild and sudden joy he screamed,
For scarce a mile was Kevan-Byres—

Sweet Kevan-Byres, dear Kevan-Byres,
That oft of old was thronged with squires
And joyous damsels blithe and gay:
Alas, alas for Kevan-Byres
That now is cold and grey.

There in her bed on linen sheet
With white soft limbs and love dreams sweet
Fair Margaret o' the Byres would be:
(Ah, when he'd lain and kissed her feet
Had she not laughed in mockery!)

Aye she had laughed, for what reck'd she
O' a' the powers of Wizardie!
"Win up, win up, guid Michael Scott,
For ye sall ne'er win boon o' me,
By plea, or sword, or spell, God wot!"

Aye, these the words that she had said:
These were the words that as he fled
Michael the Wizard muttered o'er—
"My Margaret, bow your bonnie head,
For ye sall never flout me more!"

Swiftly he raced, with gleaming eyes,
And wild, strange, sobbing, panting cries,
Dire, dire, and fell his frantic mood;
Until he gained St. Monan's Rise
Whereon the House of Kevan stood.

There looked he long and fixed his gaze
Upon a room where in past days
His very soul had pled love's boon:
Lit was it now with the wan rays
Flick-flickering from the cloud-girt moon.

"Come forth, May Margaret, come, my heart!
For thou and I nae mair sall part—
Come forth, I bid, though Christ himsel'

My bitter love should strive to thwart,
For I have a' the powers o' hell!"

What was the white wan thing that came
And lean'd from out the window-frame,
And waved wild arms against the sky?
What was the hollow echoing name,
What was the thin despairing cry?

Adown the long and dusky stair,
And through the courtyard bleak and bare,
And past the gate, and out upon
The whistling; moaning, midnight air—
What is't that Michael Scott has won!

Across the moat it seems to flee,
It speeds across the windy lea,
And through the ruin'd abbey-arch;
Now like a mist all waveringly
It stands beneath a lonely larch.

"Come Margaret, my Margaret,
Ye see my vows I ne'er forget:
Come win wi' me across the waste—
Lang lang I've wandered cauld and wet,
An' now thy sweet warm lips would taste!"

But as a whirling drift of snow,
Or flying foam the sea-winds blow,
Or smoke swept thin before a gale
It flew across the waste—and oh
'Twas Margaret's voice in that long wail!

Swift as the hound upon the deer,
Swift as the stag when nigh the mere,
Michael the Wizard followed fast—
What though May Margaret fled in fear,
She should be his, be his, at last!—

O'er broom and whin and bracken high,
Where the peat bog lay gloomily,
Where sullenly the bittern boomed
And startled curlews swept the sky,
Until St. Monan's Water loomed!

"The cauld wet water sall na be
The bride-bed for my love and me—
For now upon St. Monan's shore
May Margaret her love sall gie
To him she mocked and jeered of yore!"

Was that a heron in its flight?
Was that a mere-mist wan and white?
What thing from lonely kirkyard grave?
Forlorn it trails athwart the night
With arms that writhe and wring and wave!

Deep down within the mere it sank,
Among the slimy reeds and rank,
And all the leagues-long loch was bare—
One vast, grey, moonlit, lifeless blank
Beneath a silent waste of air.

"O God, O God! her soul it is!
Christ's saved her frae my blasting kiss!
Her soul frae out her body drawn,
The body I maun have for bliss!
O body dead and spirit gaun!"

Hours long o'er Monan's wave he stared;
The fire-flaughts flashed and gleamed and glared,
The death-lights o' the lonely place:
And aye, dead still, he watch'd, till flared
The sunrise on his haggard face.

Full well he knew that with its fires
Loud was the tumult 'mong the squires,
And fierce the bitter pain of all

Where stark and stiff in Kevan-Byres
May Margaret lay beneath her pall.

Then once he laughed, and twice, and thrice,
Though deep within his hollow eyes
Dull-gleamed a light of fell despair.
Around, Earth grew a Paradise
In the sweet golden morning air.

Slowly he rose at last, and swift
One gaunt and frantic arm did lift
And curs'd God in his heav'n o'erhead:
Then, like a lonely cloud adrift,
Far from St. Monan's wave he fled.

PART III.

All day the curlew wailed and screamed,
All day the cushat crooned and dreamed,
All day the sweet muir-wind blew free:
Beyond the grassy knowes far gleamed
The splendour of the singing sea.

Above the myriad gorse and broom
And miles of golden kingcup-bloom
The larks and yellowhammers sang:
Where the scaur cast an hour-long gloom
The lintie's liquid notes out-rang.

Oft as he wandered to and fro—
As idly as the foam-bells flow
Hither and thither on the deep—
Michael the Wizard's face would grow
From death to life, and he would weep—

Weep, weep wild tears of bitter pain
For what might never be again:
Yet even as he wept his face
Would gleam with mockery insane
And with fierce laughter on he'd race.

At times he watched the white clouds sail
Across the wastes of azure pale;
Or oft would haunt some moorland pool
Fringed round with thyme and fragrant gale
And canna-tufts of snow-white wool.

Long in its depths would Michael stare,
As though some secret thing lay there:
Mayhap the moving water made
A gloom where crouched a Kelpie fair
With death-eyes gleaming through the shade.

Then on with weary listless feet
He fared afar, until the sweet
Cool sound of mountain brooks drew nigh,
And loud he heard the strayed lambs bleat
And the white ewes responsive cry.

High up among the hills full clear
He heard the belling of the deer
Amid the corries where they browsed,
And, where the peaks rose gaunt and sheer,
Fierce swirling echoes eagle-roused.

He watched the kestrel wheel and sweep,
He watched the dun fox glide and creep,
He heard the whaup's long-echoing call,
Watched in the stream the brown trout leap
And the grilse spring the waterfall.

Along the slopes the grouse-cock whirred;
The grey-blue heron scarcely stirred
Amid the mossed grey tarn-side stones:
The burns gurg-gurgled through the yird
Their sweet clear bubbling undertones.

Above the tarn the dragon-fly
Shot like a flashing arrow by;
And in a moving shifting haze

The gnat-clouds sank or soared on high
And danced their wild aërial maze.

As the day waned he heard afar
The hawking fern-owl's dissonant jar
Disturb the silence of the hill:
The gloaming came: star after star
He watched the skiey spaces fill.

But as the darkness grew and made
Forest and mountain one vast shade,
Michael the Wizard moaned in dread—
A long white moonbeam like a blade
Swept after him where'er he fled.

Swiftly he leapt o'er rock and root,
Swift o'er the fern his flying foot,
But swifter still the white moonbeam:
Wild was the grey-owl's dismal hoot,
But wilder still his maniac scream.

Once in his flight he paused to hear
A hollow shriek that echoed near:—
The louder were his dreadful cries,
The louder rang adown the sheer
Gaunt cliffs the echoing replies.

As though a hunted wolf, he raced
To the lone woods across the waste
Steep granite slopes of Crammond-Low—
The haunted forest where none faced
The terror that no man might know.

Betwixt the mountains and the sea
Dark leagues of pine stood solemnly,
Voiceful with grim and hollow song,
Save when each tempest-stricken tree
A savage tumult would prolong.

Beneath the dark funereal plumes,
Slow waving to and fro—death-blooms
Within the void dim wood of death—
Oft shuddering at the fearful glooms
Sped Michael Scott with failing breath.

Once, as he passed a dreary place,
Between two trees he saw a face—
A white face staring at his own:
A weird strange cry he gave for grace,
And heard an echoing moan.

"Whate'er you be, O thing that hides
Among the trees—O thing that bides
In yonder moving mass o' shade
Come forth tae me!"—wan Michael glides
Swift, as he speaks, athrough the glade:

"Whate'er you be, I fear ye nought!
Michael the Wizard has na fought
Wi' men and demons year by year
To shirk ae thing he has na sought
Or blanch wi' any mortal fear!"

But not a sound thrilled thro' the air—
Not even a she-fox in her lair
Or brooding bird made any stir—
All was as still and blank and bare
As is a vaulted sepulchre.

Then awe, and fear, and wild dismay
O'ercame mad Michael, ashy grey,
With eyes as of one newly dead:
"If wi' my sword I canna slay,
Thou'lt dree my weird when it is said!"

"Whate'er you be, man, beast, or sprite,
I wind ye round wi' a sheet o' light—
Aye, round and round your burning frame

I cast by spell o' wizard might
A fierce undying sheet of flame!"

Swift as he spoke a thing sprang out,
A man-like thing, all hemmed about
With blazing blasting burning fire!
The wind swoop'd wi' a demon-shout
And whirled the red flame higher and higher!

And as, appalled, wan Michael stood
The flying flaughts swift fired the wood;
And even as he shook and stared
The gaunt pines turned the hue of blood
And all the waving branches flared.

Then with wild leaps the accursed thing
Drew nigh and nigher: with a spring
Michael escaped its fiery clasp,
Although he felt the fierce flame sting
And all the horror of its grasp.

Swift as an arrow far he fled,
But swifter still the flames o'erhead
Rushed o'er the waving sea of pines,
And hollow noises crashed and sped
Like splitting blasts in ruin'd mines.

A burning league—leagues, leagues of fire
Arose behind, and ever higher
The flying semi-circle came:
And aye beyond this dreadful pyre
There leapt a man-like thing in flame.

With awful scream doom'd Michael saw
The flying furnace reach Black-Law?
"Blood, bride, and bier, the auld rune saith
Hell's wind tae me ae nicht sall blaw,
The nicht I ride unto my death!

"The blood of Stair is round me now:
My bride can laugh to scorn my vow:
My bier, my bier, ah sall it be
Wi' a crown o' fire around my brow
Or deep within the cauld saut sea!"

Like lightning, over Black-Law's slope
Michael fled swift with sudden hope:
What though the forest roared behind—
He yet might gain the cliff and grope
For where the sheep-paths twist and wind.

The air was like a furnace-blast
And all the dome of heaven one vast
Expanse of flame and fiery wings:
To the cliff's edge, ere all be past,
With shriek on shriek lost Michael springs.

But none can hear his bitter call,
None, none can see him sway and fall
Yea, one there is that shrills his name!
"O God, it is my ain lost saul
That I hae girt wi' deathless flame!"

With waving arms and dreadful cries
He cowers beneath those glaring eyes
But all in vain—in vain—in vain!
His own soul clasps him as its prize
And scorches death upon his brain.

Body and soul together swing
Adown the night until they fling
The hissing sea-spray far and wide:
At morn the fresh sea-wind will bring
A black corpse tossing on the tide.

The Deith-Tide

"Wi' a risin' win',
An' a flowin' tide,
There's a deith tae be;
When the win gaes back
An' the tide's at the slack,
There's a spirit free."
— F<small>RAGMENT OF A</small> H<small>IGHLAND</small> F<small>OLKSONG</small>.

The weet saut wind is blawing
Upon the misty shore:
And like a stormy snawing
The deid go streaming o'er:—

    The wan drown'd deid sail wildly
    Frae out each drumly wave:
    It's O and O for the weary sea
    And O for a quiet grave.

"Whose voice is that is calling
Frae out the deid-wrack there,
What saut tears these aye falling
Upon my rain-weet hair?

"What white thing blawing, blawing
Before the moaning gale,
The grey thing 'mid the snawing,
The white thing 'mid the hail?"

    The wan drown'd deid sail wildly
    Frae oot each drumly wave:
    It's O and O for the weary sea
    And O for a quiet grave.

"O wha be ye that's mournin'
Down by the saut sea-shore—
Mournin', mournin', mournin'
Alang the saut sea-shore:

"O weel I ken my dearie,
My dear love lost lang-syne:
O weep nae mair my dearie
Your tears o' bitter brine:

"The weet saut win' is falling,
An' hear ye not the tide,
The deith-tide calling, calling?
O come wi' me, my bride!

"O come wi' me, my marrow,
Ye'll sleep love's sleep at last,
No in a cauld bed narrow
But swirlin' on the blast—

"O come wi' me my ain ain Jean—
What gars ye grow sae chill?"
"O I fear your hollow burnin' een,
An' your voice sae thin an' shrill!"

"O come wi' me my marrow,
Sae sweet sall be your sleep,
No in a cauld bed narrow
But in the swayin' deep."

    The wan drown'd deid sail wildly
    Frae back the weary land:
    It's O and O for the saut deep sea
    Ayont the barren strand.

"O weel my soul is flying
Abune the faem wi' thee:
My bodie white cauld cauld is lying
Beside the gurly sea:

"O gie tae me your shadowy han'
  An' swift your phantom-kiss,
  It's drear, sae drear, within the mirk
  Here where the white waves hiss!"

     The wan drown'd deid sail wildly
     Frae back the weary land;
     It's O and O for the saut deep sea
     Ayont the barren strand.

The Willis-Dancers

The moonlight floods the hollow dell:—
The dell where all the city's dead
Were laid, when oft the loud plague-bell
Filled wayfarers with sudden dread:
The accursed plague it was that swept
The young from life, and spared the old—
Who wept and lived, and lived and wept
And mourned the silent sleepers in the dell's chill fold.

The hollow dell is fill'd with light,
The frosty radiance of the moon;
Yet gleams there are, more weirdly bright—
And what is that slow swelling tune?
It is not any wind that blows,
For not a wafted leaf doth fall;
What is the rustling sound that grows,
As if a low wind stirred amid the poplars tall?

Yon white, yon pale green hues that shine—
Are they but fungus-growths that beam:
What moves by yon funereal pine—
What haunts the pool where marsh-fires gleam?
From out the shadow-haunted trees,
Along the nested hedgerows dumb,
And o'er the moonlit sloping leas
Singing a thin strange song the Willis-dancers come.

The *Willi* or Willis-Dancers are the spirits of those who have died untimely,
youths and maidens who on earth had no fulfilment of their desires. On certain
nights they hold wild phantasmal revelry on earth.

In hurrying scores, with silent feet,
In weird processional array
They pass, with motions wild and fleet:
And now they gain the common way.
Adown the long white road they flit,
Slow-singing their unechoing song,
Till, where the Calvary, moonlit,
Crowns the low hill—round whose white base the dancers throng.

Fair, fair, unutterably fair,
With wild and gleaming eyes they pray
O for the breath of mortal air,
O for the joys grown faint and gray!
But never the carven god commands;
The frozen eyes nor gleam nor glance—
The Willis-folk ring phantom-hands,
Then laugh and mock and whirl away in frantic dance.

Wild, wild the dance, with blazing eyes,
With flowing hair, and faun-like leaps,
With thrilling shouts, and ecstasies.
Now one withdraws, and wails, and weeps:
Her grave-blanch'd hair around her thrown,
Her white hands claspt, she doth not hear
A voice that claims her for his own,
Nor hearkens her dead Lover call in awful fear.

For oft when from the grave they've fled
To gain phantasmal joys on earth—
Fair youths and maids who ne'er were wed
But died within their spring-time mirth—
A fearful thing hath happ'd to some:
A joyous dancer hath withdrawn,
Hath wailed and wept, and then grown dumb,
And paled, and pass'd away ev'n as the stars at dawn.

The wan soul, with its burning gaze
From hollow eyes with anguish fill'd,

Would fain the lapsing maiden raise:
One moment all her being is thrilled
With one wild passionate desire—
Then, as a flame that is blown out,
Or as a mist in the sun's fire
She fades into the silence round the whirling rout.

Still wilder, swifter grows the fray:
Youths who on earth had lived in vain,
Maids who had yearned the livelong day
For ease to love's imperious pain,
All whose high hopes had come to nought,
All who for life's delights had striven,
All who had suffered, dreamt, or wrought
To make of our common Earth a glowing Heaven—

All, all, with eager, frantic haste
Swift dart and glide and dance and spring—
As gnats above a stagnant waste
Will interweave in a mazy ring—
With locks that once were living gold
Tossed wildly in the moonlit air,
With panting breasts that ne'er were cold
In the dear vanish'd days ere death came unaware:

Lovers who knew no joy of love
In the old barren years of life,
Together now enraptured move—
Claspt each to each with rapture rife:
Bosom to panting bosom pressed,
Hot lips athirst on thirsting lips,
Strange joys and languors doubly blest
Snatch'd from the sombre grave, yea even from Death's eclipse!

Swift, swifter grows the mystic dance
More wild, more wild, each fierce embrace:
The woe of death's inheritance
Gleams ghastly on each wildered face;

A wan grey light illumes the head
Of the carv'd god to whom they prayed:
A halt—a hush—among the dead!
A long-drawn sigh—and lo, the Willis-dancers fade!

A Dream

Last night thro' a haunted land I went,
Upon whose margins Ocean leant
   Waveless and soundless save for sighs
That with the twilight airs were blent.

And passing, hearing never stir
Of footfall, or the startled whirr
   Of birds, I said, "In this land lies
Sleep's home, the secret haunt of her."

And then I came upon a stone
Whereon these words were writ alone,
   The soul who reads, its body dies
Far hence that moment without moan.

And then I knew that I was dead,
And that the shadow overhead
   Was not the darkness of the skies
But that from which my soul had fled.

The Twin-Soul

In the dead of the night a spirit came:
Her moonwhite face and her eyes of flame
Were known to me:—I called her name—
    The name that shall not be spoken at all
    Till Death hath this body of mine in thrall!

And she laughed to see me lying there,
Wrapped in the living-corpse bloody and fair,
And my soul 'mid its thin films shining bare—
    And I rose and followed her glance so sweet
    And passed from the house with noiseless feet.

I know not myself what I knew, what I saw:
I know that it filled me with trouble and awe,
With pain that still at my heart doth gnaw:
    That she with her wild eyes witched my soul
    And whispered the name of the Unknown Goal.

O wild was her laugh, and wild was my cry
When with one long flash and a weary sigh
I awoke as from sleep bewilderingly:
    Her voice, her eyes, they are with me still,
    O Spirit-Enchantress, O Demon-Will!

The Isle of Lost Dreams

There is an isle beyond our ken,
Haunted by Dreams of weary men.
Grey Hopes enshadow it with wings
Weary with burdens of old things:
There the insatiate water-springs
Rise with the tears of all who weep:
And deep within it, deep, oh deep
The furtive voice of Sorrow sings.
    There evermore,
    Till Time be o'er,
Sad, oh so sad, the Dreams of men
Drift through the isle beyond our ken.

The Death-Child

She sits beneath the elder-tree
And sings her song so sweet,
And dreams o'er the burn that darksomely
Runs by her moonwhite feet.

Her hair is dark as starless night,
Her flower-crown'd face is pale,
But O her eyes are lit with light
Of dread ancestral bale.

She sings an eerie song, so wild
With immemorial dule—
Though young and fair Death's mortal child
That sits by that dark pool.

And oft she cries an eldritch scream
When red with human blood
The burn becomes a crimson stream,
A wild, red, surging flood:

Or shrinks, when some swift tide of tears—
The weeping of the world—
Dark eddying 'neath man's phantom-fears
Is o'er the red stream hurl'd.

For hours beneath the elder-tree
She broods beside the stream;
Her dark eyes filled with mystery,
Her dark soul rapt in dream.

The lapsing flow she heedeth not
Though deepest depths she scans:

Life is the shade that clouds her thought,
As Death's the eclipse of man's.

Time seems but as a bitter thing
Remember'd from of yore:
Yet ah (she thinks) her song she'll sing
When Time's long reign is o'er.

Erstwhiles she bends alow to hear
What the swift water sings,
The torrent running darkly clear
With secrets of all things.

And then she smiles a strange sad smile,
And lets her harp lie long;
The death-waves oft may rise the while,
She greets them with no song.

Few ever cross that dreary moor,
Few see that flower-crown'd head;
But whoso knows that wild song's lure
Knoweth that he is dead.

Stories by Fiona Macleod

The Sin-Eater

SIN.

Taste this bread, this substance; tell me
Is it bread or flesh?

[*The Senses approach.*]

THE SMELL.

Its smell
Is the smell of bread.

SIN.

Touch, come. Why tremble?
Say what's this thou touchest?

THE TOUCH.

Bread.

SIN.

Sight, declare what thou discernest
In this object.

THE SIGHT.

Bread alone.

CALDERON,
Los Encantos de la Culpa.

A wet wind out of the south mazed and moaned through the sea-mist that hung over the Ross. In all the bays and creeks was a continuous weary lapping of water. There was no other sound anywhere.

Thus was it at daybreak: it was thus at noon: thus was it now in the darkening of the day. A confused thrusting and falling of sounds through the silence betokened the hour of the setting. Curlews wailed in the mist:

93

on the seething limpet-covered rocks the skuas and terns screamed, or uttered hoarse, rasping cries. Ever and again the prolonged note of the oyster-catcher shrilled against the air, as an echo flying blindly along a blank wall of cliff. Out of weedy places, wherein the tide sobbed with long, gurgling moans, came at intervals the barking of a seal.

Inland by the hamlet of Contullich, there is a reedy tarn called the Loch-a-chaoruinn.* By the shores of this mournful water a man moved. It was a slow, weary walk that of the man Neil Ross. He had come from Duninch, thirty miles to the eastward, and had not rested foot, nor eaten, nor had word of man or woman since his going west an hour after dawn.

At the bend of the loch nearest the clachan he came upon an old woman carrying peat. To his reiterated question as to where he was, and if the tarn were Feur-Lochan above Fionnaphort that is on the strait of Iona on the west side of the Ross of Mull, she did not at first make any answer. The rain trickled down her withered brown face, over which the thin grey locks hung limply. It was only in the deep-set eyes that the flame of life still glimmered, though that dimly.

The man had used the English when first he spoke, but as though mechanically. Supposing that he had not been understood, be repeated his question in the Gaelic.

After a minute's silence the old woman answered in the native tongue, but only to put a question in return.

"I am thinking it is a long time since you have been in Iona?"

The man stirred uneasily.

"And why is that, mother?" he asked, in a weak voice hoarse with damp and fatigue; "how is it you will be knowing that I have been in Iona at all?"

"Because I knew your kith and kin there, Neil Ross."

"I have not been bearing that name, mother, for many a long year. And as for the old face o' you, it is unbeknown to me."

"I was at the naming of you, for all that. Well do I remember the day that Silis Macallum gave you birth; and I was at the house on the croft of Ballyrona when Murtagh Ross—that was your father—laughed. It

---

* *Contillich: i.e.* Ceann-nan-talaich, "the end of the hillocks." *Loch-a-chaoruinn* means the loch of the rowan-trees.

was an ill laughing, that."

"I am knowing it. The curse of God on him!"

"'Tis not the first, nor the last, though the grass is on his head three years agone now."

"You that know who I am will be knowing that I have no kith or kin now on Iona?"

"Ay, they are all under grey stone or running wave. Donald your brother, and Murtagh your next brother, and little Silis, and mother Silis herself, and your two brothers of your father, Angus and Ian Macallum, and your father Murtagh Ross, and his lawful childless wife, Dionaid, and his sister Anna—one and all they lie beneath the green wave or in the brown mould. It is said there is a curse upon all who live at Bally-rona. The owl builds now in the rafters, and it is the big sea-rat that runs across the fireless hearth."

"It is there I am going."

"The foolishness is on you, Neil Ross."

"Now it is that I am knowing who you are. It is old Sheen Macar-thur I am speaking to."

"*Tha mise* . . . it is I."

"And you will be alone now, too, I am thinking, Sheen?"

"I am alone. God took my three boys at the one fishing ten years ago; and before there was moonrise in the blackness of my heart my man went. It was after the drowning of Anndra that my croft was taken from me. Then I crossed the Sound, and shared with my widow sister Elsie McVurie: till *she* went: and then the two cows had to go; and I had no rent: and was old."

In the silence that followed, the rain dribbled from the sodden bracken and dripping loneroid. Big tears rolled slowly down the deep lines on the face of Sheen. Once there was a sob in her throat, but she put her shaking hand to it, and it was still.

Neil Ross shifted from foot to foot. The ooze in that marshy place squelched with each restless movement he made. Beyond them a plover wheeled a blurred splatch in the mist, crying its mournful cry over and over and over.

It was a pitiful thing to hear: ah, bitter loneliness, bitter patience of poor old women. That he knew well. But he was too weary, and his heart was nigh full of its own burthen. The words could not come to his lips. But at last he spoke.

"Tha mo chridhe goirt," he said with tears in his voice, as he put his hand on her bent shoulder; "my heart is sore."

She put up her old face against his.

"'S tha e ruidhinn mo chridhe," she whispered; "it is touching my heart you are."

After that they walked on slowly through the dripping mist, each dumb and brooding deep.

"Where will you be staying this night?" asked Sheen suddenly, when they had traversed a wide boggy stretch of land; adding, as by an afterthought—"Ah, it is asking you were if the tarn there were Feur-Lochan. No; it is Loch-a-chaoruinn, and the clachan that is near is Contullich."

"Which way?"

"Yonder: to the right."

"And you are not going there?"

"No. I am going to the steading of Andrew Blair. Maybe you are for knowing it? It is called Le-Baile-na-Chlais-nambuidheag."*

"I do not remember. But it is remembering a Blair I am. He was Adam, the son of Adam, the son of Robert. He and my father did many an ill deed together."

"Ay, to the stones be it said. Sure, now, there was, even till this weary day, no man or woman who had a good word for Adam Blair."

"And why that . . . why till this day?"

"It is not yet the third hour since he went into the silence."

Neil Ross uttered a sound like a stifled curse. For a time he trudged wearily on.

"Then I am too late," he said at last, but as though speaking to himself. "I had hoped to see him face to face again, and curse him between the eyes. It was he who made Murtagh Ross break his troth to my mother, and marry that other woman, barren at that, God be praised! And they say ill of him, do they?"

"Ay, it is evil that is upon him. This crime and that, God knows; and

---

*The farm in the hollow of the yellow flowers.

the shadow of murder on his brow and in his eyes. Well, well, 'tis ill to be speaking of a man in corpse, and that near by. 'Tis Himself only that knows, Neil Ross."

"Maybe ay and maybe no. But where is it that I can be sleeping this night, Sheen Macarthur?"

"They will not be taking a stranger at the farm this night of the nights, I am thinking. There is no place else for seven miles yet, when there is the clachan before you will be coming to Fionnaphort. There is the warm byre, Neil, my man; or, if you can bide by my peats, you may rest and welcome, though there is no bed for you, and no food either save some of the porridge that is over."

"And that will do well enough for me, Sheen; and Himself bless you for it."

And so it was.

After old Sheen Macarthur had given the wayfarer food—poor food at that, but welcome to one nigh starved, and for the heartsome way it was given, and because of the thanks to God that was upon it before even spoon was lifted—she told him a lie. It was the good lie of tender love.

"Sure now, after all, Neil my man," she said, "it is sleeping at the farm I ought to be, for Maisie Macdonald, the wise woman, will be sitting by the corpse, and there will be none to keep her company. It is there I must be going; and if I am weary, there is a good bed for me just beyond the dead-board, which I am not minding at all. So, if it is tired you are sitting by the peats, lie down on my bed there, and have the sleep, and God be with you."

With that she went, and soundlessly, for Neil Ross was already asleep, where he sat on an upturned *claar,* with his elbows on his knees, and his flame-lit face in his hands.

The rain had ceased; but the mist still hung over the land, though in thin veils now, and these slowly drifting seaward. Sheen stepped wearily along the stony path that led from her bothy to the farm-house. She stood still once, the fear upon her, for she saw three or four blurred yellow gleams moving beyond her, eastward, along the dyke. She knew what they were—the corpse-lights that on the night of death go between the bier and the place of burial. More than once she had seen them before the last hour, and by that token had known the end to be near.

Good Catholic that she was, she crossed herself and took heart. Then, muttering

> *Crois nan naoi aingeal leam*
> *'O mhullach mo chinn*
> *Gu craican mo bhonn*

> (The cross of the nine angels be about me,
> From the top of my head
> To the soles of my feet),

she went on her way fearlessly.

When she came to the White House, she entered by the milk-shed that was between the byre and the kitchen. At the end of it was a paved place, with washing-tubs. At one of these stood a girl that served in the house,—an ignorant lass called Jessie McFall, out of Oban. She was ignorant, indeed, not to know that to wash clothes with a newly dead body nearby was an ill thing to do. Was it not a matter for the knowing that the corpse could hear, and might rise up in the night and clothe itself in a clean white shroud?

She was still speaking to the lassie when Maisie Macdonald, the deid-watcher, opened the door of the room behind the kitchen, to see who it was that was come. The two old women nodded silently. It was not till Sheen was in the closed room, midway in which something covered with a sheet lay on a board, that any word was spoken.

"Duit sìth mòr, Beann Macdonald."

"And deep peace to you, too, Sheen; and to him that is there."

"Och, ochone, mise'n dingh; 'tis a dark hour this."

"Ay, it is bad. Will you have been hearing or seeing anything?"

"Well, as for that, I am thinking I saw lights moving betwixt here and the green place over there."

"The corpse-lights?"

"Well, it is calling them that they are."

"I *thought* they would be out. And I have been hearing the noise of the planks—the cracking of the boards, you know, that will be used for the coffin to-morrow."

A long silence followed. The old women had seated themselves by the corpse, their cloaks over their heads. The room was fireless, and was lit only by a tall wax death-candle, kept against the hour of the going.

At last Sheen began swaying slowly to and fro, crooning low the while. "I would not be for doing that, Sheen Macarthur," said the deid-watcher in a low voice, but meaningly; adding, after a moment's pause, *"The mice have all left the house."*

Sheen sat upright, a look half of terror half of awe in her eyes.

"God save the sinful soul that is hiding," she whispered.

Well she knew what Maisie meant. If the soul of the dead be a lost soul it knows its doom. The house of death is the house of sanctuary; but before the dawn that follows the death-night the soul must go forth, whosoever or whatsoever wait for it in the homeless, shelterless plains of air around and beyond. If it be well with the soul, it need have no fear; if it be not ill with the soul, it may fare forth with surety; but if it be ill with the soul, ill will the going be. Thus is it that the spirit of an evil man cannot stay, and yet dare not go; and so it strives to hide itself in secret places anywhere, in dark channels and blind walls; and the wise creatures that live near man smell the terror, and flee. Maisie repeated the saying of Sheen; then, after a silence, added—

"Adam Blair will not lie in his grave for a year and a day because of the sins that are upon him; and it is knowing that, they are, here. He will be the Watcher of the Dead for a year and a day."

"Ay, sure, there will be dark prints in the dawn-dew over yonder."

Once more the old women relapsed into silence. Through the night there was a sighing sound. It was not the sea, which was too far off to be heard save in a day of storm. The wind it was, that was dragging itself across the sodden moors like a wounded thing, moaning and sighing.

Out of sheer weariness, Sheen twice rocked forward from her stool, heavy with sleep. At last Maisie led her over to the niche-bed opposite, and laid her down there, and waited till the deep furrows in the face relaxed somewhat, and the thin breath laboured slow across the fallen jaw.

"Poor old woman," she muttered, heedless of her own grey hairs and greyer years; "a bitter bad thing it is to be old, old and weary. 'Tis the sorrow, that. God keep the pain of it!"

As for herself, she did not sleep at all that night, but sat between the living and the dead, with her plaid shrouding her. Once, when Sheen gave a low, terrified scream in her sleep, she rose, and in a loud voice cried *"Sheeach-ad! Away with you!"* And with that she lifted the shroud from the dead man, and took the pennies off the eyelids, and lifted each lid; then, staring into these filmed wells, muttered an ancient incantation that would compel the soul of Adam Blair to leave the spirit of Sheen alone, and return to the cold corpse that was its coffin till the wood was ready.

The dawn came at last. Sheen slept, and Adam Blair slept a deeper sleep, and Maisie stared out of her wan, weary eyes against the red and stormy flares of light that came into the sky.

When, an hour after sunrise, Sheen Macarthur reached her bothy, she found Neil Ross, heavy with slumber, upon her bed. The fire was not out, though no flame or spark was visible; but she stooped and blew at the heart of the peats till the redness came, and once it came it grew. Having done this, she kneeled and said a rune of the morning, and after that a prayer, and then a prayer for the poor man Neil. She could pray no more because of the tears. She rose and put the meal and water into the pot for the porridge to be ready against his awaking. One of the hens that was there came and pecked at her ragged skirt. "Poor beastie," she said. "Sure, that will just be the way I am pulling at the white robe of the Mother o' God. 'Tis a bit meal for you, cluckie, and for me a healing hand upon my tears. O, och, ochone, the tears, the tears!"

It was not till the third hour after sunrise of that bleak day in the winter of the winters, that Neil Ross stirred and arose. He ate in silence. Once he said that he smelt the snow coming out of the north. Sheen said no word at all.

After the porridge, he took his pipe, but there was no tobacco. All that Sheen had was the pipeful she kept against the gloom of the Sabbath. It was her one solace in the long weary week. She gave him this, and held a burning peat to his mouth, and hungered over the thin, rank smoke that curled upward.

It was within half-an-hour of noon that, after an absence, she returned.

"Not between you and me, Neil Ross," she began abruptly, "but just for the asking, and what is beyond. Is it any money you are having upon you?"

"No."

"Nothing?"

"Nothing."

"Then how will you be getting across to Iona? It is seven long miles to Fionnaphort, and bitter cold at that, and you will be needing food, and then the ferry, the ferry across the Sound, you know."

"Ay, I know."

"What would you do for a silver piece, Neil, my man?"

"You have none to give me, Sheen Macarthur, and if you had, it would not be taking it I would."

"Would you kiss a dead man for a crown-piece—a crown-piece of five good shillings?"

Neil Ross stared. Then he sprang to his feet.

"It is Adam Blair you are meaning, woman! God curse him in death now that he is no longer in life!"

Then, shaking and trembling, he sat down again, and brooded against the dull red glow of the peats.

But, when he rose, in the last quarter before noon, his face was white.

"The dead are dead, Sheen Macarthur. They can know or do nothing. I will do it. It is willed. Yes, I am going up to the house there. And now I am going from here. God Himself has my thanks to you, and my blessing too. They will come back to you. It is not forgetting you I will be. Good-bye."

"Good-bye, Neil, son of the woman that was my friend. A south wind to you! Go up by the farm. In the front of the house you will see what you will be seeing. Maisie Macdonald will be there. She will tell you what's for the telling. There is no harm in it, sure; sure, the dead are dead. It is praying for you I will be, Neil Ross. Peace to you!"

"And to you, Sheen."

And with that the man went.

When Neil Ross reached the byres of the farm in the wide hollow, he saw two figures standing as though awaiting him, but each separate and unseen of the other. In front of the house was a man he knew to be Andrew Blair; behind the milk-shed was a woman he guessed to be Maisie Macdonald.

It was the woman he came upon first.

"Are you the friend of Sheen Macarthur?" she asked in a whisper, as she beckoned him to the doorway.

"I am."

"I am knowing no names or anything. And no one here will know you, I am thinking. So do the thing and begone."

"There is no harm to it?"

"None."

"It will be a thing often done, is it not?"

"Ay, sure."

"And the evil does not abide?"

"No. The . . . the . . . person . . . the person takes them away, and . . ."

"Them?"

"For sure, man! Them . . . the sins of the corpse. He takes them away, and are you for thinking God would let the innocent suffer for the guilty? No . . . the person . . . the Sin-Eater, you know . . . takes them away on himself, and one by one the air of heaven washes them away till he, the Sin-Eater, is clean and whole as before."

"But if it is a man you hate . . . if it is a corpse that is the corpse of one who has been a curse and a foe . . . if . . ."

"*Sst!* Be still now with your foolishness. It is only an idle saying, I am thinking. Do it, and take the money, and go. It will be hell enough for Adam Blair, miser as he was, if he is for knowing that five good shillings of his money are to go to a passing tramp because of an old ancient silly tale."

Neil Ross laughed low at that. It was for pleasure to him.

"Hush wi' ye! Andrew Blair is waiting round there. Say that I have sent you round, as I have neither bite nor bit to give."

Turning on his heel, Neil walked slowly round to the front of the house. A tall man was there, gaunt and brown, with hairless face and lank brown hair, but with eyes cold and grey as the sea.

"Good day to you, an' good faring. Will you be passing this way to anywhere?"

"Health to you. I am a stranger here. It is on my way to Iona I am. But I have the hunger upon me. There is not a brown bit in my pocket. I asked at the door there, near the byres. The woman told me she could give me nothing—not a penny even, worse luck,—nor, for that, a drink of warm milk. 'Tis a sore land this."

"You have the Gaelic of the Isles. Is it from Iona you are?"

"It is from the Isles of the West I come."

"From Tiree? . . . from Coll?"

"No."

"From the Long Island . . . or from Uist . . . or maybe from Benbecula?"

"No."

"Oh well, sure it is no matter to me. But may I be asking your name?"

"Macallum."

"Do you know there is a death here, Macallum?"

"If I didn't, I would know it now, because of what lies yonder."

Mechanically Andrew Blair looked round. As he knew, a rough bier was there, that was made of a dead-board laid upon three milking-stools. Beside it was a *claar,* a small tub to hold potatoes. On the bier was a corpse, covered with a canvas sheeting that looked like a sail.

"He was a worthy man, my father," began the son of the dead man, slowly; "but he had his faults, like all of us. I might even be saying that he had his sins, to the Stones be it said. You will be knowing, Macallum, what is thought among the folk . . . that a stranger, passing by, may take away the sins of the dead, and that too without any hurt whatever—any hurt whatever."

"Ay, sure."

"And you will be knowing what is done?"

"Ay."

"With the bread . . . and the water . . . ?"

"Ay."

"It is a small thing to do. It is a Christian thing. I would be doing it myself, and that gladly, but the . . . the . . . passer-by who . . ."

"It is talking of the Sin-Eater you are?"

"Yes, yes, for sure. The Sin-Eater as he is called—and a good Christian act it is, for all that the ministers and the priests make a frowning at it—the Sin-Eater must be a stranger. He must be a stranger, and should know nothing of the dead man, above all bear him no grudge."

At that Neil Ross's eyes lightened for a moment.

"And why that?"

"Who knows? I have heard this, and I have heard that. If the Sin-Eater was hating the dead man he could take the sins and fling them into the sea, and they would be changed into demons of the air that would harry the flying soul till Judgment-Day."

"And how would that thing be done?"

The man spake with flashing eyes and parted lips, the breath coming swift. Andrew Blair looked at him suspiciously, and hesitated, before, in a cold voice, he spoke again.

"That is all folly, I am thinking, Macallum. Maybe it is all folly, the whole of it. But, see here, I have no time to be talking with you. If you will take the bread and the water you shall have a good meal if you want it, and . . . and . . . yes, look you, my man, I will be giving you a shilling too, for luck."

"I will have no meal in this house, Anndra-mhic-Adam; nor will I do this thing unless you will be giving me two silver half-crowns. That is the sum I must have, or no other."

"Two half-crowns! Why, man, for one half-crown . . ."

"Then be eating the sins o' your father yourself, Andrew Blair! It is going I am."

"Stop, man! Stop, Macallum. See here: I will be giving you what you ask."

"So be it. Is the . . . Are you ready?"

"Ay, come this way."

With that the two men turned and moved slowly towards the bier.

In the doorway of the house stood a man and two women; farther in, a woman; and at the window to the left, the serving-wench, Jessie McFall, and two men of the farm. Of those in the doorway, the man was Peter, the half-witted youngest brother of Andrew Blair; the taller and older woman was Catreen, the widow of Adam, the second brother; and the thin, slight woman, with staring eyes and drooping mouth, was Muireall, the wife of Andrew. The old woman behind these was Maisie Macdonald.

Andrew Blair stooped and took a saucer out of the *claar*. This he put upon the covered breast of the corpse. He stooped again, and brought forth a thick square piece of new-made bread. That also he placed upon the breast of the corpse. Then he stooped again, and with that he emptied a spoonful of salt alongside the bread.

"I must see the corpse," said Neil Ross simply.

"It is not needful, Macallum."

"I must be seeing the corpse, I tell you—and for that, too, the bread and the water should be on the naked breast."

"No, no, man, it . . ."

But here a voice, that of Maisie the wise woman, came upon them, saying that the man was right, and that the eating of the sins should be done in that way and no other.

With an ill grace the son of the dead man drew back the sheeting. Beneath it, the corpse was in a clean white shirt, a death-gown long ago prepared, that covered him from his neck to his feet, and left only the dusky yellowish face exposed.

While Andrew Blair unfastened the shirt and placed the saucer and the bread and the salt on the breast, the man beside him stood staring fixedly on the frozen features of the corpse. The new laird had to speak to him twice before he heard.

"I am ready. And you, now? What is it you are muttering over against the lips of the dead?"

"It is giving him a message I am. There is no harm in that, sure?"

"Keep to your own folk, Macallum. You are from the West you say, and we are from the North. There can be no messages between you and a Blair of Strathmore, no messages for *you* to be giving."

"He that lies here knows well the man to whom I am sending a message"—and at this response Andrew Blair scowled darkly. He would fain have sent the man about his business, but he feared he might get no other.

"It is thinking I am that you are not a Macallum at all. I know all of that name in Mull, Iona, Skye, and the near isles. What will the name of your naming be, and of your father, and of his place?"

Whether he really wanted an answer, or whether be sought only to divert the man from his procrastination, his question had a satisfactory result.

"Well, now, it's ready I am, Anndra-mhic-Adam."

With that, Andrew Blair stooped once more and from the *claar* brought a small jug of water. From this he filled the saucer.

"You know what to say and what to do, Macallum."

There was not one there who did not have a shortened breath because of the mystery that was now before them, and the fearfulness of it. Neil Ross drew himself up, erect, stiff, with white, drawn face. All who waited, save Andrew Blair, thought that the moving of his lips was because of the prayer that was slipping upon them, like the last lapsing of the ebb-tide. But Blair was watching him closely, and knew that it was no prayer which stole out against the blank air that was around the dead.

Slowly Neil Ross extended his right arm. He took a pinch of the salt and put it in the saucer, then took another pinch and sprinkled it upon the bread. His hand shook for a moment as he touched the saucer. But there was no shaking as he raised it towards his lips, or when he held it before him when he spoke.

"With this water that has salt in it, and has lain on thy corpse, O Adam mhic Anndra mhic Adam Mòr, I drink away all the evil that is upon thee . . ."

There was throbbing silence while he paused.

". . . And may it be upon me and not upon thee, if with this water it cannot flow away."

Thereupon he raised the saucer and passed it thrice round the head of the corpse sun-ways; and, having done this, lifted it to his lips and drank as much as his mouth would hold. Thereafter he poured the remnant over his left hand, and let it trickle to the ground. Then he took the piece of bread. Thrice, too, he passed it round the head of the corpse sun-ways.

He turned and looked at the man by his side, then at the others who watched him with beating hearts.

With a loud clear voice he took the sins.

"*Thoir dhomh do ciontachd, O Adam mhic Anndra mhic Adam Mòr!* Give me thy sins to take away from thee! Lo, now, as I stand here, I break this bread that has lain on thee in corpse, and I am eating it, I am, and in that eating I take upon me the sins of thee, O man that was alive and is now white with the stillness!"

Thereupon Neil Ross broke the bread and ate of it, and took upon himself the sins of Adam Blair that was dead. It was a bitter swallowing, that. The remainder of the bread he crumbled in his hand, and threw it on the ground, and trod upon it. Andrew Blair gave a sigh of relief. His cold eyes lightened with malice.

"Be off with you, now, Macallum. We are wanting no tramps at the farm here, and perhaps you had better not be trying to get work this side Iona; for it is known as the Sin-Eater you will be, and that won't be for the helping, I am thinking! There: there are the two half-crowns for you . . . and may they bring you no harm, you that are *Scapegoat* now!"

The Sin-Eater turned at that, and stared like a hill-bull. *Scapegoat!* Ay, that's what he was. Sin-Eater, Scapegoat! Was he not, too, another Judas, to have sold for silver that which was not for the selling? No, no, for sure Maisie Macdonald could tell him the rune that would serve for the easing of this burden. He would soon be quit of it.

Slowly he took the money, turned it over, and put it in his pocket.

"I am going, Andrew Blair," he said quietly, "I am going, now. I will not say to him that is there in the silence, *A chuid do Pharas da!*—nor will I say to you, *Gu'n gleidheadh Dia thu,*—nor will I say to this dwelling that is the home of thee and thine, *Gu'n beannaicheadh Dia an tigh!*"*

Here there was a pause. All listened. Andrew Blair shifted uneasily, the furtive eyes of him going this way and that, like a ferret in the grass.

"But, Andrew Blair, I will say this; when you fare abroad, *Droch caoidh ort!* and when you go upon the water, *Gaoth gun direadh ort!* Ay, ay, Anndra-mhic-Adam, *Dia ad aghaidh 's ad aodann . . . agus bas*

---

* (1) *A chuid do Pharas da!* "His share of heaven be his." (2) *Gu'n gleidheadh Dia thu!* "May God preserve you." (3) *Gu'n beannaicheadh Dia an tigh!* "God's blessing on this house."

dunach ort! Dhonas 's dholas ort, agus leat-sa!"

The bitterness of these words was like snow in June upon all there. They stood amazed. None spoke. No one moved.

Neil Ross turned upon his heel, and, with a bright light in his eyes, walked away from the dead and the living. He went by the byres, whence he had come. Andrew Blair remained where he was, now glooming at the corpse, now biting his nails and staring at the damp sods at his feet.

When Neil reached the end of the milk-shed he saw Maisie Macdonald there, waiting.

"These were ill sayings of yours, Neil Ross," she said in a low voice, so that she might not be overheard from the house.

"So, it is knowing me you are."

"Sheen Macarthur told me."

"I have good cause."

"That is a true word. I know it."

"Tell me this thing. What is the rune that is said for the throwing into the sea of the sins of the dead? See here, Maisie Macdonald. There is no money of that man that I would carry a mile with me. Here it is. It is yours, if you will tell me that rune."

Maisie took the money hesitatingly. Then, stooping, she said slowly the few lines of the old, old rune.

"Will you be remembering that?"

"It is not forgetting it I will be, Maisie."

"Wait a moment. There is some warm milk here."

With that she went, and then, from within, beckoned to him to enter.

"There is no one here, Neil Ross. Drink the milk."

He drank; and while he did so she drew a leather pouch from some hidden place in her dress.

"And now I have this to give you."

---

*(1) *Droch caoidh ort!* "May a fatal accident happen to you" (*lit.* "bad moan on you"). (2) *Gaoth gun direadh ort!* "May you drift to your drowning" (*lit.* "wind without direction on you"). (3) *Dia ad aghaidh, etc.,* "God against thee and in thy face . . . and may a death of woe be yours. . . . Evil and sorrow to thee and thine!"

She counted out ten pennies and two farthings.

"It is all the coppers I have. You are welcome to them. Take them, friend of my friend. They will give you the food you need, and the ferry across the Sound."

"I will do that, Maisie Macdonald, and thanks to you. It is not forgetting it I will be, nor you, good woman. And now, tell me, is it safe that I am? He called me a 'scapegoat'; he, Andrew Blair! Can evil touch me between this and the sea?"

"You must go to the place where the evil was done to you and yours—and that, I know, is on the west side of Iona. Go, and God preserve you. But here, too, is a sian that will be for the safety."

Thereupon, with swift mutterings, she said this charm: an old, familiar Sian against Sudden Harm:—

"Sian a chuir Moire air Mac ort,
Sian ro' marbhadh, sian ro' lot ort,
Sian eadar a' chlioch 's a' ghlun,
Sian nan Tri ann an aon ort,
O mhullach do chinn gu bonn do chois ort:
Sian seachd eadar a h-aon ort,
Sian seachd eadar a dha ort,
Sian seachd eadar a tri ort,
Sian seachd eadar a ceithir ort,
Sian seachd eadar a coig ort,
Sian seachd eadar a sia ort,
Sian seachd paidir nan seach paidir dol deiseil ri diugh narach ort,
ga do ghleidheadh bho bheud 's bho mhi-thapadh!

Scarcely had she finished before she heard heavy steps approaching.

"Away with you," she whispered, repeating in a loud angry tone, "Away with you! *Seachad! Seachad!*"

And with that Neil Ross slipped from the milk-shed and crossed the yard, and was behind the byres before Andrew Blair, with sullen mien and swift wild eyes, strode from the house.

It was with a grim smile on his face that Neil tramped down the wet heather till he reached the high road, and fared thence as through marsh because of the rains there had been.

For the first mile he thought of the angry mind of the dead man, bitter at paying of the silver. For the second mile he thought of the evil that had been wrought for him and his. For the third mile he pondered over all that he had heard and done and taken upon him that day.

Then he sat down upon a broken granite heap by the way, and brooded deep till one hour went, and then another, and the third was upon him.

A man driving two calves came towards him out of the west. He did not hear or see. The man stopped: spoke again. Neil gave no answer. The drover shrugged his shoulders, hesitated, and walked slowly on, often looking back.

An hour later a shepherd came by the way he himself had tramped. He was a tall, gaunt man with a squint. The small, pale-blue eyes glittered out of a mass of red hair that almost covered his face. He stood still, opposite Neil, and leaned on his *cromak.*

"*Latha math leat,*" he said at last, "I wish you good day."

Neil glanced at him, but did not speak.

"What is your name, for I seem to know you?"

But Neil had already forgotten him. The shepherd took out his snuff-mull, helped himself, and handed the mull to the lonely wayfarer. Neil mechanically helped himself.

"*Am bheil thu 'dol do Fhionphort?*" cried the shepherd again. "Are you going to Fionnaphort?"

"*Tha mise 'dol a dh' I-challum-chille,*" Neil answered in a low, weary voice, and as a man adream: "I am on my way to Iona."

"I am thinking I know now who you are. You are the man Macallum."

Neil looked, but did not speak. His eyes dreamed against what the other could not see or know. The shepherd called angrily to his dogs to keep the sheep from straying; then, with a resentful air, turned to his victim.

"You are a silent man for sure, you are. I'm hoping it is not the curse upon you already."

"What curse?"

"Ah, *that* has brought the wind against the mist! I was thinking so!"

"What curse?"

"You are the man that was the Sin-Eater over there?"

"Ay."

"The man Macallum?"

"Ay."

"Strange it is, but three days ago I saw you in Tobermory, and heard you give your name as Neil Ross to an Iona man that was there."

"Well?"

"Oh, sure, it is nothing to me. But they say the Sin-Eater should not be a man with a hidden lump in his pack."*

"Why?"

"For the dead know, and are content. There is no shaking off any sins, then—for that man."

"It is a lie."

"Maybe ay and maybe no."

"Well, have you more to be saying to me? I am obliged to you for your company, but it is not needing it I am, though no offence."

"Och, man, there's no offence between you and me. Sure, there's Iona in me, too; for the father of my father married a woman that was the granddaughter of Tomais Macdonald, who was a fisherman there. No, no; it is rather warning you I would be."

"And for what?"

"Well, well, just because of that laugh I heard about."

"What laugh?"

"The laugh of Adam Blair that is dead."

Neil Ross stared, his eyes large and wild. He leaned a little forward. No word came from him. The look that was on his face was the question.

"Yes: it was this way. Sure, the telling of it is just as I heard it. After you ate the sins of Adam Blair, the people there brought out the coffin. When they were putting him into it, he was as stiff as a sheep dead in the snow—and just like that, too, with his eyes wide open. Well, some one saw you trampling the heather down the slope that is in front of the house, and said, 'It is the Sin-Eater!' With that, Andrew Blair sneered, and said—'Ay, 'tis the scapegoat he is!' Then, after a while, he went on: 'The Sin-Eater they call him: ay, just so: and a bitter good bargain it is,

---

* *i.e.* with a criminal secret, or an undiscovered crime.

too, if all's true that's thought true!' And with that he laughed, and then his wife that was behind him laughed, and then . . ."

"Well, what then?"

"Well, 'tis Himself that hears and knows if it is true! But this is the thing I was told:—After that laughing there was a stillness, and a dread. For all there saw that the corpse had turned its head and was looking after you as you went down the heather. Then, Neil Ross, if that be your true name, Adam Blair that was dead put up his white face against the sky, and laughed."

At this, Ross sprang to his feet with a gasping sob.

"It is a lie, that thing!" he cried, shaking his fist at the shepherd. "It is a lie!"

"It is no lie. And by the same token, Andrew Blair shrank back white and shaking, and his woman had the swoon upon her, and who knows but the corpse might have come to life again had it not been for Maisie Macdonald, the deid-watcher, who clapped a handful of salt on his eyes, and tilted the coffin so that the bottom of it slid forward, and so let the whole fall flat on the ground, with Adam Blair in it sideways, and as likely as not cursing and groaning, as his wont was, for the hurt both to his old bones and his old ancient dignity."

Ross glared at the man as though the madness was upon him. Fear and horror and fierce rage swung him now this way and now that.

"What will the name of you be, shepherd?" he stuttered huskily.

"It is Eachainn Gilleasbuig I am to ourselves; and the English of that for those who have no Gaelic is Hector Gillespie; and I am Eachainn mac Ian mac Alasdair of Srathsheean that is where Sutherland lies against Ross."

"Then take this thing—and that is, the curse of the Sin-Eater! And a bitter bad thing may it be upon you and yours."

And with that Neil the Sin-Eater flung his hand up into the air, and then leaped past the shepherd, and a minute later was running through the frightened sheep, with his head low, and a white foam on his lips, and his eyes red with blood as a seal's that has the death wound on it.

On the third day of the seventh month from that day, Aulay Macneill, coming into Balliemore of Iona from the west side of the island, said to old Ronald MacCormick, that was the father of his wife, that he had seen Neil Ross again, and that he was "absent"—for though he had spoken to him, Neil would not answer, but only gloomed at him from the wet weedy rock where he sat.

The going back of the man had loosed every tongue that was in Iona. When, too, it was known that he was wrought in some terrible way, if not actually mad, the islanders whispered that it was because of the sins of Adam Blair. Seldom or never now did they speak of him by his name, but, simply, "The Sin-Eater." The thing was not so rare as to cause this strangeness, nor did many (and perhaps none did) think that the sins of the dead ever might or could abide with the living who had merely done a good Christian charitable thing. But there was a reason.

Not long after Neil Ross had come again to Iona, and had settled down in the ruined roofless house on the croft of Ballyrona, just like a fox or a wild-cat, as the saying was, he was given fishing-work to do by Aulay Macneill, who lived at Ard-an-teine, at the rocky north end of the *machar* or plain that is on the west Atlantic coast of the island.

One moonlit night, either the seventh or the ninth after the earthing of Adam Blair at his own place in the Ross, Aulay Macneill saw Neil Ross steal out of the shadow of Ballyrona and make for the sea. Macneill was there by the rocks, mending a lobster-creel. He had gone there because of the sadness. Well, when he saw the Sin-Eater he watched.

Neil crept from rock to rock till he reached the last fang that churns the sea into yeast when the tide sucks the land just opposite.

Then he called out something that Aulay Macneill could not catch. With that he springs up, and throws his arms above him.

"Then," says Aulay when he tells the tale, "it was like a ghost he was. The moonshine was on his face like the curl o' a wave. White! there is no whiteness like that of the human face. It was whiter than the foam about the skerry it was; whiter than the moonshining; whiter than . . . well, as white as the painted letters on the black boards of the fishing-cobles. There he stood, for all that the sea was about him, the slip-slop waves leapin' wild, and the tide making, too, at that. He was shaking like a sail two points off the wind. It was then that, all of a sudden, he called in a womany, screamin' voice—

"'I am throwing the sins of Adam Blair into the midst of ye, white dogs o' the sea! Drown them, tear them, drag them away out into the black deeps! Ay, ay, ay, ye dancin' wild waves, this is the third time I am doing it, and now there is none left, no, not a sin, not a sin!

> "'O-hi, O-ri, dark tide o' the sea,
>   I am giving the sins of a dead man to thee!
>   By the Stones, by the Wind, by the Fire, by the Tree,
>   From the dead man's sins set me free, set me free!
>   Adam mhic Anndra mhic Adam and me,
>   Set us free! Set us free!'

"Ay, sure, the Sin-Eater sang that over and over; and after the third singing he swung his arms and screamed—

> "'And listen to me, black waters an' running tide,
>   That rune is the good rune told me by Maisie the wise,
>   And I am Neil the son of Silis Macallum
>   By the black-hearted evil man Murtagh Ross,
>   That was the friend of Adam mac Anndra, God against him!'

And with that he scrambled and fell into the sea. But, as I am Aulay mac Luais and no other, he was up in a moment, an' swimmin' like a seal, and then over the rocks again, an' away back to that lonely roofless place once more, laughing wild at times, an' muttering an' whispering."

It was this tale of Aulay Macneill's that stood between Neil Ross and the islefolk. There was something behind all that, they whispered one to another.

So it was always the Sin-Eater he was called at last. None sought him. The few children who came upon him now and again fled at his approach, or at the very sight of him. Only Aulay Macneill saw him at times, and had word of him.

After a month had gone by, all knew that the Sin-Eater was wrought to madness because of this awful thing: the burden of Adam Blair's sins would not go from him! Night and day he could hear them laughing low, it was said.

But it was the quiet madness. He went to and fro like a shadow in the grass, and almost as soundless as that, and as voiceless. More and more the name of him grew as a terror. There were few folk on that wild west coast of Iona, and these few avoided him when the word ran that he had knowledge of strange things, and converse, too, with the secrets of the sea.

One day Aulay Macneill, in his boat, but dumb with amaze and terror for him, saw him at high tide swimming on a long rolling wave right into the hollow of the Spouting Cave. In the memory of man, no one had done this and escaped one of three things: a snatching away into oblivion, a strangled death, or madness. The islanders know that there swims into the cave, at full tide, a Mar-Tarbh, a dreadful creature of the sea that some call a kelpie; only it is not a kelpie, which is like a woman, but rather is a sea-bull, offspring of the cattle that are never seen. Ill indeed for any sheep or goat, ay, or even dog or child, if any happens to be leaning over the edge of the Spouting Cave when the Mar-Tarbh roars: for, of a surety, it will fall in and straightway be devoured.

With awe and trembling Aulay listened for the screaming of the doomed man. It was full tide, and the sea-beast would be there.

The minutes passed, and no sign. Only the hollow booming of the sea, as it moved like a baffled blind giant round the cavern-bases: only the rush and spray of the water flung up the narrow shaft high into the windy air above the cliff it penetrates.

At last he saw what looked like a mass of sea-weed swirled out on the surge. It was the Sin-Eater. With a leap, Aulay was at his oars. The boat swung through the sea. Just before Neil Ross was about to sink for the second time, he caught him, and dragged him into the boat.

But then, as ever after, nothing was to be got out of the Sin-Eater save a single saying: *"Tha e lamhan fuar: Tha e lamhan fuar!*–It has a cold, cold hand!"

The telling of this and other tales left none free upon the island to look upon the "scapegoat" save as one accursed.

It was in the third month that a new phase of his madness came upon Neil Ross.

The horror of the sea and the passion for the sea came over him at the same happening. Oftentimes he would race along the shore, screaming wild names to it, now hot with hate and loathing, now as the pleading of a man with the woman of his love. And strange chants to it, too, were upon his lips. Old, old lines of forgotten runes were overheard by Aulay Macneill, and not Aulay only: lines wherein the ancient sea-name of the island, *Ioua,* that was given to it long before it was called Iona, or any other of the nine names that are said to belong to it, occurred again and again.

The flowing tide it was that wrought him thus. At the ebb he would wander across the weedy slabs or among the rocks: silent, and more like a lost duinshee than a man.

Then again after three months a change in his madness came. None knew what it was, though Aulay said that the man moaned and moaned because of the awful burden he bore. No drowning seas for the sins that could not be washed away, no grave for the live sins that would be quick till the Day of the Judgment!

For weeks thereafter he disappeared. As to where he was, it is not for the knowing.

Then at last came that third day of the seventh month when, as I have said, Aulay Macneill told old Ronald MacCormick that he had seen the Sin-Eater again.

It was only a half-truth that he told, though. For, after he had seen Neil Ross upon the rock, he had followed him when he rose, and wandered back to the roofless place which be haunted now as of yore. Less wretched a shelter now it was, because of the summer that was come, though a cold, wet summer at that.

"Is that you, Neil Ross?" he had asked, as he peered into the shadows among the ruins of the house.

"That is not my name," said the Sin-Eater; and he seemed as strange then and there, as though he were a castaway from a foreign ship.

"And what will it be then, you that are my friend, and sure knowing me as Aulay mac Luais—Aulay Macneill that never grudges you bit or sup?"

"I am Judas."

"And at that word," says Aulay Macneill, when he tells the tale, "at that word the pulse in my heart was like a bat in a shut room. But after a bit I took up the talk.

"'Indeed,' I said; 'and I was not for knowing that. May I be so bold as to ask whose son, and of what place?'

"But all he said to me was, *'I am Judas.'*

"Well, I said, to comfort him, 'Sure, it's not such a bad name in it-self, though I am knowing some which have a more home-like sound.' But no, it was no good.

"'I am Judas. And because I sold the Son of God for five pieces of silver . . .'

"But here I interrupted him and said,—'Sure now, Neil—I mean, Ju-das—it was eight times five.' Yet the simpleness of his sorrow prevailed, and I listened with the wet in my eyes.

"'I am Judas. And because I sold the Son of God for five silver shil-lings, He laid upon me all the nameless black sins of the world. And that is why I am bearing them till the Day of Days.'"

And this was the end of the Sin-Eater; for I will not tell the long sto-ry of Aulay Macneill, that gets longer and longer every winter, but only the unchanging close of it.

I will tell it in the words of Aulay.

"A bitter, wild day it was, that day I saw him to see him no more. It was late. The sea was red with the flamin' light that burned up the air betwixt Iona and all that is west of West. I was on the shore, looking at the sea. The big green waves came in like the chariots in the Holy Book. Well, it was on the black shoulder of one of them, just short of the ton o' foam that swept above it, that I saw a spar surgin' by.

"'What is that?' I said to myself. And the reason of my wondering was this: I saw that a smaller spar was swung across it. And while I was watching that thing another great billow came in with a roar, and hurled the double-spar back, and not so far from me but I might have gripped it. But who would have gripped that thing if he were for seeing what I saw?

"It is Himself knows that what I say is a true thing.

"On that spar was Neil Ross, the Sin-Eater. Naked he was as the day he was born. And he was lashed, too—ay, sure he was lashed to it by ropes round and round his legs and his waist and his left arm. It was the Cross he was on. I saw that thing with the fear upon me. Ah, poor drift-ing wreck that he was! *Judas on the Cross:* It was his *eric!*

"But even as I watched, shaking in my limbs, I saw that there was life in him still. The lips were moving, and his right arm was ever for swinging this way and that. 'Twas like an oar, working him off a lee shore: ay, that was what I thought.

"Then all at once he caught sight of me. Well, he knew me, poor man, that has his share of heaven now, I am thinking!

"He waved, and called, but the hearing could not be, because of a big surge o' water that came tumbling down upon him. In the stroke of an oar he was swept close by the rocks where I was standing. In that flounderin', seethin' whirlpool I saw the white face of him for a moment, an' as he went out on the re-surge like a hauled net, I heard these words fallin' against my ears,—

"'*An eirig m'anama . . .* In ransom for my soul!'

"And with that I saw the double-spar turn over and slide down the back-sweep of a drowning big wave. Ay, sure, it went out to the deep sea swift enough then. It was in the big eddy that rushes between Skerry-Mòr and Skerry-Beag. I did not see it again—no, not for the quarter of an hour, I am thinking. Then I saw just the whirling top of it rising out of the flying yeast of a great, black, blustering wave that was rushing northward before the current that is called the Black-Eddy.

"With that you have the end of Neil Ross: ay, sure, him that was called the Sin-Eater. And that is a true thing, and may God save us the sorrow of sorrows.

"And that is all."

The Anointed Man

Of the seven Achannas—sons of Robert Achanna of Achanna in Galloway, self-exiled in the far north because of a bitter feud with his kindred—who lived upon Eilanmore in the Summer Isles, there was not one who was not, in more or less degree, or at some time or other, fëy.

Doubtless I shall have occasion to allude to, one and all again, and certainly to the eldest and youngest; for they were the strangest folk I have known or met anywhere in the Celtic lands, from the sea-pastures of the Solway to the kelp-strewn beaches of the Lews. Upon James, the seventh son, the doom of his people fell last and most heavily. Some day I may tell the full story of his strange life and tragic undoing, and of his piteous end. As it happened, I knew best the eldest and youngest of the brothers, Alison and James. Of the others, Robert, Allan, William, Marcus, and Gloom, none save the last-named survives, if peradventure *he* does, or has been seen of man for many years past. Of Gloom (strange and unaccountable name, which used to terrify me, the more so as, by the savagery of fate, it was the name of all names suitable for Robert Achanna's sixth son) I know nothing beyond the fact that ten years or more ago, he was a Jesuit priest in Rome, a bird of passage, whence come and whither bound no inquiries of mine could discover. Two years ago a relative told me that Gloom was dead, that he had been slain by some Mexican noble in an old city of Hispaniola beyond the seas. Doubtless the news was founded on truth, though I have ever a vague unrest when I think of Gloom, as though he were travelling hitherward, as though his feet, on some urgent errand, were already white with the dust of the road that leads to my house.

But now I wish to speak only of Alison Achanna. He was a friend whom I loved, though he was a man of close on forty and I a girl less than half his years. We had much in common, and I never knew any one more companionable, for all that he was called "Silent Ally." He was tall, gaunt, loosely-built. His eyes were of that misty blue which smoke takes when it rises in the woods, I used to think them like the tarns that lay amid the canna and gale-surrounded swamps in Uist, where I was wont to dream as a child.

I had often noticed the light on his face when he smiled—a light of such serene joy as young mothers have sometimes over the cradles of their firstborn. But, for some reason I had never wondered about it, not even when I heard and understood the half-contemptuous, half-reverent mockery with which, not only Alison's brothers, but even his father, at times used towards him. Once, I remember, I was puzzled when, on a bleak day in a stormy August, I overheard Gloom say, angrily and scoffingly, "There goes the Anointed Man!" I looked; but all I could see was that, despite the dreary cold, despite the ruined harvest, despite the rotting potato-crop, Alasdair walked slowly onward, smiling, and with glad eyes brooding upon the grey lands around and beyond him.

It was nearly a year thereafter—I remember the date, because it was that of my last visit to Eilanmore—that I understood more fully. I was walking westward with Alison, towards sundown. The light was upon his face as though it came from within; and when I looked again, half in awe, I saw that there was no glamour out of the west, for the evening was dull and threatening rain. He was in sorrow. Three months before, his brothers, Allan and William, had been drowned; a month later, his brother Robert had sickened, and now sat in the ingle from morning till the covering of the peats, a skeleton almost, shivering, and morosely silent, with large staring eyes. On the large bed in the room above the kitchen old Robert Achanna lay, stricken with paralysis. It would have been unendurable for me but for Alison and James, and, above all, for my loved girl-friend, Anne Gillespie, Achanna's niece, and the sunshine of his gloomy household.

As I walked with Alison I was conscious of a well-nigh intolerable depression. The house we had left was so mournful, the bleak sodden pastures were so mournful; so mournful was the stony place we were crossing, silent but for the thin crying of the curlews; and, above all, so mournful was the sound of the ocean as, unseen, it moved sobbingly round the isle—so beyond words distressing was all this to me, that I stopped abruptly, meaning to go no farther, but to return to the house, where at least there was warmth, and where Anne would sing for me as she spun.

But when I looked up into my companion's face I saw in truth the light that shone from within. His eyes were upon a forbidding stretch of ground, where the blighted potatoes rotted among a wilderness of round skull-white stones. I remember them still, these strange far-blue eyes, lamps of quiet joy, lamps of peace they seemed to me.

"Are you looking at Achnacarn?" (as the tract was called), I asked, in what I am sure was a whisper.

"Yes," replied Alasdair, slowly; "I am looking. It is beautiful—beautiful. O God, how beautiful is this lovely world!"

I know not what made me act so, but I threw myself on a heathery ridge close by, and broke out into convulsive sobbings.

Alison stooped, lifted me in his strong arms, and soothed me with soft caressing touches and quieting words.

"Tell me, my fawn, what is it? What is the trouble?" he asked again and again.

"It is *you*—it is *you,* Alison," I managed to say coherently at last. "It terrifies me to hear you speak as you did a little ago. You must be fëy. Why—why do you call that hateful, hideous field beautiful on this dreary day—and—and after all that has happened, O Alison?"

At this, I remember, he took his plaid and put it upon the wet heather, and then drew me thither, and seated himself and me beside him.

"Is it not beautiful, my fawn?" he asked, with tears in his eyes. Then, without waiting for my answer, he said quietly, "Listen, dear, and I will tell you."

He was strangely still—breathless he seemed to me—for a minute or more. Then he spoke.

"I was little more than a child—a boy just in my teens—when something happened, something that came down the Rainbow-Arches of Cathair-Sith." He paused here, perhaps to see if I followed, which I did, familiar as I was with all fairy-lore. "I was out upon the heather, in the time when the honey oozes in the bells and cups. I had always loved the island and the sea. Perhaps I was foolish, but I was so glad with my joy that golden day that I threw myself on the ground and kissed the hot, sweet ling, and put my hands and arms into it, sobbing the while with my vague, strange yearning. At last I lay still, nerveless, with my eyes closed. Suddenly I was aware that two tiny hands had come up through the spires of the heather, and were pressing something soft and fragrant upon my eyelids. When I opened them, I could see nothing unfamiliar. No one was visible. But I heard a whisper: 'Arise and go away from this place at once; and this night do not venture out, lest evil befall you.' So I rose, trembling, and went home. Thereafter I was the same, and yet not the same. Never could I see as they saw, what my father and brothers or the isle-folk looked upon as ugly or dreary. My father was wroth with me many times, and called me a fool. Whenever my eyes fell upon those waste and desolate spots, they seemed to me passing fair, radiant with lovely light. At last my father grew so bitter that, mocking me the while, he bade me go to the towns and see there the squalor and sordid hideousness wherein men dwelled. But thus it was with me: in the places they call slums, and among the smoke of factories and the grime of destitution, I could see all that other men saw, only as vanishing shadows. What I saw was lovely, beautiful with strange glory, and the faces of men and women were sweet and pure, and their souls were white. So, weary and bewildered with my unwilling quest, I came back to Eilanmore. And on the day of my home-coming, Morag was there—Morag of the Falls. She turned to my father and called him blind and foolish. 'He has the white light upon his brows,' she said of me; 'I can see it, like the flicker-light in a wave when the wind's from the south in thunder-weather. He has been touched with the Fairy Ointment. The Guid Folk know him. It will be thus with him till the day of his death, if a *duinshee* can die, being already a man dead yet born anew. He upon whom the Fairy Ointment has been laid must see all that is ugly and hideous and dreary and bitter through a glamour of beauty. Thus it hath been since the Mhic-Alpine ruled from sea to sea, and thus it is with the man Alison your son.'

"That is all, my fawn, and that is why my brothers, when they are angry, sometimes call me the Anointed Man."

"That is all." Yes, perhaps. But oh, Alasdair Achanna, how often have I thought of that most precious treasure you found in the heather, when the bells were sweet with honey-ooze! Did the wild bees know of it? Would that I could hear the soft hum of their gauzy wings.

Who of us would not barter the best of all our possessions—and some there are who would surrender all—to have one touch laid upon the eyelids—one touch of the Fairy Ointment? But the place is far, and the hour is hidden. No man may seek that for which there can be no quest.

Only the wild bees know of it; but I think they must be the bees of Magh-Mell. And there no man that liveth may wayfare—*yet*.

The Dàn-nan-Ròn

I

When Anne Gillespie, that was my friend in Eilanmore, left the island after the death of her uncle, the old man Robert Achanna, it was to go far west.

Among the men of the outer isles who for three summers past had been at the fishing off Eilanmore, there was one named Mànus Mac-Codrum. He was a fine lad to sea, but though most of the fisher-folk of the Lewis and North Uist are fair, either with reddish hair and grey eyes or blue-eyed and yellow-haired, he was of a brown skin with dark hair and dusky brown eyes. He was, however, as unlike to the dark Celts of Arran and the Inner Hebrides as to the Northmen. He came of his people, sure enough. All the MacCodrums of North Uist had been brown-skinned and brown-haired and brown-eyed: and herein may have lain the reason why, in bygone days, this small clan of Uist was known throughout the Western Isles as the *Sliochd nan Ròn,* the offspring of the Seals.

Not so tall as most of the men of North Uist and Long Island men, Mànus MacCodrum was of a fair height and supple and strong. No man was a better fisherman than he, and he was well liked of his fellows, for all the morose gloom that was upon him at times. He had a voice as sweet as a woman's when he sang, and he sang often, and knew all the old runes of the islands, from the Obb of Harris to the Head of Mingulay. Often, too, he chanted the beautiful *orain sporadail* of the Catholic priests and Christian Brothers of South Uist and Barra, though where he lived in North Uist he was the sole man who adhered to the ancient faith.

It may have been because Anne was a Catholic too, though, sure, the Achannas were so also, notwithstanding that their forbears and kindred in Galloway were Protestant (and this because of old Robert Achanna's love for his wife, who was of the old Faith, so it is said)—it may have been for this reason, though I think her lover's admiring eyes and soft speech and sweet singing had more to do with it, that she pledged her troth to Mànus. It was a south wind for him, as the saying is; for with her rippling brown hair and soft grey eyes and cream-white skin, there was no comelier lass in the isles.

So when Achanna was laid to his long rest, and there was none left upon Eilanmore save only his three youngest sons, Mànus MacCodrum sailed north-eastward across the Minch to take home his bride. Of the four eldest sons, Alison had left Eilanmore some months before his father died, and sailed westward, though no one knew whither, or for what end, or for how long, and no word had been brought from him, nor was he ever seen again in the island, which had come to be called Eilan-nan-Allmharachain, the Isle of the Strangers. Allan and William had been drowned in a wild gale in the Minch; and Robert had died of the white fever, that deadly wasting disease which is the scourge of the isles. Marcus was now "Eilanmore," and lived there with Gloom and Sheumais, all three unmarried, though it was rumoured among the neighbouring islanders that each loved Marsail nic Ailpean,* in Eilan-Rona of the Summer Isles, hard by the coast of Sutherland.

When Mànus asked Anne to go with him she agreed. The three brothers were ill-pleased at this, for apart from their not wishing their cousin to go so far away, they did not want to lose her, as she not only cooked for them and did all that a woman does, including spinning and weaving, but was most sweet and fair to see, and in the long winter nights sang by the hour together, while Gloom played strange wild airs upon his *feadan,* a kind of oaten pipe or flute.

She loved him, I know; but there was this reason also for her going, that she was afraid of Gloom. Often upon the moor or on the hill she turned and hastened home, because she heard the lilt and fall of that *feadan.* It was an eerie thing to her, to be going through the twilight when she thought the three men were in the house smoking after their supper, and suddenly to hear beyond and coming towards her the shrill song of that oaten flute playing "The Dance of the Dead," or "The Flow and Ebb," or "The Shadow-Reel."

---

*Marsail nic Ailpean is the Gaelic of which an English translation would be Marjory MacAlpine. *Nic* is a contraction for *nighean mhic,* "daughter of the line of."

That, sometimes at least, he knew she was there was clear to her, because as she stole rapidly through the tangled fern and gale she would hear a mocking laugh follow her like a leaping thing.

Mànus was not there on the night when she told Marcus and his brothers that she was going. He was in the haven on board the *Luath,* with his two mates, he singing in the moonshine as all three sat mending their fishing gear.

After the supper was done, the three brothers sat smoking and talking over an offer that had been made about some Shetland sheep. For a time Anne watched them in silence. They were not like brothers, she thought. Marcus, tall, broad-shouldered, with yellow hair and strangely dark blue-black eyes and black eyebrows; stern, with a weary look on his sun-brown face. The light from the peats glinted upon the tawny curve of thick hair that trailed from his upper lip, for he had the *caisean-feusag* of the Northmen. Gloom, slighter of build, dark of hue and hair, but with hairless face; with thin, white, long-fingered hands, that had ever a nervous motion as though they were tide-wrack. There was always a frown on the centre of his forehead, even when he smiled with his thin lips and dusky, unbetraying eyes. He looked what he was, the brain of the Achannas. Not only did he have the English as though native to that tongue, but could and did read strange unnecessary books. Moreover, he was the only son of Robert Achanna to whom the old man had imparted his store of learning, for Achanna had been a schoolmaster in his youth in Galloway, and he had intended Gloom for the priesthood. His voice, too, was low and clear, but cold as pale-green water running under ice. As for Sheumais, he was more like Marcus than Gloom, though not so fair. He had the same brown hair and shadowy hazel eyes, the same pale and smooth face, with something of the same intent look which characterised the long-time missing and probably dead eldest brother, Alison. He, too, was tall and gaunt. On Sheumais' face there was that indescribable, as to some of course imperceptible, look which is indicated by the phrase, "the dusk of the shadow," though few there are who know what they mean by that, or, knowing, are fain to say.

Suddenly, and without any word or reason for it, Gloom turned and spoke to her.

"Well, Anne, and what is it?"

"I did not speak, Gloom."

"True for you *mo cailinn.* But it's about to speak you were."

"Well, and that is true. Marcus, and you Gloom, and you Sheumais, I have that to tell which you will not be altogether glad for the hearing. 'Tis about . . . about . . . me and . . . and Mànus."

There was no reply at first. The three brothers sat looking at her like the kye at a stranger on the moorland. There was a deepening of the frown on Gloom's brow, but when Anne looked at him his eyes fell and dwelt in the shadow at his feet. Then Marcus spoke in a low voice:

"Is it Mànus MacCodrum you will be meaning?"

"Ay, sure."

Again, silence. Gloom did not lift his eyes, and Sheumais was now staring at the peats. Marcus shifted uneasily.

"And what will Mànus MacCodrum be wanting?"

"Sure, Marcus, you know well what I mean. Why do you make this thing hard for me? There is but one thing he would come here wanting; and he has asked me if I will go with him, and I have said yes. And if you are not willing that he come again with the minister, or that we go across to the kirk in Berneray of Uist in the Sound of Harris, then I will not stay under this roof another night, but will go away from Eilanmore at sunrise in the *Luath,* that is now in the haven. And that is for the hearing and knowing, Marcus and Gloom and Sheumais!"

Once more, silence followed her speaking. It was broken in a strange way. Gloom slipped his *feadan* into his hands, and so to his mouth. The clear, cold notes of the flute filled the flame-lit room. It was as though white polar birds were drifting before the coming of snow.

The notes slid in to a wild remote air: cold moonlight on the dark o' the sea, it was. It was the *Dàn-nan-Ròn.*

Anne flushed, trembled, and then abruptly rose. As she leaned on her clenched right hand upon the table, the light of the peats showed that her eyes were aflame.

"Why do you play *that,* Gloom Achanna?"

The man finished the bar, then blew into the oaten pipe, before, just glancing at the girl, he replied:

"And what harm will there be in *that,* Anna-ban?"

"You know it is harm. That is the Dàn-nan-Ròn!"

"Ay; and what then, Anna-ban?"

"What then? Are you thinking I don't know what you mean by playing the Song o' the Seal?"

With an abrupt gesture Gloom put the *feadan* aside. As he did so, he rose.

"See here, Anne," he began roughly—when Marcus intervened.

"That will do just now, Gloom. Ann-à-ghraidh, do you mean that you are going to do this thing?"

"Ay sure."

"Do you know why Gloom played the Dàn-nan-Ròn?"

"It was a cruel thing."

"You know what is said in the isles about . . . about . . . this or that man, who is under *gheasan*—who is spell-bound . . . and . . . and . . . about the seals and . . ."

"Yes, Marcus, it is knowing it that I am: *'Tha iad a' cantuinn gur h-e daoine fo gheasan a th' anns no roin.'*"

"*'They say that seals,'* he repeated slowly; "*'they say that seals are men under magic spells.'* And have you ever pondered that thing, Anne, my cousin?"

"I am knowing well what you mean."

"Then you will know that the MacCodrums of North Uist are called the Sliochd-nan-Ròn?"

"I have heard."

"And would you be for marrying a man that is of the race of the beasts, and himself knowing what that *geas* means, and who may any day go back to his people?"

"Ah, now, Marcus, sure it is making a mock of me you are. Neither you nor any here believe that foolish thing, How can a man born of a woman be a seal, even though his *sinnsear* were the offspring of the sea-people,—which is not a saying I am believing either, though it may be: and not that it matters much, whatever, about the far-back forebears."

Marcus frowned darkly, and at first made no response. At last he answered, speaking sullenly.

"You may be believing this or you may be believing that, Anna-nic-Gilleasbuig, but two things are as well known as that the east wind brings the blight and the west wind the rain. And one is this: that long ago a

Seal-man wedded a woman of North Uist, and that he or his son was called Neil MacCodrum; and that the sea-fever of the seal was in the blood of his line ever after. And this is the other: that twice within the memory of living folk a MacCodrum has taken upon himself the form of a seal, and has so met his death—once Neil MacCodrum of Ru' Tormaid, and once Anndra MacCodrum of Berneray in the Sound. There's talk of others, but these are known of us all. And you will not be forgetting now that Neil-donn was the grandfather, and that Anndra was the brother of the father of Mànus MacCodrum?"

"I am not caring what you say, Marcus: It is all foam of the sea."

"There's no foam without wind or tide, Anne. An' it's a dark tide that will be bearing you away to Uist; and a black wind that will be blowing far away behind the East, the wind that will be carrying his death-cry to your ears."

The girl shuddered. The brave spirit in her, however, did not quail.

"Well, so be it. To each his fate. But, seal or no seal, I am going to wed Mànus MacCodrum, who is a man as good as any here, and a true man at that, and the man I love, and that will be my man, God willing, the praise be His!"

Again Gloom took up the *feadan,* and sent a few cold white notes floating through the hot room, breaking suddenly into the wild fantastic opening air of the Dàn-nan-Ròn.

With a low cry and passionate gesture Anne sprang forward, snatched the oat-flute from his grasp, and would have thrown it in the fire. Marcus held her in an iron grip, however.

"Don't you be minding Gloom, Anne," he said quietly, as he took the *feadan* from her hand, and handed it to his brother; "sure, he's only telling you in *his* way what I am telling you in mine."

She shook herself free, and moved to the other side of the table. On the opposite wall hung the dirk which had belonged to old Achanna. This she unfastened. Holding it in her right hand, she faced the three men.

"On the cross of the dirk I swear I will be the woman of Mànus MacCodrum."

The brothers made no response. They looked at her fixedly.

"And by the cross of the dirk I swear that if any man come between me and Mànus, this dirk will be for his remembering in a certain hour of the day of the days."

As she spoke, she looked meaningly at Gloom, whom she feared more than Marcus or Sheumais.

"And by the cross of the dirk I swear that if evil come to Mànus, this dirk will have another sheath, and that will be my milkless breast: and by that token I now throw the old sheath in the fire."

As she finished, she threw the sheath on to the burning peats.

Gloom quietly lifted it, brushed off the sparks of flame as though they were dust, and put it in his pocket.

"And by the same token, Anne," he said, "your oaths will come to nought."

Rising, he made a sign to his brothers to follow. When they were outside he told Sheumais to return, and to keep Anne within, by peace if possible—by force if not. Briefly they discussed their plans, and then separated. While Sheumais went back, Marcus and Gloom made their way to the haven.

Their black figures were visible in the moonlight, but at first they were not noticed by the men on board the *Luath,* for Mànus was singing.

When the islesman stopped abruptly, one of his companions asked him jokingly if his song had brought a seal alongside, and bid him beware lest it was a woman of the sea-people.

He gloomed morosely, but he made no reply. When the others listened they heard the wild strain of the Dàn-nan-Ròn stealing through the moonshine. Staring against the shore, they could discern the two brothers.

"What will be the meaning of that?" asked one of the men uneasily.

"When a man comes instead of a woman," answered Mànus, slowly, "the young corbies are astir in the nest."

So, it meant blood. Aulay MacNeil and Donull MacDonull put down their gear, rose, and stood waiting for what Mànus would do.

"Ho, there!" he cried.

"Ho-ro!"

"What will you be wanting, Eilanmore?"

"We are wanting a word of you, Mànus MacCodrum. Will you come ashore?"

"If you want a word of me, you can come to me."

"There is no boat here."

"I'll send the *bàta-beag*."

When he had spoken, Mànus asked Donull, the younger of his mates, a lad of seventeen, to row to the shore.

"And bring back no more than one man," he added, "whether it be Eilanmore himself or Gloom-mhic-Achanna."

The rope of the small boat was unfastened. and Donull rowed it swiftly through the moonshine. The passing of a cloud dusked the shore, but they saw him throw a rope for the guiding of the boat alongside the ledge of the landing-place; then the sudden darkening obscured the vision. Donull must be talking, they thought; for two or three minutes elapsed without sign: but at last the boat put off again, and with two figures only. Doubtless the lad had had to argue against the coming of both Marcus and Gloom.

This, in truth, was what Donull had done. But while he was speaking, Marcus was staring fixedly beyond him.

"Who is it that is there?" he asked, "there, in the stern?"

"There is no one there."

"I thought I saw the shadow of a man."

"Then it was my shadow, Eilanmore."

Achanna turned to his brother.

"I see a man's death there in the boat."

Gloom quailed for a moment, then laughed low.

"I see no death of a man sitting in the boat, Marcus, but if I did, I am thinking it would dance to the air of the Dàn-nan-Ròn, which is more than the wraith of you or me would do."

"It is not a wraith I was seeing, but the death of a man."

Gloom whispered, and his brother nodded sullenly. The next moment a heavy muffler was round Donull's mouth, and before he could resist, or even guess what had happened, he was on his face on the shore, bound and gagged. A minute later the oars were taken by Gloom, and the boat moved swiftly out of the inner haven.

As it drew near Mànus stared at it intently.

"That is not Donull that is rowing, Aulay!"

"No; it will be Gloom Achanna, I'm thinking."

MacCodrum started. If so, that other figure at the stern was too big for Donull. The cloud passed just as the boat came alongside. The rope was made secure, and then Marcus and Gloom sprang on board.

"Where is Donull MacDonull?" demanded Mànus sharply.

Marcus made no reply, so Gloom answered for him.

"He has gone up to the house with a message to Anna-nic-Gilleasbuig."

"And what will that message be?"

"That Mànus MacCodrum has sailed away from Eilanmore, and will not see her again."

MacCodrum laughed. It was a low, ugly laugh.

"Sure, Gloom Achanna, you should be taking that *feadan* of yours and playing the Codhail-nan-Pairtean, for I'm thinkin' the crabs are gathering about the rocks down below us, an' laughing wi' their claws."

"Well, and that is a true thing," Gloom replied slowly and quietly. "Yes, for sure I might, as you say, be playing the Meeting of the Crabs. Perhaps," he added, as by a sudden afterthought, "perhaps, though it is a calm night, you will be hearing the *comh-thonn.* The 'slapping of the waves' is a better thing to be hearing than the Meeting of the Crabs."

"If I hear the *comh-thonn,* it is not in the way you will be meaning, Gloom 'ic Achanna. 'Tis not the 'up sail and good-bye' they will be saying, but 'Home wi' the Bride.'"

Here Marcus intervened.

"Let us be having no more words, Mànus MacCodrum. The girl Anne is not for you. Gloom is to be her man. So get you hence. If you will be going quiet, it is quiet we will be. If you have your feet on this thing, then you will be having that too which I saw in the boat."

"And what was it you saw in the boat, Achanna?"

"The death of a man."

"So . . . And now" (this after a prolonged silence, wherein the four men stood facing each other), "is it a blood-matter, if not of peace?"

"Ay. Go, if you are wise. If not, 'tis your own death you will be making."

There was a flash as of summer lightning. A bluish flame seemed to leap through the moonshine. Marcus reeled, with a gasping cry; then, leaning back till his face blanched in the moonlight, his knees gave way. As he fell, he turned half round. The long knife which Mànus had hurled at him had not penetrated his breast more than two inches at most, but as he fell on the deck it was driven into him up to the hilt.

In the blank silence that followed, the three men could hear a sound like the ebb-tide in sea-weed. It was the gurgling of the bloody froth in the lungs of the dead man.

The first to speak was his brother, and then only when thin reddish-white foam-bubbles began to burst from the blue lips of Marcus.

"It is murder."

He spoke low, but it was like the surf of breakers in the ears of those who heard.

"You have said one part of a true word, Gloom Achanna. It is mur-der . . . that you and he came here for."

"The death of Marcus Achanna is on you, Mànus MacCodrum."

"So be it, as between yourself and me, or between all of your blood and me; though Aulay MacNeil as well as you can witness that, though in self-defence I threw the knife at Achanna, it was his own doing that drove it into him."

"You can whisper that to the rope when it is round your neck."

"And what will *you* be doing now, Gloom-nic-Achanna?"

For the first time Gloom shifted uneasily. A swift glance revealed to him the awkward fact that the boat trailed behind the *Luath,* so that he could not leap into it, while if he turned to haul it close by the rope, he was at the mercy of the two men.

"I will go in peace," he said quietly.

"Ay," was the answer, in an equally quiet tone: "in the white peace."

Upon this menace of death the two men stood facing each other.

Achanna broke the silence at last.

"You'll hear the Dàn-nan-Ròn the night before you die, Mànus MacCodrum: and, lest you doubt it, you'll hear it again in your death-hour."

"*Ma tha sin an Dàn*—if that be ordained." Mànus spoke gravely. His very quietude, however, boded ill. There was no hope of clemency. Gloom knew that.

Suddenly he laughed scornfully. Then, pointing with his right hand as if to some one behind his two adversaries, he cried out: "Put the death-hand on them, Marcus! Give them the Grave!"

Both men sprang aside, the heart of each nigh upon bursting. The death-touch of the newly slain is an awful thing to incur, for it means that the wraith can transfer all its evil to the person touched.

The next moment there was a heavy splash. Mànus realised that it was no more than a ruse, and that Gloom had escaped. With feverish haste he hauled in the small boat, leaped into it, and began at once to row so as to intercept his enemy.

Achanna rose once, between him and the *Luath.* MacCodrum crossed the oars in the thole-pins, and seized the boat-hook.

The swimmer kept straight for him. Suddenly he dived. In a flash, Mànus knew that Gloom was going to rise under the boat, seize the keel, and upset him, and thus probably be able to grip him from above. There was time and no more to leap: and, indeed, scarce had he plunged into the sea ere the boat swung right over, Achanna clambering over it the next moment.

At first Gloom could not see where his foe was. He crouched on the upturned craft, and peered eagerly into the moonlit water. All at once a black mass shot out of the shadow between him and the smack. This black mass laughed—the same low, ugly laugh that had preceded the death of Marcus.

He who was in turn the swimmer was now close. When a fathom away he leaned back and began to tread water steadily. In his right hand he grasped the boat-hook. The man in the boat knew that to stay where he was meant certain death. He gathered himself together like a crouching cat. Mànus kept treading the water slowly, but with the hook ready so that the sharp iron spike at the end of it should transfix his foe if he came at him with a leap. Now and again he laughed. Then in his low sweet voice, but brokenly at times, between his deep breathings, he began to sing:

The tide was dark, an' heavy with the burden that it bore,
I heard it talkin', whisperin', upon the weedy shore:
Each wave that stirred the sea-weed was like a closing door,
'Tis closing doors they hear at last who hear no more, no more,
My Grief,
No more!

The tide was in the salt sea-weed, and like a knife it tore;
The wild sea-wind went moaning, sooing, moaning o'er and o'er;
The deep sea-heart was brooding deep upon its ancient lore,
I heard the sob, the sooing sob, the dying sob at its core,
My Grief,
Its core!

The white sea-waves were wan and grey, its ashy lips before,
The yeast within its ravening mouth was red with streaming gore—
O red sea-weed, O red sea-waves, O hollow baffled roar,
Since one thou hast, O dark, dim sea, why callest thou for more,
My Grief,
For more!

In the quiet moonlight the chant, with its long slow cadences, sung as no other man in the Isles could sing it, sounded sweet and remote beyond words to tell. The glittering shine was upon the water of the haven, and moved in waving lines of fire along the stone ledges. Sometimes a fish rose, and spilt a ripple of pale gold; or a sea-nettle swan to the surface, and turned its blue or greenish globe of living jelly to the moon dazzle.

The man in the water made a sudden stop in his treading, and listened intently. Then once more the phosphorescent light gleamed about his slow-moving shoulders. In a louder chanting voice came once again,

Each wave that stirs the sea-weed is like a closing door,
'Tis closing doors they hear at last who hear no more, no more,
My Grief,
No more!

Yes, his quick ears had caught the inland strain of a voice he knew. Soft and white as the moonshine came Anne's singing, as she passed along the corrie leading to the haven. In vain his travelling gaze sought her: she was still in the shadow, and, besides, a slow drifting cloud obscured the moonlight. When he looked back again, a stifled exclamation came from his lips. There was not a sign of Gloom Achanna. He had slipped noiselessly from the boat, and was now either behind it, or had dived beneath it, or was swimming under water this way or that. If only the cloud would sail by, muttered Mànus, as he held himself in readiness for an attack from beneath or behind. As the dusk lightened, he swam slowly towards the boat, and then swiftly round it. There was no one there. He climbed on to the keel, and stood, leaning forward as a salmon-leisterer by torchlight, with his spear-pointed boat-hook raised. Neither below nor beyond could he discern any shape. A whispered call to Aulay MacNeill showed that he, too, saw nothing. Gloom must have swooned, and sunk deep as he slipped through the water. Perhaps the dog-fish were already darting about him.

Going behind the boat, Mànus guided it back to the smack. It was not long before, with MacNeill's help, he righted the punt. One oar had drifted out of sight, but as there was a sculling hole in the stern, that did not matter.

"What shall we do with it?" he muttered, as he stood at last by the corpse of Marcus. "This is a bad night for us, Aulay!"

"Bad it is; but let us be seeing it is not worse. I'm thinking we should have left the boat."

"And for why that?"

"We could say that Marcus Achanna and Gloom Achanna left us again, and that we saw no more of them nor of our boat."

MacCodrum pondered a while. The sound of voices, borne faintly across the water, decided him. Probably Anne and the lad Donull were talking. He slipped into the boat, and with a sail-knife soon ripped it here and there. It filled, and then, heavy with the weight of a great ballast-stone which Aulay had first handed to his companion, and surging with a foot-thrust from the latter, it sank.

"We'll bide the . . . the man there . . . behind the windlass, below the spare sail, till we're out at sea, Aulay. Quick, give me a hand!"

It did not take the two men long to lift the corpse and do as Mànus had suggested. They had scarce accomplished this when Anne's voice came hailing silver-sweet across the water.

With death-white face and shaking limbs MacCodrum stood holding the mast, while with a loud voice, so firm and strong that Aulay MacNeill smiled below his fear, he asked if the Achannas were back yet, and, if so, for Donull to row out at once, and she with him if she would come.

It was nearly half-an-hour thereafter that Anne rowed out towards the *Luath.* She had gone at last along the shore to a creek where one of Marcus' boats was moored, and returned with it. Having taken Donull on board, she made way with all speed, fearful lest Gloom or Marcus should intercept her.

It did not take long to explain how she had laughed at Sheumais' vain efforts to detain her, and had come down to the haven. As she approached, she heard Mànus singing, and so had herself broken into a song she knew he loved. Then, by the water-edge she had come upon Donull lying upon his back, bound and gagged. After she had released him, they waited to see what would happen, but as in the moonlight they could not see any small boat come in—bound to or from the smack—she had hailed to know if Mànus were there.

On his side, he said briefly that the two Achannas had come to persuade him to leave without her. On his refusal, they had departed again, uttering threats against her as well as himself. He heard their quarrelling voices as they rowed into the gloom, but could not see them at last because of the obscured moonlight.

"And now, Ann-mochree," he added, "is it coming with me you are, and just as you are? Sure, you'll never repent it, and you'll have all you want that I can give. Dear of my heart, say that you will be coming away this night of the nights! By the Black Stone on Icolmkill I swear it, and by the Sun, and by the Moon, and by Himself!"

"I am trusting you, Mànus dear. Sure, it is not for me to be going back to that house after what has been done and said. I go with you, now and always, God save us."

"Well, dear lass o' my heart, it's farewell to Eilanmore it is, for by the Blood on the Cross I'll never land on it again!"

"And that will be no sorrow to me, Mànus my home!"

And this was the way that my friend Anne Gillespie left Eilanmore to go to the isles of the west.

It was a fair sailing in the white moonshine with a whispering breeze astern. Anne leaned against Mànus, dreaming her dream. The lad Donull sat drowsing at the helm. Forward, Aulay MacNeill, with his face set against the moonshine to the west, brooded dark.

Though no longer was land in sight, and there was peace among the deeps of the quiet stars and upon the sea, the shadow of fear was upon the face of Mànus MacCodrum.

This might well have been because of the as yet unburied dead that lay beneath the spare sail by the windlass. The dead man, however, did not affright him. What went moaning in his heart, and sighing and calling in his brain, was a faint falling echo he had heard as the *Luath* glided slow out of the haven. Whether from the water or from the shore he could not tell, but he heard the wild fantastic air of the Dàn-nan-Ròn, as he had heard it that very night upon the *feadan* of Gloom Achanna.

It was his hope that his ears had played him false. When he glanced about him and saw the sombre flame in the eyes of Aulay MacNeill, staring at him out of the dusk, he knew that which Oisin, the son of Fionn, cried in his pain: "his soul swam in mist."

II

For all the evil omens, the marriage of Anne and Mànus MacCodrum went well. He was more silent than of yore, and men avoided rather than sought him; but he was happy with Anne, and content with his two mates, who were now Callum MacCodrum and Ranald MacRanald. The youth Donull had bettered himself by joining a Skye skipper, who was a kinsman, and Aulay MacNeill had surprised every one except Mànus by going away as a seaman on board one of the *Loch* line of ships which sail for Australia from the Clyde.

Anne never knew what had happened, though it is possible she suspected somewhat. All that was known to her was that Marcus and Gloom Achanna had disappeared, and were supposed to have been drowned. There was now no Achanna upon Eilanmore, for Sheumais had taken a horror of the place and his loneliness. As soon as it was commonly admitted that his two brothers must have drifted out to sea, and been drowned, or at best picked up by some ocean-going ship, he disposed of the island-farm, and left Eilanmore for ever. All this confirmed the thing said among the islanders of the west—that old Robert Achanna had brought a curse with him. Blight and disaster had visited Eilanmore over and over in the many years he had held it, and death, sometimes tragic

or mysterious, had overtaken six of his seven sons, while the youngest
bore upon his brows the "dusk of the shadow." True, none knew for
certain that three out of the six were dead, but few for a moment believed in the possibility that Alison and Marcus and Gloom were alive.
On the night when Anne had left the island with Mànus MacCodrum
he, Sheumais, had heard nothing to alarm him. Even when, an hour after she had gone down to the haven, neither she nor his brothers had
returned, and the *Luath* had put out to sea, he was not in fear of any ill.
Clearly, Marcus and Gloom had gone away in the smack, perhaps determined to see that the girl was duly married by priest or minister. He
would have perturbed himself little for days to come, but for a strange
thing that happened that night. He had returned to the house because of
a chill that was upon him, and convinced too that all had sailed in the
Luath. He was sitting brooding by the peat-fire, when he was startled by
a sound at the window at the back of the room. A few bars of a familiar
air struck painfully upon his ear, though played so low that they were
just audible. What could it be but the Dàn-nan-Ròn; and who would be
playing that but Gloom? What did it mean? Perhaps, after all, it was
fantasy only, and there was no *feadan* out there in the dark. He was
pondering this when, still low, but louder and sharper than before, there
rose and fell the strain which he hated, and Gloom never played before
him, that of the Dàvsa-na-mairv, the Dance of the Dead. Swiftly and silently he rose and crossed the room. In the dark shadows cast by the
byre he could see nothing; but the music ceased. He went out, and
searched everywhere, but found no one. So he returned, took down the
Holy Book, and with awed heart read slowly, till peace came upon him,
soft and sweet as the warmth of the peat-glow.

But as for Anne, she had never even this hint that one of the supposed dead might be alive; or that, being dead, Gloom might yet touch a
shadowy *feadan* into a wild remote air of the Grave.

When month after month went by, and no hint of ill came to break
upon their peace, Mànus grew light-hearted again. Once more his songs
were heard as he came back from the fishing or loitered ashore mending his nets. A new happiness was nigh to them, for Anne was with
child. True, there was fear also, for the girl was not well at the time
when her labour was near, and grew weaker daily. There came a day

when Mànus had to go to Loch Boisdale in South Uist; and it was with pain and something of foreboding, that he sailed away from Berneray in the Sound of Harris, where he lived. It was on the third night that he returned. He was met by Katreen MacRanald, the wife of his mate, with the news that, on the morrow after his going, Anne had sent for the priest who was staying at Loch Maddy, for she had felt the coming of death. It was that very evening she died, and took the child with her.

Mànus heard as one in a dream. It seemed to him that the tide was ebbing in his heart, and a cold sleety rain falling, falling through a mist in his brain.

Sorrow lay heavily upon him. After the earthing of her whom he loved he went to and fro solitary; often crossing the Narrows and going to the old Pictish Tower under the shadow of Ban Breac. He would not go upon the sea, but let his kinsman Callum do as he liked with the *Luath.*

Now and again Father Allan MacNeill sailed northward to see him. Each time he departed sadder. "The man is going mad, I fear," he said to Callum, the last time he saw Mànus.

The long summer nights brought peace and beauty to the isles. It was a great herring-year, and the moon-fishing was unusually good. All the Uist men who lived by the sea-harvest were in their boats whenever they could. The pollack, the dogfish, the otters, and the seals, with flocks of sea-fowl beyond number, shared in the common joy. Mànus MacCodrum alone paid no heed to herring or mackerel. He was often seen striding along the shore, and more than once had been heard laughing. Sometimes, too, he was come upon at low tide by the great Reef of Berneray, singing wild strange runes and songs, or crouching upon a rock and brooding dark.

The midsummer moon found no man on Berneray except Mac-Codrum, the Reverend Mr. Black, the minister of the Free Kirk, and an old man named Anndra McIan. On the night before the last day of the middle month, Anndra was reproved by the minister for saying that he had seen a man rise out of one of the graves in the kirkyard, and steal down by the stone-dykes towards Balnahunnur-sa-mona,* where Mànus MacCodrum lived.

---

* *Baille-'na-aonar'sa mhonadh,* "the solitary farm on the hill-slope."

"The dead do not rise and walk, Anndra."

"That may be, maighstir, but it may have been the Watcher of the Dead. Sure it is not three weeks since Padruic McAlistair was laid beneath the green mound. He'll be wearying for another to take his place."

"Hoots, man, that is an old superstition. The dead do not rise and walk, I tell you."

"It is right you may be, maighstir, but I heard of this from my father, that was old before you were young, and from his father before him. When the last buried is weary with being the Watcher of the Dead he goes about from place to place till he sees man, woman, or child with the death-shadow in the eyes, and then he goes back to his grave and lies down in peace, for his vigil it will be over now."

The minister laughed at the folly, and went into his house to make ready for the Sacrament that was to be on the morrow. Old Anndra, however, was uneasy. After the porridge he went down through the gloaming to Balnahunnur-sa-mona. He meant to go in and warn Mànus MacCodrum. But when he got to the west wall, and stood near the open window, he heard Mànus speaking in a loud voice, though he was alone in the room.

*"B'ionganntach do ghràdh dhomhsa, a' toirt barrachd air gràdh nam ban! . . ."**

This Mànus cried in a voice quivering with pain. Anndra stopped still, fearful to intrude, fearful also, perhaps, to see some one there beside MacCodrum whom eyes should not see. Then the voice rose into a cry of agony.

"Aoram dhuit, ay an déigh dhomh fàs aosda!"†

With that Anndra feared to stay. As he passed the byre he started, for he thought he saw the shadow of a man. When he looked closer he could see nought, so went his way trembling and sore troubled.

It was dusk when Mànus came out. He saw that it was to be a cloudy night, and perhaps it was this that, after a brief while, made him turn in

---

* "Thy love to me was wonderful, surpassing the love of women."

† "I shall worship thee, ay, even after I have become old."

his aimless walk and go back to the house. He was sitting before the flaming heart of the peats, brooding in his pain, when suddenly he sprang to his feet.

Loud and clear, and close as though played under the very window of the room, came the cold white notes of an oaten flute. Ah, too well he knew that wild fantastic air. Who could it be but Gloom Achanna, playing upon his *feadan;* and what air of all airs could that be but the Dàn-nan-Ròn?

Was it the dead man, standing there unseen in the shadow of the grave? Was Marcus beside him—Marcus with the knife still thrust up to the hilt, and the lung-foam upon his lips? Can the sea give up its dead? Can there be strain of any *feadan* that ever was made of man—there in the Silence?

In vain Mànus MacCodrum tortured himself thus. Too well he knew that he had heard the Dàn-nan-Ròn, and that no other than Gloom Achanna was the player.

Suddenly an access of fury wrought him to madness. With an abrupt lilt the tune swung into the Davsà-na-mairv, and thence, after a few seconds, and in a moment, into that mysterious and horrible *Codhail-nan-Pairtean* which none but Gloom played.

There could be no mistake now, nor as to what was meant by the muttering, jerking air of the "Gathering of the Crabs."

With a savage cry Mànus snatched up a long dirk from its place by the chimney, and rushed out.

There was not the shadow of a sea-gull even in front: so he sped round by the byre. Neither was anything unusual discoverable there.

"Sorrow upon me," he cried; "man or wraith, I will be putting it to the dirk!"

But there was no one; nothing; not a sound.

Then, at last, with a listless droop of his arms, MacCodrum turned and went into the house again. He remembered what Gloom Achanna had said: *"You'll hear the Dàn-nan-Ròn the night before you die, Mànus MacCodrum, and lest you doubt it, you'll hear it in your death-hour."*

He did not stir from the fire for three hours; then he rose, and went over to his bed and lay down without undressing.

He did not sleep, but lay listening and watching. The peats burned low, and at last there was scarce a flicker along the floor. Outside he could hear the wind moaning upon the sea. By a strange rustling sound he knew that the tide was ebbing across the great reef that runs out from Berneray. By midnight the clouds had gone. The moon shone clear and full. When he heard the clock strike in its worm-eaten, rickety case, he sat up, and listened intently. He could hear nothing. No shadow stirred. Surely if the wraith of Gloom Achanna were waiting for him it would make some sign, now, in the dead of night.

An hour passed. Mànus rose, crossed the room on tip-toe, and soundlessly opened the door. The salt-wind blew fresh against his face. The smell of the shore, of wet sea-wrack and pungent gale, of foam and moving water, came sweet to his nostrils. He heard a skua calling from the rocky promontory. From the slopes behind, the wail of a moon-restless lapwing rose and fell mournfully.

Crouching, and with slow, stealthy step, he stole round by the seaward wall. At the dyke he stopped, and scrutinised it on each side. He could see for several hundred yards, and there was not even a sheltering sheep. Then, soundlessly as ever, he crept close to the byre. He put his ear to chink after chink; but not a stir of a shadow even. As a shadow, himself, he drifted lightly to the front, past the hayrick: then, with swift glances to right and left, opened the door and entered. As he did so, he stood as though frozen. Surely, he thought, that was a sound as of a step, out there by the hayrick. A terror was at his heart. In front, the darkness of the byre, with God knows what dread thing awaiting him: behind, a mysterious walker in the night, swift to take him unawares. The trembling that came upon him was nigh overmastering. At last, with a great effort, he moved towards the ledge, where he kept a candle. With shaking hand he struck a light. The empty byre looked ghostly and fearsome in the flickering gloom. But there was no one, nothing. He was about to turn, when a rat ran along a loose hanging beam, and stared at him, or at the yellow shine. He saw its black eyes shining like peat-water in moonlight.

The creature was curious at first, then indifferent. At least, it began to squeak, and then make a swift scratching with its forepaws. Once or twice came an answering squeak: a faint rustling was audible here and there among the straw.

With a sudden spring Mànus seized the beast. Even in the second in which he raised it to his mouth and scrunched its back with his strong teeth, it bit him severely. He let his hands drop, and grope furtively in the darkness. With stooping head he shook the last breath out of the rat, holding it with his front teeth, with back-curled lips. The next moment he dropped the dead thing, trampled upon it, and burst out laughing. There was a scurrying of pattering feet, a rustling of straw. Then silence again. A draught from the door had caught the flame and extinguished it. In the silence and darkness MacCodrum stood, intent but no longer afraid. He laughed again, because it was so easy to kill with the teeth. The noise of his laughter seemed to him to leap hither and thither like a shadowy ape. He could see it: a blackness within the darkness. Once more he laughed. It amused him to see the *thing* leaping about like that.

Suddenly he turned, and walked out into the moonlight. The lapwing was still circling and wailing. He mocked it, with loud, shrill *pēē-wēēty, pēē-wēēty, pēē-wēēt.* The bird swung waywardly, alarmed: its abrupt cry, and dancing flight, aroused its fellows. The air was full of the lamentable crying of plovers.

A sough of the sea came inland. Mànus inhaled its breath with a sigh of delight. A passion for the running wave was upon him. He yearned to feel green water break against his breast. Thirst and hunger, too, he felt at last, though he had known neither all day. How cool and sweet, he thought, would be a silver haddock, or even a brown-backed liath, alive and gleaming wet with the sea-water still bubbling in its gills. It would writhe, just like the rat; but then how he would throw his head back, and toss the glittering thing up into the moonlight, catch it on the downwhirl just as it neared the wave on whose crest he was, and then devour it with swift voracious gulps!

With quick jerky steps he made his way past the landward side of the small thatch-roofed cottage. He was about to enter, when he noticed that the door, which he had left ajar, was closed. He stole to the window and glanced in.

A single thin, wavering moonbeam flickered in the room. But the flame at the heart of the peats had worked its way through the ash, and there was now a dull glow, though that was within the "smooring," and threw scarce more than a glimmer into the room.

There was enough light, however, for Mànus MacCodrum to see that a man sat on the three-legged stool before the fire. His head was bent, as though he were listening. The face was away from the window. It was his own wraith, of course—of that Mànus felt convinced. What was it doing there? Perhaps it had eaten the Holy Book, so that it was beyond his putting a *rosad* on it! At the thought, he laughed loud. The shadow-man leaped to his feet.

The next moment MacCodrum swung himself on to the thatched roof, and clambered from rope to rope, where these held down the big stones which acted as dead-weight for thatch against the fury of tempests. Stone after stone he tore from its fastenings, and hurled to the ground over beyond the door. Then, with tearing hands, he began to burrow an opening in the thatch. All the time he whined like a beast.

He was glad the moon shone full upon him. When he had made a big enough hole, he would see the evil thing out of the grave that sat in his room, and would stone it to death.

Suddenly he became still. A cold sweat broke out upon him. The *thing,* whether his own wraith, or the spirit of his dead foe, or Gloom Achanna himself, had begun to play, low and slow, a wild air. No piercing, cold music like that of the *feadan!* Too well he knew it, and those cool white notes that moved here and there in the darkness like snow-flakes. As for the air, though he slept till Judgment Day and heard but a note of it amidst all the clamour of heaven and hell, sure he would scream because of the Dàn-nan-Ròn.

The Dàn-nan-Ròn: the *Roin!* the Seals! Ah, what was he doing there, on the bitter-weary land! Out there was the sea. Safe would he be in the green waves.

With a leap he was on the ground. Seizing a huge stone he hurled it through the window. Then, laughing and screaming, he fled towards the Great Reef, along whose sides the ebb-tide gurgled and sobbed, with glistening white foam.

He ceased screaming or laughing as he heard the Dàn-nan-Ròn behind him, faint, but following; sure, following. Bending low, he raced towards the rock-ledges from which ran the reef.

When at last he reached the extreme ledge, he stopped abruptly. Out on the reef he saw from ten to twenty seals, some swimming to and fro, others clinging to the reef, one or two making a curious barking sound, with round heads lifted against the moon. In one place there was a surge and lashing of water. Two bulls were fighting to the death.

With swift stealthy movements Mànus unclothed himself. The damp had clotted the leathern thongs of his boots, and he snarled with curled lip as he tore at them. He shone white in the moonshine, but was sheltered from the sea by the ledge behind which he crouched. "What did Gloom Achanna mean by that?" he muttered savagely, as he heard the nearing air change into the "Dance of the Dead." For a moment Mànus was a man again. He was nigh upon turning to face his foe, corpse or wraith or living body, to spring at this thing which followed him, and tear it with hands and teeth. Then, once more, the hated Song of the Seal stole mockingly through the night.

With a shiver he slipped into the dark water. Then, with quick, powerful strokes, he was in the moon-flood, and swimming hard against it out by the leeside of the reef.

So intent were the seals upon the fight of the two great bulls that they did not see the swimmer, or, if they did, took him for one of their own people. A savage snarling and barking and half-human crying came from them. Mànus was almost within reach of the nearest, when one of the combatants sank dead, with torn throat. The victor clambered on to the reef, and leaned high, swaying its great head and shoulders to and fro. In the moonlight its white fangs were like red coral. Its blinded eyes ran with gore.

There was a rush, a rapid leaping and swirling, as Mànus surged in among the seals, which were swimming round the place where the slain bull had sunk.

The laughter of this long white seal terrified them.

When his knees struck against a rock, MacCodrum groped with his arms, and hauled himself out of the water.

From rock to rock and ledge to ledge he went, with a fantastic, dancing motion, his body gleaming foam-white in the moonshine.

As he pranced and trampled along the weedy ledges, he sang snatches of an old rune—the lost rune of the MacCodrums of Uist. The seals on the rocks crouched spell-bound; those slow-swimming in the water stared with brown unwinking eyes, with their small ears strained against the sound:—

> It is I, Mànus MacCodrum,
> I am telling you that, you, Anndra of my blood,
> And you, Neil my grandfather, and you, and you, and you!
> Ay, ay, Mànus my name is, Mànus Mac Mànus!
> It is I myself, and no other.
> Your brother, O Seals of the Sea!
> Give me blood of the red fish,
> And a bite of the flying sgadan:
> The green wave on my belly,
> And the foam in my eyes!
> I am your bull-brother, O Bulls of the Sea,
> Bull-better than any of you, snarling bulls!
> Come to me, mate, seal of the soft furry womb,
> White am I still, though red shall I be,
> Red with the streaming red blood if any dispute me!
> Aoh, aoh, aoh, arò, arò, ho-rò!
> A man was I, a seal am I,
> My fangs churn the yellow foam from my lips:
> Give way to me, give way to me, Seals of the Sea;
> Give way, for I am fëy of the sea
> And the sea-maiden I see there,
> And my name, true, is Mànus MacCodrum,
> The bull-seal that was a man, Arà! Arà!

By this time he was close upon the great black seal, which was still monotonously swaying its gory head, with its sightless eyes rolling this way and that. The sea-folk seemed fascinated. None moved, even when the dancer in the moonshine trampled upon them.

When he came within arm-reach he stopped.

"Are you the Ceann-Cinnidh?" he cried. "Are you the head of this clan of the sea-folk?"

The huge beast ceased its swaying. Its curled lips moved from its fangs.

"Speak, Seal, if there's no curse upon you! Maybe, now, you'll be Anndra himself, the brother of my father! Speak! *H'st—are you hearing that music on the shore?* 'Tis the Dàn-nan-Ròn! Death o' my soul, it's the Dàn-nan-Ròn! Aha, 'tis Gloom Achanna out of the Grave. Back, beast, and let me move on!"

With that, seeing the great bull did not move, he struck it full in the face with clenched fist. There was a hoarse strangling roar, and the seal-champion was upon him with lacerating fangs.

Mànus swayed this way and that. All he could hear now was the snarling and growling and choking cries of the maddened seals. As he fell, they closed in upon him. His screams wheeled through the night like mad birds. With desperate fury he struggled to free himself. The great bull pinned him to the rock; a dozen others tore at his white flesh, till his spouting blood made the rocks scarlet in the white shine of the moon.

For a few seconds he still fought savagely, tearing with teeth and hands. Once, a red irrecognisable mass, he staggered to his knees. A wild cry burst from his lips, when from the shore-end of the reef came loud and clear the lilt of the rune of his fate.

The next moment he was dragged down and swept from the reef into the sea. As the torn and mangled body disappeared from sight, it was amid a seething crowd of leaping and struggling seals, their eyes wild with affright and fury, their fangs red with human gore.

And Gloom Achanna, turning upon the reef, moved swiftly inland, playing low on his *feadan* as he went.

Green Branches

In the year that followed the death of Mànus MacCodrum, James Achanna saw nothing of his brother Gloom. He might have thought himself alone in the world, of all his people, but for a letter that came to him out of the west. True, he had never accepted the common opinion that his brothers had both been drowned on that night when Anne Gillespie left Eilanmore with Mànus. In the first place, he had nothing of that inner conviction concerning the fate of Gloom which he had concerning that of Marcus; in the next, had he not heard the sound of the *feadan,* which no one that he knew played, except Gloom; and, for further token, was not the tune that which he hated above all others—the Dance of the Dead—for who but Gloom would be playing that, he hating it so, and the hour being late, and no one else on Eilanmore? It was no sure thing that the dead had not come back; but the more he thought of it the more Achanna believed that his sixth brother was still alive. Of this, however, he said nothing to any one.

It was as a man set free that, at last, after long waiting and patient trouble with the disposal of all that was left of the Achanna heritage, he left the island. It was a grey memory for him. The bleak moorland of it, the blight that had lain so long and so often upon the crops, the rains that had swept the isle for grey days and grey weeks and grey months, the sobbing of the sea by day and its dark moan by night, its dim relinquishing sigh in the calm of dreary ebbs, its hollow, baffling roar when the storm-shadow swept up out of the sea, one and all oppressed him, even in memory. He had never loved the island, even when it lay green and fragrant in the green and white seas under white and blue skies, fresh and sweet as an Eden of the sea. He had ever been lonely and weary, tired of the mysterious shadow that lay upon his folk, caring little for any of his brothers except the eldest—long since mysteriously gone out of the ken of man—and almost hating Gloom, who had ever borne him a grudge because of his beauty, and because of his likeness to and reverent heed for Alison. Moreover, ever since he had come to love Katreen Macarthur, the daughter of Donald Macarthur who lived in Sleat of Skye, he had been eager to live near her; the more eager as he knew that Gloom loved the girl also, and wished for success not only for his own sake, but so as to put a slight upon his younger brother.

So, when at last he left the island, he sailed southward gladly. He was leaving Eilanmore; he was bound to a new home in Syke, and perhaps he was going to his long-delayed, long dreamed-of happiness. True, Katreen was not pledged to him; he did not even know for sure if she loved him. He thought, hoped, dreamed, almost believed that she did; but then there was her cousin Ian, who had long wooed her, and to whom old Donald Macarthur had given his blessing. Nevertheless, his heart would have been lighter than it had been for long, but for two things. First, there was the letter. Some weeks earlier he had received it, not recognising the writing, because of the few letters he had ever seen, and, moreover, as it was in a feigned hand. With difficulty he had deciphered the manuscript, plain printed though it was. It ran thus:—

"Well, Sheumais, my brother, it is wondering if I am dead, you will be. Maybe ay and maybe no. But I send you this writing to let you see that I know all you do and think of. So you are going to leave Eilanmore without an Achanna upon it? And you will be going to Sleat in Skye? Well, let me be telling you this thing. *Do not go.* I see blood there. And there is this, too: neither you nor any man shall take Katreen away from me. *You* know that; and Ian Macarthur knows it; and Katreen knows it: and that holds whether I am alive or dead. I say to you: do not go. It will be better for you and for all. Ian Macarthur is away in the north-sea with the whaler-captain who came to us at Eilanmore, and will not be back for three months yet. It will be better for him not to come back. But if he comes back he will have to reckon with the man who says that Katreen Macarthur is his. I would rather not have two men to speak to, and one my brother. It does not matter to you where I am. I want no money just now. But put aside my portion for me. Have it ready for me against the day I call for it. I will not be patient that day; so have it ready for me. In the place that I am I am content. You will be saying: why is my brother away in a remote place (I will say this to you: that it is not farther north than St. Kilda nor far-

ther south than the Mull of Cantyre!), and for what reason? That is between me and silence. But perhaps you think of Anne sometimes. Do
you know that she lies under the green grass? And of Mànus Mac-
Cordrum? They say that he swam out into the sea and was drowned;
and they whisper of the seal-blood, though the minister is wrath with
them for that. He calls it a madness. Well, I was there at that madness,
and I played to it on my *feadan.* And now, Sheumais, can you be thinking of what the tune was that I played?

"Your brother, who waits his own day,
"GLOOM."

"Do not be forgetting this thing: *I would rather not be playing the
'Damhsà-na-mairbh.'* It was an ill hour for Mànus when he heard the
Dàn-nan-Ròn; it was the song of his soul, that; and yours is the Davsa-na-
Mairv."

This letter was ever in his mind: this, and what happened in the
gloaming when he sailed away for Skye in the herring-smack of two men
who lived at Armadale in Sleat. For, as the boat moved slowly out of the
haven, one of the men asked him if he was sure that no one was left upon the island; for he thought he had seen a figure on the rocks, waving a
black scarf. Achanna shook his head, but just then his companion cried
that at that moment he had seen the same thing. So the smack was put
about, and when she was moving slow through the haven again, Achanna sculled ashore in the little coggly punt. In vain he searched here and
there, calling loudly again and again. Both men could hardly have been
mistaken, he thought. If there were no human creature on the island,
and if their eyes had not played them false, who could it be? The wraith
of Marcus, mayhap; or might it be the old man himself (his father), risen
to bid farewell to his youngest son, or to warn him?

It was no use to wait longer, so, looking often behind him, he made
his way to the boat again, and rowed slowly out towards the smack.

Jerk—jerk—jerk across the water came, low but only too loud for
him, the opening motif of the Damhsà-na-Mairbh. A horror came upon
him, and he drove the boat through the water so that the sea splashed
over the bows. When he came on deck he cried in a hoarse voice to the
man next him to put up the helm, and let the smack swing to the wind.

"There is no one there, Callum Campbell," he whispered.

"And who is it that will be making that strange music?"

"What music?"

"Sure it has stopped now, but I heard it clear, and so did Anndra MacEwan. It was like the sound of a reed-pipe, and the tune was an ee-rie one at that."

"It was the Dance of the Dead."

"And who will be playing that?" asked the man, with fear in his eyes.

"No living man."

"No living man?"

"No. I'm thinking it will be one of my brothers who was drowned here, and by the same token that it is Gloom, for he played upon the *feadan;* but if not, then . . . then . . ."

The two men waited in breathless silence, each trembling with su-perstitious fear; but at last the elder made a sign to Achanna to finish.

"Then . . . it will be the Kelpie."

"Is there . . . is there one of the . . . the cave-women here?"

"It is said; and you know of old that the Kelpie sings or plays a strange tune to wile seamen to their death."

At that moment, the fantastic jerking music came loud and clear across the bay. There was a horrible suggestion in it, as if dead bodies were moving along the ground with long jerks, and crying and laughing wild. It was enough; the men, Campbell and MacEwan, would not now have waited longer if Achanna had offered them all he had in the world. Nor were they, or he, out of their panic haste till the smack stood well out at sea, and not a sound could be heard from Eilanmore.

They stood watching, silent. Out of the dusky mass that lay in the seaward way to the north came a red gleam. It was like an eye staring af-ter them with blood-red glances.

"What is that, Achanna?" asked one of the men at last.

"It looks as though a fire had been lit in the house up in the island. The door and the window must be open. The fire must be fed with wood, for no peats would give that flame; and there were none lit when I left. To my knowing, there was no wood for burning except the wood of the shelves and the bed."

"And who would be doing that?"

"I know of that no more than you do, Callum Campbell."

No more was said, and it was a relief to all when the last glimmer of the light was absorbed in the darkness.

At the end of the voyage Campbell and MacEwan were well pleased to be quit of their companion; not so much because he was moody and distraught, as because they feared that a spell was upon him—a fate in the working of which they might become involved. It needed no vow of the one to the other for them to come to the conclusion that they would never land in Eilanmore, or, if need be, only in broad daylight and never alone.

The days went well for James Achanna, where he made his home at Ranza-beag, on Ranza Water in the Sleat of Skye. The farm was small but good, and he hoped that with help and care he would soon have the place as good a farm as there was in all Skye.

Donald Macarthur did not let him see much of Katreen, but the old man was no longer opposed to him. Sheumais must wait till Ian Macarthur came back again, which might be any day now. For sure, James Achanna of Ranza-beag was a very different person from the youngest of the Achanna-folk who held by on lonely Eilanmore; moreover, the old man could not but think with pleasure that it would be well to see Katreen able to walk over the whole land of Ranza, from the cairn at the north of his own Ranza-Mòr to the burn at the south of Ranza-beag, and know it for her own.

But Achanna was ready to wait. Even before he had the secret word of Katreen he knew from her beautiful dark eyes that she loved him. As the weeks went by they managed to meet often, and at last Katreen told him that she loved him too, and would have none but him; but that they must wait till Ian came back, because of the pledge given to him by her father. They were days of joy for him. Through many a hot noontide hour, through many a gloaming, he went as one in a dream. Whenever he saw a birch swaying in the wind, or a wave leaping upon Loch Liath, that was near his home, or passed a bush covered with wild roses, or saw the moonbeams lying white on the holes of the pines, he thought of Katreen: his fawn for grace, and so lithe and tall, with sun-brown face and wavy dark mass of hair and shadowy eyes and rowan-red lips. It is said that there is a god clothed in shadow who goes to and fro among the human kind, putting silence between lovers with his waving hands and breathing a chill out of his cold breath, and leaving a gulf of deep water flowing between them because of the passing of his feet. That shadow never came their way. Their love grew as a flower fed by rains and warmed by sunlight.

When midsummer came, and there was no sign of Ian Macarthur, it was already too late. Katreen had been won.

During the summer months, it was the custom for Katreen and two of the farm-girls to go up Maol-Ranza, to reside at the shealing of Cnoc-an-Fhraoch: and this because of the hill-pasture for the sheep. Cnoc-an-Fhraoch is a round, boulder-studded hill covered with heather, which has a precipitous corrie on each side, and in front slopes down to Loch-an Fraoch, a lochlet surrounded by dark woods. Behind the hill, or great hillock rather, lay the shealing. At each week-end Katreen went down to Ranza-Mòr, and on every Monday morning at sunrise returned to her heather-girt eyrie. It was on one of these visits that she endured a cruel shock. Her father told her that she must marry some one else than Sheumais Achanna. He had heard words about him which made a union impossible, and, indeed, he hoped that the man would leave Ranza-beag. In the end, he admitted that what he had heard was to the effect that Achanna was under a doom of some kind; that he was involved in a blood feud; and, moreover, that he was fëy. The old man would not be explicit as to the person from whom his information came, but hinted that he was a stranger of rank, probably a laird of the isles. Besides this, there was word of Ian Macarthur. He was at Thurso, in the far north, and would be in Skye before long, and he—her father—had written to him that he might wed Katreen as soon as was practicable.

"Do you see that lintie yonder, father?" was her response to this.

"Ay, lass; and what about the birdeen?"

"Well, when she mates with a hawk, so will I be mating with Ian Macarthur, but not till then."

With that she turned, and left the house, and went back to Cnoc-an-Fhraoch. On the way she met Achanna.

It was that night that, for the first time, he swam across Lochan Fraoch to meet Katreen.

The quickest way to reach the shealing was to row across the lochlet, and then ascend by a sheep-path that wound through the hazel copses at the base of the hill. Fully half-an-hour was thus saved, because of the steepness of the precipitous corries to right and left. A boat was kept for this purpose, but it was fastened to a shore-boulder by a padlocked iron chain, the key of which was kept by Donald Macarthur. Latterly he had refused to let this key out of his possession. For one thing, no doubt, he believed he could thus restrain Achanna from visiting his daughter. The young man could not approach the shealing from either side without being seen.

But that night, soon after the moon was whitening slow in the dark, Katreen stole down to the hazel copse and awaited the coming of her lover. The lochan was visible from almost any point on Cnoc-an-Fhraoch, as well as from the south side. To cross it in a boat unseen, if any watcher were near, would be impossible, nor could even a swimmer hope to escape notice unless in the gloom of night, or, mayhap, in the dusk. When, however, she saw, half way across the water, a spray of green branches slowly moving athwart the surface, she knew that Sheumais was keeping his tryst. If, perchance, any one else saw, he or she would never guess that those derelict rowan-branches shrouded Sheumais Achanna.

It was not till the estray had drifted close to the ledge, where, hid among the bracken and the hazel undergrowth, she awaited him, that Katreen descried the face of her lover, as with one hand he parted the green sprays and stared longingly and lovingly at the figure he could just discern in the dim fragrant obscurity.

And as it was this night so was it many of the nights that followed. Katreen spent the days as in a dream. Not even the news of her cousin Ian's return disturbed her much.

One day the inevitable meeting came. She was at Ranza-Mòr, and when a shadow came into the dairy where she was standing she looked up, and saw Ian before her. She thought he appeared taller and stronger than ever, though still not so tall as Sheumais, who would appear slim beside the Herculean Skye man. But as she looked at his close curling black hair, and thick bull neck, and the sullen eyes in his dark wind-red face, she wondered that she had ever tolerated him at all.

He broke the ice at once.

"Tell me, Katreen, are you glad to see me back again?"

"I am glad that you are home once more safe and sound."

"And will you make it my home for me by coming to live with me, as I've asked you again and again?"

"No: as I've told you again and again."

He gloomed at her angrily for a few moments before he resumed.

"I will be asking you this one thing, Katreen, daughter of my father's brother: do you love that man Achanna who lives at Ranza-beag?"

"You may ask the wind why it is from the east or the west, but it won't tell you. You're not the wind's master."

"If you think I will let this man take you away from me, you are thinking a foolish thing."

"And you saying a foolisher."

"Ay?"

"Ay, sure. What could you do, Ian-mhic-Ian? At the worst, you could do no more than kill James Achanna. What then? I too would die. You cannot separate us. I would not marry you, now, though you were the last man on the world and I the last woman."

"You're a fool, Katreen Macarthur. Your father has promised you to me, and I tell you this: if you love Achanna you'll save his life only by letting him go away from here. I promise you he will not be here long."

"Ay, you promise *me;* but you will not say that thing to James Achanna's face. You are a coward."

With a muttered oath the man turned on his heel.

"Let him beware o' me, and you, too, Katreen-mo-nighean-donn. I swear it by my mother's grave and by St. Martin's Cross that you will be mine by hook or by crook."

The girl smiled scornfully. Slowly she lifted a milk-pail.

"It would be a pity to waste the good milk, Ian-gòrach; but if you don't go it is that I will be emptying the pail on you, and then you'll be as white without as your heart is within."

"So you call me witless, do you? *Ian-gòrach!* Well, we shall be seeing as to that; and as for the milk, there will be more than milk spilt because of *you,* Katreen-donn."

From that day, though neither Sheumais nor Katreen knew of it, a watch was set upon Achanna.

It could not be long before their secret was discovered; and it was with a savage joy overmastering his sullen rage that Ian Macarthur knew himself the discoverer, and conceived his double vengeance. He dreamed, gloatingly, on both the black thoughts that roamed like ravenous beasts through the solitudes of his heart. But he did not dream that another man was filled with hate because of Katreen's lover—another man who had sworn to make her his own; the man who, disguised, was known in Armadale as Donald McLean, and in the north isles would have been hailed as Gloom Achanna.

There had been steady rain for three days, with a cold, raw wind. On the fourth the sun shone, and set in peace. An evening of quiet beauty followed, warm, fragrant, dusky from the absence of moon or star, though the thin veils of mist promised to disperse as the night grew.

There were two men that eve in the undergrowth on the south side of the lochlet. Sheumais had come earlier than his wont. Impatient for the dusk, he could scarce await the waning of the afterglow. Surely, he thought, he might venture. Suddenly his ears caught the sound of cautious footsteps. Could it be old Donald, perhaps, with some inkling of the way in which his daughter saw her lover, in despite of all; or, mayhap, might it be Ian Macarthur, tracking him, as a hunter stalking a stag by the water-pools? He crouched, and waited. In a few minutes he saw Ian carefully picking his way. The man stopped as he descried the green branches; smiled as, with a low rustling, he raised them from the ground.

Meanwhile, yet another man watched and waited, though on the farther side of the lochan, where the hazel copses were. Gloom Achanna half hoped, half feared the approach of Katreen. It would be sweet to see her again, sweet to slay her lover before her eyes, brother to him though he was. But, there was the chance that she might descry him, and, whether recognisingly or not, warn the swimmer. So it was that he had come there before sundown, and now lay crouched among the bracken underneath a projecting mossy ledge close upon the water, where it could scarce be that she or any should see him.

As the gloaming deepened, a great stillness reigned. There was no breath of wind. A scarce audible sigh prevailed among the spires of the heather. The churring of a night-jar throbbed through the darkness.

Somewhere a corncrake called its monotonous *crik-craik*—the dull harsh sound emphasising the utter stillness. The pinging of the gnats hovering over and among the sedges made an incessant rumour through the warm sultry air.

There was a splash once as of a fish; then silence. Then a lower but more continuous splash, or rather wash of water. A slow susurrus rustled through the dark.

Where he lay among the fern Gloom Achanna slowly raised his head, stared through the shadows, and listened intently. If Katreen were waiting there she was not near.

Noiselessly he slid into the water. When he rose it was under a clump of green branches. These he had cut and secured three hours before. With his left hand he swam slowly, or kept his equipoise in the water; with his right he guided the heavy rowan bough. In his mouth were two objects, one long and thin and dark, the other with an occasional glitter as of a dead fish.

His motion was scarce perceptible. None the less he was nigh the middle of the loch almost as soon as another clump of green branches. Doubtless the swimmer beneath it was confident that he was now safe from observation.

The two clumps of green branches drew nearer. The smaller seemed a mere estray—a spray blown down by the recent gale. But all at once the larger clump jerked awkwardly and stopped. Simultaneously a strange low strain of music came from the other.

The strain ceased. The two clumps of green branches remained motionless. Slowly at last the larger moved forward. It was too dark for the swimmer to see if any one lay hid behind the smaller. When he reached it he thrust aside the leaves.

It was as though a great salmon leaped. There was a splash, and a narrow dark body shot through the gloom. At the end of it something gleamed. Then suddenly there was a savage struggle. The inanimate green branches tore this way and that, and surged and swirled. Gasping cries came from the leaves. Again and again the gleaming thing leaped. At the third leap an awful scream shrilled through the silence. The echo of it wailed thrice with horrible distinctness in the corrie beyond Cnoc-an-Fhraoch. Then, after a faint splashing, there was silence once more. One clump of green branches drifted loosely up the lochlet. The other moved steadily towards the place whence, a brief while before, it had stirred.

Only one thing lived in the heart of Gloom Achanna—the joy of his exultation, He had killed his brother Sheumais. He had always hated him because of his beauty; of late he had hated him because he had stood between him, Gloom, and Katreen Macarthur, because he had become her lover. They were all dead now except himself—all the Achannas. He was "Achanna." When the day came that he would go back to Galloway there would be a magpie on the first birk, and a screaming jay on the first rowan, and a croaking raven on the first fir. Ay, he would be their suffering, though they knew nothing of him meanwhile! He would be Achanna of Achanna again. Let those who would stand in his way beware. As for Katreen: perhaps he would take her there, perhaps not. He smiled.

These thoughts were the wandering fires in his brain while he slowly swam shoreward under the floating green branches, and as he disengaged himself from them, and crawled upward through the bracken. It was at this moment that a third man entered the water from the farther shore.

Prepared as he was to come suddenly upon Katreen, Gloom was startled when, in a place of dense shadow, a hand touched his shoulder, and her voice whispered *"Sheumais, Sheumais!"*

The next moment she was in his arms. He could feet her heart beating against his side.

"What was it, Sheumais? What was that awful cry?" she whispered.

For answer he put his lips to hers, and kissed her again and again.

The girl drew back. Some vague instinct warned her.

"What is it, Sheumais? Why don't you speak?"

He drew her close again.

"Pulse of my heart, it is I who love you—I who love you best of all. It is I, Gloom Achanna!"

With a cry, she struck him full in the face. He staggered, and in that moment she freed herself.

"You *coward!*"

"Katreen, I . . ."

"Come no nearer. If you do, it will be the death of you!"

"The death o' me! Ah, bonnie fool that you are, and it is you that will be the death o' me?"

"Ay, Gloom Achanna, for I have but to scream and Sheumais will be here, an' he would kill you like a dog if he knew you did me harm."

"Ah, but if there were no James, or any man, to come between me an' my will!"

"Then there would be a woman! Ay, if you overbore me I would strangle you with my hair, or fix my teeth in your false throat!"

"I was not for knowing you were such a wild-cat! But I'll tame you yet, my lass! Aha, wild-cat!" and, as he spoke, he laughed low.

"It is a true word, Gloom of the black heart. I *am* a wild-cat, and like a wild-cat I am not to be seized by a fox, and that you will be finding to your cost, by the holy St. Briget! But now, off with you, brother of my man!"

"Your man . . . ha! ha! . . ."

"Why do you laugh?"

"Sure, I am laughing at a warm white lass like yourself having a dead man as your lover!"

"A . . . dead . . . man?"

No answer came. The girl shook with a new fear. Slowly she drew closer till her breath fell warm against the face of the other. He spoke at last.

"Ay, a dead man."

"It is a lie."

"Where would you be that you were not hearing his goodbye? I'm thinking it was loud enough!"

"It is a lie . . . it is a lie!"

"No, it is no lie. Sheumais is cold enough now. He's low among the weeds by now. Ay, by now; down there in the lochan."

"*What* . . . you, *you devil!* Is it for killing your own brother you would be?"

"I killed no one. He died his own way. Maybe the cramp took him. Maybe . . . maybe a kelpie gripped him. I watched. I saw him beneath the green branches. He was dead before he died. I saw it in the white face o' him. Then he sank. He's dead—James is dead. Look here, girl, I've always loved you. I swore the oath upon you—you're mine. Sure, you're mine now, Katreen! It is loving you I am! It will be a south wind for you from this day, *muirnean mochree!* See here, I'll show you how I . . ."

"Back . . . back . . . *murderer!*"

"Be stopping that foolishness now, Katreen Macarthur! By the Book, I am tired of it! I am loving you, and it's having you for mine I am! And if you won't come to me like the dove to its mate, I'll come to you like the hawk to the dove!"

With a spring he was upon her. In vain she strove to beat him back. His arms held her as a stoat grips a rabbit.

He pulled her head back, and kissed her throat till the strangulating breath sobbed against his ear. With a last despairing effort she screamed the name of the dead man—"*Shumais! Sheumais! Sheumais!*" The man who struggled with her laughed.

"Ay, call away! The herrin' will be coming through the bracken as soon as Sheumais comes to your call! Ah, it is mine you are now, Katreen! He's dead an' cold . . . an' you'd best have a living man . . . an' . . ."

She fell back, her balance lost in the sudden releasing. What did it mean? Gloom still stood there, but as one frozen. Through the darkness she saw at last that a hand gripped his shoulder—behind him a black mass vaguely obtruded.

For some moments there was absolute silence. Then a hoarse voice came out of the dark.

"You will be knowing now who it is, Gloom Achanna!"

The voice was that of Sheumais, who lay dead in the lochan. The murderer shook as in a palsy. With a great effort, slowly he turned his head. He saw a white splatch—the face of the corpse. In this white splatch flamed two burning eyes, the eyes of the soul of the brother whom he had slain.

He reeled, staggered as a blind man, and, free now of that awful clasp, swayed to and fro as one drunken. Slowly Sheumais raised an arm, and pointed downward through the wood towards the lochan. Still pointing, he moved swiftly forward.

With a cry like a beast, Gloom Achanna swung to one side, stumbled, rose, and leaped into the darkness.

For some minutes Sheumais and Katreen stood, silent, apart, listening to the crashing sound of his flight—the race of the murderer against the pursuing shadow of the Grave.

Silk o' the Kine

What I shall now be telling you," said Ian Mòr to me once—and indeed, I should remember the time of it well: for it was in the last year of his life, when rarely any other than myself saw aught of Ian of the Hills—"What I shall now be telling you is an ancient forgotten tale of a man and woman of the old heroic days. The name of the man was Isla, and the name of the woman was Eilidh."

"Ah, yes, for sure," Ian added, as I interrupted him; "I knew you would be saying that: but it is not of Eilidh that loved Cormac that I am now speaking. Nor am I taking the hidden way with Isla, that was my friend, nor with Eilidh that is my name-child, whom you know. Let the Birdeen be, bless her bonnie heart! No, what I am for telling you is all as new to you as the green grass to a lambkin: and no one has heard it from these tired lips o' mine since I was a boy, and learned it off the mouth of old Barabol MacAodh that was my foster-mother."

Of all the many tales of the olden time that Ian Mòr told me, and are to be found in no book, this was the last. That is why I give it here, where I have spoken much of him.

Ian told me this thing one winter night, while we sat before the peats, where the ingle was full of warm shadows. We were in the croft of the small hill-farm of Glenivore, which was held by my cousin, Silis Macfarlane. But we were alone then, for Silas was over at the far end of

---

Silk o' the Kine, one of the poetic "secret" names of conquered Erin, was in ancient days, there and in the Scottish Isles, a designation for a woman of rare beauty. The name Eilidh (pronouncec *Eil-ih*, with a long accent on the first syllable) is also ancient, but lingers in the Isles still, and indeed throughout the Western Highlands, as also, I understand, in Connaught and Connemara. Somhairle (Somerled) is pronounced *So-irl-ū*.

the Strath, because of the baffling against death of her dearest friend, Giorsal MacDiarmid.

It was warm there, before the peats, with a thick wedge of spruce driven into the heart of them. The resin crackled and sent blue sparks of flame up through the red and yellow tongues that licked the sooty chimney-slopes, in which, as in a shell, we could hear an endless soughing of the wind.

Outside, the snow lay deep. It was so hard on the surface that the white hares, leaping across it, went soundless as shadows, and as trackless.

In the far-off days, when Somhairle was Maormor of the Isles, the most beautiful woman of her time was named Eilidh.

The king had sworn that whosoever was his best man in battle, when next the Fomorian pirates out of the north came down upon the isles, should have Eilidh to wife.

Eilidh, who, because of her soft, white beauty, for all the burning brown of her by the sun and wind, was also called Silk o' the Kine, laughed low when she heard this. For she loved the one man in all the world for her, and that was Isla, the son of Isla Mòr, the blind chief of Islay. He, too, loved her even as she loved him. He was a poet as well as a warrior, and scarce she knew whether she loved best the fire in his eyes when, girt with his gleaming weapons and with his fair hair unbound, he went forth to battle: or the shine in his eyes when, harp in hand, he chanted of the great deeds of old, or made a sweet song to her, Eilidh, his queen of women: or the flame in his eyes when, meeting her at the setting of the sun, he stood speechless, wrought to silence because of his worshipping love of her.

One day she bade him go to the Isle of the Swans to fetch her enough of the breast-down of the wild cygnets for her to make a white cloak of. While he was still absent—and the going there, and the faring thereupon, and the returning took three days—the Fomorians came down upon the Long Island.

It was a hard fight that was fought, but at last the Norlanders were driven back with slaughter. Somhairle, the Maormor, was all but slain in that fight, and the corbies would have had his eyes had it not been for

Osra mac Osra, who with his javelin slew the spearman who had waylaid the king while he slipped in the Fomorian blood he had spilt.

While the ale was being drunk out of the great horns that night, Somhairle called for Eilidh.

The girl came to the rath where the king and his warriors feasted; white and beautiful as moonlight among turbulent black waves.

A murmur went up from many bearded lips. The king scowled. Then there was silence.

"I am here, O King," said Eilidh. The sweet voice of her was like soft rain in the woods at the time of the greening.

Somhairle looked at her. Sure, she was fair to see. No wonder men called her Silk o' the Kine. His pulse beat against the stormy tide in his veins. Then, suddenly, his gaze fell upon Osra. The heart of his kinsman that had saved him was his own: and he smiled, and lusted after Eilidh no more.

"Eilidh, that art called Silk o' the Kine, dost thou see this man here before me?"

"I see the man."

"Let the name of him then be upon your lips."

"It is Osra mac Osra."

"It is this Osra and no other man that is to wind thee, fair Silk o' the Kine. And by the same token, I have sworn to him that he shall lie breast to breast with thee this night. So go hence to where Osra has his sleeping-place, and await him there upon the deer-skins. From this hour thou art his wife. It is said."

Then a silence fell again upon all there, when, after a loud surf of babbling laughter and talk, they saw that Eilidh stood where she was, heedless of the king's word.

Somhairle gloomed. The great black eyes under his cloudy mass of hair flamed upon her.

"Is it dumb you are, Eilidh," he said at last, in a cold, hard voice; "or do you wait for Osra to take you hence?"

"I am listening," she answered; and that whisper was heard by all there. It was as the wind in the heather, low and sweet.

Then all listened.

The playing of a harp was heard. None played like that save Isla mac Isla Mòr.

Then the deer-skins were drawn aside, and Isla came among those who feasted there.

"Welcome, O thou who wast afar off when the foe came," began Somhairle, with bitter mocking.

But Isla took no note of that. He went forward till he was nigh upon the Maormor. Then he waited.

"Well, Isla that is called Isla-Aluinn, Isla fair-to-see, what is the thing you want of me, that you stand there, close-kin to death I am warning you?"

"I want Eilidh that is called Silk o' the Kine."

"Eilidh is the wife of another man."

"There is no other man, O King."

"A brave word that! And who says it, O Isla, my over-lord!"

"I say it."

Somhairle, the great Maormor, laughed, and his laugh was like a black bird of omen let loose against a night of storm.

"And what of Eilidh?"

"Let her speak."

With that the Maormor turned to the girl, who did not quail.

"Speak, Silk o' the Kine!"

"There is no other man, O King."

"Fool, I have this moment wedded you and Osra mac Osra."

"I am wife to Isla-Aluinn."

"Thou canst not be wife to two men."

"That may be, O King. I know not. But I am wife to Isla-Aluinn."

The king scowled darkly. None at the board whispered even. Osra shifted uneasily, clasping his sword-hilt. Isla stood, his eyes ashine as they rested on Eilidh. He knew nothing in life or death could come between them.

"Art thou not still a maid, Eilidh?" Somhairle asked at last.

"No."

"Shame to thee, wanton."

The girl smiled; but in her eyes, darkened now, there shone a flame.

"Is Isla-Aluinn the man?"

"He is the man."

With that the king laughed a bitter laugh.

"Seize him!" he cried.

But Isla made no movement. So those who were about to bind him, stood by, ready with naked swords.

"Take up your harp," said Somhairle.

Isla stooped, and lifted the harp.

"Play now the wedding song of Osra mac Osra and Eilidh Silk o' the Kine."

Isla smiled; but it was a grim smile that, and only Eilidh understood. Then he struck the harp, and he sang thus far this song out of his heart to the woman he loved better than life.

Eilidh, Eilidh, heart of my life, my pulse, my flame,
There are two men loving thee and two who are calling thee wife:

But only one husband to thee, Eilidh, that art my wife, and my joy;
Ay, sure thy womb knows me, and the child thou bearest is mine.

Thou to me, I to thee, there is nought else in the world, Eilidh Silk o'
  the Kine,—
Nought else in the world, no, no other man for thee, no woman for me!

But with that Somhairle rose, and dashed the hilt of his great spear upon the ground.

"Let the twain go," he shouted.

Then all stood or leaned back as Isla and Eilidh slowly moved through their midst, hand in hand. Not one there but knew they went to their death.

"This night shall be theirs," cried the king with mocking wrath; "then, Osra, you can have your will of Silk o' the Kine, that is your wife, and have Isla-Aluinn to be your slave; and this for the rising and setting of three moons from to-night. Then they shall each be blinded and made dumb, and that for the same space of time; and at the end of that time they shall be thrown upon the snow to the wolves."

Nevertheless, Osra groaned in his heart because of that night of Isla with Eilidh. Not all the years of the years could give him a joy like unto that.

In the silence of the mid-dark he went stealthily to where the twain lay.

It was there he was found in the morning, where he had died soundlessly, with Eilidh's dagger up to the hilt in his heart.

But none saw them go, save one, and that was Sorch, the brother of Isla—Sorch who, in later days, was called Sorch Mouth o' Honey because of his sweet songs. Of all songs that he sang none was so sweet against the ears as that of the love of Eilidh and Isla. Two lovers these that loved as few love: and deathless, too, because of that great love.

And what Sorch saw was this. Just before the rising of the sun, Isla and Eilidh came hand in hand from out of the rath, where they had lain awake all night because of their deep joy.

Silently, but unhasting, fearless still as of yore, they moved across the low dunes that withheld the sea from the land.

The waves were just frothed, so low were they. The loud glad singing of them filled the morning. Eilidh and Isla stopped when the first waves met their feet. They cast their raiment from them. Eilidh flung the gold fillet of her dusky hair far into the sea. Isla broke his sword, and saw the two halves shelve through the moving greenness. Then they turned and kissed each other upon the lips.

And the end of the song of Sorch is this: that neither he nor any man knows whether they went to life or to death; but that Isla and Eilidh swam out together against the sun, and were seen never again by any of their kin or race. Two strong swimmers were these who swam out together into the sunlight—Eilidh and Isla.

The Washer of the Ford

I

When Torcall the Harper heard of the death of his friend, Aodh-of-the-Songs, he made a vow to mourn for him for three seasons—a green time, an apple time, and a snow time.

There was sorrow upon him because of that death. True, Aodh was not of his kindred, but the singer had saved the harper's life when his friend was fallen in the Field of Spears.

Torcall was of the people of the north—of the men of Lochlin. His song was of the fjords and of strange gods, of the sword and the war-galley, of the red blood and the white breast, of Odin and Thor and Freya, of Balder and the Dream-God that sits in the rainbow, of the starry North, of the flames of pale blue and flushing rose that play around the Pole, of sudden death in battle, and of Valhalla.

Aodh was of the south isles, where these shake under the thunder of the western seas. His clan was of the isle that is now called Barra, and was then Aoidû; but his mother was a woman out of a royal rath in Banba, as men of old called Eiré or Eireann. She was so fair that a man died of his desire of her. He was named Ulad, and was a prince. "The Melancholy of Ulad" was long sung in his land after his end in the dark swamp, where he heard a singing, and went laughing glad to his death. Another man was made a prince because of her. This was Aodh the Harper, out of the Hebrid Isles. He won the heart out of her, and it was his from the day she heard his music and felt his eyes flame upon her. Before the child was born, she said, "He shall be the son of love. He shall be called Aodh. He shall be called Aodh-of-the-Songs." And so it was.

Sweet were his songs. He loved, and he sang, and he died.

And when Torcall that was his friend knew this sorrow, he rose and made his vow, and went out for evermore from the place where he was.

Since the hour of the Field of Spears he had been blind. Torcall

Dall he was upon men's lips thereafter. His harp had a moonshine wind upon it from that day, it was said: a beautiful strange harping when he went down through the glen, or out upon the sandy machar by the shore, and played what the wind sang, and the grass whispered, and the tree murmured, and the sea muttered or cried hollowly in the dark.

Because there was no sight to his, eyes, men said he saw and he heard. What was it he heard and saw that they saw not and heard not? It was in the voice that sighed in the strings of his harp, so the saying was.

When he rose and went away from his place, the Maormor asked him if he went north, as the blood sang; or south, as the heart cried; or west, as the dead go; or east, as the light comes.

"I go east," answered Torcall Dall.

"And why so, Blind Harper?"

"For there is darkness always upon me, and I go where the light comes."

On that night of the nights, a fair wind blowing out of the west, Torcall the Harper set forth in a galley. It splashed in the moonshine as it was rowed swiftly by nine men.

"Sing us a song, O Torcall Dall!" they cried.

"Sing us a song, Torcall of Lochlin," said the man who steered. He and all his company were of the Gael: the Harper only was of the Northmen.

"What shall I sing?" he asked. "Shall it be of war that you love, or of women that twine you like silk o' the kine; or shall it be of death that is your meed; or of your dread, the Spears of the North?"

A low sullen growl went from beard to beard.

"We are under *ceangal,* Blind Harper," said the steersman, with downcast eyes because of his flaming wrath; "we are under bond to take you safe to the mainland, but we have sworn no vow to sit still under the lash of your tongue. 'Twas a wind-fleet arrow that sliced the sight out of your eyes: have a care lest a sudden sword-wind sweep the breath out of your body."

Torcall laughed a low, quiet laugh.

"Is it death I am fearing now—I who have washed my hands in blood, and had love, and known all that is given to man? But I will sing you a song, I will."

And with that he took his harp, and struck the strings.

A lonely stream there is, afar in a lone dim land:
It hath white dust for shore it has, white bones bestrew the strand:
The only thing that liveth there is a naked leaping sword;
But I, who a seer am, have seen the whirling hand
    Of the Washer of the Ford.

A shadowy shape of cloud and mist, of gloom and night, she stands,
    The Washer of the Ford:
She laughs, at times, and strews the dust through the hollow of her hands.

She counts the sins of all men there, and slays the red-stained horde—
The ghosts of all the sins of men must know the whirling sword
    Of the Washer of the Ford.

She stoops and laughs when in the dust she sees a writhing limb:
"Go back into the ford," she says, "and hither and thither swim;
Then I shall wash you white as snow, and shall take you by the hand,
And slay you here in the silence with this my whirling brand,
And trample you into the dust of this white windless sand"—
    This is the laughing word
    Of the Washer of the Ford
    Along that silent strand.

There was silence for a time after Torcall Dall sang that song. The oars took up the moonshine and flung it hither and thither like loose shining crystals. The foam at the prow curled and leaped.

Suddenly one of the rowers broke into a long, low chant—

 Yo, eily-a-ho, ayah-a-ho, eily-ayah-a-ho,
  Singeth the Sword
 Eily-a-ho, ayah-a-ho, eily-ayah-a-ho,
  Of the Washer of the Ford!

And at that all ceased from rowing. Standing erect, they lifted up their oars against the stars, and the wild voices of them flew out upon the night—

 Yo, eily-a-ho, ayah-a-ho, eily-ayah-a-ho,
  Singeth the Sword
 Eily-a-ho, ayah-a-ho, eily-ayah-a-ho,
  Of the Washer of the Ford!

Torcall Dall laughed. Then he drew his sword from his side and plunged it into the sea. When he drew the blade out of the water and whirled it on high, all the white shining drops of it swirled about his head like a sleety rain.

And at that the steersman let go the steering-oar and drew his sword, and clove a flowing wave. But with the might of his blow the sword spun him round, and the sword sliced away the ear of the man who had the sternmost oar. Then there was blood in the eyes of all there. The man staggered, and felt for his knife, and it was in the heart of the steersman.

Then because these two men were leaders, and had had a blood-feud, and because all there, save Torcall, were of one or the other side, swords and knives sang a song.

The rowers dropped their oars; and four men fought against three.

Torcall laughed, and lay back in his place. While out of the wandering wave the death of each man clambered into the hollow of the boat, and breathed its chill upon its man, Torcall the Blind took his harp. He sang this song, with the swirling spray against his face, and the smell of blood in his nostrils, and the feet of him dabbling in the red tide that rose there.

> Oh 'tis a good thing the red blood, by Odin his word!
> And a good thing it is to hear it bubbling deep.
> And when we hear the laughter of the Sword,
> Oh, the corbies croak, and the old wail, and the women weep!
> And busy will she be there where she stands,
> Washing the red out of the sins of all this slaying horde;
> And trampling the bones of them into white powdery sands,
>   And laughing low at the thirst of her thirsty sword—
>   The Washer of the Ford!

When he had sung that song there was only one man whose pulse still beat, and he was at the bow.

"A bitter black curse upon you, Torcall Dall!" he groaned out of the ooze of blood that was in his mouth.

"And who will you be?" said the blind Harper.

"I am Fergus, the son of Art, the son of Fergus of the Two Dûns."

"Well, it is a song for your death I will make, Fergus mac Art mhic Fheargus: and because you are the last."

With that Torcall struck a sob out of his harp, and he sang—

Oh, death of Fergus, that is lying in the boat here,
    Betwixt the man of the red hair and him of the black beard,
Rise now, and out of your cold white eyes take out the fear,
    And let Fergus mac Art mhic Fheargus see his weird!

Sure, now, it's a blind man I am, but I'm thinking I see
    The shadow of you crawling across the dead.
Soon you will twine your arm around his shaking knee,
    And be whispering your silence into his listless head.

And that is why, O Fergus—

But here the man hurled his sword into the sea and with a choking cry fell forward; and upon the White Sands he was, beneath the trampling feet of the Washer of the Ford.

II

It was a fair wind that blew beneath the stars that night. At dawn the mountains of Skye were like turrets of a great Dûn against the east.

But Torcall the blind Harper did not see that thing. Sleep, too, was upon him. He smiled in that sleep, for in his mind he saw the dead men, that were of the alien people, his foes, draw near the stream that was in a far place. The shaking of them, poor tremulous frostbit leaves they were, thin and sere, made the only breath there was in that desert.

At the ford—this is what he saw in his vision—they fell down like stricken deer with the hounds upon them.

"What is this stream?" they cried in the thin voice of rain across the moors.

"The River of Blood," said a voice.

"And who are you that are in the silence?"

"I am the Washer of the Ford."

And with that each red soul was seized and thrown into the water of the ford; and when white as a sheep-bone on the hill, was taken in one hand by the Washer of the Ford and flung into the air, where no wind was and where sound was dead, and was then severed this way and that, in four whirling blows of the sword from the four quarters of the world.

Then it was that the Washer of the Ford trampled upon what fell to the ground, till under the feet of her was only a white sand, white as powder, light as the dust of the yellow flowers that grow in the grass.

It was at that Torcall Dall smiled in his sleep. He did not hear the washing of the sea; no, nor any idle splashing of the unoared boat. Then he dreamed, and it was of the woman he had left, seven summer-sailings ago in Lochlin. He thought her hand was in his, and that her heart was against his.

"Ah, dear beautiful heart of woman," he said, "and what is the pain that has put a shadow upon you?"

It was a sweet voice that he heard coming out of sleep.

"Torcall, it is the weary love I have."

"Ah, heart o' me, dear! sure 'tis a bitter pain I have had too, and I away from you all these years."

"There's a man's pain, and there's a woman's pain."

"By the blood of Balder, Hildyr, I would have both upon me to take it off the dear heart that is here."

"Torcall!"

"Yes, white one."

"We are not alone, we two in the dark."

And when she had said that thing, Torcall felt two baby arms go round his neck, and two leaves of a wild-rose press cool and sweet against his lips.

"Ah! what is this?" he cried, with his heart beating, and the blood in his body singing a glad song.

A low voice crooned in his ear: a bitter-sweet song it was, passing-sweet, passing-bitter.

"Ah, white one, white one," he moaned; "ah, the wee fawn o' me! Baby o' foam, bonnie wee lass, put your sight upon me that I may see the blue eyes that are mine too and Hildyr's."

But the child only nestled closer. Like a fledgling in a great nest she was. If God heard her song, He was a glad God that day. The blood that was in her body called to the blood that was in his body. He could say no word. The tears were in his blind eyes.

Then Hildyr leaned into the dark, and took his harp, and played upon it. It was of the fonnsheen he had learned, far, far away, where the isles are.

She sang: but he could not hear what she sang.

Then the little lips, that were like a cool wave upon the dry sand of his life, whispered into a low song: and the wavering of it was like this in his brain—

> Where the winds gather
>   The souls of the dead,
> O Torcall, my father,
>   My soul is led!
>
> In Hildyr-mead
>   I was thrown, I was sown:
> Out of thy seed
>   I am sprung, I am blown!
>
> But where is the way
>   For Hildyr and me,
> By the hill-moss grey
>   Or the grey sea?
>
> For a river is here,
>   And a whirling Sword—
> And a Woman washing
>   By a Ford!

With that, Torcall Dall gave a wild cry, and sheathed an arm about the wee white one, and put out a hand to the bosom that loved him. But there was no white breast there, and no white babe: and what was against his lips was his own hand red with blood.

"O Hildyr!" he cried.

But only the splashing of the waves did he hear.

"O white one!" he cried.

But only the scream of a sea-mew, as it hovered over that boat filled with dead men, made answer.

III

All day the Blind Harper steered the galley of the dead. There was a faint wind moving out of the west. The boat went before it, slow, and with a low, sighing wash.

Torcall saw the red gaping wounds of the dead, and the glassy eyes of the nine men.

"It is better not to be blind and to see the dead," he muttered, "than to be blind and to see the dead."

The man who had been steersman leaned against him. He took him in his shuddering grip and thrust him into the sea.

But when, an hour later, he put his hand to the coolness of the water, he drew it back with a cry, for it was on the cold, stiff face of the dead man that it had fallen. The long hair had caught in a cleft in the leather where the withes had given.

For another hour Torcall sat with his chin in his right hand, and his unseeing eyes staring upon the dead. He heard no sound at all, save the lap of wave upon wave, and the *suss* of spray against spray, and a bubbling beneath the boat, and the low, steady swish of the body that trailed alongside the steering oar.

At the second hour before sundown he lifted his head. The sound he heard was the sound of waves beating upon rocks.

At the hour before sundown he moved the oar rapidly to and fro, and cut away the body that trailed behind the boat. The noise of the waves upon the rocks was now a loud song.

When the last sunfire burned upon his neck, and made the long hair upon his shoulders ashine, he smelt the green smell of grass. Then it was too that he heard the muffled fall of the sea, in a quiet haven, where shelves of sand were.

He followed that sound, and while he strained to hear any voice the boat grided upon the sand, and drifted to one side. Taking his harp, Torcall drove an oar into the sand, and leaped on to the shore. When he was there, he listened. There was silence. Far, far away he heard the falling of a mountain-torrent, and the thin, faint cry of an eagle, where the sun-flame dyed its eyrie as with streaming blood.

So he lifted his harp, and, harping low, with a strange, wild song on his lips, moved away from that place, and gave no more thought to the dead.

It was deep gloaming when he came to a wood. He felt the cold green breath of it.

"Come," said a voice, low and sweet.

"And who will *you* be?" asked Torcall the Harper, trembling because of the sudden voice in the stillness.

"I am a child, and here is my hand, and I will lead you, Torcall of Lochlin."

The blind man had fear upon him.

"Who are you that in a strange place are for knowing who I am?"

"Come."

"Ay, sure, it is coming I am, white one; but tell me who you are, and whence you came, and whither we go."

Then a voice that he knew sang:

> O where the winds gather
> The souls of the dead,
> O Torcall, my father,
> My soul is led!
>
> But a river is here,
> And a whirling Sword—
> And a Woman washing
> By a Ford!

Torcall Dall was as the last leaf on a tree at that.

"Were you on the boat?" he whispered hoarsely.

But it seemed to him that another voice answered: *"Yea, even so."*

"Tell me, for I have blindness: Is it peace?"

"It is peace."

"Are you man, or child, or of the Hidden People?"

"I am a shepherd."

"A shepherd? Then, sure, you will guide me through this wood? And what will be beyond this wood?"

"A river."

"And what river will that be?"

"Deep and terrible. It runs through the Valley of the Shadow."

"And is there no ford there?"

"Ay, there is a ford."

"And who will guide me across that ford?"

"She."

"Who?"

"The Washer of the Ford."

But hereat Torcall Dall gave a sore cry and snatched his hand away, and fled sidelong into an alley of the wood.

It was moonshine when he lay down, weary. The sound of flowing water filled his ears.

"Come," said a voice.

So he rose and went. When the cold breath of the water was upon his face, the guide that led him put a fruit into his hand.

"Eat, Torcall Dall!"

He ate. He was no more Torcall Dall. He felt his sight coming upon him again. Out of the blackness shadows came; out of the shadows, the great boughs of trees; from the boughs, dark branches and dark clusters of leaves; above the branches, white stars; below the branches, white flowers; and beyond these, the moonshine on the grass and the moon-fire on the flowing of a river dark and deep.

"Take your harp, O Harper, and sing the song of what you see."

Torcall heard the voice, but saw no one. No shadow moved. Then he walked out upon the moonlit grass; and at the ford he saw a woman stooping and washing shroud after shroud of woven moonbeams: washing them there in the flowing water, and singing low a song that he did not hear. He did not see her face. Bnt she was young, and with long black hair that fell like the shadow of night over a white rock.

So Torcall took his harp, and he sang:

> Glory to the great Gods, it is no Sword I am seeing;
> Nor do I see aught but the flowing of a river.
> And I see shadows on the flow that are ever fleeing,
> And I see a woman washing shrouds for ever and ever.

Then he ceased, for he heard the woman sing:
Glory to God on high, and to Mary, Mother of Jesus,
Hcrc am I washing away the sins of the shriven,
O Torcall of Lochlin, throw off the red sins that ye cherish
And I will be giving you the washen shroud that they wear in Heaven.

Filled with a great awe, Torcall bowed his head. Then once more he took his harp, and he sang:

O well it is I am seeing, Woman of the Shrouds,
That you have not for me any whirling of the Sword;
I have lost my gods, O woman, so what will the name be
Of thee and thy gods, O woman that art Washer of the Ford?

But the woman did not look up from the dark water, nor did she cease from washing the shrouds made of the woven moonbeams. The Harper heard this song above the sighing of the water:

It is Mary Magdalene my name is, and I loved Christ.
And Christ is the Son of God and of Mary the Mother of Heaven.
And this river is the river of death, and the shadows
Are the fleeing souls that are lost if they be not shriven.

Then Torcall drew nigher to the stream. A melancholy wind was upon it.

"Where are all the dead of the world?" he said.

But the woman answered not.

"And what is the end, you that are called Mary?"

Then the woman rose.

"Would you cross the Ford, O Torcall the Harper?"

He made no word upon that. But he listened. He heard a woman singing faint and low, far away in the dark. He drew more near.

"Would you cross the Ford, O Torcall?"

He made no word upon that; but once more he listened. He heard a little child crying in the night.

"Ah, lonely heart of the white one," he sighed, and his tears fell.

Mary Magdalene turned and looked upon him.

It was the face of Sorrow she had. She stooped and took up the tears.

"They are bells of joy," she said. And he heard a faint, sweet ringing in his ears.

A prayer came out of his heart. A blind prayer it was, but God gave it wings. It flew to Mary, who took and kissed it, and gave it song.

"It is the Song of Peace," she said. And Torcall had peace.

"What is best, O Torcall?" she asked,—rustling-sweet as rain among the trees her voice was. "What is best?" The sword, or peace?"

"Peace," he answered; and he was white now, and was old.

"Take your harp," Mary said, "and go in unto the Ford. But, lo, now I clothe you with a white shroud. And if you fear the drowning flood, follow the bells that were your tears; and if the dark affright you, follow the song of the prayer that came out of your heart."

So Torcall the Harper moved into the whelming flood, and he played a new strauge air like the laughing of a child.

Deep silence there was. The moonshine lay upon the obscure wood, and the darkling river flowed sighing through the soundless gloom.

The Washer of the Ford stooped once more. Low and sweet, as of yore and for ever, over the drowning souls she sang her immemorial song.

The Last Supper

"... and there shall be
Beautiful things made new ..."
(*Hyperion.*)

The last time that the Fisher of Men was seen in Strath-Nair was not of Alasdair Macleod but of the little child, Art Macarthur, him that was born of the woman Mary Gilchrist, that had known the sorrow of women.

He was a little child, indeed, when, because of his loneliness and having lost his way, he lay sobbing among the bracken by the streamside in the Shadowy Glen.

When he was a man, and had reached the gloaming of his years, he was loved of men and women, for his songs are many and sweet, and his heart was true, and he was a good man and had no evil against any one.

It is he who saw the Fisher of Men when he was but a little lad: and some say that it was on the eve of the day that Alasdair Og died, though of this I know nothing. And what he saw, and what he heard, was a moonbeam that fell into the dark sea of his mind, and sank therein, and filled it with light for all the days of his life. A moonlit mind was that of Art Macarthur: him that is known best as Ian Mòr, Ian mòr of the Hills, though why he took the name of Ian Cameron is known to none now but one person, and that need not be for the telling here. He had music always in his mind. I asked him once why he heard what so few heard, but he smiled and said only: "When the heart is full of love, cool dews of peace rise from it and fall upon the mind: and that is when the song of Joy is heard."

It must have been because of this shining of his soul that some who loved him thought of him as one illumined. His mind was a shell that held the haunting echo of the deep seas: and to know him was to catch a

180

breath of the infinite ocean of wonder and mystery and beauty of which he was the quiet oracle. He has peace now, where he lies under the heather upon a hillside far away: but the Fisher of Men will send him hitherward again, to put a light upon the wave and a gleam upon the brown earth.

I will try to tell this *sgeul* much as Ian Mòr that was the little child of Art Macarthur, told it to me.

Often and often it is to me all as a dream that comes unawares. Often and often have I striven to see into the green glens of the mind whence it comes, and whither, in a flash, in a rainbow gleam, it vanishes. When I seek to draw close to it, to know whether it is a winged glory out of the soul, or was indeed a thing that happened to me in my tender years, lo— it is a dawn drowned in day, a star lost in the sun, the falling of dew.

But I will not be forgetting: no, never: no, not till the silence of the grass is over my eyes: I will not be forgetting that gleaming.

Bitter tears are those that children have. All that we say with vain words is said by them in this welling spray of pain. I had the sorrow that day. Strange hostilities lurked in the familiar bracken. The soughing of the wind among the trees, the wash of the brown water by my side, that had been companionable, were voices of awe. The quiet light upon the grass flamed.

The fierce people that lurked in shadow had eyes for my helplessness. When the dark came I thought I should be dead, devoured of I knew not what wild creature. Would mother never come, never come with saving arms, with eyes like soft candles of home?

Then my sobs grew still, for I heard a step. With dread upon me, poor wee lad that I was, I looked to see who came out of the wilderness. It was a man, tall and thin and worn, with long hair hanging adown his face. Pale he was as a moonlit cot on the dark moor, and his voice was low and sweet. When I saw his eyes I had no fear upon me at all. I saw the mother-look in the grey shadow of them.

"And is that you, Art lennavan-mo?" he said, as he stooped and lifted me.

I had no fear. The wet was out of my eyes.

"What is it you will be listening to now, my little lad?" he whispered, as he saw me lean, intent, to catch I know not what.

"Sure," I said, "I am not for knowing: but I thought I heard a music away down there in the wood."

I heard it, for sure. It was a wondrous sweet air, as of one playing the *feadan* in a dream. Callum Dall, the piper, could give no rarer music than that was; and Callum was a seventh son, and was born in the moonshine.

"Will you come with me this night of the nights, little Art?" the man asked me, with his lips touching my brow and giving me rest.

"That I will indeed and indeed," I said. And then I fell asleep.

When I awoke we were in the huntsman's booth, that is at the far end of the Shadowy Glen.

There was a long rough-hewn table in it, and I stared when I saw bowls and a great jug of milk and a plate heaped with oat-cakes, and beside it a brown loaf of rye-bread.

"Little Art," said he who carried me, "are you for knowing now who I am?"

"You are a prince, I'm thinking," was the shy word that came to my mouth.

"Sure, lennav-aghrày, it is so. It is called the Prince of Peace I am."

"And who is to be eating all this?" I asked.

"This is the last supper," the prince said, so low that I could scarce hear; and it seemed to me that he whispered, "For I die daily, and ever ere I die the Twelve break bread with me."

It was then I saw that there were six bowls of porridge on the one side and six on the other.

"What is your name, O Prince?"

"Iosa."

"And will you have no other name than that?"

"I am called Iosa mac Dhe."

"And is it living in this house you are?"

"Ay. But Art, my little lad, I will kiss your eyes, and you shall see who sup with me."

And with that the prince that was called Iosa kissed me on the eyes, and I saw.

"You will never be quite blind again," he whispered, and that is why all the long years of my years I have been glad in my soul.

What I saw was a thing strange and wonderful. Twelve men sat at that table, and all had eyes of love upon Iosa. But they were not like any men I had ever seen. Tall and fair and terrible they were, like morning in a desert place; all save one, who was dark, and had a shadow upon him and in his wild eyes.

It seemed to me that each was clad in radiant mist. The eyes of them were as stars through that mist.

And each, before he broke bread, or put spoon to the porridge that was in the bowl before him, laid down upon the table three shuttles.

Long I looked upon the company, but Iosa held me in his arms, and I had no fear.

"Who are these men?" he asked me.

"The Sons of God," I said, I not knowing what I said, for it was but a child I was.

He smiled at that. "Behold," he spoke to the twelve men who sat at the table, "behold the little one is wiser than the wisest of ye." At that all smiled with the gladness and the joy, save one; him that was in the shadow. He looked at me, and I remembered two black lonely tarns upon the hillside, black with the terror because of the kelpie and the drowner.

"Who are these men?" I whispered, with the tremor on me that was come of the awe I had.

"They are the Twelve Weavers, Art, my little child."

"And what is their weaving?"

"They weave for my Father, whose web I am."

At that I looked upon the prince, but I could see no web.

"Are you not Iosa the Prince?"

"I am the Web of Life, Art lennavan-mo."

"And what are the three shuttles that are beside each Weaver?"

I know now that when I turned my child's-eyes upon these shuttles I saw that they were alive and wonderful, and never the same to the seeing.

"They are called *Beauty* and *Wonder* and *Mystery*."

And with that Iosa mac Dhe sat down and talked with the Twelve. All were passing fair, save him who looked sidelong out of dark eyes. I thought each as I looked at him, more beautiful than any of his fellows: but most I loved to look at the twain who sat on either side of Iosa.

"He will be a Dreamer among men," said the prince; "so tell him who ye are."

Then he who was on the right turned his eyes upon me. I leaned to him, laughing low with the glad pleasure I had because of his eyes and shining hair, and the flame as of the blue sky that was his robe.

"I am the Weaver of Joy," he said. And with that he took his three shuttles that were called Beauty and Wonder and Mystery, and he wove an immortal shape, and it went forth of the room and out into the green world, singing a rapturous sweet song.

Then he that was upon the left of Iosa the Life looked at me, and my heart leaped. He, too, had shining hair, but I could not tell the colour of his eyes for the glory that was in them. "I am the Weaver of Love," he said, "and I sit next the heart of Iosa." And with that he took his three shuttles that were called Beauty and Wonder and Mystery and he wove an immortal shape, and it went forth of the room and into the green world singing a rapturous sweet song.

Even then, child as I was, I wished to look on no other. None could be so passing fair, I thought, as the Weaver of Joy and the Weaver of Love.

But a wondrous sweet voice sang in my ears, and a cool, soft hand laid itself upon my head, and the beautiful lordly one who had spoken said, "I am the Weaver of Death," and the lovely whispering one who had lulled me with rest said, "I am the Weaver of Sleep." And each wove with the shuttles of Beauty and Wonder and Mystery, and I knew not which was the more fair, and Death seemed to me as Love, and in the eyes of Dream I saw Joy.

My gaze was still upon the fair wonderful shapes that went forth from these twain—from the Weaver of Sleep, an immortal shape of star-eyed Silence, and from the Weaver of Death a lovely Dusk with a heart of hidden flame—when I heard the voice of two others of the Twelve. They were like the laughter of the wind in the corn, and like the golden fire upon that corn. And the one said, "I am the Weaver of Passion," and when he spoke I thought that he was both Love and Joy, and Death and Life, and I put out my hands. "It is Strength I give," he said, and he took and kissed me. Then, while Iosa took me again upon his knee, I saw the Weaver of Passion turn to the white glory beside him, him that Iosa whispered to me was the secret of the world, and that was called "The Weaver of Youth," I know not whence nor how it came, but there was a singing of skiey birds when these twain took the shuttles of Beauty and Wonder and Mystery, and wove each an immortal shape, and bade it go forth out of the room into the green world, to sing there for ever and ever in the ears of man a rapturous sweet song.

"O Iosa," I cried, "are these all thy brethren? for each is fair as thee, and all have lit their eyes at the white fire I see now in thy heart."

But, before he spake, the room was filled with music. I trembled with the joy, and in my ears it has lingered ever, nor shall ever go. Then I saw that it was the breathing of the seventh and eighth, of the ninth and the tenth of those star-eyed ministers of Iosa whom he called the Twelve: and the names of them were the Weaver of Laughter, the Weaver of Tears, the Weaver of Prayer, and the Weaver of Peace. Each rose and kissed me there. "We shall be with you to the end, little Art," they said and I took hold of the hand of one, and cried, "O beautiful one, be likewise with the woman my mother," and there came back to me the whisper of the Weaver of Tears: "I will, unto the end."

Then, wonderingly, I watched him likewise take the shuttles that were ever the same and yet never the same, and weave an immortal shape. And when this Soul of Tears went forth of the room, I thought it was my mother's voice singing that rapturous sweet song, and I cried out to it.

The fair immortal turned and waved to me. "I shall never be far from thee, little Art," it sighed, like summer rain falling on leaves: "but I go now to my home in the heart of women."

There were now but two out of the Twelve. Oh the gladness and the joy when I looked at him who had his eyes fixed on the face of Iosa that was the Life! He lifted the three shuttles of Beauty and Wonder and Mystery, and he wove a Mist of Rainbows in that room; and in the glory I saw that even the dark twelfth one lifted up his eyes and smiled.

"O what will the name of you be?" I cried, straining my arms to the beautiful lordly one. But he did not hear, for he wrought Rainbow after Rainbow out of the mist of glory that he made, and sent each out into the green world, to be for ever before the eyes of men.

"He is the Weaver of Hope," whispered Iosa mac Dhe; "and he is the soul of each that is here."

Then I turned to the twelfth, and said: "Who art thou, O lordly one with the shadow in the eyes."

But he answered not, and there was silence in the room. And all there, from the Weaver of Joy to the Weaver of Peace, looked down, and said nought. Only the Weaver of Hope wrought a rainbow, and it drifted into the heart of the lonely Weaver that was twelfth.

"And who will this man be, O Iosa mac Dhe?" I whispered.

"Answer the little child," said Iosa, and his voice was sad.

Then the Weaver answered:

"I am the Weaver of Glory—," he began, but Iosa looked at him, and he said no more.

"Art, little lad," said the Prince of Peace, "he is the one who betrayeth me for ever. He is Judas, the Weaver of Fear."

And at that the sorrowful shadowed-eyed man that was the twelfth took up the three shuttles that were before him.

"And what are these, O Judas?" I cried eagerly, for I saw that they were black.

When he answered not, one of the Twelve leaned forward and looked at him. It was the Weaver of Death who did this thing.

"The three shuttles of Judas the Fear-Weaver, O little Art," said the Weaver of Death, "are called Mystery, and Despair, and the Grave."

And with that Judas rose and left the room. But the shape that he had woven went forth with him as his shadow: and each fared out into the dim world, and the Shadow entered into the minds and into the hearts of men, and betrayed Iosa that was the Prince of Peace.

Thereupon, Iosa rose and took me by the hand, and led me out of that room. When, once, I looked back I saw none of the Twelve save only the Weaver of Hope, and he sat singing a wild sweet song that he had learned of the Weaver of Joy, sat singing amid a mist of rainbows and weaving a radiant glory that was dazzling as the sun.

And at that I woke, and was against my mother's heart, and she with the tears upon me, and her lips moving in a prayer.

Cathal of the Woods

(THE ANNIR CHOILLE.)

I

When Cathal mac Art, that was called Cathal Gille-Mhoire, Cathal the Servant of Mary, walked by the sea, one night of the nights in a green May, there was trouble in his heart.

It was not long since he had left Iona. The good St Colum, in sending the youth to the Isle of Â-rinn, as it was then called, gave him a writing for St Molios, the holy man who lived in the sea-cave of the small Isle of the Peak, that is in the eastward hollow at the south end of Arran. A sorrow it was to him to leave the fair isle in the west. He had known glad years there—since, in one of the remote isles of the north, he had seen his father slain by a man of Lochlin, and his mother carried away in a galley oared by fierce yellow-haired men, No kith or kin had he but the old priest, that was the brother of his father, Cathal Gille-Chriosd, Cathal the Servant of Christ.

On Iona he had learned the way of Christ. He had a white robe; and could, with a shaven stick and a thin tuft of seal-fur, or with the feather-quill of a wild swan or a solander, write the holy words upon strained lambskin or parchment, and fill the big letters, that were here and there, with earth-brown and sky-blue and shining green, with scarlet of blood and gold of sun-warm sands. He could sing the long holy hymns, too, that Colum loved to hear; and it was his voice that had the sweetest clear-call of any on the island. He was in the nineteenth year of his years when a Frankish prince, who had come to Iona for the blessing

---

The English equivalent of Annir-Choille would be the Wood-nymph. The word *Annir* is an ancient compound Gaelic word for a maiden.

of the Saint, wanted him to go back with him to the Southlands. He promised many things because of that voice. Cathal dreamed often, in the hot drowsy afternoons of the month that followed, of the long white sword that would slay so well; and of the white money that might be his to buy fair apparel with, and a great black stallion accoutred with trappings wrought with gold, and a bed of down; and of white hands, and white breasts, and the white song of youth.

He had not gone with the Frankish prince, nor wished to go. But he dreamed often. It was on a day of dream that he lay on his back in the hot grass upon a dune, near where the cells of the monks were. The sun-glow bathed the isle in a golden haze. The strait was a shimmering dazzle, and the blue wavelets that made curves in the soft white sand seemed to spill gold flakes and change them straightway into little jets of foam or bubbles of rainbow-spray. Cathal had made a song for his delight. His pain was less when he had made it. Now, lying there, and dreaming at times of the words of the Frankish prince, and remembering at times the stranger words of the old pagan helot, Neis, who had come with him out of the north, he felt fire burn in his veins and he sang:

O where in the north, or where in the south, or where in the east or
    west
Is she who hath the flower-white hands and the swandown breast?
O, if she be west, or east she be, or in the north or south,
A sword will leap, a horse will prance, ere I win to Honey-Mouth.

She has great eyes, like the doe on the hill, and warm and sweet she is,
O, come to me, Honey-Mouth, bend to me, Honey-Mouth, give me
    thy kiss!
White Hands her name is, where she reigns amid the princes fair:

White hands she moves like swimming swans athrough her dusk-wave
    hair:
White hands she puts about my heart, white hands fan up my breath:
White hands take out the heart of me, and grant me life or death!

White hands make better songs than hymns, white hands are young
    and sweet:
O, a sword for me, O Honey-Mouth, and a war-horse fleet!

O wild sweet eyes! O glad wild eyes! O mouth, how sweet it is!
O, come to me, Honey-Mouth! bend to me, Honey-Mouth! give me
    thy kiss!

When he had ceased he saw a shadow fall upon the white sand beyond the dune. He looked up, and beheld Colum the Saint.

"Who taught you that song?" said the white holy one, in a voice
hard and stern.

"No one, O Colum."

"Then the Evil One is indeed here. Cathal, I promised that you
would be having a holy name soon, but that name I will not be giving
you now. You must come to me in sackcloth and with dust upon your
head, with pain upon you, and with deep grief in your heart. Then only
shall I bless you before the brothers and call you Cathal Gille-Mhoire,
Cathal the Servant of Mary."

A bitter, sad waiting it was for him who had fire in his young blood
and was told to weave frost there, and to put silence upon the welling
song in his heart. But at the end of the week Cathal was a holy monk
again, and sang the hymns that Colum had taught him.

It was on the eve of the day when Colum blessed him before the
brethren, and called him Gille-Mhoire, that he walked alone, brooding
upon the evil of women and the curse they brought, and praying to
Mary to save him from the sins of which he scarce knew the meaning.
On his way back to his cell he passed old Neis, the helot, who said to
him mockingly:

"It is a good thing that sorrow, Cathal mac Art,—and yet, sure, it is
true that but for the hot love the slain man your father had for Foam
that was your mother, you would not be here to praise your God or
serve the woman whom the Arch-Druid yonder says is the Mother of
God."

Cathal bade the man eat silence, or it would go ill with him. But the
words rankled. That night in his cell he woke, with on his lips his own
sinful words:

White hands make better songs than hymns, white hands are young
    and sweet;
O, a sword for me, O Honey-Mouth, and a war-horse fleet!

On the morrow he went to Colum and told him that the Evil One would not give him peace. That night the Saint bade him make ready to go east to the Isle of Arran—the sole isle, then, where the Pictish folk would let the white robes of the Culdees go scatheless. To the holy Molios he was to go, him that dwelled in the sea-cave of the Isle of the Peak, that men already called the Holy Isle because of the preaching and the miracles of Molios.

"He is a wise man," said Colum to himself, "and he was a pagan Cruithne once, and a prince at that, and he knows the sweetness of sin, and will keep Cathal away from the snares that are set. With fasting, and much peril by day and weariness by night, the blood of the youth will forget the songs the Evil One has put into his mind and it will sing holy hymns. Great will be the glory. Cathal Gille-Mhoire will be a holy man while he has yet his youth upon him; and he will be a martyr to the flesh by day and by night and by night and by day, till the heathen put him to death because of the faith that is his."

Thus it was that Cathal was blessed by Colum, and sent east among the wild Picts.

It was with joy that he served Molios. For four months he gave him all he had to give. The old saint passed word to Colum that Cathal was a saint and was assured of the crown of martyrdom, and lovingly he urged that the youth should be sent to the Isle of Mist in the north, the great isle that was ruled by Scathach the Queen. There, at the last Summer-sailing, the pagans had flayed a monk alive. A fair happy end: and Cathal was now worthy—and withal might triumph, and might even convert the heathen queen. "She is wondrous fair to see," he added, "and Cathal is a comely youth."

But Colum had answered that the young monk was to bide where he was, and to seek to win souls in the pagan Isle of Arran, where the Cross was still feared.

But with the coming of May and golden weather, the blood of Cathal grew warm. At times, even, he dreamed of the Frankish prince and the evil sweet words he had said.

Then a day of the days came. Molios and Cathal went to a hill-dûn where the Pict chieftain lived, and converted him and all the people in the dûn and all in the rath that was beyond the dûn. That eve the daughter of the warrior came upon Cathal walking in a solitary place, among the green pines beyond the rath. She was most sweet to look upon: tall and fair, with eyes like the sea in a cloudless noon, and hair like westward wheat turned back upon itself.

"What is the name men call you by, young Druid?" she said. "I am Ardanna, the daughter of Ecta."

"Your beauty is sweet to look upon, Ardanna. I am Cathal the son of Art the son of Aodh of the race of Alpein, from the isles of the sea. But I am not a Druid. I am a priest of Christ, a servant of Mary the Mother of God, and a son of God."

Ardanna looked at him. A flush came into his face. In his eyes the same light flamed that was there when the Frankish prince told him of the delights of the world.

"Is it true, O Cathal, that the Druids—that the priests of Christ and the two other gods, the white-robed men whom we call Culdees, and of whom you are one, is it true that they will have nought to do with women?"

Cathal looked upon the woman no more, but on the ground at his feet.

"It is true, Ardanna."

The girl laughed. It was a low, sweet, mocking laugh, but it went along Cathal's blood like cloud-fire along the sky. It was to him as though somewhat he had not seen was revealed.

"And is it a true thing that you holy men look at women askance, and as snares of peril and evil?"

"It is true, Ardanna; but not so upon those who are sisters of Christ, and whose eyes are upon heavenly things."

"But what of those who are not sisters of your god, and are only women, fair to look upon, fair to woo, fair to love?"

Cathal again flushed. His eyes were still upon the ground. He made no answer.

Ardanna laughed low.

"Cathal!"

"Yes, fair daughter of Ecta?"

"Is it never longing for love you are?"

"There is but one love for us who have taken the vows of chastity."

"What is chastity?"

Cathal raised his eyes and glanced at Ardanna. Her dark-blue eyes looked at him pure and sweet, though a smile was upon her mouth. He sighed.

"It is the sanctity of the body, Ardanna."

"I do not understand," she said simply. "But tell me this, poor Cathal—"

"Why do you call me poor Cathal?"

"Because you have put your manhood from you—and you so young, and strong, and comely—and are not a warrior, and care neither for the sword, nor the chase, nor the harp, nor for women."

Cathal was troubled. He looked again and again at Ardanna. The sunset light was in her yellow hair, which was about her as a glory. He had seen the moon as wondrous pale as her beautiful face. Like lilies her white hands were. He had dreamed of that flamelight in the eyes.

"I care," he said.

She drew nearer, and leaned a little forward, and looked at him.

"You are good to look upon, Cathal—the comeliest youth I have ever seen."

The monk flushed. This was the devil-tongue of which Colum had warned him. But how sweet the words were: like a harp that low voice. Sure, sweeter is a waking dream than a dream in sleep.

"I care," he repeated dully.

"Look, Cathal."

Slowly he raised his eyes. As his gaze moved upward it rested on the white breast which was like sea-foam swelling out of brown sea-weed, for she had a tanned fawn-skin belted and gold-claspt over the white robe she wore, and that had disparted for the warm air to play upon her bosom.

It troubled him. He let his eyes fall again. The red was on his face.

"Cathal!"

"Yes, Ardanna."

"And you will never put your kiss upon a woman's lips? Never put your heart upon a woman's heart? Is it of cold sea water you are made—for even the running water in the streams is warmed by the sun? Tell me, Cathal, would you leave Molios the Culdee,—if—"

The monk of Christ suddenly flashed his eyes upon the woman.

"If what, Ardanna?" he asked abruptly: "if what, Ardanna that is so witching fair?"

"If *I* loved you, Cathal? If I, the daughter of Ecta the chief, loved you, and took you to be my man, and you took me to be your woman, would you be content so?"

He stared at her as one in a dream. Then suddenly all the foolish madness that had been put upon him by Colum fell away. What did these old men, Colum and Molios, know? It is only the young who know what life is. They were old, and their blood was gelid.

He put up his arms, as though in prayer. Then he smiled. Ardanna saw a light in his eyes that sprang into her heart and sang a song there that whirled in her ears and dazzled her eyes and made her feel as though she had fallen over a great height and were still falling.

Cathal was no longer pale. A red flame burned in either cheek. The sunset-light behind him filled his hair with fire. His eyes were beacons.

"Cathal, Cathal!"

"Come, Ardanna!"

That was all. What need to say more. She was in his arms, and her heart throbbing against his that leapt in his body like a wolf fallen in a snare.

He stooped and kissed her. She lifted her eyes, and his brain swung. She kissed him, and he kissed her till she gave a low cry and gently thrust him back. He laughed.

"Why do you laugh, Cathal?"

"I? It is I who laugh now. The old men put a spell upon me. I am no more Cathal Gille-Mhoire, but Cathal mac Art. Nay, I am Cathal Gille-Ardanna."

With that he plucked the branch of a rowan that grew near. He stripped it of its leaves, and threw them from him north, south, east, and west.

"Why do you that, Cathal-aluinn?" Ardanna asked, looking at him with eyes of love, and she like a summer morning there, because of the sunshine in her hair, and the wild roses on her face, and the hill-tarn blue of her eyes.

"These are all the hymns that Colum taught me. I give them back. I am knowing them no more. They are idle, foolish songs."

Then the monk took the branch and broke it, and threw the pieces upon the ground and trampled upon them.

"Why do you that, Cathal-aluinn?" asked Ardanna, wondering at him with her home-call eyes.

"That is the branch of all the wisdom Colum taught me. Old Neis, the helot, was wise. It is a madness, all that. See, it is gone; it is beneath my feet. I am a man now."

"But O Cathal, Cathal! this very day of the days, Ecta, my father, has become a man of the Christ-faith, him and his; and he would do what Molios asked now. And Molios would ask your death."

"Death is a dream."

With that Cathal leaned forward and kissed Ardanna upon the lips twice. "A kiss for life that," he said; "and that a kiss for death."

Ardanna laughed a low laugh. "The monk can kiss," she whispered; "can the monk love?"

He put his arm about her, and they went into the dim dark greenness.

The moon rose slowly, a globe of pale golden fire which spilled unceasingly a yellow flame upon the suspended billows of the forest. Star after star emerged. Deep silence was in the woods, save for the strange, passionate churring of a night-jar, where he leaned low from a pine branch and called to his mate, whose heart throbbed a flight-away amid the dewy shadows.

The wind was still. The white rays of the stars wandered over the moveless, over the shadowless and breathless green lawns of the tree-tops.

"What is that sound?" said Ardanna, a dim shape in the darkness, where she lay in the arms of Cathal.

"I know not," said the youth; for the fevered blood in his veins sang a song against his ears.

"Listen!"

Cathal listened. He heard nothing. His eyes dreamed again into the silence.

"What is that sound?" she whispered against his heart once again. "It is not from the sea, nor is it of the woods."

"It is the moan of Heaven," answered Cathal wearily; *"an acain Pharais."*

II

They found them there in the twilight of the dawn. For long Ecta looked at them and pondered. Then he glanced at Molios. There were tears in the heart of the holy man, but in his eyes a deep anger.

"Bind him," said Ecta.

Cathal woke with the thongs. His gaze fell upon Molios. He made no sign, and spake never a word; but he smiled.

"What now, O Molios?" asked Ecta.

"Take the woman away. Do with her as you will—spare or slay. It matters not. She is but a woman, and she hath wrought evil upon this man. To slay were well."

"She is my daughter."

"Spare, then, if you will; but take her away. Give her to a man. She shall never see this renegade again."

With that, two men led Ardanna away. She gave a glance at Cathal, who smiled. No tears were in her eyes; but a proud fire was there, and she brooked no man's hand upon her, and walked free.

When she was gone, Molios spake,

"Cathal, that was called Cathal Gille-Mhoire, why have you done this thing?"

"Because I was weary of vain imaginings, and I am young; and Ardanna is fair, and we loved."

"Such love is death."

"So be it, Molios. Such death is sweet as love."

"No ordinary death shalt thou have, blasphemer. Yet even now I would be merciful if I could. Dost thou call upon God?"

"I call upon the gods of my fathers."

"Fool, they shall not save you."

"Nevertheless, I call. I have nought to do with thy three gods, O Christian."

"Hast thou no fear of hell?"

"I am a warrior, and the son of my father, and of a race of heroes. Why should I fear?"

Molios brooded a while.

"Take him," he said at last, "and bury him alive where his gods perchance will hear his cries and come and save him! Find me a hollow tree."

"There is a great oak near here," said Ecta, wondering, "a great hollow oak whose belly would hold five men, each standing upon the other."

With that he led them to an ancient tree.

"Dost thou repent, Cathal?" Molios asked.

"Ay," the young man answered grimly; "I repent. I repent that I wasted the good days serving you and your three false gods."

"Blaspheme no more. Thou knowest that these three are one God."

Cathal laughed mockingly.

"Hearken to him, Ecta," he cried; "this old Druid would have you believe that two men and a woman make one person! Believe that if you will! As for me, I laugh."

But with that, at a sign from Molios, they lifted and slung him amid the branches of the oak, and let him slide feet foremost into the deep hollow heart of the tree.

When the law was done, Molios bade all near kneel in a circle round the oak. Then he prayed for the soul of the doomed man. As he ended this prayer, a laugh flew up among the high wind-swayed leaves. It was as though an invisible bird were there, mocking like a jay.

One by one, with bowed heads, Molios and Ecta and those with him withdrew, all save two young men who were bidden to stay. Upon these was bond laid, that they would not stir from that place for three days. They were to let none draw nigh: and no food was to be given to the victim: and if he cried to them, they were to take no heed,—nay, not though he called upon God or the Mother of God or upon the White Christ.

All that day there was no sound from the hollow tree. At the setting of the sun a blackbird lit upon a small branch that drooped over the aperture, and sang a brave lilt. Then the dark came, and the moon rose, and the stars glimmered through the dew.

At midnight the moon was overhead. A flood of pale gold rays lit up the branches of the oak, and turned the leaves into a lustrous bronze. The watchers heard a voice singing in the silence of the night—a voice muffled and obscure, as from one in a pit, or as that of a shepherd straying in a narrow corrie. Words they caught, though not all; and this was what they heard:*

> O yellow lamp of Ioua that is having a cold pale flame there,
> Put thy honey-sheen upon me who am close-caverned with Death:
> Sure it is nought I see now who have seen too much and too little:
> O moon, thy breast is softer and whiter than hers who burneth the day.
>
> Put thy white light on the grave where the dead man my father is,
>   And waken him, waken him, wake!
> And put thy soft shining on the breast of the woman my mother,
> So that she stir in her sleep and say to the Viking beside her,
> "Take up thy sword, and let it lap blood, for it thirsts with long thirst."
>
> And O Ioua, be as the sea-calm upon the hot heart of Ardanna, the girl:
> Tell her that Cathal loves her, and that memory is sweeter than life.
> I list her heart beating here in the dark and the silence,
> And it is not lonely I am, because of that, and remembrance.
>
> O yellow flame of Ioua, be a spilling of blood out of the heart of Ecta,
> So that he fall dead, inglorious, slain from within, as a grey-beard;
> And light a fire in the brain of Molios, so that he shall go moonstruck,
> And men will jeer at him, and he will die at the last, idly laughing.
>
> For lo, I worship thee, Ioua; and if you can give my message to Neis,—
> Neis the helot out of Aoidû, who is in Iona, bondman to Colum,—
> Tell him I hail you as Bandia, as god-queen and mighty,
> And that he had the wisdom and I was a fool with trickling ears of moss.
>
> But grant me this, O goddess, a bitter moon-drinking for Colum!
> May he have the moonsong in his brain, and in his heart the moonfire:
> Flame burn him in heart of flame, and may he wane as wax at the furnace,
> And his soul drown in tears, and his body be a nothingness upon the
>   sands!

The watchers looked at each other, but said no word. On the pale face of each was fear and awe. What if this new god-teaching were false, and if Cathal was right, and the old gods were the lords of life and death? The moonlight fell upon them, and they saw doubt in the eyes of

---

* *Ioua* was one of the early Celtic names of the moon. The allusion (in the fourth line) to the sun, in the feminine, is in accordance with ancient usage.

each other. Neither looked at the white fire. Out of the radiance, cold eyes might stare upon them: when at that, sure they would leap to the woods, laughing, wild, and be as the beasts of the forest.

While it was still dark, an hour before the dawn, one of the twain awoke from a brief slumber. His gaze wandered from vague tree to tree. Thrice he thought he saw dim shapes glide from bole to bole or from thicket to thicket. Suddenly he discerned a tall figure, silent as a shadow, standing at the verge of the glade.

His low cry aroused his companion.

"What is it, Mûrta?" the young man asked in a whisper.

"A woman."

When they looked again she was gone.

"It was one of the Hidden People," said Mûrta, with restless eyes roaming from dusk to dusk.

"How are you for knowing that, Mûrta?"

"She was all in green, just like a green shadow she was, and I saw the green fire in her eyes."

"Have you not thought of one that it might be?"

"Who?"

"Ardanna."

With that the young man rose and ran swiftly to the place where he had seen the figure. But he could see no one. Looking at the ground he was troubled: for in the moonshine-dew he descried the imprint of small feet.

Thereafter they saw or heard nought, save the sights and sounds of the woodland.

At sunrise the two youths rose. Mûrta lifted up his arms, then sank upon his knees with bowed head.

"Why do you do that forbidden thing?" said Diarmid, that was his companion. "Have you forgotten Cathal the monk that is up there alone with death? If Molios the holy one saw you worshipping the Light he would do unto you as he had done unto Cathal."

But before Mûrta answered they heard the voice of Cathal once more—hoarse and dry it was, but scarce weaker than when it thrilled them at the rising of the moon.

This was what he chanted in his muffled voice out of his grave there in the hollow oak:

O hot yellow fire that streams out of the sky, sword-white and golden,
Be a flame upon the monks who are praying in their cells in Ioua!
Be a fire in the veins of Colum, and the hell that he preacheth be his,
And be a torch to the men of Lochlin, that they discover the isle and
   destroy it!

For I see this thing, that the old gods are the gods that die not:
All else is a seeming, a dream, a madness, a tide ever ebbing.
Glory to thee, O Grian, lord of life, first of the gods Allfather,
Swords and spears are thy beams, thy breath a fire that consumeth.

And upon this isle of Â-rinn send sorrow and death and disaster,
Upon one and all save Ardanna, who gave me her bosom,
Upon one and all send death, the curse of a death slow and swordless,
From Molios of the Cave to Mûrta and Diarmid my doomsmen!

At that Mûrta moved close to the oak.

"Hail, O Cathal!" he cried. There was silence.

"Art thou a living man still, or is it the death of thee that is singing there in the hollow oak?"

"My limbs perish, but I die not yet," answered the muffled voice that had greeted the sun.

"I am Mûrta mac Mûrta mac Neisa, and my heart is sore for thee, Cathal!"

There was no word to this. A thrush upon a branch overhead lifted its wings, sang a wild sweet note, and swooped arrowly through the greengloom of the leaves.

"Cathal, that wert a monk, which is the true thing? Is it Christ, or the gods of our fathers?"

Silence. Three oaks away a woodpecker thrust its beak into the soft bark, tap-tapping, tap-tapping.

"Cathal, is it death you are having, there in the dark and the silence?"

Mûrta strained his ears, but he could hear no sound. Over the woodlands a voice floated, drowsy-warm and breast-white—the voice of a cuckoo calling a love-note from cool green shadow to shadow across a league of windless blaze.

Then Mûrta that was a singer, went to where the bulrushes grew by a little tarn that was in the moss an arrow-flight away. He plucked a last-year reed, straight and brown, and with his knife cut seven holes in it. With a thinner reed he scooped the hollow clean.

Thereupon he returned to the oak. Diarmid, who had begun to eat of the food that had been left with them, sat still, with his eyes upon him.

Mûrta put his hollow reed to his lips, and he played. It was a for-lorn, sweet air that he had heard from a shepherding woman upon the hills. Then he played a burying-song of the islanders, wherein the wash of the sea and the rippling of the waves upon the shore was heard. Then he played the song of love, and the beating of hearts was heard, and sighs, and a voice like a distant bird-song rose and fell.

When he ceased, a voice came out of the hollow oak—

"Play me a death-song, Mûrta mac Mûrta mac Neisa."

Mûrta smiled, and he played again the song of love.

After that there was silence for a brief while. Then Mûrta played upon his reed for the time it takes a heron to mount her seventh spiral. Then he ceased, and threw away the reed, and stood erect, stating into the greenness. In his eyes was a strange shine. He sang:

Out of the wild hills I am hearing a voice, O Cathal!
And I am thinking it is the voice of a bleeding sword.
Whose is that sword? I know it well: it is the sword of the Slayer—
Him that is called Death, and the song that it sings I know:—
O where is Cathal mac Art, that is the cup for the thirst of my lips?

Out of the cold greyness of the sea I am hearing, O Cathal,
I am hearing a wave-muffled voice, as of one who drowns in the
    depths:
Whose is that voice? I know it well: it is the voice of the Shadow—
Her that is called the Grave, and the song that she sings I know:—
O where is Cathal mac Art, he has warmth for the chill that I have!

Out of the hot greenness of the wood I am hearing, O Cathal,
I am hearing a rustling step, as of one stumbling blind.

Whose is that rustling step? I know it well: the rustling walk of the
    Blind One—
She that is called Silence, and the song that she sings I know:—
O where is Cathal mac Art, that has tears to water my stillness?

After that there was silence. Mûrta moved away. When he sat by
Diarmid and ate, there was no word spoken. Diarmid did not look at
him, for he had sung a song of death, and the shadow was upon him.
He kept his gaze upon the moss: if he raised his eyes might he not see
the Slayer, or the Shadow, or the Blind One?

Noon came. None drew nigh: not a face was seen shadowily afar off.
Sometimes the hoofs of the deer rustled among the bracken. The snarling of young foxes in an oak-root hollow was like a red pulse in the heat.
At times, in the sheer abyss of blue sky to the north, a hawk suspended:
in the white-blaze southerly a blotch like swirled foam appeared for a
moment at long intervals, as a gannet swung from invisible pinnacles of
air to the invisible sea.

The afternoon drowsed through the sunflood. The green leaves
grew golden, saturated with light. At sundown a flight of wild doves rose
out of the pines, wheeled against the shine of the west and flashed out of
sight, flames of purple and rose, of foam-white and pink.

The gloaming came, silvery. The dew glistened on the fronds of the
ferns, in the cups of the moss. From glade to glade the cuckoos called.
The stars emerged delicately, as the eyes of fawns shining through the
green gloom of the forest. Once more the moon snowed the easter
frondage of the pines and oaks.

No one came nigh. Not a sound had sighed from the oak since
Mûrta had sung at the goldening of the day. At sunset Mûrta had risen,
to lean, intent, against the vast bole. His keen ears caught the jar of a
beetle burrowing beneath the bark. There was no other sound.

At the fall of dark the watchers heard the confused far noise of a festival. It waned as a lost wind. Dim veils of cloud obscured the moon; a
low rainy darkness suspended over the earth.

Thus went the second day and the second night.

When, after the weary vigil of the hours, dawn came at last, Mûrta
rose and struck the oak with a stone.

"Cathal!" he cried, "Cathal!"

There was no sound: not a stir, not a sigh.

"Cathal! Cathal!"

Mûrta looked at Diarmid. Then, seeing his own thought in the eyes of his friend, he returned to his side.

"The Blind One has been here," said Diarmid in a low voice.

At noon there was thunder, and great heat. The noise of rustling wings filled the underwood.

Diarmid fell into a deep sleep. When the thunder had travelled into the hills, and a soft rain fell, Mûrta climbed into the branches of the oak. He stared down into the hollow, but could see nothing save a green dusk that became brown shadow, and brown shadow that grew into a blackness.

"Cathal!" he whispered.

Not a breath of sound ascended like smoke.

"Cathal! Cathal!"

The slow drip of the rain slipped and pattered among the leaves. The cry of a sea-bird flying inland came mournfully across the woods. A distant clang, as of a stricken anvil, iterated from the barren mountain beyond the forest.

"Cathal! Cathal!"

Mûrta broke a straight branch, stripped it of the leaves, and, forcing the thicker end downward, let it fall sheer.

It struck with a dull, soft thud. He listened: there was not a sound.

"A quiet sleep to you, monk," he whispered, and slipped down through the boughs, and was beside Diarmid again.

At dusk the rain ceased. A cool green freshness came into the air. The stars were as wind-whirled fruit blown upward from the tree-tops. The moon, full-orbed and with a pulse of flame, led a tide of soft light across the brown shores of the world.

The vigils of the watchers were over. Mûrta and Diarmid rose. Without a word they moved across the glade: the faint rustle of their feet stirred the bracken: then they left the undergrowth, and were among the pines. Their shadows lapsed into the obscure wilderness. A doe, heavy with fawn, lay down among the dewy fern, and was at peace there.

III

At midnight, when the whole isle lay in the full flood of the moon, Cathal stirred.

For three days and three nights he had been in that dark hollow, erect, wedged as a spear imbedded in the jaws of a dead beast. He had died thrice: with hunger, with thirst, with weariness. Then when hunger was slain in its own pain, and thirst perished of its own agony, and weariness could no more endure, he stirred with the death-throe.

"I die," he moaned.

"Die not, O white one," came a floating whisper, he knew not whence, though it was to him as though the crushing walls of oak breathed the sound.

"I die," he gasped, and the froth bubbled upon his nether lip. With that his last strength went. No more could he hold his head above his shoulder, nor would his feet sustain him. Like a stricken deer he sank. So thin was he, so worn, that he slipt into a narrow crevice where dead leaves had been, and lay there, drowning in the dark.

Was that death, or a cold air about his feet, he wondered? With a dull pain he moved them: they came against no tree-wood—the coolness about them was of dewy moss. A wild hope flashed into his mind. With feeble hands he strove to sink farther into the crevice.

"I die," he gasped, "I die now at the last."

"Die not, O white one," breathed the same low sweet whisper, like leaves stirred by a nesting bird.

"Save, O save," muttered the monk, hoarse with the death-dew.

Then a blackness came down upon him from a great height, and he swung in that blank gulf as a feather swirled this way and that in the void of an abyss.

When the darkness lifted again, Cathal was on his back, and breathing slow, but without pain. A sweet wonderful coolness and ease, that he knew now! Where was he? he wondered. Was he in that Pàras that Colum and Molios had spoken of? Was he in Hy Bràsil, of which he had heard Aodh the Harper sing? Was he in Tir-na'n-Òg, where all men and women are young for evermore, and there is joy in the heart and peace in the mind and gladness by day and by night?

Why was his mouth so cool, that had burned dry as ash? Why were his lips moist, with a bitter-sweet flavour, as though the juice of fruit was there still?

He pondered, with closed eyes. At last he opened them, and stared upward. The profound black-blue dome of the sky held group after group of stars that he knew: was not that sword and belt yonder the sword-gear of Fionn? Yon shimmering cluster, were they not the dust of the feet of Alldai? That leaping green and blue planet, what could it be but the harp of Brigidh, where she sang to the gods?

A shadow crossed his vision. The next moment a cool hand was upon his eyes. It brought rest, and healing. He felt the blood move in his veins: his heart beat: a throbbing was in his throat.

Then he knew that he had strength to rise. With a great effort he put his weariness from off him, and staggered to his feet.

Cathal gave a low sob. A fair beautiful woman stood by him.

"Ardanna!" he cried, though even as the word leaped from his lips he knew that he looked upon no Pictish woman.

She smiled. All his heart was glad because of that. The light in her eyes was like the fire of the moon, bright and wonderful. The delicate body of her was pale green, and luminous as a leaf, with soft earth-brown hair falling down her shoulders and over the swelling breast; even as the small green mounds over the dead the two breasts were. She was clad only in her own loveliness, though the moonshine was about her as a garment.

"Like a green leaf: like a green leaf," Cathal muttered over and over below his breath.

"Are you a dream?" he asked simply, having no words for his wonder.

"No, Cathal, I am no dream. I am a woman."

"A woman? But . . . but . . . you have no body as other women have: and I see the moonbeam that is on your breast shining upon the moss behind you!"

"Is it thinking you are, poor Cathal, that there are no women and no men in the world except those who are in thick flesh, and move about in the suntide?"

Cathal stared wonderingly.

"I am of the green people, Cathal. We are of the woods. I am a woman of the woods."

"Hast thou a name, fair woman?"

"I am called Deòin."*

"That is well. Truly 'Green Life' is a good name for thee. Are there others of thy kin in this place?"

"Look!" and at that she stooped, lifted the dew of a white flower in the moonshine, and put it upon his eyes.

Cathal looked about him. Everywhere he saw tall, fair pale-green lives moving to and fro: some passing out of trees, swift and silent as rain out of a cloud; some passing into trees, silent and swift as shadows. All were fair to look upon: tall, lithe, graceful, moving this way and that in the moonshine, pale green as the leaves of the lime, soft shining, with radiant eyes, and delicate earth-brown hair.

"Who are these, Deòin?" Cathal asked in a low whisper of awe.

"They are my people the folk of the woods: the green people."

"But they come out of trees: they come and they go like bees in and out of a hive."

"Trees? That is your name for us of the woods. *We* are the trees."

"*You* the trees, Deòin! How can that be?"

"There is life in your body. Where does it go when the body sleeps, or when the sap rises no more to heart or brain, and there is chill in the blood, and it is like frozen water? Is there a life in your body?"

"Ay, so. I know it."

"The flesh is *your* body; the tree is *my* body."

"Then you are the green life of a tree?"

"I am the green life of a tree."

"And these?"

"They are as I am."

"I see those that are men and those that are women and their offspring too I see."

"They are as I am."

"And some are crowned with pale flowers."

"They love."

---

* *Deo-uaine.*

"And hast thou no crown, Deòin, who art so fair?"

"Neither hast thou, Cathal, though thy face is fair. Thy body I cannot see, because thou hast a husk about thee."

With a low laugh Cathal removed his raiment from him. The whiteness of his body was like a flower there in the moonshine.

"That shall not be against me," he said. "Truly, I am a man no longer, if thou and thine will have me as one of the wood-folk."

At that Deòin called. Many green phantoms glided out of the trees, and others, hand-in-hand, flower-crowned, crossed the glade.

"Look, green lives," Deòin cried in her sweet leaf-whisper, rising now like a wind-song among birchen boughs; "look, here is a human. His life is mine, for I saved him. I have put the moonshine dew upon his eyes. He sees as we see. He would be one of us, for all that he has no tree for his body, but flesh, white over red."

One who had moved thitherward out of an ancient oak looked at Cathal.

"Wouldst thou be of the wood-folk, man?"

"Ay, fain am I; for sure, for sure, O Druid of the trees."

"Wilt thou learn and abide by our laws, the first of which is that none may stir from his tree until the dusk has come, nor linger away from it when the dawn opens grey lips and drinks up the shadows?"

"I have no law now but the law of green life."

"Good. Thou shalt live with us. Thy home will be the hollow oak where thy kin left thee to die. Why did they do that evil deed?"

"Because I did not believe in the new gods."

"Who are thy gods, man whom this green one here calls Cathal?"

"They are the Sun, and the Moon, and the Wind, and others that I will tell you of."

"Hast thou heard of Keithoir?"

"No."

"He is the god of the green world. He dreams, and his dreams are Springtide and Summertime and Appletide. When he sleeps, without dream there is winter."

"Have you no other god but this earth-god?"

"Keithoir is our god. We know no other."

"If he is thy god, he is my god."

"I see in the eyes of Deòin that she loves thee, Cathal the human. Wilt thou have her love?"

Cathal looked at the girl. His heart swam in light.

"Ay, if Deòin will give me her love, my love shall be hers."

The Annir-Coille moved forward and brushed softly against him as a green branch.

He put his arms around her. She had a cool, sweet body to feel. He was glad she was no moonshine phantom. The beating of her heart against his made a music that filled his ears.

Deòin stooped and plucked white, dewy flowers. Of these she wove a wreath for Cathal. He, likewise, plucked the white blooms, and made a coronal of foam for the brown wave of her hair.

Then, hand in hand, they fared slowly forth across the moonlit glade. None crossed their path, though everywhere delicate green lives flitted from tree to tree. They heard a wonderful sweet singing, aerial, with a ripple as of leaves lipping a windy shore of light. A green glamour was in the eyes of Cathal. The green fire of life flamed in his veins.

IV

Molios, the saint of Christ, that lived in the sea-cave of the Isle of the Peak, so that even in his own day it was called the Holy Isle, endured to a great age.

Some say of him that before his hair was bleached white as the hog-cotton, he was slain by the heathen Picts, or by the fierce summer-sailors out of Lochlin. But that is an idle tale. His end was not thus. A Culdee, who had the soul of a bat, feared the truth, though that gave glory to God, and wrote both in ogham and lambskin the truthless tale that Molios went forth with the cross and was slain in a north isle.

On a day of the days every year, Molios fared to the Hollow Oak that was in the hill-forest beyond the rath of Ecta MacEcta. There he spake long upon the youth that had been his friend, and upon how the Evil One had prevailed with Cathal, and how the islander had been done to death there in the oak. Then he and all his company sang the hymns of peace, and great joy there was over the doom of Cathal the monk, and many would have cleft the great tree or burned it, so that the dust of the sinner might be scattered to the four winds: only this was banned by Molios.

It was well for Cathal, who slept there through the hours of light! Deep slumber was his, for never once did he hear the moontide voices, nor ever in his ears was the long rise and fall of the holy hymns.

But when, in the twentieth year after Cathal had been thrust into the hollow oak, Molios came at sundown, being weary with the heat, the saint heard a low, faint laughter issuing from the tree, like fragrance from a flower.

None other heard it. He saw that with gladness. Quietly he went with the islanders.

When the moon was over the pines, and all in the rath slept, Molios arose and went silently back into the forest.

When he came to the Doom-Tree he listened long, with his ear against the bark. There was no sound.

His voice was old and quavering, but fresh and young in the courts of heaven, when it reached there like a fluttering bird tired from long flight. He sang a holy hymn.

He listened. There was no laughter. He was glad of that. All had been a dream, for sure.

Then it was that he heard once again the low, mocking laughter. He started back, trembling.

"Cathal!" he cried, with his voice like a wuthering wind.

"I am here, O Molios," said a voice behind him.

The old Culdee turned, as though arrow-nipped. Before him, white in the moonshine, stood a man, naked.

At first, Molios knew him not. He was so tall and strong, so fair and wonderful. Long locks of ruddy hair hung upon his white shoulders: his eyes were lustrous, and had the lovely, soft light of the deer. When he moved, it was swiftly and silently. No stag upon the hills was more fair to see.

Then, slowly, Cathal the monk swam into Cathal of the Woods. Molios saw him whom he knew of old, as a blue flame is visible within the flame of yellow.

"I am here, O Molios."

Strange was the voice: faint and far the tone of it: yet it was that of a living man.

"Is it a spirit you are, Cathal?"

"I am no spirit. I am Cathal the monk that was, Cathal the man now."

"How came you out of hell, you that are dead, and the dust of whose crumbling bones is in the hollow of this oak?"

"There is no hell, Culdee."

"No hell!" Molios the Saint stared at the woodman in blank amaze.

"No hell," he said again; "and is there no heaven?"

"A hell there is, and a heaven there is: but not what Colum taught, and you taught."

"Doth Christ live?"

"I know not."

"And Mary?"

"I know not."

"And God the Father?"

"I know not."

"It is a lie that you have upon your lips. Sure, Cathal, you shall be dead indeed soon, to the glory of God. For I shall have thy dust scattered to the four winds, and thy bones consumed in flame, and a stake be driven through the place where thou wast."

Once more Cathal laughed.

"Go back to thy sea-cave, Molios. Thou hast much to learn. Brood there upon the ways of thy God before thou judgest if He knoweth no more than thou dost. And see, I will show you a wonder. Only, first, tell me this one thing. What of Ardanna, whom I loved?"

"She was accursed. She would not believe. When Ecta took the child from her, that was born in sin, to have the water put upon it with the sign of the Cross, she went north beyond the Hill of the Pinnacles. There she saw the young king of the Picts of Argyll, and he loved her, and she went to his dûn. He took her to his rath in the north, and she was his queen. He, and she, and the two sons she bore to him are all under the hill-moss now: and their souls are in hell."

Cathal laughed, low and mocking.

"It is a good hell that, I am thinking, Molios. But come . . . I will show you a wonder."

With that he stooped, and took the moonshine dew out of a white flower, and put it upon the eyes of the old man.

Then Molios saw.

And what he saw was a strangeness and a terror to him. For everywhere were green lives, fair and comely, gentle-eyed, lovely, of a soft shining. From tree to tree they flitted, or passed to and fro from the tree-boles, as wild bees from their hives.

Beside Cathal stood a woman. Beautiful she was, with eyes like stars in the gloaming. All of green flame she seemed, though the old monk saw her breast rise and fall, and the light lift of her earth-brown hair by a wind-breath eddying there, and the hand of her clasped in that of Cathal. Beyond her were fair and beautiful beings, lovely shapes like unto men and women, but soulless, though loving life and hating death, which, of a truth, is all that the vain human clan does.

"Who is this woman, Cathal?" asked the saint, trembling.

"It is Deòin, whom I love, and who has given me life."

"And these . . . that are neither green phantoms out of trees, nor yet men as we are?"

"These are the offspring of our love."

Molios drew back in horror.

But Cathal threw up his arms, and with glad eyes cried:

"O green flame of life, pulse of the world! O Love! O Youth! O Dream of Dreams!"

"O bitter grief," Molios cried, "O bitter grief, that I did not slay thee utterly on that day of the days! Flame to thy flesh, and a stake through thy belly—that is the doom thou shouldst have had! My ban upon thee, Cathal, that was a monk, and now art a wild man of the woods: upon thee, and thy Annir-Coille, and all thy brood, I put the ban of fear and dread and sorrow, a curse by day and a curse by night!"

But with that a great dizziness swam into the brain of the saint, and he fell forward, and lay his length upon the moss, and there was no sight to his eyes, or hearing to his ears, or knowledge upon him at all until the rising of the sun.

When the yellow light was upon his face he rose. There was no face to see anywhere. Looking in the dew for the myriad feet that had been there, he saw none.

The old man knelt and prayed.

At the first praying God filled his heart with peace. At the second praying God filled his heart with wonder. At the third praying God whispered mysteriously, and he knew. Humble in his new knowledge, he rose. The tears were in his old eyes. He went up to the Hollow Oak, and blessed it, and the wild man that slept within it, and the Annir-Coille that Cathal loved, and the offspring of their love. He took the curse away, and he blessed all that God had made.

All the long weary way to the shore he went as one in a dream. Wonder and mystery were in his eyes.

At the shore he entered the little coracle that brought him daily from the Holy Isle, a triple arrow-flight seaward.

A child sat in it, playing with pebbles. It was Ardan, the son of Ardanna.

"Ardan mac Cathal," began the saint, weary now, but glad with a strange new gladness.

"Who is Cathal?" said the boy.

"He that was thy father. Tell me, Ardan, hast thou ever seen aught moving in the woods—green lives out of the trees?"

"I have seen a green shine come out of the trees."

Molios bowed his head.

"Thou shalt be as my son, Ardan; and when thou art a man thou shalt choose thy own way, and let no man hinder thee."

That night Molios could not sleep. Hearing the loud wash of the sea, he went to the mouth of the cave. For a long while he watched the seals splashing in the silver radiance of the moonshine. Then he called them.

"O seals of the sea, come hither!"

At that all the furred swimmers drew near.

"Is it for the curse you give us every year of the years, O holy Molios?" moaned a great black seal.

"O Ron dubh, it is no curse I have for thee or thine, but a blessing and peace. I have learned a wonder of God, because of an Annir-Coille in the forest that is upon the hill. But now I will be telling you the white story of Christ."

So there, in the moonshine, with the flowing tide stealing from his feet to his knees, the old saint preached the gospel of love. The seals crouched upon the rocks, with their great brown eyes filled with glad tears.

When Molios ceased, each slipped again into the shadowy sea. All that night, while he brooded upon the mystery of Cathal and the Annir-Coille, with deep knowledge of hidden things, and a heart filled with the wonder and mystery of the world, he heard them splashing to and fro in the moon-dazzle, and calling, one to the other, "We, too, are the sons of God."

At dawn a shadow came into the cave. A white frost grew upon the face of Molios. Still was he, and cold, when Ardan, the child, awoke. Only the white lips moved. A ray of the sun slanted across the sea, from the great disc of whirling golden flame new risen. It fell softly upon the moving lips. They were still then, and Ardan kissed them because of the smile that was there.

Mircath

When Haco the Laugher saw the islanders coming out of the west in their birlinns, he called to his vikings, "Now of a truth we shall hear the Song of the Sword!"

The ten galleys of the summer-sailors spread out into two lines of five boats, each boat an arrow-flight from that on either side.

The birlinns came on against the noon. In the sun-dazzle they loomed black as a shoal of pollack. There were fifteen in all, and from the largest, midway among them, flew a banner. On this banner was a disc of gold.

"It is the Banner of the Sunbeam!" shouted Olaf the Red, who with Torquil the One-Armed was hero-man to Haco. "I know it well. The Gael who fight under that are warriors indeed."

"Is there a saga-man here?" cried Haco. At that a great shout went up from the vikings: "Harald the Smith!"

A man rose among the bow-men in Olaf's boat. It was Harald. He took a small square harp, and he struck the strings. This was the song he sang:

> Let loose the hounds of war,
> > The whirling swords!
> Send them leaping afar,
> Red in their thirst for war;
> Odin laughs in his car
> > At the screaming of the swords!

> Far let the white ones fly,
> > The whirling swords!
> Afar off the ravens spy
> Death-shadows cloud the sky.

The *Mire Chath* was the name given to the war-frenzy that often preceded and accompanied battle.

> Let the wolves of the Gael die
>   'Neath the screaming swords!
>
> The Shining Ones yonder
>   High in Valhalla
> Shout now, with thunder,
> *Drive the Gaels under,*
> *Cleave them asunder,—*
>   *Swords of Valhalla!*

A shiver passed over every viking. Strong men shook as a child when lightning plays. Then the trembling passed. The mircath, the war-frenzy came on them. Loud laughter went from boat to boat. Many tossed the great oars, and swung them down upon the sea, splashing the sun-dazzle into a yeast of foam. Others sprang up and whirled their javelins on high, catching them with bloody mouths: others made sword-play, and stammered thick words through a surf of froth upon their lips. Olaf the Red towered high on the steering-plank of the *Calling Raven,* swirling round and round a mighty battle-axe: on the *Sea-Wolf,* Torquil One-Arm shaded his eyes, and screamed hoarsely wild words that no one knew the meaning of. Only Haco was still for a time. Then he, too, knew the mircath; and he stood up in the *Red-Dragon* and laughed loud and long. And when Haco the Laugher laughed, there was ever blood and to spare.

The birlinns of the islanders drove on apace. They swayed out into a curve, a black crescent there in the gold-sprent blue meads of the sea. From the great birlinn that carried the Sunbeam came a chanting voice:

> O, 'tis a good song the sea makes when blood is on the wave,
> And a good song the wave makes when its crest of foam is red!
> For the rovers out of Lochlin the sea is a good grave,
> And the bards will sing to-night to the sea-moan of the dead!
>
>   Yo-ho-a-h'eily-a-yo, eily, ayah, a yo!
>   Sword and spear and Battle-axe sing the Song of Woe!
>   Ayah, eily, a yo!
>   Eily, ayah, a yo!

Then there was a swirling and dashing of foam. Clouds of spray filled the air from the thresh of the oars.

No man knew aught of the last moments ere the birlinns bore down upon the viking-galleys. Crash and roar and scream, and a wild surging; the slashing of swords, the whistle of arrows, the fierce hiss of whirled spears, the rending crash of battle-axe and splintering of the javelins; wild cries, oaths, screams, shouts of victors, and yells of the dying; shrill taunts from the spillers of life, and savage choking cries from those drowning in the bloody yeast that bubbled and foamed in the maelstrom where the war-boats swung and reeled this way and that; and, over all, the loud death-music of Haco the Laugher.

Olaf the Red went into the sea, red indeed, for the blood streamed from head and shoulders, and fell about him as a scarlet robe. Torquil One-Arm fought, blind and arrow-sprent, till a spear went through his neck, and he sank among the dead. Louder and louder grew the fierce shouts of the Gael; fewer the savage screaming cries of the vikings. Thus it was till two galleys only held living men. The *Calling Raven* turned and fled, with the nine men who were not wounded to the death. But, on the *Red-Dragon,* Haco the Laugher still laughed. Seven men were about him. These fought in silence.

Then Toscar mac Aonghas, that was leader of the Gael, took his bow. None was arrow-better than Toscar of the Nine Battles. He laid down his sword and took his bow, and an arrow went through the right eye of Haco the Laugher. He laughed no more. The seven died in silence. Swaran Swiftfoot was the last. When he fell, he wiped away the blood that streamed over his face.

"Skoal!" he cried to the hero of the Gael, and with that he whirled his battle-axe at Toscar mac Aonghas; and the soul of Toscar met his, in the dark mist, and upon the ears of both fell at one and the same time the glad laughter of the gods in Valhalla.

The Laughter of Scathach the Queen

In the year when Cuchullin left the Isle of Skye, where Scathach the warrior-Queen ruled with the shadow of death in the palm of her sword-hand, there was sorrow because of his beauty. He had fared back to Eiré, at the summons of Concobar mac Nessa, Ard-Righ of Ulster. For the Clan of the Red Branch was wading in blood, and there were seers who beheld that bitter tide rising and spreading.

Cuchullin was only a youth in years; but he had come to Skye a boy, and he had left it a man. None fairer had ever been seen of Scathach or of any woman. He was tall and lithe as a young pine; his skin was as white as a woman's breast; his eyes were of a fierce bright blue, with a white light in them as of the sun. When bent, and with arrow half-way drawn, he stood on the heather, listening against the belling of the deer; or when he leaned against a tree, dreaming not of eagle-chase or wolf-hunt, but of the woman whom he had never met; or, when by the dûn, he played at sword-whirl or spear-thrust, or raced the war-chariot across the machar—then, and ever there were eyes upon his beauty, and there were some who held him to be Angus Ogue himself. For there was a light about him, such as the hills have in sun-glow an hour before set. His hair was the hair of Angus and of the fair gods, earth-brown shot with gold next his head, ruddy as flame midway, and, where it sprayed into a golden mist of fire, yellow as windy sunshine.

But Cuchullin loved no woman upon Skye, and none dared openly to love Cuchullin, for Scathach's heart yearned for him, and to cross the Queen was to put the shroud upon oneself. Scathach kept an open face for the soil of Lerg. There was no dark frown above the storm in her eyes when she looked at his sunbright face. Gladly she slew a woman

---

Scathach (pronounced Scá-ya or Sky´-ya) was an Amazonian Queen of the Island of Skye, and is supposed to have given her name to that island.

because Cuchullin had lightly reproved the maid for some idle thing; and once, when the youth looked in grave silence at three viking captives whom she had spared because of their comely manhood, she put her sword through the heart of each, and sent him the blade, dripping red, as the flower of love.

But Cuchullin was a dreamer, and he loved what he dreamed of, and that woman was not Scathach, nor any of her warrior-women who made the Isle of Mist a place of terror for those cast upon the wild shores, or stranded there in the ebb of inglorious battle.

Scathach brooded deep upon her vain desire. Once, in a windless, shadowy gloaming, she asked him if he loved any woman.

"Yes," he said. "Etáin."

Her breath came quick and hard. It was for pleasure to her then to think of Cuchullin lying white at her feet, with the red blood spilling from the whiteness of his breast. But she bit her under lip, and said quietly—

"Who is Etáin?"

"She is the wife of Mídir."

And with that the youth turned and moved haughtily away. She did not know that the Etáin of whom Cuchullin dreamed was no woman that he had seen in Eiré, but the wife of Mídir, the King of Faerie, who was so passing fair that Mac Greine, the beautiful god, had made for her a grianan all of shining glass, where she lives in a dream, and in that sun-bower is fed at dawn upon the bloom of flowers and at dusk upon their fragrance. *O ogham mhic Gréine, tha e boidheach,** she sighs for ever in her sleep; and that sigh is in all sighs of love for ever and ever.

Scathach watched him till he was lost behind the flare of the camp fires of the rath. For long she stood there, brooding deep, till the sickle of the new moon, which had been like a brown feather over the sun as it sank stood out in silver-shine against the blue-black sky, now like a wake in the sea because of the star-dazzle that was there. And what the Queen brooded upon was this: Whether to send emissaries to Eirèann, under bond to seek in that land till they found Mídir and Etáin, and to slay Mídir and to bring to her the corpse, for a gift from her to lay before

---

*"O beauty of my love the Sun-lord" (*lit.* "O youth, son of the Sun, how fair he is!").

Cuchullin; or to bring Etáin to Skye, where the Queen might see her lose her beauty and wane into death. Neither way might win the heart of Cuchullin. The dark tarn of the woman's mind grew blacker with the shadow of that thought.

Slowly she moved dûn-ward through the night.

"As the moon sometimes is seen rising out of the east," she muttered, "and sometimes, as now, is first seen in the west, so is the heart of love. And if I go west, lo, the moon may rise along the sunway; and if I go east, lo, the moon may be a white light over the setting sun. And who that knoweth the heart of man or woman can tell when the moon of love is to appear full-orbed in the east, or sickle-wise in the west?"

It was on the day following that tidings came out of Eirèann. An Ultonian brought a sword to Cuchullin from Concobar the Ard-Righ.

"The sword has ill upon it, and will die unless you save it, Cuculain, son of Lerg," said the man.

"And what is that ill, Ultonian?" asked the youth.

"It is thirst."

Then Cuchullin understood.

On the night of his going none looked at Scathach. She had a flame in her eyes.

At moonrise she came back into the rath. No one meeting her looked in her face. Death lay there, like the levin behind a cloud. But Maev, her chief captain, sought her, for she had glad news.

"I would slay you for that glad news, Maev," said the dark Queen to the warrior-woman, "for there is no glad news unless it be that Cuchullin is come again; only, I spare, for you saved my life that day the summer-sailors burned my rath in the south."

Nevertheless Scathach had gladness because of the tidings. Three viking galleys had been driven into Loch Scavaig, and been dashed to death there by the whirling wind and the narrow, furious seas. Of the ninety men who had sailed in them, only a score had reached the rocks, and these were now lying bound at the dûn, awaiting death.

"Call out my warriors," said Scathach, "and bid all meet at the oak near the Ancient Stones. And bring thither the twenty men that lie bound in the dûn."

There was a scattering of fire and a clashing of swords and spears when the word went from Maev. Soon all were at the Stones beneath the great oak.

"Cut the bonds from the feet of the sea-rovers, and let them stand." Thus commanded the Queen.

The tall, fair men out of Lochlin stood with their hands bound behind them. In their eyes burned wrath and shame, because that they were the sport of women. A bitter death theirs, with no sword-song for music. "Take each by his long yellow hair," said Scathach, "and tie the hair of each to a down-caught bough of the oak."

In silence this thing was done. A shadow was in the paleness of each viking face.

"Let the boughs go," said Scathach.

The five score warrior women who held the great boughs downward sprang back. Up swept the branches, and from each swung a living man, swaying in the wind by his long yellow hair.

Great men they were, strong warriors; but stronger was the yellow hair of each, and stronger than the hair the bough wherefrom each swung, and stronger than the boughs the wind that swayed them idly like drooping fruit, with the stars silvering their hair and the torch-flares reddening the white soles of their dancing feet.

Then Scathach the Queen laughed loud and long. There was no other sound at all there, for none ever uttered sound when Scathach laughed that laugh, for then her madness was upon her.

But at the last, Mael strode forward and struck a small clarsach that she carried, and to the wild notes of it sang the death-song of the vikings:

> O arone, a-ree, eily arone, arone!
> 'Tis a good thing to be sailing across the sea!
> How the women smile and the children are laughing glad
> When the galleys go out into the blue sea—arone!
> O eily arone, arone!
>
> But the children may laugh less when the wolves come,
> And the women may smile less in the winter-cold;
> For the Summer-sailors will not come again, arone!
> O arone a-ree, eily arone, arone!

I am thinking they will not sail back again, O no!
The yellow-haired men that came sailing across the sea:
For 'tis wild apples they would be, and swing on green branches,
And sway in the wind for the corbies to preen their eyne,
            O eily arone, eily a-ree!

And it is pleasure for Scathach the Queen to see this:
To see the good fruit that grows upon the Tree of the Stones.
Long, speckled fruit it is, wind-swayed by its yellow roots,
And like men they are with their feet dancing in the void air!
            O, O, arone, a-ree, eily arone!

When she ceased, all there swung swords and spears, and flung flaring torches into the night, and cried out—

O arone a-ree, eily arone, arone,
O, O, arone, a-ree, eily arone!

Scathach laughed no more. She was weary now. Of what avail any joy of death against the pain she had in her heart, the pain that was called Cuchullin?

Soon all was dark in the rath. Flame after flame died out. Then there was but one red glare in the night, the watch-fire by the dûn. Deep peace was upon all. Not a heifer lowed, not a dog bayed against the moon. The wind fell into a breath, scarce enough to lift the fragrance from flower to flower. Upon the branches of a great oak swung motionless a strange fruit, limp and grey as the hemlock that hangs from ancient pines.

Ula and Urla

"Rose of all Roses, Rose of all the World!
 You, too, have come where the dim tides are hurled
 Upon the wharves of sorrow, and heard ring
 The bell that calls us on: the sweet far thing.
 Beauty grown sad with its eternity
 Made you of us, and of the dim grey sea."

Ula and Urla were under vow to meet by the Stone of Sorrow. But Ula, dying first, stumbled blindfold when he passed the Shadowy Gate; and till Urla's hour was upon her, she remembered not.

These were the names that had been given to them in the north isles, when the birlinn that ran down the war-galley of the vikings brought them before the Maormor.

No word had they spoken that day, and no name. They were of the Gael, though Ula's hair was yellow, and though his eyes were blue as the heart of a wave. They would ask nothing, for both were in love with death. The Maormor of Siol Tormaid looked at Urla, and his desire gnawed at his heart. But he knew what was in her mind, because he saw into it through her eyes, and he feared the sudden slaying in the dark.

Nevertheless, he brooded night and day upon her beauty. Her skin was more white than the foam of the moon: her eyes were as a star-lit dewy dusk. When she moved, he saw her like a doe in the fern: when she stooped, it was as the fall of wind-swayed water. In his eyes there was a shimmer as of the sun-flood in a calm sea. In that dazzle he was led astray.

"Go," he said to Ula, on a day of the days. "Go: the men of Siol

---

The first part of the story of Ula and Urla, as Isla and Eilidh, is told in "Silk o' the Kine."

Torquil will take you to the south isles, and so you can hale to your own place, be it Eirèann or Manannan, or wherever the south wind puts its hand upon your home."

It was on that day Ula spoke for the first time.

"I will go, Coll mac Torcall; but I go not alone. Urla that I love goes whither I go."

"She is my spoil. But, man out of Eirèann—for so I know you to be, because of the manner of your speech—tell me this: Of what clan and what place are you, and whence is Urla come; and by what shore was it that the men of Lochlin whom we slew took you and her out of the sea, as you swam against the sun, with waving swords upon the strand when the viking-boat carried you away?"

"How know you these things?" asked Ula, that had been Isla, son of the king of Islay.

"One of the sea-rovers spoke before he died."

"Then let the viking speak again. I have nought to say."

With that the Maormor frowned, but said no more. That eve Ula was seized, as he walked in the dusk by the sea, singing low to himself an ancient song.

"Is it death?" he said, remembering another day when he and Eilidh, that they called Urla, had the same asking upon their lips.

"It is death."

Ula frowned, but spake no word for a time. Then he spake.

"Let me say one word with Urla."

"No word canst thou have. She, too, must die."

Ula laughed low at that.

"I am ready," he said. And they slew him with a spear.

When they told Urla, she rose from the deer-skins and went down to the shore. She said no word then. But she stooped, and she put her lips upon his cold lips, and she whispered in his unhearing ear.

That night Coll mac Torcall went secretly to where Urla was. When he entered, a groan came to his lips and there was froth there: and that was because the spear that had slain Ula was thrust betwixt his shoulders by one who stood in the shadow. He lay there till the dawn. When they found Coll the Maormor he was like a seal speared upon a rock, for he had his hands out, and his head was between them, and his face was downward.

"Eat dust, slain wolf," was all that Eilidh, whom they called Urla, said, ere she moved away from that place in the darkness of the night.

When the sun rose, Urla was in a glen among the hills. A man who shepherded there took her to his mate. They gave her milk, and because of her beauty and the frozen silence of her eyes, bade her stay with them and be at peace.

They knew in time that she wished death. But first, there was the birthing of the child.

"It was Isla's will," she said to the woman. Ula was but the shadow of a bird's wing: an idle name. And she, too, was Eilidh once more.

"It was death he gave you when he gave you the child," said the woman once.

"It was life," answered Eilidh, with her eyes filled with the shadow of dream. And yet another day the woman said to her that it would be well to bear the child and let it die: for beauty was like sunlight on a day of clouds, and if she were to go forth young and alone and so wondrous fair, she would have love, and love is best.

"Truly, love is best," Eilidh answered. "And because Isla loved me, I would that another Isla came into the world and sang his songs—the songs that were so sweet, and the songs that he never sang, because I gave him death when I gave him life. But now he shall live again, and he and I shall be in one body, in him that I carry now."

At that the woman understood, and said no more. And so the days grew out of the nights, and the dust of the feet of one month was in the eyes of that which followed after; and this until Eilidh's time was come.

Dusk after dusk, Ula that was Isla the Singer, waited by the Stone of Sorrow. Then a great weariness came upon him. He made a song there, where he lay in the narrow place; the last song that he made, for after that he heard no trampling of the hours.

The swift years slip and slide adown the steep;
    The slow years pass; neither will come again.
Yon huddled years have weary eyes that weep,
    These laugh, these moan, these silent frown, these plain,

These have their lips acurl with proud disdain.

O years with tears, and tears through weary years,
    How weary I who in your arms have lain:
Now, I am tired: the sound of slipping spears
    Moves soft, and tears fall in a bloody rain,
    And the chill footless years go over me who am slain.

I hear, as in a wood, dim with old light, the rain,
    Slow falling; old, old, weary, human tears:
And in the deepening dark my comfort is my Pain,
    Sole comfort left of all my hopes and fears,
    Pain that alone survives, gaunt hound of the shadowy years.

But, at the last, after many days, he stirred. There was a song in his ears.

He listened. It was like soft rain in a wood in June. It was like the wind laughing among the leaves.

Then his heart leaped. Sure, it was the voice of Eilidh!

"Eilidh! Eilidh! Eilidh!" he cried. But a great weariness came upon him again. He fell asleep, knowing not the little hand that was in his, and the small, flower-sweet body that was warm against his side.

Then the child that was his looked into the singer's heart, and saw there a mist of rainbows, and midway in that mist was the face of Eilidh, his mother.

Thereafter, the little one looked into his brain that was so still, and he saw the music that was there: and it was the voice of Eilidh his mother.

And, again, the birdeen, that had the blue of Isla's eyes and the dream of Eilidh's, looked into Ula's sleeping soul: and he saw that it was not Isla nor yet Eilidh, but that it was like unto himself, who was made of Eilidh and Isla.

For a long time the child dreamed. Then he put his ear to Isla's brow, and listened. Ah, the sweet songs that he heard. Ah, bitter-sweet moonseed of song! Into his life they passed, echo after echo, strain after strain, wild air after wild sweet air.

"Isla shall never die," whispered the child, "for Eilidh loved him. And I am Isla and Eilidh."

Then the little one put his hands above Isla's heart. There was a flame there, that the Grave quenched not.

"O flame of love!" sighed the child, and he clasped it to his breast: and it was a moonshine glory about the two hearts that he had, the heart of Isla and the heart of Eilidh, that were thenceforth one.

At dawn he was no longer there. Already the sunrise was warm upon him where he lay, new-born, upon the breast of Eilidh.

"It is the end," murmured Isla when he waked. "She has never come. For sure, now, the darkness and the silence."

Then he remembered the words of Maol the Druid, he that was a seer, and had told him of Orchil, the dim goddess who is under the brown earth, in a vast cavern, where she weaves at two looms. With one hand she weaves life upward through the grass; with the other she weaves death downward through the mould; and the sound of the weaving is Eternity, and the name of it in the green world is Time. And, through all, Orchil weaves the weft of Eternal Beauty, that passeth not, though its soul is Change.

And these were the words of Orchil, on the lips of Maol the Druid, that was old, and knew the mystery of the Grave.

When thou journeyest toward the Shadowy Gate take neither Fear with thee nor Hope, for both are abashed hounds of silence in that place; but take only the purple nightshade for sleep, and a vial of tears and wine, tears that shall be known unto thee and old wine of love. So shalt thou have thy silent festival, ere the end.

So therewith Isla, having, in his weariness, the nightshade of sleep, and in his mind the slow dripping rain of familiar tears, and deep in his heart the old wine of love, bowed his head.

It was well to have lived, since life was Eilidh. It was well to cease to live, since Eilidh came no more.

Then suddenly he raised his head. There was music in the green world above. A sunray opened the earth about him: staring upward he beheld Angus Ogue.

"Ah, fair face of the god of youth," he sighed. Then he saw the white birds that fly about the head of Angus Ogue, and he heard the music that his breath made upon the harp of the wind.

"Arise," said Angus; and, when he smiled, the white birds flashed their wings and made a mist of rainbows.

"Arise," said Angus Ogue again, and, when he spoke, the spires of the grass quivered to a wild, sweet haunting air.

So Isla arose, and the sun shone upon him, and his shadow passed into the earth. Orchil wove into it her web of death.

"Why dost thou wait here by the Stone of Sorrow, Isla that was called Ula at the end?"

"I wait for Eilidh, who cometh not."

At that the wind-listening god stooped and laid his head upon the grass.

"I bear the coming of a woman's feet," he said, and he rose.

"Eilidh! Eilidh!" cried Isla, and the sorrow of his cry was a moan in the web of Orchil.

Angus Ogue took a branch, and put the cool greenness against his cheek.

"I hear the beating of a heart," he said.

"Eilidh! Eilidh! Eilidh!" Isla cried, and the tears that were in his voice were turned by Angus into dim dews of remembrance in the babe-brain that was the brain of Isla and Eilidh.

"I hear a word," said Angus Ogue, "and that word is a flame of joy."

Isla listened. He heard a singing of birds. Then, suddenly, a glory came into the shine of the sun.

"I have come, Isla my king!"

It was the voice of Eilidh. He bowed his head, and swayed; for it was his own life that came to him.

"Eilidh!" he whispered.

And so, at the last, Isla came into his kingdom.

But are they gone, these twain, who loved with deathless love? Or is this a dream that I have dreamed?

Afar in an island-sanctuary that I shall not see again, where the wind chants the blind oblivious rune of Time, I have heard the grasses whisper: *Time never was, time is not.*

By the Yellow Moonrock

I

Rory MacAlpine the piper had come down the Strath on St. Bride's Eve, for the great wedding at the farm of his kinsman Donald Macalister. Every man and woman, every boy and girl, who could by hook or by crook get to the big dance at the barns was to be seen there: but no one that danced till he or she could dance no more had a wearier joy than Rory with the pipes. Reels and strathspeys that every one knew gave way at last to wilder strathspeys that no one had ever heard before . . . and why should they, since it was the hill-wind and the mountain-torrent and the roar of pines that had got loose in Rory's mind, and he not knowing it any more than a leaf that sails on the yellow wind.

He played with magic and pleasure, and had never looked handsomer, in his new grandeur of clothes, and with his ruddy hair aflame in the torchlight, and his big blue eyes shining as with a lifting, shifting fire. But those who knew him best saw that he was strangely subdued for Rory MacAlpine, or at least, that he laughed and shouted (in the rare intervals when he was not playing, and there were two other pipers present to help the Master) more by custom than from the heart.

"What is't, Rory?" said Dalibrog to him, after a heavy reel wherein he had nearly killed a man by swinging upon and nigh flattening him against the wall.

"Nothing, foster-brother dear; it's just nothing at all. Fling away, Dalibrog; you're doing fine."

Later old Dionaid took him aside to bid him refresh himself from a brew of rum and lemons she had made, with spice and a flavour of old brandy—"Barra Punch" she called it—and then asked him if he had any sorrow at the back of his heart.

"Just this," he said in a whisper, "that Rory MacAlpine's fëy."

"Fëy, my lad, an' for why that? For sure, I'm thinking it's fëy with the good drink you have had all day, an' now here am I spoiling ye with more."

"Hush, woman; I'm not speaking of what comes wi' a drop to the bad. But I had a dream, I had; a powerful strange dream, for sure. I had it a month ago; I had it the night before I left Strathanndra; and I had it this very day of the days, as I lay sleepin' off the kindness I had since I came into Strathraonull."

"An' what will that dream be, now?"

"Sure, it's a strange dream, Dionaid Alacalister. You know the great yellow stone that rises out of the heather on the big moor of Dalmonadh, a mile or more beyond Tom-na-shee?"

"Ay, the Moonrock they call it: it that fell out o' the skies, they say."

"The Yellow Moonrock. Ay, the Yellow Moonrock; that's its name, for sure. Well, the first time I dreamed of it I saw it standing fair yellow in the moonshine. There was a moorfowl sitting on it, and it flew away. When it flew away I saw it was a ptarmigan, but she was as clean brown as though it were summer and not midwinter, and I thought that strange."

"How did you know it was a ptarmigan? It might have been a moorhen or a—"

"Hoots, woman, how do I know when it's wet or fine, when it's day or night? Well, as I was saying, I though it strange; but I hadn't turned over that thought on its back before it was gone like the shadow o' a peewit, and I saw standing before me the beautifullest woman I ever saw in all my life. I've had sweethearts here and sweethearts there, Dionaid-nic-Tormod, and long ago I loved a lass who died, Sinè MacNeil; but not one o' these, not sweet Sine herself, was like the woman I saw in my dream, who had more beauty upon her than them altogether, or than all the women in Strathraonull and Stratharmdra."

"Have some more Barra punch, Rory," said Miss Macalister drily.

"Whist, ye old fule, begging your pardon for that same. She was as white as new milk, an' her eyes were as dark as the two black pools below Annora Linn, an' her hair was as long an' wavy as the shadows o' a willow in the wind; an' she sat an' she sang, an' if I could be remembering that song now it's my fortune I'd be making, an' that quick too."

"And where was she?"

"Why, on the Moonrock, for sure. An' if I hadn't been a good Christian I'd have bowed down before her, because o'—because—well, because o' that big stare out of her eyes she had, an' the beauty of her, an' all. An' what's more, by the Black Stone of Iona, if I hadn't been a God-fearin' man I'd have run to her, an' put my arms round her, an' kissed the honey lips of her till she cried out, 'For the Lord's sake, Rory MacAlpine, leave off!'"

"It's well seen you were only in a dream, Rory MacAlpine."

At another time Rory would have smiled at that, but now he just stared.

"She said no word," he added, "but lifted a bit of hollow wood or thick reed. An' then all at once she whispered, 'I'm bonnie St. Bride of the Mantle,' an' wi' that she began to play, an' it was the finest, sweet, gentle, little music in the world. But a big fear was on me, an' I just turned an' ran."

"No man'll ever call ye a fool again to my face, Rory MacAlpine. I never had the thought you had so much sense."

"She didna let me run so easy, for a grey bitch went yapping and yowling at my heels; an' just as I tripped an' felt the bad hot breath of the beast at my throat, I woke, an' was wet wi' sweat."

"An' you've had that dream three times?"

"I've had it three times, and this very day, to the Stones be it said. Now, you're a wise woman, Dionaid Macalister, but can you tell me what that dream means?"

"If you're really fëy, I'm thinking I can, Rory MacAlpine."

"It's a true thing: Himself knows it."

"And what are you fëy of?"

"I'm fëy with the beauty o' that woman."

"There's good women wi' the fair looks on them in plenty, Rory; an' if you prefer them bad, you needna wear out new shoon before you'll find them."

"I'm fëy wi' the beauty o' that woman. I'm fëy wi' the beauty o' that woman that had the name o' Bride to her."

Dionaid Macalister looked at him with troubled eyes.

"When she took up the reed, did you see anything that frighted you?"

"Ay. I had a bit fright when I saw a big black adder slip about the Moonrock as the ptarmigan flew off; an' I had the other half o' that fright when I thought the woman lifted the adder, but it was only wood or a reed, for amn't I for telling you about the gentle, sweet music I heard?"

Old Dionaid hesitated; then, looking about her to see that no one was listening, she spoke in a whisper:

"An' you've been fëy since that hour because o' the beauty o' that woman?"

"Because o' the sore beauty o' that woman."

"An' it's not the drink?"

"No, no, Dionaid Macalister. You women are always for hurting the feelin's o' the drink. It is not the innycent drink, I am telling you; for sure, no; no, no, it is not the drink."

"Then I'll tell you what it means, Rory MacAlpine. It wasn't Holy St. Bride—"

"I know that, ye old—, I mean, Miss Macalister."

"It was the face of the *Bhean-Nimhir* you saw, the face of *Nighean-Imhir,* an' this is St. Bride's Night, an' it is on this night of the nights she can be seen, an' beware o' that seeing, Rory MacAlpine."

"The *Bean-Nimhir,* the *Nighean-Imhir* . . . the Serpent Woman, the Daughter of Ivor—" muttered Rory; "where now have I heard tell o' the Daughter of Ivor?" Then he remembered an old tale of the isles, and his heart sank, because the tale was of a woman of the underworld who could suck the soul out of a man through his lips, and send it to slavery among the people of ill-will, whom there is no call to speak of by name; and if she had any spite, or any hidden wish that is not for our knowing, she could put the littleness of a fly's bite on the hollow of his throat, and take his life out of his body, and nip it and sting it till it was no longer a life, and till that went away on the wind that she chased with screams and laughter.

"Some say she's the wife of the Amadan-Dhu, the Dark Fool," murmured Dionaid, crossing herself furtively, for even at Dalibrog it was all Protestantry now.

But Rory was not listening. He sat intent, for he heard music—a strange music.

Dionaid shook him by the shoulder.

"Wake up, Rory, man; you'll be having sleep on you in another minute."

Just then a loud calling for the piper was heard, and Rory went back to the dancers. Soon his pipes were heard, and the reels swung to that good glad music, and his face lighted up as he strode to and fro, or stopped and tap-tapped away with his right foot, while drone and chanter all but burst with the throng of sound in them.

But suddenly he began to play a reel that nigh maddened him, and his own face was wrought so that Dalibrog came up and signed to stop, and then asked him what in the name o' Black Donald he was playing.

Rory laughed foolishly.

"Oh, for sure, it's just a new reel o' my own. I call it 'The Reel of Ivor's Daughter.' An' a good reel it is too, although it's Rory MacAlpine says it."

"Who is she, an' what Ivor will you be speaking of?"

"Oh, ask the Amadan-Dhu; it's he will be knowing that. No, no, now, I will not be naming it that name; sure, I will call it instead the Serpent-Reel."

"Come now, Rory, you've played enough, an' if your wrist's not tired wi' the chanter, sure, it must be wi' lifting the drink to your lips. An' it's time, too, these lads an' lasses were off."

"No, no, they're waiting to bring in the greying of the day—St. Bride's Day. They'll be singing the hymn for that greying, 'Bride bhoidheach muime Chriosda.'"

"Not they, if Dalibrog has a say in it! Come, now, have a drink with me, your own foster-brother, an' then lie down an' sleep it off, an' God's blessing be on you."

Whether it was Dalibrog's urgency, or the thought of the good drink he would have, and he with a terrible thirst on him after that lung-bursting reel of his, Rory went quietly away with the host, and was on a mattress on the floor of a big, empty room, and snoring hard, long before the other pipers had ceased piping, or the last dancers flung their panting breaths against the frosty night.

II

An hour after midnight Rory woke with a start. He had "a spate of a headache on," he muttered, as he half rose and struck a match against the floor. When he saw that he was still in his brave gear, and had lain down "just as he was," and also remembered all that had happened and the place he was in, he wondered what had waked him.

Now that he thought of it, he had heard music: yes, for sure, music— for all that it was so late, and after every one had gone home. What was it? It was not any song of his own, nor any air he had. He must have dreamed that it came across great lonely moors, and had a laugh and a moan and a sudden cry in it.

He was cold. The window was open. That was a stupid, careless thing of Donald Macalister to do, and he sober, as he always was, though he could drink deep; on a night of frost like this Death could slip in on the back of a shadow and get his whisper in your ear before you could rise for the stranger.

He stumbled to his feet and closed the window. Then he laid down again, and was nearly asleep, and was confused between an old prayer that rose in his mind like a sunken spar above a wave; and whether to take Widow Sheen a packet of great thick Sabbath peppermints, or a good heavy twist of tobacco; and a strange delightsome memory of Dionaid Macalister's brew of rum and lemons with a touch of old brandy in it; when again he heard that little, wailing, fantastic air, and sat up with the sweat on his brow.

The sweat was not there only because of the little thin music he heard, and it the same, too, as he had heard before; but because the window was wide open again, though the room was so heavy with silence that the pulse of his heart made a noise like a jumping rat.

Rory sat, as still as though he were dead, staring at the window. He could not make out whether the music was faint because it was so far away, or because it was played feebly, like a child's playing, just under the sill.

He was a big, strong man, but he leaned and wavered like the flame of a guttering candle in that slow journey of his from the mattress to the window. He could hear the playing now quite well. It was like the beautiful, sweet song of "Bride bhoidheach muime Chriosda," but with the holy peace out of it, and with a little, evil, hidden laugh flapping like a wing against the blessed name of Christ's foster-mother. But when it sounded under the window, it suddenly was far; and when it was far, the last circling pee-wit-lilt would be at his ear like a skiffing bat.

When he looked out, and felt the cold night lie on his skin, he could not see because he saw too well. He saw the shores of the sky filled with dancing lights, and the great lighthouse of the moon sending a foam-white stream across the delicate hazes of frost which were too thin to be seen, and only took the sharp edges off the stars, or sometimes splintered them into sudden dazzle. He was like a man in a sailless, rudderless boat, looking at the skies because he lay face upward and dared not stoop and look into the dark, slipping water alongside.

He saw, too, the hornlike curve of Tom-na-shee black against the blueness, and the inky line of Dalmonadh Moor beyond the plumy mass of Dalibrog woods, and the near meadows where a leveret jumped squealing, and then the bare garden with ragged gooseberry-bushes like scraggy, hunched sheep, and at last the white gravel-walk bordered with the withered roots of pinks and southernwood.

Then he looked from all these great things and these little things to the ground beneath the window. There was nothing there. There was no sound. Not even far away could he hear any faint, devilish music. At least—

Rory shut the window, and went back to his mattress and lay down.

"By the sun an' wind," he exclaimed, "a man gets fear on him nowadays, like a cold in the head when a thaw comes."

Then he lay and whistled a blithe catch. For sure, he thought, he would rise at dawn and drown that thirst of his in whatever came first to hand.

Suddenly he stopped whistling, and on the uplift of a lilting turn. In a moment the room was full of old silence again.

Rory turned his head slowly. The window was wide open.

A sob died in his throat. He put his hands to his dry mouth; the back of it was wet with the sweat on his face.

White and shaking, he rose and walked steadily to the window. He looked out and down: there was no one, nothing.

He pulled the ragged cane chair to the sill, and sat there, silent and hopeless.

Soon big tears fell one by one, slowly, down his face. He understood now. His heart filled with sad, bitter grief, and brimmed over, and that was why the tears fell.

It was his hour that had come and opened the window.

He was cold, and as faint with hunger and heavy with thirst as though he had not put a glass to his lips or a bit to his mouth for days instead of for hours; but for all that, he did not feel ill, and he wondered and wondered why he was to die so soon, and he so well-made and handsome, and unmarried too, and now with girls as eager to have him as trouts for a May fly.

And after a time Rory began to dream of that great beauty that had troubled his dreams; and while he thought of it, and the beautiful, sweet wonder of the woman who had it, she whom he had seen sitting in the moonshine on the yellow rock, he heard again the laughing, crying, fall and lilt of that near and far song. But now it troubled him no more.

He stooped, and swung himself out of the window, and at the noise of his feet on the gravel a dog barked. He saw a white hound running swiftly across the pasture beyond him. It was gone in a moment, so swiftly did it run. He heard a second bark, and knew that it came from the old deerhound in the kennel. He wondered where that white hound he had seen came from, and where it was going, and it silent and white and swift as a moonbeam, with head low and in full sleuth.

He put his hand on the sill, and climbed into the room again; lifted the pipes which he or Donald Macalister had thrown down beside the mattress; and again, but stealthily, slipped out of the window.

Rory walked to the deerhound and spoke to it. The dog whimpered, but barked no more. When the piper walked on, and had gone about a score yards, the old hound threw back his head and gave howl upon howl, long and mournful. The cry went from stead to stead; miles and miles away the farm-dogs answered.

Perhaps it was to drown their noise that Rory began to finger his pipes, and at last let a long drone go out like a great humming cockchafer on the blue frosty stillness of the night. The crofters at Moor Edge heard his pibroch as he walked swiftly along the road that leads to

Dalmonadh Moor. Some thought it was uncanny; some that one of the pipers had lost his way, or made an early start; one or two wondered if Rory MacAlpine were already on the move, like a hare that could not be long in one form.

The last house was the gamekeeper's, at Dalmonadh Toll, as it was still called. Duncan Grant related next day that he was wakened by the skreigh of the pipes, and knew them for Rory MacAlpine's by the noble, masterly fashion in which drone and chanter gave out their music, and also because that music was the strong, wild, fearsome reel that Rory had played last in the byres, that which he had called "The Reel of the Daughter of Ivor."

"At that," he added, each time he told the tale, "I rose and opened the window, and called to MacAlpine. 'Rory,' I cried, 'is that you?'

"'Ay,' he said, stopping short, an' giving the pipes a lilt. 'Ay, it's me an' no other, Duncan Grant.'

"'I thought ye would be sleeping sound at Dalibrog?'

"But Rory made no answer to that, and walked on. I called to him in the English: 'Dinna go out on the moor, Rory! Come in, man, an' have a sup o' hot porridge an' a mouthful with them.' But he never turned his head; an' as it was cold an' dark, I said to myself that doited fools must gang their ain gait, an' so turned an' went to my bed again, though I hadn't a wink so long as I could hear Rory playing."

But Duncan Grant was not the last man who heard "The Reel of the Daughter of Ivor."

A mile or more across Dalmonadh Moor the heather-set road forks. One way is a cartway to Balnaree; the other is the drover's way to Tom-na-shee and the hill countries beyond. It is up this, a mile from the fork, that the Yellow Moonrock rises like a great fang out of purple lips. Some say it is of granite, and some marble, and that it is an old cromlech of the forgotten days; others that it is an unknown substance, a meteoric stone believed to have fallen from the moon.

Not near the Moonrock itself, but five score yards or more away, and perhaps more ancient still, there is a group of three lesser fang-shaped boulders of trap, one with illegible runic writing or signs. These are familiar to some as the Stannin' Stanes; to others, who have the Gaelic, as the Stone Men, or simply as the Stones, or the Stones of

Dalmonadh. None knows anything certain of this ancient cromlech, though it is held by scholars to be of Pictish times.

Here a man known as Peter Lamont, though commonly as Peter the Tinker, an idle, homeless vagrant, had taken shelter from the hill-wind which had blown earlier in the night, and had heaped a bed of dry bracken. He was asleep when he heard the wail and hum of the pipes.

He sat up in the shadow of one of the Stones. By the stars he saw that it was still the black of the night, and that dawn would not be astir for three hours or more. Who could be playing the pipes in that lonely place at that hour?

The man was superstitious, and his fears were heightened by his ignorance of what the unseen piper played (and Peter the Tinker prided himself on his knowledge of pipe music) and by the strangeness of it. He remembered, too, where he was. There was not one in a hundred who would lie by night among the Stannin' Stanes, and he had himself been driven to it only by heavy weariness and fear of death from the unsheltered cold. But not even that would have made him lie near the Moonrock. He shivered as memories of wild stories rose ghastly one after the other.

The music came nearer. The tinker crawled forward, and hid behind the Stone next the path, and cautiously, under a tuft of bracken, stared in the direction whence the sound came.

He saw a tall man striding along in full Highland gear, with his face death-white in the moonshine, and his eyes glazed like those of a leistered salmon. It was not till the piper was close that Lamont recognised him as Rory MacAlpine.

He would have spoken—and gladly, in that lonely place, to say nothing of the curiosity that was on him—had it not been for those glazed eyes and that set, death-white face. The man was fëy. He could see that. It was all he could do not to keep away like a rabbit.

Rory MacAlpine passed him, and played till he was close on the Moonrock. Then he stopped, and listened, leaning forward as though straining his eyes to see into the shadow.

He heard nothing, saw nothing, apparently. Slowly he waved a hand across the heather.

Then suddenly the piper began a rapid talking. Peter the Tinker could not hear what he said, perhaps because his own teeth chattered with the fear that was on him. Once or twice Rory stretched his arms, as though he were asking something, as though he were pleading.

Suddenly he took a step or two forward, and in a loud, shrill voice cried:

"By Holy St. Bride, let there be peace between us, white woman!

"I do not fear you, white woman, because I too am of the race of Ivor:

"My father's father was the son of Ivor mhic Alpein, the son of Ivor the Dark, the son of Ivor Honeymouth, the son of Ruaridh, the son of Ruaridh the Red, of the straight, unbroken line of Ivor the King:

"I will do you no harm, and you will do me no harm, white woman:

"This is the Day of Bride, the day for the daughter of Ivor. It is Rory MacAlpine who is here, of the race of Ivor. I will do you no harm, and you will do me no harm:

"Sure, now, it was you who sang. It was you who sang. It was you who played. It was you who opened my window:

"It was you who came to me in a dream, daughter of Ivor. It was you who put your beauty upon me. Sure, it is that beauty that is my death, and I am hungering and thirsting for it."

Having cried thus, Rory stood, listening, like a crow on a furrow when it sees the wind coming.

The tinker, trembling, crept a little nearer. There was nothing, no one.

Suddenly Rory began singing in a loud, chanting, monotonous voice:

> "An diugh La' Bride
> Thig nighean Imhir as a chnoc,
> Cha bhean mise do nighean Imhir,
> 'S cha bhean Imhir dhomh."

> (To-day the day of Bride,
> The daughter of Ivor shall come from the knoll;
> I will not touch the daughter of Ivor,
> Nor shall the daughter of Ivor touch me.)

Then, bowing low, with fantastic gestures, and with the sweep of his plaid making a shadow like a flying cloud, he sang again:

> "La' Bride nam brig ban
> Thig an rigen ran a tom
> Cha bhoin mise ris an rigen ran,
> 'S cha bhoin an rigen ran ruim."

> (On the day of Bride of the fair locks,
> The noble queen will come from the hill;
> I will not molest the noble queen,
> Nor will the noble queen molest me.)

"An' I, too, Nighean Imhir," he cried in a voice more loud, more shrill, more plaintive yet, "will be doing now what our own great forbear did, when he made *tabhartas agus tuis* to you, so that neither he nor his seed for ever should die of you; an' I, too, Ruaridh MacDhonuill mhic Alpein, will make offering and incense." And with that Rory stepped back, and lifted the pipes, and flung them at the base of the Yellow Moonrock, where they caught on a jagged spar and burst with a great wailing screech that made the hair rise on the head of Peter the Tinker, where he crouched sick with the white fear.

"That for my *tabhartas*," Rory cried again, as though he were calling to a multitude; "an' as I've no *tuis,* an' the only incense I have is the smoke out of my pipe, take the pipe an' the tobacco too, an' it's all the smoke I have or am ever like to have now, an' as good incense too as any other, daughter of Ivor."

Suddenly Peter Lamout heard a thin, strange, curling, twisting bit of music, so sweet for all its wildness that cold and hunger went below his heart. It grew louder, and he shook with fear. But when he looked at Rory MacAlpine, and saw him springing to and fro in a dreadful reel, and snapping his fingers and flinging his arms up and down like flails, he could stand no more, but with a screech rose and turned across the heather, and fluttered and fell and fell and fluttered like a wounded snipe.

He lay still once, after a bad fall, for his breath was like a thistle-down blown this way and that above his head. It was on a heathery knoll, and he could see the Moonrock yellow-white in the moonshine.

The savage lilt of that jigging wild air still rang in his ears, with never a sweetness in it now, though when he listened it grew fair and lightsome, and put a spell of joy and longing in him. But he could see nothing of Rory.

He stumbled to his knees and stared. There was something on the road.

He heard a noise as of men struggling. But all he saw was Rory MacAlpine swaying and swinging, now up and now down; and then at last the piper was on his back in the road and tossing like a man in a fit, and screeching with a dreadful voice, "Let me go! let me go! Take your lips off my mouth! take your lips off my mouth!"

Then, abruptly, there was no sound but only a dreadful silence; till he heard a rush of feet, and heard the heather-sprigs break and crack, and something went past him like a flash of light.

With a scream he flung himself down the heather knoll, and ran like a driven hare till he came to the white road beyond the moor; and just as dawn was breaking, he fell in a heap at the byre-edge at Dalmonadh Toll, and there Duncan Grant found him an hour later, white and senseless still.

Neither Duncan Grant nor any one else believed Peter Lamont's tale, but at noon the tinker led a reluctant few to the Yellow Moonrock.

The broken pipes still hung on the jagged spar at the base. Half on the path and half on the heather was the body of Rory MacAlpine. He was all but naked to the waist, and his plaid and jacket were as torn and ragged as Lamont's own, and the bits were scattered far and wide. His lips were blue and swelled. In the hollow of his hairy, twisted throat was a single drop of black blood.

"It's an adder's bite," said Duncan Grant.

None spoke.

The Herdsman

I

On the night when Alan Carmichael with his old servant and friend, Ian M'Ian, arrived in Balnaree ("Baile'-na-Righ"), the little village wherein was all that Borosay had to boast of in the way of civic life, he could not disguise from himself that he was regarded askance.

Rightly or wrongly, he took this to be resentment because of his having wed (alas, he recalled, wed and lost) the daughter of the man who had killed Ailean Carmichael in a duel. So possessed was he by this idea, that he did not remember how little likely the islanders were to know anything of him or his beyond the fact that Ailean MacAlasdair Rhona had died abroad.

The trouble became more than an imaginary one when, on the morrow, he tried to find a boat for the passage to Rona. But for the Frozen Hand, as the triple-peaked hill to the south of Balnaree was called, Rona would have been visible; nor was it, with a fair wind, more than an hour's sail distant.

Nevertheless, he could detect in every one to whom he spoke a strange reluctance. At last he asked an old man of his own surname why there was so much difficulty.

In the island way, Sheumas Carmichael replied that the people on Elleray, the island adjacent to Rona, were unfriendly.

"But unfriendly at what?"

"Well, at this and at that. But for one thing, they are not having any dealings with the Carmichaels. They are all Macneils there, Macneils of Barra. There is a feud, I am thinking; though I know nothing of it; no, not I."

"But Sheumas mac Eachainn, you know well yourself that there are almost no Carmichaels to have a feud with! There are you and your brother, and there is your cousin over at Sgòrr-Bhan on the other side of Borosay. Who else is there?"

To this the man could say nothing. Distressed, Alan sought Ian and bade him find out what he could. He also was puzzled and uneasy. That some evil was at work could not be doubted, and that it was secret boded ill.

Ian was a stranger in Borosay because of his absence since boyhood; but, after all, Ian mac Iain mhic Dhonuill was to the islanders one of themselves; and though he came there with a man under a shadow (though this phrase was not used in Ian's hearing), that was not his fault.

And when he reminded them that for these many years he had not seen the old woman, his sister Giorsal; and spoke of her, and of their long separation, and of his wish to see her again before he died, there was no more hesitation, but only kindly willingness to help.

Within an hour a boat was ready to take the homefarers to the Isle of Caves, as Rona is sometimes called. Before the hour was gone, they, with the stores of food and other things, were slipping seaward out of Borosay Haven.

The moment the headland was rounded, the heights of Rona came into view. Great gaunt cliffs they are, precipices of black basalt; though on the south side they fall away in grassy declivities which hang a greenness over the wandering wave for ever sobbing round that desolate shore. But it was not till the Sgòrr-Dhu, a conical black rock at the south-east end of the island, was reached, that the stone keep, known as Caisteal-Rhona, came in sight.

It stands at the landward extreme of a rocky ledge, on the margin of a green *àiridh.* Westward is a small dark-blue sea loch, no more than a narrow haven. To the north-west rise precipitous cliffs; northward, above the green pasture and a stretch of heather, is a woodland belt of some three or four hundred pine-trees. It well deserves its poetic name of I-monair, as Aodh the Islander sang of it; for it echoes ceaselessly with wind and wave. If the waves dash against it from the south or east, a loud crying is upon the faces of the rocks; if from the north or north-east, there are unexpected inland silences, but amid the pines a continual voice. It is when the wind blows from the south-west, or the huge Atlantic billows surge out of the west, that Rona is given over to an indescribable tumult. Through the whole island goes the myriad echo of a continuous booming; and within this a sound as though waters were pouring through vast hidden conduits in the heart of every precipice, every rock, every boulder. This is because of the sea-arcades of which it consists, for from the westward the island has been honeycombed by the waves. No living man has ever traversed all those mysterious, winding sea-galleries. Many have perished in the attempt. In the olden days the Uisteans and Barrovians sought refuge there from the marauding Danes and other pirates out of Lochlin; and in the time when the last Scottish king took shelter in the west, many of his island followers found safety among these perilous arcades.

Some of them reach an immense height. These are filled with a pale green gloom which in fine weather, and at noon or toward sundown, becomes almost radiant. But most have only a dusky green obscurity, and some are at all times dark with a darkness that has seen neither sun nor moon nor star for unknown ages. Sometimes, there, a phosphorescent wave will spill a livid or a cold blue flame, and for a moment a vast gulf of dripping basalt be revealed; but day and night, night and day, from year to year, from age to age, that awful wave-clamant darkness is unbroken.

To the few who know some of the secrets of the passages, it is possible, except when a gale blows from any quarter but the north, to thread these dim arcades in a narrow boat, and so to pass from the Hebrid Seas to the outer Atlantic. But for the unwary there might well be no return; for in that maze of winding galleries and sea-washed, shadowy arcades, confusion is but another name for death. Once bewildered, there is no hope; and the lost adventurer will remain there idly drifting from barren passage to passage, till he perish of hunger and thirst, or, maddened by the strange and appalling gloom and the unbroken silence—for there the muffled voice of the sea is no more than a whisper—leap into the green waters which for ever slide stealthily from ledge to ledge.

Now, as Alan approached his remote home, he thought of these death-haunted corridors, avenues of the grave, as they are called in the "Cumha Fhir-Mearanach Aonghas mhic Dhonuill"—the Lament of mad Angus Macdonald.

When at last the unwieldy brown coble sailed into the little haven, it was to create unwonted excitement among the few fishermen who put in there frequently for bait. A group of eight or ten was upon the rocky ledge beyond Caisteal-Rhona, among them the elderly woman who was sister to Ian mac Iain.

At Alan's request, Ian went ashore in advance in a small punt. He was to wave his hand if all were well, for Alan could not but feel apprehensive on account of the strange ill-will that had shown itself at Borosay.

It was with relief that he saw the signal when, after Ian had embraced his sister, and shaken hands with all the fishermen, he had explained that the son of Ailean Carmichael was come out of the south, and had come to live a while at Caisteal-Rhona.

All there uncovered and waved their hats. Then a shout of welcome went up, and Alan's heart was glad. But the moment he had set foot on land he saw a startled look come into the eyes of the fishermen—a look that deepened swiftly into one of aversion, almost of fear.

One by one the men moved away, awkward in their embarrassment. Not one came forward with outstretched hand, or said a word of welcome.

At first amazed, then indignant, Ian reproached them. They received his words in shamed silence. Even when with a bitter tongue he taunted them, they answered nothing.

"Giorsal," said Ian, turning in despair to his sister, "is it madness that you have?"

But even she was no longer the same. Her eyes were fixed upon Alan with a look of dread, and indeed of horror. It was unmistakable, and Alan himself was conscious of it with a strange sinking of the heart. "Speak, woman!" he demanded. "What is the meaning of this thing? Why do you and these men look at me askance?"

"God forbid!" answered Giorsal Macdonald with white lips; "God forbid that we look at the son of Ailean Carmichael askance. But—"

"But what?"

With that the woman put her apron over her head and moved away, muttering strange words.

"Ian, what is this mystery?"

"How am I for knowing, Alan mac Ailean? It is all a darkness to me also. But I will be finding that out soon."

That, however, was easier for Ian to say than to do. Meanwhile, the brown coble tacked back to Borosay, and the fisherman sailed away to the Barra coasts, and Alan and Ian were left solitary in their wild and remote home.

But in that very solitude Alan found healing. From what Giorsal hinted, he came to believe that the fishermen had experienced one of those strange dream-waves which, in remote isles, occur at times, when whole communities will be wrought by the self-same fantasy. When day by day went past, and no one came near, he at first was puzzled, and even resentful; but this passed, and soon he was glad to be alone. Ian, however, knew that there was another cause for the inexplicable aversion that had been shown. But he was silent, and kept a patient watch for the hour that the future held in its shroud. As for Giorsal, she was dumb; but no more looked at Alan askance.

And so the weeks went. Occasionally a fishing smack came with the provisions, for the weekly despatch of which Alan had arranged at Loch Boisdale, and sometimes the Barra men put in at the haven, though they would never stay long, and always avoided Alan as much as was possible.

In that time Alan and Ian came to know and love their strangely beautiful island home. Hours and hours at a time they spent exploring the dim, green, winding sea-galleries, till at last they knew the chief arcades thoroughly.

They had even ventured into some of the narrow, snake-like inner passages, but never for long, because of the awe and dread these held, silent estuaries of the grave.

Week after week passed, and to Alan it was as the going of the grey owl's wing, swift and silent.

Then it was that, on a day of the days, he was suddenly stricken with a new and startling dread.

II

In the hour that this terror came upon him Alan was alone upon the high slopes of Rona, where the grass fails and the lichen yellows at close on a thousand feet above the sea.

The day had been cloudless since sunrise. The sea was as the single vast petal of an azure flower, all of one unbroken blue save for the shadows of the scattered isles and the slow-drifting mauve or purple of floating weed. Countless birds congregated from every quarter. Guillemots and puffins, cormorants and northern divers, everywhere darted, swam, or slept upon the listless ocean, whose deep breathing no more than lifted a league-long calm here and there, to lapse breathlike as it rose. Through the not less silent quietudes of air the grey skuas swept with curving flight, and the narrow-winged terns made a constant white shimmer. At remote altitudes the gannet motionlessly drifted. Oceanward the great widths of calm were rent now and again by the shoulders of the porpoises which followed the herring trail, their huge, black, revolving bodies looming large above the silent wave. Not a boat was visible anywhere; not even upon the most distant horizons did a brown sail fleck itself duskily against the skyward wall of steely blue.

In the great stillness which prevailed, the noise of the surf beating around the promontory of Aonaig was audible as a whisper; though even in that windless hour the confused rumour of the sea, moving through the arcades of the island, filled the hollow of the air overhead. Ever since the early morning Alan had moved under a strange gloom. Out of that golden glory of midsummer a breath of joyous life should have reached his heart, but it was not so. For sure, there is sometimes in the quiet beauty of summer an air of menace, a premonition of suspended force—a force antagonistic and terrible. All who have lived in these lonely isles know the peculiar intensity of this summer melancholy. No noise of wind, no prolonged season of untimely rains, no long baffling of mists in all the drear inclemencies of that remote region, can produce the same ominous and even paralysing gloom sometimes born of ineffable peace and beauty. Is it that in the human soul there is a mysterious kinship with the outer soul which we call Nature; and that in these few supreme hours which come at the full of the year, we are, sometimes, suddenly aware of the tremendous forces beneath and behind us, momently quiescent?

Determined to shake off this dejection, Alan wandered high among the upland solitudes. There a cool air moved always, even in the noons of August; and there, indeed, often had come upon him a deep peace. But whatsoever the reason, only a deeper despondency possessed him. An incident, significant in that mood, at that time, happened then. A few hundred yards away from where he stood, half hidden in a little glen where a fall of water tossed its spray among the shadows of rowan and birch, was the bothie of a woman, the wife of Neil MacNeill, a fisherman of Aonaig. She was there, he knew, for the summer pasturing; and even as he recollected this, he heard the sound of her voice as she sang somewhere by the burnside. Moving slowly toward the corrie, he stopped at a mountain ash which overhung a pool. Looking down, he saw the woman, Morag MacNeill, washing and peeling potatoes in the clear brown water. And as she washed and peeled, she sang an old-time shealing hymn of the Virgin-Shepherdess, of Michael the White, and of Columan the Dove. It was a song that, years ago, far away in Brittany, he had heard from his mother's lips. He listened now to every word of the doubly familiar Gaelic; and when Morag ended, the tears were in his eyes, and he stood for a while as one under a spell*—

"A Mhicheil mhin! nan steud geala,
 A choisin cios air Dragon fala,
 Air ghaol Dia 'us Mhic Muire,
 Sgaoil do sgiath oirnn than sinn uile,
 Sagoil do sgiath oirnn than sinn uile.

A Mhoire ghradhach! Mathair Uain-ghil,
 Cobhair oirnne, Oigh na h-uaisle;
 A rioghainn uai'reach! a bhuachaille nan treud!
 Cum ar cuallach cuartaich sinn le cheil,
 Cum ar cuallach cuartaich sinn le cheil.

---

*This hymn was taken down in the Gaelic and translated by Mr. Alexander Carmichael of South Uist.

A Chalum-Chille! chairdeil, chaoimh,
An ainm Athar, Mic, 'us Spioraid Naoimh,
Trid na Trithinn! trid na Triath!
Comraig sinne, gleidh ar trial,
Comraig sinne, gleidh ar trial.

Athair! A Mhic! A Spioraid Naoimh!
Bi 'eadh an Tri-Aon leinn, a la's a dh-oidhche!
'S air chul nan tonn, no air thaobh nan beann,
Bi 'dh ar Mathair leinn' 's bith a lamh fo'r ceann,
Bi 'dh ar Mathair leinn, 's bith a lamh fo'r ceann.

Thou gentle Michael of the white steed,
Who subdued the Dragon of blood,
For love of God and the Son of Mary,
Spread over us thy wing, shield us all!
Spread over us thy wing, shield us all!

Mary beloved! Mother of the White Lamb,
Protect us, thou Virgin of nobleness,
Queen of beauty! Shepherdess of the flocks!
Keep our cattle, surround us together,
Keep our cattle, surround us together.

Thou Columba, the friendly, the kind,
In name of the Father, the Son, and the Spirit Holy,
Through the Three-in-One, through the Three,
Encompass us, guard our procession,
Encompass us, guard our procession.

Thou Father! thou Son! thou Spirit Holy!
Be the Three-in-One with us day and night.
And on the crested wave, or on the mountain-side.
Our Mother is there, and her arm is under our head,
Our Mother is there, and her arm is under our head."

Alan found himself repeating whisperingly, and again and again—

"Bi 'eadh an Tri-Aon leinn, a la's a dh-oidhche!
'S air chul nan tonn, no air thaobh nam beann."

Suddenly the woman glanced upward, perhaps because of the shadow that moved against the green bracken below. With a startled gesture she sprang to her feet. Alan looked at her kindly, saying, with a smile, "Sure, Morag nic Tormod, it is not fear you need be having of one who is your friend." Then, seeing that the woman stared at him with something of terror as well as surprise, he spoke to her again.

"Sure, Morag, I am no stranger that you should be looking at me with those foreign eyes." He laughed as he spoke, and made as though he were about to descend to the burnside. Unmistakably, however, the woman did not desire his company. He saw this, with the pain and bewilderment which had come upon him whenever the like happened, as so often it had happened since he had come to Rona.

"Tell me, Morag MacNeill, what is the meaning of this strangeness that is upon you? Why do you not speak? Why do you turn away your head?"

Suddenly the woman flashed her black eyes upon him.

"Have you ever heard of *am Buachaill Bàn–am Buachaill Buidhe?*"

He looked at her in amaze. *Am Buachaill Bàn!* . . . The fair-haired Herdsman, the yellow-haired Herdsman! What could she mean? In days gone by, he knew, the islanders, in the evil time after Culloden, had so named the fugitive Prince who had sought shelter in the Hebrides; and in some of the runes of an older day still the Saviour of the World was sometimes so called, just as Mary was called *Bhuachaile man treud*–Shepherdess of the Flock. But it could be no allusion to either of these that was intended.

"Who is the Herdsman of whom you speak, Morag?"

"Is it no knowledge you have of him at all, Alan MacAilean?"

"None. I know nothing of the man, nothing of what is in your mind. Who is the Herdsman?"

"You will not be putting evil upon me because that you saw me here by the pool before I saw you?"

"Why should I, woman? Why do you think that I have the power of the evil eye? Sure, I have done no harm to you or yours, and wish none. But if it is for peace to you to know it, it is no evil I wish you, but only good. The Blessing of Himself be upon you and yours and upon your house!"

The woman looked relieved, but still cast her furtive gaze upon Alan, who no longer attempted to join her.

"I cannot be speaking the thing that is in my mind, Alan MacAilean. It is not for me to be saying that thing. But if you have no knowledge of the Herdsman, sure it is only another wonder of the wonders, and God has the sun on that shadow, to the Stones be it said."

"But tell me, Morag, who is the Herdsman of whom you speak?"

For a minute or more the woman stood regarding him intently. Then slowly, and with obvious reluctance, she spoke—

"Why have you appeared to the people upon the isles, sometimes by moonlight, sometimes by day or in the dusk, and have foretold upon one and all who dwell here black gloom and the red flame of sorrow? Why have you, who are an outcast because of what lies between you and another, pretended to be a messenger of the Son—ay, for sure, even, God forgive you, to be the Son Himself?"

Alan stared at the woman. For a time he could utter no word. Had some extraordinary delusion spread among the islanders, and was there in the insane accusation of this woman the secret of that which had so troubled him?

"This is all an empty darkness to me, Marag. Speak more plainly, woman. What is all this madness that you say? When have I spoken of having any mission, or of being other than I am? When have I foretold evil upon you or yours, or upon the isles beyond? What man has ever dared to say that Alan MacAilean of Rona is an outcast? And what sin is it that lies between me and another of which you know?"

It was impossible for Morag MacNeill to doubt the sincerity of the man who spoke to her. She crossed herself, and muttered the words of a *seun* for the protection of the soul against the demon powers. Still, even while she believed in Alan's sincerity, she could not reconcile it with that terrible and strange mystery with which rumour had filled her ears. So, having nothing to say in reply to his eager questions, she cast down her eyes and kept silence.

"Speak, Morag, for Heaven's sake! Speak if you are a true woman; you that see a man in sore pain, in pain, too, for that of which he knows nothing, and of the ill of which he is guiltless!"

But, keeping her face averted, the woman muttered simply, "I have no more to say." With that she turned and moved slowly along the pathway which led from the pool to her hillside bothie.

With a sigh, Alan walked slowly away. What wonder, he thought, that deep gloom had been upon him that day? Here, in the woman's mysterious words, was the shadow of that shadow.

Slowly, brooding deep over what he had heard, he crossed the Monadh-nan-Con, as the hill-tract there was called, till he came to the rocky wilderness known as the Slope of the Caverns.

There for a time he leaned against a high boulder, idly watching a few sheep nibbling the short grass which grew about some of the many caves which opened in slits or wide hollows. Below and beyond he saw the pale blue silence of the sea meet the pale blue silence of the sky; south-westward, the grey film of the coast of Ulster; westward, again the illimitable vast of sea and sky, infinitudes of calm, as though the blue silence of heaven breathed in that one motionless wave, as though that wave sighed and drew the horizons to its heart. From where he stood he could hear the murmur of the surge whispering all round the isle; the surge that, even on days of profound stillness, makes a murmurous rumour among the rocks and shingle of the island shores. Not upon the moor-side, but in the blank hollows of the eaves around him, he heard, as in gigantic shells, the moving of a strange and solemn rhythm: wave-haunted shells indeed, for the echo that was bruited from one to the other came from beneath, from out of those labyrinthine passages and dim, shadowy sea-arcades, where among the melancholy green glooms the Atlantic waters lose themselves in a vain wandering.

For long he leaned there, revolving in his mind the mystery of Morag MacNeill's words. Then, abruptly, the stillness was broken by the sound of a dislodged stone. So little did he expect the foot of fellow-man, that he did not turn at what he thought to be the slip of a sheep. But when upon the slope of the grass, a little way beyond where he stood, a dusky blue shadow wavered fantastically, he swung round with a sudden instinct of dread.

And this was the dread which, after these long weeks since he had come to Rona, was upon Alan Carmichael.

For there, standing quietly by another boulder, at the mouth of another cave, was a man in all appearance identical with himself. Looking at this apparition, he beheld one of the same height as himself, with hair of the same hue, with eyes the same and features the same, with the same carriage, the same smile, the same expression. No, there, and there alone, was any difference.

Sick at heart, Alan wondered if he looked upon his own wraith. Familiar with the legends of his people, it would have been no strange thing to him that there, upon the hillside, should appear the wraith of himself. Had not old Ian McIain—and that, too, though far away in a strange land—seen the death of his mother moving upward from her feet to her knees, from her knees to her waist, from her waist to her neck, and, just before the end, how the shroud darkened along the face until it hid the eyes? Had he not often heard from her, from Ian, of the second self which so often appears beside the living when already the shadow of doom is upon him whose hours are numbered? Was this, then, the reason of what had been his inexplicable gloom? Was he indeed at the extreme of life? Was his soul amid shallows, already a rock upon a blank, inhospitable shore? If not, who or what was this second self which leaned there negligently, looking at him with scornful smiling lips, but with intent, unsmiling eyes?

Slowly there came into his mind this thought: How could a phantom, that was itself intangible, throw a shadow upon the grass, as though it were a living body? Sure, a shadow there was indeed. It lay between the apparition and himself. A legend heard in boyhood came back to him; instinctively he stooped and lifted a stone and flung it midway into the shadow.

"Go back into the darkness," he cried, "if out of the darkness you came; but if you be a living thing, put out your hands!"

The shadow remained motionless. When Alan looked again at his second self, he saw that the scorn which had been upon the lips was now in the eyes also. Ay, for sure, scornful silent laughter it was that lay in those cold wells of light. No phantom that; a man he, even as Alan himself. His heart pulsed like that of a trapped bird, but with the spoken word his courage came back to him.

"Who are you?" he asked, in a voice strange even in his own ears.

"*Am Buachaill,*" replied the man in a voice as low and strange. "I am the Herdsman."

A new tide of fear surged in upon Alan. That voice, was it not his own? that tone, was it not familiar in his ears? When the man spoke, he heard himself speak; sure, if he were *Am Buachaill Bàn,* Alan, too, was the Herdsman, though what fantastic destiny might be his was all unknown to him.

"Come near," said the man, and now the mocking light in his eyes was wild as cloudfire—"come near, oh *Buachaill Bàn!"*

With a swift movement, Alan sprang forward; but as he leaped, his foot caught in a spray of heather, and he stumbled and fell. When he rose, he looked in vain for the man who had called him. There was not a sign, not a trace of any living being. For the first few moments he believed it had all been a delusion. Mortal being did not appear and vanish in that ghostly way. Still, surely he could not have mistaken the blank of that place for a speaking voice, or out of nothingness have fashioned the living phantom of himself? Or could he? With that, he strode forward and peered into the wide arch of the cavern by which the man had stood. He could not see far into it; but so far as it was possible to see, he discerned neither man nor shadow of man, nor anything that stirred; no, not even the gossamer bloom of a beàrnan-bride, that grew on a patch of grass a yard or two within the darkness, had lost one of its delicate filmy spires. He drew back, dismayed. Then, suddenly, his heart leaped again, for beyond all question, all possible doubt, there, in the bent thyme, just where the man had stood, was the imprint of his feet. Even now the green sprays were moving forward.

III

An hour passed, and Alan Carmichael had not moved from the entrance to the cave. So still was he that a ewe, listlessly wandering in search of cooler grass, lay down after a while, drowsily regarding him with her amber-coloured eyes. All his thought was upon the mystery of what he had seen. No delusion this, he was sure. That was a man whom he had seen. But who could he be? On so small an island, inhabited by less than a score of crofters, it was scarcely possible for one to live for many weeks and not know the name and face of every soul. Still, a stranger might have come. Only, if this were so, why should he call himself the Herdsman? There was but one herdsman on Rona and he Angus MacCormic, who lived at Einaval on the north side. In these outer isles, the shepherd and the herdsman are appointed by the community, and no man is allowed to be one or the other at will, any more than to be a *maor*. Then, too, if this man were indeed herdsman, where was his *iomair-ionailtair,* his browsing tract? Looking round him, Alan could perceive nowhere any fitting pasture. Surely no herdsman would be content with such an *iomair a bhuachaill*—rig of the herdsman—as that rocky wilderness where the soft green grass grew in patches under this or that boulder, on the sun side of this or that rocky ledge. Again, he had given no name, but called himself simply *Am Buachaill.* This was how the woman Morag had spoken; did she indeed mean this very man? and if so, what lay in her words? But far beyond all other bewilderment for him was that strange, that indeed terrifying likeness to himself—a likeness so absolute, so convincing, that he knew he might himself easily have been deceived, had he beheld the apparition in any place where it was possible that a reflection could have misled him.

Brooding thus, eye and ear were both alert for the faintest sight or sound. But from the interior of the cavern not a breath came. Once, from among the jagged rocks high on the west slope of Ben Einaval, he fancied he heard an unwonted sound—that of human laughter, but laughter so wild, so remote, so unmirthful, that fear was in his heart. It could not be other than imagination, he said to himself; for in that lonely place there was none to wander idly at that season, and none who, wandering, would laugh there solitary.

It was with an effort that Alan at last determined to probe the mystery. Stooping, he moved cautiously into the cavern, and groped his way along the narrow passage which led, as he thought, into another larger cave. But this proved to be one of the innumerable blind ways which intersect the honeycombed slopes of the Isle of Caves. To wander far in these lightless passages would be to track death. Long ago the piper whom the Prionnsa-Bàn, the Fair Prince, loved to hear in his exile—he that was called Rory M'Vurich—penetrated one of the larger hollows to seek there for a child that had idly wandered into the dark. Some of the clansmen, with the father and mother of the little one, waited at the entrance to the cave. For a time there was silence; then, as agreed upon, the sound of the pipes was heard, to which a man named Lachlan M'Lachlan replied from the outer air. The skirl of the pipes within grew fainter and fainter. Louder and louder Lachlan played upon his chanter; deeper and deeper grew the wild moaning of the drone; but for all that, fainter and fainter waned the sound of the pipes of Rory M'Vurich. Generations have come and gone upon the isle, and still no man has heard the returning air which Rory was to play. He may have found the little child, but he never found his backward path, and in the gloom of that honeycombed hill he and the child and the music of the pipes lapsed into the same stillness. Remembering this legend, familiar to him since his boyhood, Alan did not dare to venture further. At any moment, too, he knew he might fall into one of the crevices which opened into the sea-corridors hundreds of feet below. Ancient rumour had it that there were mysterious passages from the upper heights of Ben Einaval which led into the heart of this perilous maze. But for a time he lay still, straining every sense. Convinced at last that the man whom he sought had evaded all possible quest, he turned to regain the light. Brief way as he had gone, this was no easy thing to do. For a few moments, indeed, Alan lost his self-possession when he found a uniform dusk about him, and could not discern which of the several branching narrow corridors was that by which he had come. But following the greener light, he reached the cave, and soon, with a sigh of relief, was upon the sun-sweet warm earth again.

How more than ever beautiful the world seemed! how sweet to the eyes were upland and cliff, the wide stretch of ocean, the flying birds, the sheep grazing on the scanty pastures, and, above all, the homely blue smoke curling faintly upward from the fisher crofts on the headland east of Aonaig!

Purposely he retraced his steps by the way of the glen: he would see the woman Morag MacNeill again, and insist on some more explicit word. But when he reached the burnside once more, the woman was not there. Possibly she had seen him coming, and guessed his purpose; half he surmised this, for the peats in the hearth were brightly aglow, and on the hob beside them the boiling water hissed in a great iron pot wherein were potatoes. In vain he sought, in vain called. Impatient, he walked around the bothie and into the little byre beyond. The place was deserted. This, small matter as it was, added to his disquietude. Resolved to sift the mystery, he walked swiftly down the slope. By the old shealing of Cnoc-na-Monie, now forsaken, his heart leaped at sight of Ian coming to meet him.

When they met, Alan put his hands lovingly on the old man's shoulders, and looked at him with questioning eyes. He found rest and hope in those deep pools of quiet light, whence the faithful love rose comfortingly to meet his own yearning gaze.

"What is it, Alan-mo-ghray; what is the trouble that is upon you?"

"It is a trouble, Ian, but one of which I can speak little, for it is little I know."

"Now, now, for sure you must tell me what it is."

"I have seen a man here upon Rona whom I have not seen or met before, and it is one whose face is known to me, and whose voice too, and one whom I would not meet again."

"Did he give you no name?"

"None."

"Where did he come from? Where did he go to?"

"He came out of the shadow, and into the shadow he went."

Ian looked steadfastly at Alan, his wistful gaze searching deep into his unquiet eyes, and thence from feature to feature of the face which had become strangely worn of late.

But he questioned no further.

"I, too, Alan MacAilean, have heard a strange thing to-day. You know old Marsail Macrae? She is ill now with a slow fever, and she thinks that the shadow which she saw lying upon her hearth last Sabbath, when nothing was there to cause any shadow, was her own death, come for her, and now waiting there. I spoke to the old woman, but she would not have peace, and her eyes looked at me.

"'What will it be now, Marsail?' I asked.

"'Ay, ay, for sure,' she said, 'it was I who saw you first.'

"'Saw me first, Marsail?'

"'Ay, you and Alan MacAilean.'

"'When and where was this sight upon you?'

"'It was one month before you and he came to Rona.'

"I asked the poor old woman to be telling me her meaning. At first I could make little of what was said, for she muttered low, an' moved her head this way and that, and moaned like a stricken ewe. But on my taking her hand, she looked at me again, and then told me this thing—

"'On the seventh day of the month before you came—and by the same token it was on the seventh day of the month following that you and Alan McAilean came to Caisteal-Rhona—I was upon the shore at Aonaig, listening to the crying of the wind against the great cliff of Biola-creag. With me were Ruaridh Macrae and Neil MacNeill, Morag Mac-Neill, and her sister Elsa; and we were singing the hymn for those who were out on the wild sea that was roaring white against the cliffs of Berneray, for some of our people were there, and we feared for them. Sometimes one sang, and sometimes another. And sure, it is remembering I am, how, when I had called out with my old wailing voice—

"'Bi 'eadh an Tri-aon leinn, a la's a dh-oidche;
'S air chul nan tonn, A Mhoire ghradhach!

(Be the Three-in-One with us day and night;
And on the crested wave, O Mary Belovëd!)

"'Now when I had just sung this, and we were all listening to the sound of it caught by the wind and blown up against the black face of Biola-creag, I saw a boat come sailing into the haven. I called out to those about me, but they looked at me with white faces, for no boat was there, and it was a rough, wild sea it was in that haven.

"'And in that boat I saw three people sitting; and one was you, Ian MacIain, and one was Alan MacAilean, and one was a man who had his face in shadow, and his eyes looked into the shadow at his feet. I saw you clear, and told those about me what I saw. And Seumas MacNeill, him that is dead now, and brother to Neil here at Aonaig, he said to me, "Who was that whom you saw walking in the dusk the night before last"—"Ailean MacAlasdair Carmichael," answered one at that. Seumas muttered, looking at those about him, "Mark what I say, for it is a true thing—that Ailean Carmichael of Rona is dead now, because Marsail saw him walking in the dusk when he was not upon the island; and now, you Neil, and you Rory, and all of you, will be for thinking with me that one of the men in the boat whom Marsail sees now will be the son of him who has changed."

"'Well, well, it is a true thing that we each of us thought that thought, but when the days went and nothing more came of it, the memory of the seeing went too. Then there came the day when the coble of Aulay MacAulay came out of Borosay into Caisteal-Rhona haven. Glad we were to see your face again, Ian McIain, and to hear the sob of joy coming out of the heart of Giorsal your sister; but when you and Alan MacAilean came on shore, it was my voice that then went from mouth to mouth, for I whispered to Morag MacNeill who was next me that you were the men I had seen in the boat.'

"Well, after that," Ian added, with a grave smile, "I spoke gently to old Marsail, and told her that there was no evil in that seeing, and that for sure it was nothing at all, at all, to see two people in a boat, and nothing coming of that, save happiness for those two, and glad content to be here.

"Marsail looked at me with big eyes.

"But when I asked her what she meant by that, she would say no more. No asking of mine would bring the word to her lips, only she shook her head and kept her gaze from my face. Then, seeing that it was useless, I said to her—

"'Marsail, tell me this: Was this sight of yours the sole thing that made the people here on Rona look askance at Alan MacAilean?'

"For a time she stared at me with dim eyes, then suddenly she spoke—

"'It is not all.'

"'Then what more is there, Marsail Macrae?'

"'That is not for the saying. I have no more to say. Let you, or Alan MacAilean, go elsewhere. That which is to be, will be. To each his own end.'

"'Then be telling me this now at least,' I asked: 'is there danger for him or me in this island?'

"But the poor old woman would say no more, and then I saw a swoon was on her."

After this, Alan and Ian walked slowly home together, both silent, and each revolving in his mind as in a dim dusk that mystery which, vague and unreal at first, had now become a living presence, and haunted them by day and night.

IV

"In the shadow of pain, one may hear the footsteps of joy." So runs a proverb of old.

It was a true saying for Alan. That night he lay down in pain, his heart heavy with the weight of a mysterious burden. On the morrow he woke blithely to a new day—a day of absolute beauty. The whole wide wilderness of ocean was of living azure, aflame with gold and silver. Around the promontories of the isles the brown-sailed fishing-boats of Barra and Berneray, of Borosay and Seila, moved blithely hither and thither. Everywhere the rhythm of life pulsed swift and strong. The first sound which had awakened Alan was of a loud singing of fishermen who were putting out from Aonaig. The coming of a great shoal of mackerel had been signalled, and every man and woman of the near isles was alert for the take. The watchers had known it by the swift congregation of birds, particularly the gannets and skuas. And as the men pulled at the oars, or hoisted the brown sails, they sang a snatch of an old-world tune, still chanted at the first coming of the birds when spring-tide is on the flow again—

> "Bui' cheas dha 'n Ti thaine na Gugachan
> Thaine's na h-Eoin-Mhora cuideriu,
> Cailin dugh ciaru bo's a chro;
> Bo dhonn! bo dhonn! bo dhonn bheadarrach!
> Bo dhonn a ruin a bhlitheadh am baine dhuit
> Ho ro! mo gheallag! ni gu rodagach!
> Cailin dugh ciaru bo's a chro—
> Na h-eoin air tighinn! cluinneam an ceol!"

> (Thanks to the Being, the Gannets have come,
> Yes! and the Great Auks along with them.
> Dark-haired girl!—a cow in the fold!
> Brown cow! brown cow! brown cow, beloved ho!
> Brown cow! my love! the milker of milk to thee!
> Ho ro! my fair-skinned girl—a cow, in the fold,
> And the birds have come!—glad sight, I see!)

Eager to be of help, Ian put off in his boat, and was soon among the fishermen, who in their new excitement were forgetful of all else than that the mackerel were come, and that every moment was precious. For the first time Ian found himself no unwelcome comrade. Was it, he wondered, because that, there upon the sea, whatever of shadow dwelled about him, or rather about Alan MacAilean, on the land, was no longer visible.

All through that golden noon he and the others worked hard. From isle to isle went the chorus of the splashing oars and splashing nets; of the splashing of the fish and the splashing of gannets and gulls; of the splashing of the tide leaping blithely against the sun-dazzle, and the illimitable rippling splash moving out of the west;—all this blent with the loud, joyous cries, the laughter, and the hoarse shouts of the men of Barra and the adjacent islands. It was close upon dusk before the Rona boats put into the haven of Aonaig again; and by that time none was blither than Ian MacIain, who in that day of happy toil had lost all the gloom and apprehension of the day before, and now returned to Caisteal-Rhona with lighter heart than he had known for long.

When, however, he got there, there was no sign of Alan. He had gone, said Giorsal, he had gone out in the smaller boat midway in the afternoon, and had sailed around to Aoidhu, the great scaur which ran out beyond the precipices at the south-west of Rona.

This Alan often did, and of late more and more often. Ever since he had come to the Hebrid Isles his love of the sea had deepened and had grown into a passion for its mystery and beauty. Of late, too, something impelled to a more frequent isolation, a deep longing to be where no eye could see and no ear hearken.

So at first Ian was in no way alarmed. But when the sun had set, and over the faint blue film of the Isle of Tiree the moon had risen, and still no sign of Alan, he became restless and uneasy. Giorsal begged him in vain to eat of the supper she had prepared. Idly he moved to and fro along the rocky ledge, or down by the pebbly shore, or across the green *àiridh,* eager for a glimpse of him whom he loved so well.

At last, unable longer to endure a growing anxiety, he put out in his boat, and sailed swiftly before the slight easterly breeze which had prevailed since moonrise. So far as Aoidhu, all the way from Aonaig, there was not a haven anywhere, nor even one of the sea caverns which honeycombed the isle beyond the headland. A glance, therefore, showed him that Alan had not yet come back that way. It was possible, though unlikely, that he had sailed right round Rona; unlikely, because in the narrow straits to the north, between Rona and the scattered islets known as the Innsemhara, strong currents prevailed, and particularly at the full of the tide, when they swept north-eastward dark and swift as a mill-race.

Once the headland was passed and the sheer precipitous westward cliffs loomed black out of the sea, he became more and more uneasy. As yet, there was no danger; but he saw that a swell was moving out of the west; and whenever the wind blew that way, the sea-arcades were filled with a lifting, perilous wave, Later, escape might be difficult, and often impossible. Out of the score or more great passages which opened between Aoidhu and Ardgorm, it was difficult to know into which to chance the search of Alan. Together they had examined all of them. Some twisted but slightly; others wound sinuously till the green, serpentine alleys, flanked by basalt walls hundreds of feet high, lost themselves in an indistinguishable maze.

But that which was safest, and wherein a boat could most easily make its way against wind or tide, was the huge, cavernous passage known locally as the Uaimh-nan-roin, the Cave of the Seals.

For this opening Ian steered his boat. Soon he was within the wide corridor. Like the great cave at Staffa, it was wrought as an aisle in some natural cathedral; the rocks, too, were columnar, and rose in flawless symmetry, as though graven by the hand of man. At the far end of this gigantic aisle, there diverges a long, narrow arcade, filled by day with the green shine of the water, and by night, when the moon is up, with a pale froth of light. It is one of the few where there are open gateways for the sea and the wandering light, and by its spherical shape almost the only safe passage in a season of heavy wind. Half-way along this arched arcade a corridor leads to a round cup-like cavern, midway in which stands a huge mass of black basalt, in shape suggestive of a titanic altar. Thus it must have impressed the imagination of the islanders of old; for by them, even in a remote day, it was called Teampull-Mara, the Temple of the Sea. Owing to the narrowness of the passage, and to the smooth, unbroken walls which rise sheer from the green depths into an invisible darkness, the Strait of the Temple is not one wherein to linger long, save in a time of calm.

Instinctively, however, Ian quietly headed his boat along this narrow way. When, silently, he emerged from the arcade, he could just discern the mass of basalt at the far end of the cavern. But there, seated in his boat, was Alan, apparently idly adrift, for one oar floated in the water alongside, and the other swung listlessly from the tholes.

His heart had a suffocating grip as he saw him whom he had come to seek. Why that absolute stillness, that strange, listless indifference? For a dreadful moment he feared death had indeed come to him in that lonely place where, as an ancient legend had it, a woman of old time had perished, and ever since had wrought death upon any who came thither solitary and unhappy.

But at the striking of the shaft of his oar against a ledge, Alan moved, and looked at him with startled eyes. Half rising from where he crouched in the stern, he called to him in a voice that had in it something strangely unfamiliar.

"I will not hear!" he cried. "I will not hear! Leave me! Leave me!"

Fearing that the desolation of the place had wrought upon his mind, Ian swiftly moved towards him, and the next moment his boat glided alongside. Stepping from the one to the other, he kneeled beside him.

"*Ailean mo caraid, Ailean-aghray,* what is it? What gives you dread? There is no harm here. All is well. Look! See, it is I, Ian—old Ian MacIain! Listen, *mo ghaoil;* do you not know me—do you not know who I am? It is I, Ian; Ian who loves you!"

Even in that obscure light he could clearly discern the pale face, and his heart smote him as he saw Alan's eyes turn upon him with a glance wild and mournful. Had he indeed succumbed to the sea madness which ever and again strikes into a terrible melancholy one here and there among those who dwell in the remote isles? But even as he looked, he noted another expression come into the wild strained eyes; and almost before he realised what had happened, Alan was on his feet and pointing with rigid arm.

For there, in that nigh unreachable and for ever unvisited solitude, was the figure of a man. He stood on the summit of the huge basalt altar, and appeared to have sprung from out the rock, or, himself a shadowy presence, to have grown out of the obscure unrealities of the darkness. Ian stared, fascinated, speechless.

Then with a spring he was on the ledge. Swift and sure as a wild-cat, he scaled the huge mass of the altar.

Nothing; no one! There was not a trace of any human being. Not a bird, not a bat; nothing. Moreover, even in that slowly blackening darkness, he could see that there was no direct connection between the summit or side with the blank, precipitous wall of basalt beyond. Overhead there was, so far as he could discern, a vault. No human being could have descended through that perilous gulf.

Was the island haunted? he wondered, as slowly he made his way back to the boat. Or had he been startled by some wild fantasy, and imagined a likeness where none had been? Perhaps even he had not really seen any one. He had heard of such things. The nerves can soon chase the mind into the shadow wherein it loses itself.

Or was Alan the vain dreamer? That, indeed, might well be. Mayhap he had heard some fantastic tale from Morag MacNeill, or from old Marsail Macrae; the islanders had *sgeul* after *sgeul* of a wild strangeness.

In silence he guided the boats back into the outer arcade, where a faint sheen of moonlight glistened on the water. Thence, in a few minutes, he oared that wherein he and Alan sat, with the other fastened astern, into the open.

When the moonshine lay full on Alan's face, Ian saw that he was thinking neither of himself nor of where he was. His eyes were heavy with dream.

What wind there was blew against their course, so Ian rowed unceasingly. In silence they passed once again the headland of Aoidhu; in silence they drifted past a single light gleaming in a croft near Aonaig—a red eye staring out into the shadow of the sea, from the room where the woman Marsail lay dying; and in silence their keels grided on the patch of shingle in Caisteal-Rhona haven.

For days thereafter Alan haunted that rocky, cavernous wilderness where he had seen the Herdsman.

It was in vain he had sought everywhere for some tidings of this mysterious dweller in those upland solitudes. At times he believed that there was indeed some one upon the island of whom, for inexplicable reasons, none there would speak; but at last he came to the conviction that what he had seen was an apparition, projected by the fantasy of overwrought nerves. Even from the woman Morag MacNeill, to whom he had gone with a frank appeal that won its way to her heart, he learned no more than that an old legend, of which she did not care to speak, was in some way associated with his own coming to Rona.

Ian, too, never once alluded to the mysterious incident of the green arcades which had so deeply impressed them both: never after Alan had told him that he had seen a vision.

But as the days passed, and as no word came to either of any unknown person who was on the island, and as Alan, for all his patient wandering and furtive quest, both among the upland caves and in the green arcades, found absolutely no traces of him whom he sought, the belief that he had been duped by his imagination deepened almost to conviction.

As for Ian, he, unlike Alan, became more and more convinced that what he had seen was indeed no apparition. Whatever lingering doubt he had was dissipated on the eve of the night when old Marsail Macrae died. It was dusk when word came to Caisteal-Rhona that Marsail felt the cold wind on the soles of her feet. Ian went to her at once, and it was in the dark hour which followed that he heard once more, and more fully, the strange story which, like a poisonous weed, had taken root in the minds of the islanders. Already from Marsail he had heard of the Prophet, though, strangely enough, he had never breathed word of this to Alan, not even when, after the startling episode of the apparition in the Teampull-Mara, he had, as he believed, seen the Prophet himself. But there in the darkness of the low, turfed cottage, with no light in the room save the dull red gloom from the heart of the smoored peats, Marsail, in the attenuated, remote voice of those who have already entered into the vale of the shadow, told him this thing, in the homelier Gaelic—

"Yes, Ian mac Iain-Bàn, I will be telling you this thing before I change. You are for knowing, sure, that long ago Uilleam, brother of him who was father to the lad up at the castle yonder, had a son? Yes, you know that, you say, and also that he was called Donnacha Bàn? No, mo-caraid, that is not a true thing that you have heard, that Donnacha Bàn went under the waves years ago. He was the seventh son, and was born under the full moon; 'tis Himself will be knowing whether that was for or against him. Of these seven none lived beyond childhood except the two youngest, Kenneth an' Donnacha. Kenneth was always frail as a February flower, but he lived to be a man. He and his brother never spoke, for a feud was between them, not only because that each was unlike the other, and the younger hated the older because through him he was the penniless one, but most because both loved the same woman. I am not for telling you the whole story now, for the breath in my body will soon blow out in the draught that is coming upon me; but this I will say, to you: darker and darker grew the gloom between these brothers. When Giorsal Macdonald gave her love to Kenneth, Donnacha disappeared for a time. Then, one day, he came back to Borosay, an' smiled quietly with his cold eyes when they wondered at his coming again. Now, too, it was noticed that he no longer had an ill-will upon his brother, but spoke smoothly with him and loved to be in his company. But to this day no one knows for sure what happened. For there was a gloaming when Donnacha Bàn came back alone in his sailing-boat. He and Kenneth had sailed forth, he said, to shoot seals in the sea-arcades to the west of Rona, but in these dark and lonely passages they had missed each other. At last he had heard Kenneth's voice calling for help, but when he had got to the place it was too late, for his brother had been seized with the cramps, and had sunk deep into the fathomless water. There is no getting a body again that sinks in these sea-galleries. The crabs know that.

"Well, this and much more was what Donnacha Bàn told to his people. None believed him; but what could any do? There was no proof; none had ever seen them enter the sea-caves together. Not that Donnacha Bàn sought in any way to keep back those who would fain know more. Not so; he strove to help to find the body. Nevertheless, none believed; an' Giorsal nic Dugall Mòr least of all. The blight of that sorrow went to her heart. She had death soon, poor thing! but before the cold greyness was upon her she told her father, and the minister that was there, that she knew Donnacha Bàn had murdered his brother. One might be saying these were the wild words of a woman; but, for sure, no one said that thing upon Borosay or Rona, or any of these isles. When all was done, the minister told what he knew, and what he thought, to the Lord of the South Isles, and asked what was to be put upon Donnacha Bàn. 'Exile for ever,' said the chief, 'or if he stays here, the doom of silence. Let no man or woman speak to him or give him food or drink, or give him shelter, or let his shadow cross his or hers.'

"When this thing was told to Donnacha Bàn Carmichael, he laughed at first; but as day after day slid over the rocks where all days fall, he laughed no more. Soon he saw that the chief's word was no empty word; and yet would not go away from his own place. He could not stay upon Borosay, for his father cursed him; and no man can stay upon the island where a father's curse moves this way and that, for ever seeking him. Then, some say a madness came upon him, and others that he took wildness to be his way, and others that God put upon him the shadow of loneliness, so that he might meet sorrow there and re-pent. Howsoever that may be, Donnacha Bàn came to Rona, and, by the same token, it was the year of the great blight, when the potatoes and the corn came to naught, and when the fish in the sea swam away from the isles. In the autumn of that year there was not a soul left on Rona except Giorsal and the old man Ian, her father, who had guard of Caisteal-Rhona for him who was absent. When, once more, years after, smoke rose from the crofts, the saying spread that Donnacha Bàn, the murderer, had made his home among the caves of the upper part of the isle. None knew how this saying rose, for he was seen of none. The last man who saw him—and that was a year later—was old Padruic M'Vurich the shepherd. Padruic said that, as he was driving his ewes across the north slope of Ben Einaval in the gloaming, he came upon a silent fig-ure seated upon a rock, with his chin in his hands, and his elbows on his knees—with the great, sad eyes of him staring at the moon that was lifting itself out of the sea. Padruic did not know who the man was. The shep-herd had few wits, poor man! and he had known, or remembered, little about the story of Donnacha Bàn Carmichael; so when he spoke to the man, it was as to a stranger. The man looked at him and said—

"'You are Padruic M'Vurich, the shepherd.'

"At that a trembling was upon old Padruic, who had the wonder that this stranger should know who and what he 'was.

"And who will you be, and forgive the saying?' he asked.

"'*Am Fàidh*—the Prophet,' the man said.

"'And what prophet will you be, and what is your prophecy?' asked Padruic.

"'I am here because I wait for what is to be, and that will be the coming of the Woman who is the Daughter of God.'

"And with that the man said no more, and the old shepherd went down through the gloaming, and, heavy with the thoughts that troubled him, followed his ewes down into Aonaig. But after that neither he nor any other saw or heard tell of the shadowy stranger; so that all upon Rona felt sure that Padruic had beheld no more than a vision. There were some who thought that he had seen the ghost of the outlaw Donnacha Bàn; and mayhap one or two who wondered if the stranger that had said he was a prophet was not Donnacha Bàn himself, with a madness come upon him; but at last these sayings went out to sea upon the wind, and men forgot. But, and it was months and months afterwards, an' three days before his own death, old Padruic M'Vurich was sitting in the sunset on the rocky ledge in front of his brother's croft, where then he was staying, when he heard a strange crying of seals. He thought little of that; only, when he looked closer, he saw, in the hollow of the wave hard by that ledge, a drifting body.

"*'Am Fàidh—Am Fàidh!'* he cried; 'the Prophet, the Prophet!'

"At that his brother and his brother's wife ran to see; but it was nothing that they saw. 'It would be a seal,' said Pòl M'Vurich; but at that Padruic had shook his head, and said no for sure, he had seen the face of the dead man, and it was of him whom he had met on the hillside, and that had said he was the Prophet who was waiting there for the second coming of God.

"And that is how there came about the echo of the thought that Donnacha Bàn had at last, after his madness, gone under the green wave and was dead. For all that, in the months which followed, more than one man said he had seen a figure high up on the hill. The old wisdom says that when God comes again, or the prophet who will come before, it will be as a herdsman on a lonely isle. More than one of the old people on Rona and Borosay remembered that *sgeul* out of the *Seanachas* that the tale-tellers knew. There were some who said that Donnacha Bàn had never been drowned at all, and that he was this Prophet, this Herdsman. Others would not have that saying at all, but believed that the wraith was indeed Am Buachaill Bàn, the Fair-haired Shepherd, who had come again to redeem the people out of their sorrow. There were even those who said that the Herdsman who haunted Rona was no other than Kenneth Carmichael himself, who had not died but had had the mind-dark there in the sea-caves where he had been lost, and there had come to the knowledge of secret things, and so was at last Am Fàidh Chriosd."

A great weakness came upon the old woman when she had spoken thus far. Ian feared that she would have breath for no further word; but after a thin gasping, and a listless fluttering of weak hands upon the coverlet, whereon her trembling fingers plucked aimlessly at the invisible blossoms of death, she opened her eyes once more, and stared in a dim questioning at him who sat by her bedside.

"Tell me," whispered Ian, "tell me, Marsail, what thought it is that is in your own mind?"

But already the old woman had begun to wander.

"For sure, for sure," she muttered, "*Am Fàidh . . . Am Fàidh . . .* an' a child will be born . . . the Queen of Heaven, an' . . . that will be the voice of Domhuill, my husband, I am hearing . . . an' dark it is, an' the tide comin' in . . . an'—"

Then, sure, the tide came in, and if in that darkness old Marsail Macrae heard any voice at all, it was that of Domhuill who years agone had sunk into the wild seas off the head of Barra.

An hour later Alan walked slowly under the cloudy night. All he had heard from Ian came back to him with a strange familiarity. Something of this, at least, he had known before. Some hints of this mysterious Herdsman had reached his ears. In some inexplicable way his real or imaginary presence there upon Rona seemed a pre-ordained thing for him.

He knew that the wild imaginings of the islanders had woven the legend of the Prophet, or of his mysterious message, out of the loom of the deep longing whereon is woven that larger tapestry, the shadow-thridden life of the island Gael. Laughter and tears, ordinary hopes and pleasures, and even joy itself, and bright gaiety, and the swift, spontaneous imaginations of susceptible natures—all this, of course, is to be found with the island Gael as with his fellows elsewhere. But every here and there are some who have in their minds the inheritance from the dim past of their race, and are oppressed as no other people are oppressed by the gloom of a strife between spiritual emotion and material facts. It is the brains of dreamers such as these which clear the mental life of the community; and it is in these brains are the mysterious looms which weave the tragic and sorrowful tapestries of Celtic thought. It were a madness to suppose that life in the isles consists of nothing but sadness or melancholy. It is not so, or need not be so, for the Gael is a creature of shadow and shine. But whatever the people is, the brain of the Gael hears a music that is sadder than any music there is, and has for its cloudy sky a gloom that shall not go; for the end is near, and upon the westernmost shores of these remote isles the voice of Celtic sorrow may be heard crying, *"Cha till, cha till, cha till mi tuille":* "I will return, I will return, I will return no more."

Alan knew all this well; and yet he too dreamed his dream—that, even yet, there might be redemption for the people. He did not share the wild hope which some of the older islanders held, that Christ Himself shall come again to redeem an oppressed race; but might not another saviour arise, another redeeming spirit come into the world? And if so, might not that child of joy be born out of suffering and sorrow and crime; and if so, might not the Herdsman be indeed a prophet, the Prophet of the Woman in whom God should come anew as foretold?

With startled eyes he crossed the thyme-set ledge whereon stood Caisteal-Rhona. Was it, after all, a message he had received, and was that which had appeared to him in that lonely cavern of the sea but a phantom of his own destiny? Was he himself, Alan Carmichael, indeed *Am Fàidh,* the predestined Prophet of the isles?

V

Ever since the night of Marsail's death, Ian had noticed that Alan no longer doubted, but that in some way a special message had come to him, a special revelation. On the other hand, he had himself swung further into his conviction that the vision he had seen in the cavern was, in truth, that of a living man. On Borosay, he knew, the fishermen believed that the *aonaran nan creag,* the recluse of the rocks, as commonly they spoke of him, was no other than Donnacha Bàn Carmichael, survived there through these many years, and long since mad with his loneliness and because of the burden of his crime.

But by this time the islanders had come to see that Alan MacAilean was certainly not Donnacha Bàn. Even the startling likeness no longer betrayed them in this way. The ministers and the priests on Berneray and Barra scoffed at the whole story, and everywhere discouraged the idea that Donnacha Bàn could still be among the living. But for the common belief that to encounter the Herdsman, whether the lost soul of Donnacha Bàn or indeed the strange phantom of the hills of which the old legends spoke, was to meet inevitable disaster, the islanders might have been persuaded to make such a search among the caves of Rona as would almost certainly have revealed the presence of any who dwelt therein.

But as summer lapsed into autumn, and autumn itself through its golden silences waned into the shadow of the equinox, a strange, brooding serenity came upon Alan. Ian himself now doubted his own vision of the mysterious Herdsman—if he indeed existed at all except in the imaginations of those who spoke of him either as the Buachaill Bàn, or as the *aonaran nan creag.* If a real man, Ian believed that at last he had passed away. None saw the Herdsman now; and even Morag MacNeill, who had often on moonlight nights been startled by the sound of a voice chanting among the upper solitudes, admitted that she now heard nothing unusual.

St. Martin's summer came at last, and with it all that wonderful, dreamlike beauty which bathes the isles in a flood of golden light, and draws over sea and land a veil of deeper mystery.

One late afternoon, Ian, returning to Caisteal-Rhona after an unexplained absence of several hours, found Alan sitting at a table. Spread before him were the sheets of one of the strange old Gaelic tales which he had ardently begun to translate. Alan lifted and slowly read the page or paraphrase which he had just laid down. It was after the homelier Gaelic of the *Eachdaireachd Challum mhic Cruimein.*

"And when that king had come to the island, he lived there in the shadow of men's eyes; for none saw him by day or by night, and none knew whence he came or whither he fared; for his feet were shod with silence, and his way with dusk. But men knew that he was there, and all feared him. Months, even years, tramped one on the heels of the other, and perhaps the king gave no sign, but one day he would give a sign; and that sign was a laughing that was heard somewhere, upon the lonely hills, or on the lonely wave, or in the heart of him who heard, And whenever the king laughed, he who heard would fare ere long from his fellows to join that king in the shadow. But sometimes the king laughed only because of vain hopes and wild imaginings, for upon these he lives as well as upon the strange savours of mortality."

That night Alan awakened Ian suddenly, and taking him by the hand made him promise to go with him on the morrow to the Team-pull-Mara.

In vain Ian questioned him as to why he asked this thing. All Alan would say was that he must go there once again, and with him, for he believed that a spirit out of heaven had come to reveal to him a wonder. Distressed by what he knew to be a madness, and fearful that it might prove to be no passing fantasy, Ian would fain have persuaded him against this intention. Even as he spoke, however, he realised that it might be better to accede to his wishes, and, above all, to be there with him, so that it might not be one only who heard or saw the expected revelation.

And it was a strange faring indeed, that which occurred on the morrow. At noon, when the tide was an hour turned in the ebb, they sailed westward from Caisteal-Rhona. It was in silence they made that strange journey together; for, while Ian steered, Alan lay down in the hollow of the boat, with his head against the old man's knees, and slept, or at least lay still with his eyes closed.

When at last they passed the headland and entered the first of the sea-arcades, Alan rose and sat beside him. Hauling down the now useless sale, Ian took an oar and, standing at the prow, urged the boat inward along the narrow corridor which led to the huge sea-cave of the Altar.

In the deep gloom—for even on that day of golden light and beauty the green air of the sea-cave was heavy with shadow—there was a deathly chill. What dull light there was came from the sheen of the green water which lay motionless along the black basaltic ledges. When at last the base of the Altar was reached, Ian secured the boat by a rope passed around a projecting spur, and then seated himself in the stern beside Alan.

"Tell me, Alan-a-ghaoil, what is this thing that you are thinking you will hear or see?"

Alan looked at him strangely for a while, but, though his lips moved, he said nothing.

"Tell me, my heart," Ian urged again, "who is it you expect to see or hear?"

"Am Buachaill Bàn," Alan answered, "the Herdsman."

For a moment Ian hesitated. Then, taking Alan's hand in his and raising it to his lips, he whispered in his ear—

"There is no Herdsman upon Rona. If a man was there who lived solitary, the *aonaran nan creag* is dead long since. What you have seen and heard has been a preying upon you of wild thoughts. Be thinking no more now of this vision."

"This man," Alan answered quietly, "is not Donnacha Bàn, but the Prophet of whom the people speak. He himself has told me this thing. Yesterday I was here, and he bade me come again. He spoke out of the shadow that is about the Altar, though I saw him not. I asked him if he were Donnacha Bàn, and he said 'No.' I asked him if he were *Am Fàidh,* and he said 'Yes.' I asked him if he were indeed an immortal spirit and herald of that which was to be, and he said 'Even so.'"

For a long while after this no word was spoken. The chill of that remote place began to affect Alan, and he shivered slightly at times. But more he shivered because of the silence, and because that he who had promised to be there gave no sign. Sure, he thought, it could not be all a dream; sure, the Herdsman would come again.

Then at last, turning to Ian, he said, "We must come on the morrow, for to-day he is not here."

"I will do what you ask, Alan-mo-ghaol."

But of a sudden Alan stepped on the black ledges at the base of the Altar, and slowly mounted the precipitous rock.

Ian watched him till he became a shadow in that darkness. His heart leaped when suddenly he heard a cry fall out of the gloom.

"Alan, Alan!" he cried, and a great fear was upon him when no answer came; but at last he heard him clambering slowly down the perilous slope of that obscure place. When he reached the ledge Alan stood still regarding him.

"Why do you not come into the boat?" Ian asked, terrified because of what he saw in Alan's eyes.

Alan looked at him with parted lips, his breath coming and going like that of a caged bird.

"What is it?" Ian whispered.

"Ian, when I reached the top of the Altar, and in the dim light that was there, I saw the dead body of a man lying upon the rock. His head was lain back so that the gleam from a crevice in the cliff overhead fell upon it. The man had been dead many hours. He is a man whose hair has been greyed by years and sorrow, but the man is he who is of my blood; he whom I resemble so closely; he that the fishermen call the hermit of the rocks; he that is the Herdsman."

Ian stared, with moving lips: then in a whisper he spoke—

"Would you be for following a herdsman who could lead you to no fold? This man is dead, Alan mac Alasdair; and it is well that you brought me here to-day. That is a good thing, and for sure God has willed it."

"It is not a man that is dead. It is my soul that lies there. It is dead. God called me to be His Prophet, and I hid in dreams. It is the end." And with that, and death staring out of his eyes, he entered the boat and sat down beside Ian.

"Let us go," he said, and that was all.

Slowly Ian oared the boat across the shadowy gulf of the cave, along the narrow passage, and into the pale green gloom of the outer cavern, wherein the sound of the sea made a forlorn requiem in his ears.

But the short November day was already passing to its end. All the sea westward was aflame with gold and crimson light, and in the great dome of the sky a wonderful radiance lifted above the paleness of the clouds, whose pinnacled and bastioned heights towered in the southwest.

A faint wind blew eastwardly. Raising the sail, Ian made it fast and then sat down beside Alan. But he, rising, moved along the boat to the mast, and leaned there with his face against the setting sun.

Idly they drifted onward. Deep silence lay between them; deep silence was all about them, save for the ceaseless, inarticulate murmur of the sea, the splash of low waves against the rocks of Rona, and the sigh of the surf at the base of the basalt precipices.

And this was their homeward sailing on that day of revelation: Alan, with his back against the mast, and his lifeless face irradiated by the light of the setting sun; Ian, steering, with his face in shadow.

APPENDIX

By the Yellow Moonrock [beginning]

I

When the word went through Strathraonull that the wife of Donald Macalister of Dalibrog had given birth to a child, there was rejoicing. Dalibrog himself was not so well pleased, for he had hoped that Morag his wife would have borne him a son; and as he was the most important man in the Strath, after the great Laird himself, he never doubted but that Morag would fulfil his trust in her. It was an ill thought, for him, that Seoras Macalister his brother ("an' him with such a starvin' big family behind him") should one day sit at Dalibrog, and care little whether or not the hill-rains were too heavy, whether some of the kye proved poor in milk, or if here or there a ewe or a lamb were lost. It was Seoras' way to care too little, or to say too little, about these things at the best of times; but if he were once at Dalibrog, out of that wet poor farm of his up in the hills, he would be glad every day of the days, and when he died the place would be worth less by a long way than it was now.

If only the lands of Dalibrog did not lie under entail, he could keep Seoras out. However, though Morag had failed this time, she would do better next. "It comes o' marrying a Mackenzie," he muttered to himself at times; "I never knew one of the breed yet that wouldn't be after doing just the very thing you wouldn't expect, and just because o' that same expecting."

So he made the best of it when he learned that his firstborn was a girl.

The Strath folk cared nothing about his hopes or disappointment. Their rejoicing was because there were to be festivities at Dalibrog House, and that every one from far and near was to be welcome. Donald Macalister had waited till he was forty before he married, and would not have changed his state then but that the fear of Seoras' big family was on him, for he loved Dalibrog better than kinship, or wife, or child.

The three great and as yet undivided and otherwise unfinished byres that had recently been added to the home farm—the model dairy it was already called, to the resentment of those whose dairies were painfully primitive—were to be filled with all who cared to come, and with meats and pastries and wine and beer and whisky enough to satisfy these, "and as many more again."

As the goings-on at Dalibrog fell on the popular day known throughout the Highlands as "La Fheill Bride" (the Feast-day or Festival of St. Bride or Bridget), the stir was the greater. In every shepherd-sheiling and hill-bothie to the glen-crofts and the big farmhouses, preparation of some kind was made. Among the good news which went from mouth to mouth, perhaps not the least welcome was that which told the coming of Rory M'Alpine the piper.

Every one knew Rory, and he was as welcome at each fireside along the Strath as he was at any hearth throughout the West, from the Cowal to the Torridons. There was no better piper than he, and, what was more, there was no one who had so great a store of old tales and new gossip; and he had a bad reputation, too, not for dishonesty, but for morals, though little evil against others was laid to him. "Let Rory beware o' the whisky, and let the girls beware o' Rory," had become a saying; with the result that the girls of the glens were over-curious, and that there was ever whisky and to spare for Piper Rory M'Alpine.

For more than a year, however, he had not set foot in the Strath. "Strathraonull may whistle," he said, "but the curlew's on the hill"—by which he meant that the Strath folk might look in vain for him or his pipes or tales.

For on the Hallowe'en of the preceding year Rory had been enthusiastic. That was all he would ever admit: "I had a great enthusiasm on me." There had been a big gathering at the manse of the Rev. Kenneth Maclellan to celebrate the marriage of his daughter Jessie to the son of Sir Hector MacInnes, a great laird over away from Strathraonull. Rory had played with all his genius (the words are his); he had told old tales, and invented others old and new, and had spread gossip with a splendid impartiality; and, in a word, from noon till sundown had proved beyond all doubt that Rory M'Alpine was quite the most important person present, after the bridegroom, and a good deal more entertaining. As for the bride, she meant well, but if she had not had a mighty big tocher she would never have got young Ewan MacInnes; so they said.

By sundown on that memorable day, however, Rory had become so puffed up with his own elation and the sound of continual laughing praise, that he had drunk at least thrice the great quantity he was accustomed to allow as his "measure." He said afterwards that the misfortune of that night came about through the meanness of the Reverend Kenneth, who had given him some whisky that Black Donald himself would have found a murthering poison; "for no gentleman," he added, "would get drunk all at once on good whisky," forgetting, no doubt, that six hours' preliminary appreciation was a fair allowance. Whatever the reason was, he lost his good sense and good manners, and while the Reverend Kenneth was at prayer in the schoolhouse (that had been got up as a ballroom for the wedding-party), Rory's pipes were heard coming near and nearer, jigging a blasphemous, merry dance; and then, while every one was trying to look solemn, the door swung open, and Rory himself strutted in, playing an old, wicked wedding-pibroch that was a shame there in that place given over to prayer and thanksgiving. Some smiled, some laughed, but most frowned or shook their heads with shocked reproving glances. The minister was sore angry, and at last let go his pulpit voice and shouted to the piper to take himself off.

"An' for why that?" cried Rory, stopping to take breath, and cocking his head on one side, and winking hard this way and that, as though he were in a company of shepherds and drovers in a mountain-dew cabin.

"Because we are decent folk praising the Lord, an' we want none o' your rant, Rory M'Alpine!"

"Hoots, Mr. Maclellan, we're a' men an' women the night. It's no' every night that a quean is bedded wi' a—"

"That'll do, ye sumph," shouted the minister angrily, "an' get out o' this at once, for it's shameless drunk you are, you and your pipes too."

But Rory only laughed at this. Then he threw back the pipes and tilted the chanter and let fly a long wailing screech; and in a minute or less the schoolhouse rang with the dancing, sweet, evil delight of "The Hare amongst the Corn." The tune was like a live thing, a leaping flame, and sprang this way and that, and laughed and screamed and jeered and mocked, and made men flush and stir, and the women grow white and nervous.

Suddenly two or three men, then half a dozen and more, put their arms round the waists of struggling, blushing girls; and a madness came upon every one there, and all kissed and hugged, and the younger ones swung to and fro in confused rough dance; while the minister, black in the face, thumped on the big Bible like Peter Mackechnie, the six-foot-four drummer down Fort William way, and Rory M'Alpine played an' played an' played till the veins stood out on his face, and his breath jerked like a jumping ewe at a gangway.

There is no saying what would have come of that tantarran (and evil enough came if all be true that's said, "forbye the shame of it in that place an' at that hour an' before the Lord," as Mr. Maclellan declared on the Sabbath that followed, when every one had bad headaches and stricken consciences) if Rory had not flung his pipes to the ground, and then danced on them with wild screeches and up-flung fists, and seized good Mistress Sarah, the minister's wife, and swung her this way and that in a touzled devil-may-care of a Highland reel, and had then kissed and hugged her with drunken amorous cries, and suddenly wept with loud hiccoughs and sobs, and then fallen like a wind-stricken scarecrow off its pole to lie in a shapeless, senseless heap at her feet.

Three elders and some young men carried Rory out, while Mr. Maclellan fanned his breathless, terrified wife with a hymn-book, and dried her scandalised tears with her new brown boa, and whispered blessed texts of Scripture and less holy words of marital exhortation.

The village-pond was not a score yards away, and they flung Rory into it, and John Macmillan the carpenter pitched the trampled broken pipes in after him; so that when, half sobered and panting for life, the piper struggled to his feet, and stood drenched and forlorn—"with all the enthusiasm out o' me," as he said afterwards—he appeared dripping and dishevelled with a shapeless mass over his head and shoulders, and two great prongs like horns sticking out: "for all the world like an awfu' beast in the Apocalypse," related, later, one of the elders to an understanding and sympathetic audience, who had their own associations with apocalyptic visions of the kind.

And out of all that came not only a cruel, heavy cold for Rory, and the shame of a preaching against him on the Sabbath, but the black looks of every lad and lass who had been led to sin because of his lawless bad music, and of every douce man and woman who wondered if the neighbours had seen anything forbye the common on "that awfu' night." He had no money, and his pipes were wrecked, and couldn't give out even the poor drone of a hymn, or a "Praise ye the Lord"; and he had his cruel cold on him, with hunger and a starving thirst.

He had slept that night at the warm side of a hayrick, but it was drizzly and drear chill when he woke at the greying. He looked sullenly at his drenched clothes and the tattered remnant of his pipes, and held the broken chanter in his hand, while he muttered black curses on those who lead innocent men into evil ways, and on drink in general, and whisky in particular, and, above all, on "that water o' mildew out of an old ancient ink-bottle," which Mr. Maclellan had given him; and cursed the minister, and all the folk in Strathraonull, with the coughing sickness to the cows and rot to the sheep, and a stake through the belly for that bitter misfit o' a man Macmillan who had ruined his pipes, and a black curse on the pipes themselves, and on the falling rain, and on the cold and hunger and bitter black thirst he had.

Then he sat down among the dry hay again, and tears ran down his face, because there was no pity in the world, and no God, and in his wet pockets never a pipeful of tobacco nor a match to light old cinders with for the whiff of a whiff.

He put his right hand to his breast to feel if his broken heart had still a beat to it, when his fingers touched something cold and hard. For a moment he dreamed God's mercy had left him a forgotten pipe, but the next he recognised a tin whistle he had bought three weeks before at a booth Glenshiel way, and had played on often since. He was in little mood for tin whistles or any other clamjaffry after what the pipes had led him to, but mechanically he began to blow a few dismal notes. Then an air came into the whistle and sang itself. It was like wild bees coming out of the heather, when the notes crept humming or singing or laughing out of the holes in the tin tube. Rory wondered what the air was. He played idly, and it came again. He knew it now; it was "O'er the hills and far away." While the drizzle soaked his stained rusty hair (red enough in the sunlight, or when he was talking and smiling before the peats, or playing reels in a barn to the flames of pine-torches), a shine came into his blue eyes. He played the sweet dreamy air three times. Then, with a sigh, he played a song he loved, "A' Chruinneag Ileach" (The Islay Maid), and put the tin flute on his knee when he had ended, and stared before him, with the wet in his blue eyes, while words of the song fell from his lips:—

> "Och, och mar tha mi! 's mi nam aonar
>
> .   .   .   .   .
>
> O sorrow upon me that I'm here so lonely,
> With black Despair with my heart in his grip:
> There's tears in my eyes for each drop from the skies,
> And my love is gone from me like vows from the lip."

Then he lifted the tin flute again, and played air upon air. And soon he forgot the heavy cold that was on him, and the chill and the empty belly and the bad thirst, and all the bitter evils of the world. He saw green glens waving in warm wind, and streams with fish splashing a whiteness over the running blue, and meadows filled with cattle gleaming white and red in the sunshine; or long fields of green corn or yellow wheat, lifting lances of flame under flying banners of the shadows of white clouds; or still lochs crimpled with the little dancing feet o' moonshine; or great lonely moors, with grey-brown ptarmigan fleeting from rock to rock, or a kestrel hawking like a drift of wind-blown rain, and nothing more to be seen or heard in all the waste but a woman with white shoulders and long, black hair sitting by a tarn and singing a wild forlorn song, evil-sweet; or he saw quiet places, under the stars, and an unknown folk moving blithely to and fro, and singing and laughing, all clad in green, like moonbeams in lily sheaths he thought. One of these delicate glad people came close to him, and played a little wild fantastic air, and Rory's tears fell because of his broken pipes, and because he could not capture the sighs and laughter of faëry, and he felt a sob in his heart when the slim green harper laughed, and he looked and could see nothing but a white foxglove in the moonshine, and heard nothing but a chime of little tinkling bells.

He came out of his dreams at that, and put a black curse on the slow-falling rain. Then, remembering the day it was, he played softly

"The Lord's my Shepherd," and part of a hymn called "Ye little lambs of Zion," which he had picked up not long since, one day when lying half sober to leeward of a Methodist prayer-meeting.

An old woman, passing near, heard it, and her heart went out to the poor man.

"Well, well now, an' is that you, Rory M'Alpine?" she said, half kindly, half dubious, because of the drear broken man she saw and his sore plight.

"It is just me an' no other, Widow Sheen," he answered sadly; "for sure there's none but God to have pity on a poor man that was travelling hard to see his own kith an' kin afore he died, an' fell down by the way, an' a bad fit at that, with the good pipes smashed too, an' not any tobacco upon him whatever, an' a broken heart to lift along the way."

Sheen Macgregor was a tender soul, and she knew nothing of what had happened the night before. She was too old and sad to go to the merrymaking.

She was now on her way to the kirk, but she turned and led Rory back to her turf-thatched cottage that was only a butt and a ben. Soon he grew warm before the glowing peats, and was glad to be in the dry clothes that had belonged to old Gregor Macgregor, while his own steamed in the comfortable heat. It was a true word he said when he told Widow Sheen that he had never known porridge like her porridge, or tasted them so sweet and wholesome, and that the milk was like a young cow's at clover-time. For a time he was uneasy, with restless eyes; for he had caught sight of a black bottle on a shelf. But when Sheen had taken it down, and poured him out a good glass of smoky Glenlivet, he praised God aloud, and said with tears in his eyes that his own mother had never been more tender sweet with him.

He had but slight hopes of the good thing; but when the old woman went to the drawers-head and lifted a jar, and filled his pipe for him, his gladness was a gladness indeed. When he lifted a bit of red peat and put it to the bowl of his pipe, and had his mouth and nose filled with the heavy good smoke, there was not a curse left in his heart.

After a time Widow Sheen said she would go now, but he prayed her to give him home a little longer.

"I'm hungry to hear the hymns," she said simply.

"For sure now, if that 's all you'll be hungry for," pleaded Rory eagerly, "I'll play you more hymns in an hour than you'll hear in a week"—and with that (and the more readily, because there were only ashes in the bowl now) he put down his pipe, and took his tin whistle, and played softly by the fire.

Widow Sheen sat and listened. It gave her peace and glad, holy thoughts. And if, after a time, Rory remembered no more hymns, and played old airs of love and sorrowful sweet songs of partings and regrets, the tired old woman did not know, or, knowing, showed no sign, but folded her withered hands on her lap, and closed her eyes, and dreamed old dreams.

After a time Rory saw she slept, so he rose and filled his pipe again. He had filled his pouch, too, when he remembered what he was doing, and put the tobacco back. Two hours passed. Then Widow Sheen waked and bade Rory stay and share her Sabbath stoup of leek broth with part of a neck of mutton in it—a luxury due to Miss Maclellan, who had sent the meat to the old woman, along with a packet of tea, to make up for her absence from the great doings.

That he did gladly, and all afternoon he told her stories. She cared little for any gossip save of Strathraonull, and all the decent gossip of the region was already known to her; but she loved old tales, and wild uncanny legends of kelpies and water-horses and sea-bulls, of fairy-lovers and solitary walkers in the night, of the green-clad cailleach on the hillside singing her fatal song as she milked the wild deer, of the bewitched thorns under which folk lay down to awake witless, of horns heard in the moonshine, and strange forlorn music in desolate places, and of what came of these and other omens and perversities. Rory had a good voice, too, and he sang old Gaelic songs; and when by chance he sang "Mo nighean donn," and she remembered when she had first heard it, when Gregor her lad wooed her at the summer-sheiling high on Ben Chreagan, her heart gave way, and she rose and kissed Rory.

Then she gave him tea, with as many scones and butter as he could eat, and filled his pouch and gave him a parting glass; and so he went out into the late day, sweet and fragrant now, with quiet light lying on stone and tree and warming the shadows into broad leaves or fans of living dusk.

But for a year thereafter Rory M'Alpine would have nothing to do with Strathraonull. He made many a bitter satire upon it and its folk; and these sayings went round the straths and outlying countries, till the Strathraonull people wished that Mr. Maclellan had just forborne with the poor man, and him in his natural state too, seeing the day it was; or else that he had been drowned in the pool; or that Widow Sheen had left him in the wet open, where as likely as not he would have died of his chill and his broken pipes.

Rory prospered, however, and in Strathanndra it was allowed that the piper had reformed, and was on his way to end his days in peace. He was not known to be drunk save at the quarters, and there was no scandal except on Martinmas Day, when in the market-place at Fort William he hated the law and hurled his heavy pipes at the head of Sheriff Macdougall, and brought that great and bulky gentleman to the ground like a felled steer.

For a time after the Strathraonull sorrow he had acted as a drover, an old ploy; then Strathanndra himself had given him the post of second shepherd; and if one bad night he had not piped the sheep over a broken ledge into a quarry (it was the Lammas-quarter, and he was enthusiastic), he would have been shepherd still. Since then he had acted as Strathanndra blacksmith in place of Allan Colquhoun, who had broken his leg, and was only too glad to get Rory to take his place and act for him. And when at the New Year Colquhoun celebrated Hogmanay with too great joy, and was found head foremost in a miry boghole, Rory M'Alpine succeeded him as blacksmith, and Strathanndra widows and girls looked on him as a good man and true.

For some weeks Rory worked hard at his fine reputation. But when first the Established man, and then the Free Church man, and then the new-come U.P. man, called and exhorted him, and he had to subscribe to this and subscribe to that, and had made promises to attend each of the kirks, and even to qualify for a communicant, and was finally offered the U.P. precentorship, he became restive, and longed to be up in the hills, or moving from place to place with his pipes.

The change would have come soon or late, but it was the Strathraonull message that brought it near.

When first the word came that Strathraonull was stricken with re-morse for what had happened when Rory had last honoured it, the piper snorted like an angry stot. Later, with a big slow wave of his hand, he re-marked that it was news to him to learn Strathraonull was still in existence. "I remember a poor place o' that name," he said, "but I thought it had died off, or been bought by a Glasgow man for jam or boot factories, or had emigryated at two-pound-ten a head, an' no thanks when ye get there."

A second embassy was rebuffed less bitterly. Rory was secretly over-joyed to hear that all Strathraonull was agreed on one point—that there was no piper in the Highlands to surpass Rory M'Alpine, and no teller of old tales to compare with him, and none so welcome of an evening. But he was obdurate. He sent word back that in Strathanndra the folk knew when they were well off, and that he could be a precentor when he liked, and an elder too for the matter o' that, and in any one o' the three kirks: then, fearing that this might go for laughter, and remember-ing that ill day at Fort William at Martinmas, and the prejudice of the magistracy against him ever since, he added bitterly, "A poor, poor place Strathraonull! Sure it has only one gentleman in it, an' that's a woman—old Widow Sheen Macgregor—"

But (apart from his own great longing to go back there, "the strath of his love," as he called it in one of his own songs, and dear to him for many things) two happenings moved him at last.

First there came word from Donald Macalister of Dalibrog, and that meant much, for Dalibrog was his foster-brother. That is an intimate tender bond; of old, and here and there still, it is a tie closer than blood. "Fuil gu fichead, comhaltas gu ceud," as the saying is: "Blood to the twentieth, fostership to the hundredth degree."

So that when Donald Macalister wrote affectionately, and addressed him as *comhalta,* Rory's heart melted, and he would have gone to Dalibrog gladly, if only he had not to pass through Strathraonull to get there. "There are two I want to see, an' badly," he muttered often: "my foster-brother and Sheen Macgregor." Every quarter-day (or as soon af-ter it as he was sober) he had sent Widow Sheen a small packet of tea and tobacco, and the old woman had remembered him gratefully at the New Year, and had sent him a pair of thick hose she had knitted, and a ramshorn mull filled with black snuff that had belonged to her man.

As he could not read or write, and would not own to either lack, he had to wait on opportunity; so that days passed, and Donald Macalister wrote again and urged him by the good bond of *comhaltas* to come to Dalibrog and help make the christening festivities a time for remembrance indeed.

He had received and become acquainted with this second letter, when Peter Macfarlane and Thomas M'Hardy arrived in the carrier's cart at the smithy, and gave Rory one of the proudest moments in his life. For they brought with them a beautiful new set of pipes, with silver flutings, and decked with streamers of M'Alpine tartan, and handed the brave pipes to Rory as a present from the whole of Strathraonull, and as a sign of repentance.

They took back word next day (for that night all three were too overcome with drinking healths, now to Strathraonull, and now to Strathanndra, to stir from the smithy) that Rory M'Alpine was coming to Dalibrog for the christening, and that there was not a man or woman in the Strath but that he would be glad to see again, and that he had not a sour memory left against any one, except for that poor fool of a man, John Macmillan the carpenter (the only man in the Strath who had not subscribed to the new set of pipes), and not that either, seeing the poor home he had with the scolding wife an' a heavy cold in his head three parts o' the year. As for the Reverend Kenneth Maclellan, he had had a call from the Lord, and now preached the Word (at a higher stipend) in the town of Greenock.

II

There never was a finer St. Bride's Eve in the Highlands than that which saw the return of Rory M'Alpine.

He came down by the Pass of the Lochans, at the eastern end of Strathraonull, and long before he was seen the crofters at Creggans could hear the wild pibroch he was playing. A handsome, strapping man he was always; but now he was Piper Rory M'Alpine, and came striding down the pass with his pipes on his left shoulder and skreigh upon skreigh skirling from his chanter and big drone, with the tartan streamers flying in the wind, and himself with a new jacket of braided velveteen with silver buttons and clasps, a new kilt and philabeg, new hose of his own clan, with slit and deckled shoes agleam with silver buckles, a great plaid of the finest woven M'Alpine tartan round his big chest and over and away beyond his shoulder, where sat the largest brooch in the Highlands with a yellow cairngorm in it that was like a lump of solid sunlight, and a new cap of the Glengarry men with a sprig of heather held by a silver clasp, which held also two big wing-feathers of the golden eagle.

The whole of Creggans came to the roadside to welcome the glad stranger. He looked at none; but when, still playing his new pibroch, he reached the space in front of the "Crossways Inn," he strode backwards and forwards, or stood tapping the ground with his right foot, till the glory and greatness of the man were too overcoming to be borne, and there was a rush of M'Dermids and M'Ians (for every one at Creggans was either a M'Ian or a M'Dermid), and they carried him, just as a running wave sweeps a bit of driftwood, into the laughing gape of the inn.

And what Creggans did, every hamlet along Strathraonull did or tried to do. But as he neared Dalibrog village, Rory became more and more circumspect as to the kindly drink, and so entered the place of his old shame and new triumph with no more in him than what went for comfort. Every man, woman, and child came out to greet him; and what with their laughing glad cries, and shoutings to each other, and the squealing of children and barking of dogs, and the wild ceaseless drone of the pipes and skirling cries that screamed from the chanter, there was noise enough to make the dead in Dalibrog kirkyard wonder if the last trump had sounded, and they not knowing it because of the heavy sleep on them.

It was a triumph indeed, and none ever had a welcome more true. For not only had Rory sent a brave word of thanks for the Strathraonull repentance, and made a beautiful new pibroch (which between Candlemas and Lammas would reach every hamlet in the Highlands from the Mull of Cantyre to the Ord of Sutherland) called "Strathraonull for Ever!" and had publicly repudiated, too, every curse and ill word he had put on the Strath and the men and women in it; but it was also known that in order to come here in all this glory he had sold the smithy rights to Andrew M'Andrew, the Aberdeen man who had been spying for work in Strathanndra, and was now Piper Rory M'Alpine again, and that and no other.

When he spoke at last, it was like a prince, very cordial and kind.

"Well, well, now," he said, "for sure I see well I'm in dear Strathraonull again. Sure I've never ceased to love it, or the folk within it, and where my heart 's been my thoughts have been."

There was a cheer at that, though every man and woman there knew it was a black lie. But perhaps not that either, and only a good friendly lie.

"It's Macalister land indeed," Rory added laughingly; for as he glanced about him, he saw that two-thirds at least of the company were of Mhic Alastair. "Sure we might all as well be in the Isles out yonder"— this in allusion to the fact that some generations ago a number of isles-men (Macleans and Macneils with a few Macdonalds and others) had left the Hebrides and settled on the main, and adopted the clan-name of Macalister because of a famous chieftain whom all claimed as their common ancestor, one Alasdair the Red of Storsay; a matter needless to mention here, were it not that in the region spoken of the people still adhere to certain customs that are Hebridean rather than of the main-land, and of the Southern and Catholic isles at that.

Only too gladly William Macalister of the "Raonull Arms" would have had Rory as his free guest (and this in despite of all painful memory of the shallowness of the piper's purse in comparison with his deep quenchless thirst); but, as was everywhere understood, he had, of course, to go on to Dalibrog House. But he drank abundant goodwill first.

Dalibrog himself was not an expansive man, but with Rory his coàlt he was more cordial than with any other, and had as much affection for him and pleasure in his company as he had in that of any living being after himself; and the more so as Rory never asked anything of him, save bed and board, gladly given, and was, moreover, of poor and hum-ble estate as compared with Donald Macalister of Dalibrog.

But neither Dalibrog nor his wife, nor his old half-sister Dionaid (who still had the Island Gaelic, she having come from Barra in her ear-ly womanhood), were pleased when they saw that Rory had already been so eager to show Strathraonull that it had his whole-hearted for-giveness, for he carried too obviously the signs of that repentance and his own overwilling meeting of it more than half-way. It was too wild a tune that he played as he came up Dalibrog House avenue, with a bro-ken crowd at his heels, and himself hating so many uncertain trees running at him, and he trying to play at one and the same time "The Cock of the North" and "Deil tak' the Hindmost."

Rory, however, would not hear a word of reproach, and insisted that he had never been so well in his life, save for a bit of a rheum he had got as he came down the cold pass of the Lochans; and that it would go soon, and quicker too for the help of some good warm broth and a mouthful of something with it (Glenlivet for choice), for he had not touched bite or sup since a slop of porridge and milk at daybreak.

"Well, as ye've enough breath for that lie, I suppose you'll have to reach the end your ain gate," said Dalibrog drily, and speaking the Lowland tongue to show his displeasure.

However, Rory recovered for a time, and by three of the clock was in a deep sleep in the loft beyond the kitchen, where Dionaid Macalister had given him all he wanted and more. The christening was over and the minister gone before he came out of that sleep, to the thankful content of all concerned.

Meanwhile the St. Bride preparations were carried swiftly on.

The young women of the neighbourhood had already made a fine image of a woman out of woven corn-sheafs, and had clothed this with the best that could be had; and because of the mildness of the winter they had been able to gather many snowdrops and aconites and early daisies, and even primroses and daffodils, and so made the figure of St. Bride like a delight of spring. With brightly-tinted snail shells, and with polished pebbles, and red bramble leaves and golden bracken fronds which had been carefully preserved from October, and with many little ornaments, "our Brideag dear" was made fair to see.

As soon as the ceremony was over and the great folk gone with the Laird's carriages, the *banal Bride* (the maiden band of St. Bridget) went in procession from cottage to cottage and from house to house. All were young girls, dressed in white, and with their hair down; and as they carried the figure among them, they sang the song of "Bride bhoidheach oigh nam mile beus" ("Beautiful young Bridget of a thousand charms"); and because none let St. Bride go without an offering, the figure was soon covered with shells and ribbons and flowers and little fineries of all kinds—and many besides gave presents of cheese and cakes and honey, to be given in turn to the poor of the neighbourhood.

When they came to Dalibrog House, old Dionaid Macalister (who many years before was mainly responsible for the St. Bride celebrations in Strathraonull) put a fine white cairngorm in a silver sheath over the heart of the image of St. Bride, which, she said, was for the "reul iuil Bride," the guiding star of St. Bridget—that star over the stable at Bethlehem which led St. Bride to the Virgin Mother and her little new-born Son, and made her known and loved for ever as "Bride nam brat," St. Bride of the Mantle, for the good deed she did then.

Having ended at Dalibrog, the *banal Bride* made the circuit of the house, and then went to the new byres that had been made ready for the feast, and in the third installed Bridget, "Bride bhoidheach oigh," and near the great window where she could be seen of all. Then having barred the doors, they awaited the coming of the other young men and women from the Strath. They came in twos and threes and larger groups; but because most were Protestants, and not of the old faith, and inlanders too, there were songs unsung and prayers unprayed that should have been sung and prayed; nor did more than a few of the young men make obeisance before Bride as they should have done, she being the friend of Mary and the foster-mother of Christ.

After this there was much eating and drinking, though not so much as there seemed, for each put aside something to the common table that was reserved for what was afterwards to be distributed to the poor.

Then the dancing began, and now Rory M'Alpine was again the foremost figure, for there was none in all the home straths or the countries beyond who had so great a store of reels and strathspeys.

He played . . .

Bibliography

I. Selected Books by William Sharp and Fiona Macleod

Romantic Ballads and Poems of Phantasy. London Walter Scott, 1888 (2nd ed. 1889). [*Contains:* ROMANTIC BALLADS: The Weird of Michael Scott; The Son of Allan; Mad Madge o' Cree; The Deith-Tide; POEMS OF PHANTASY: Phantasy; The Willis-Dancers; A Dream; The Wandering Voice; The Twin-Soul; The Isle of Lost Dreams; The Death-Child.]

The Gypsy Christ and Other Tales. By William Sharp. Chicago: Stone & Kimball, 1895. [*Contains:* The Gypsy Christ; Madge o' the Pool; The Coward; A Venetian Idyl; The Graven Image; The Lady in Hosea; Fröken Bergliot.]

The Sin-Eater and Other Tales. By Fiona Macleod. Edinburgh: Patrick Geddes; Chicago: Stone & Kimball, 1895. New York: Duffield, 1907 (as *The Sin-Eater and Other Tales and Episodes*). [*Contains:* Prologue (From Iona); The Sin-Eater; The Ninth Wave; The Judgment o' God; The Harping of Cravetheen; Tragic Landscapes (I. The Tempest; II. The Mist; III. Summer-Sleep); The Anointed Man; The Dàn-nan-Ròn; Green Branches; The Daughter of the Sun; The Birdeen; Silk o' the Kine.]

The Washer of the Ford and Other Legendary Moralities. By Fiona Macleod. Edinburgh: Patrick Geddes; Chicago: Stone & Kimball, 1896. [*Contains:* Prologue (To Kathia); The Washer of the Ford; Muime Chriosd; The Fisher of Men; The Last Supper; The Dark Nameless One; The Three Marvels of Hy; The Annir-Choille; The Shadow-Seers; The Song of the Sword; The Flight of the Culdees; Mircath; The Laughter of Scathach the Queen; Ula and Urla.]

The Dominion of Dreams. By Fiona Macleod. London: Constable, 1899. New York: Frederick A. Stokes Co., 1900. [Contains: Dalua; By the Yellow Moonrock; The House of Sand and Foam; Lost; The White Heron; Children of the Dark Star; Alasdair the Proud; The Adaman; The Herdsman; The Book of the Opal; The Wells of Peace; In the Shadow of the Hills; The Distant Country; A Memory of Beauty; The Sad Queen; The Woman with the Net; Enya of the Dark Eyes; Honey of the Wild Bees; The Birds of Emar; Ulad of the Dreams; The Crying Wind; Epilogue: The Wind, the Shadow, and the Soul.]

The Works of Fiona Macleod. Ed. Elizabeth Sharp. London: Heinemann, 1910. [Contains: Volume 1: *Pharais; The Mountain Lovers;* Volume 2: *The Sin-Eater; The Washer of the Ford and Other Legendary Moralities;* Volume 3: *The Dominion of Dreams; Under the Dark Star;* Volume 4: *The Divine Adventure; Iona: Studies in Spiritual History;* Volume 5: *The Winged Destiny: Studies in the Spiritual History of the Gael;* Volume 6: *The Silence of Amor; Where the Forest Murmurs;* Volume 7: *Poems and Dramas.*]

II. Original Publications of Individual Stories

"The Anointed Man." In *The Sin-Eater and Other Tales* (1895). In *The Works of Fiona Macleod,* Volume 3 (1910).

"By the Yellow Moonrock." In *The Dominion of Dreams* (1896). In *The Works of Fiona Macleod,* Volume 3 (1910).

"Cathal of the Woods." In *The Washer of the Ford and Other Legendary Moralities* (as "The Annir-Choille"). In *The Works of Fiona Macleod,* Volume 2 (1910).

"The Dàn-nan-Ròn." In *The Sin-Eater and Other Tales* (1895). In *The Works of Fiona Macleod,* Volume 3 (1910).

"The Graven Image." In *The Gypsy Christ and Other Tales* (1895).

"Green Branches." In *The Sin-Eater and Other Tales* (1895). In *The Works of Fiona Macleod,* Volume 3 (1910).

"The Gypsy Christ." In *The Gypsy Christ and Other Tales* (1895).

"The Herdsman." In *The Dominion of Dreams* (1899). In *The Works of Fiona Macleod*, Volume 6 (1910). [Early version included as part of *Green Fire* (New York: Harper & Brothers, 1896).]

"The Last Supper." In *The Washer of the Ford and Other Legendary Moralities* (1896). In *The Works of Fiona Macleod*, Volume 2 (1910).

"The Laughter of Scathach the Queen." In *The Washer of the Ford and Other Legendary Moralities* (1896). In *The Works of Fiona Macleod*, Volume 2 (1910).

"Mircath." In *The Washer of the Ford and Other Legendary Moralities* (1896). In *The Works of Fiona Macleod*, Volume 2 (1910).

"Silk o' the Kine." In *The Sin-Eater and Other Tales* (1895). In *The Works of Fiona Macleod*, Volume 2 (1910).

"The Sin-Eater." In *The Sin-Eater and Other Tales* (1895). In *The Works of Fiona Macleod*, Volume 2 (1910).

"Ula and Urla." In *The Washer of the Ford and Other Legendary Moralities* (1896). In *The Works of Fiona Macleod*, Volume 2 (1910).

"The Washer of the Ford." In *The Washer of the Ford and Other Legendary Moralities* (1896). In *The Works of Fiona Macleod*, Volume 2 (1910).

[All poems in this volume are taken from *Romantic Ballads and Poems of Phantasy*.]

ABOUT S. T. JOSHI

S. T. JOSHI is the author of *The Weird Tale* (1990), *H. P. Lovecraft: The Decline of the West* (1990), and *Unutterable Horror: A History of Supernatural Fiction* (2012). He has prepared corrected editions of H. P. Lovecraft's stories for Penguin Classics. He has also prepared editions of Lovecraft's collected fiction, essays, poetry, and letters for Hippocampus Press. His exhaustive biography *I Am Providence: The Life and Times of H. P. Lovecraft* appeared in 2010. He is the editor of such anthologies as *American Supernatural Tales* (Penguin, 2007), *Black Wings* I-VII (PS Publishing, 2010-23), *A Mountain Walked: Great Tales of the Cthulhu Mythos* (Centipede Press, 2014), *The Madness of Cthulhu* (Titan Books, 2014-15), and *The Weird Cat* (with Katherine Kerestman; Wordcrafts Press, 2023). He is the editor of the *Lovecraft Annual, Penumbra,* and *Spectral Realms* (all for Hippocampus Press). His collected mystery and horror fiction is gathered in *The Recurring Doom* (Sarnath Press, 2019).

www.ingramcontent.com/pod-product-compliance
Lightning Source LLC
Chambersburg PA
CBHW050925030726
47503CB00007BB/2465